Richmond Campus
2151 Old Brick Road
Glen Allen, Va 23060

JAN 1 1 2012

Southern Families

A Novel

Southern Families

Their Friends, Servants, Rivals, and Affairs

1901-1911

Michael V.C. Alexander

Copyright © 2011 by Michael V.C. Alexander.

Library of Congress Control Number: 2011909850
ISBN: Hardcover 978-1-4628-8794-1
       Softcover 978-1-4628-8793-4
       Ebook   978-1-4628-8795-8

All rights reserved. No part of this book may be reproduced or transmitted in any form or by any means, electronic or mechanical, including photocopying, recording, or by any information storage and retrieval system, without permission in writing from the copyright owner.

This is a work of fiction. Names, characters, places and incidents either are the product of the author's imagination or are used fictitiously, and any resemblance to any actual persons, living or dead, events, or locales is entirely coincidental.

This book was printed in the United States of America.

To order additional copies of this book, contact:
Xlibris Corporation
1-888-795-4274
www.Xlibris.com
Orders@Xlibris.com

A college professor for many years, Dr. Michael Van Cleave Alexander published four scholarly books between 1975 and 1998. Those books are the following:

Charles I's Lord Treasurer: Sir Richard Weston, Earl Of Portland (1577-1635). Published jointly in 1975 by the Macmillan Company of London and the University of North Carolina Press of Chapel Hill, NC. (This was a revision and expansion of his doctoral dissertation.)

The First of the Tudors: A Study of Henry VII and His Reign. Published in 1980 by Rowman & Littlefield of Totowa, NJ.

The Growth of English Education, 1348-1648: A Social and Cultural History. Published in 1990 by the Pennsylvania State University Press of College Park, PA.

Three Crises in Early English History. (The Norman Conquest, Magna Carta, and the Wars of the Roses.) Published in 1998 by the University Press of America of Landover, MD.

Dedication

For my wife Ann and our sons Mike and
Peter, their wives Sarah and Krista, and their children
James, Mary, and Nutmeg

Chapter 1

The third Thursday in January 1901 was unusually warm and clear in Perquimmons City, a town of roughly 5,500 people in the extreme northeastern part of North Carolina. To Chip and Rhonda Summerlin, a couple in their mid thirties with two small children, one only a baby, the spring-like weather seemed perfect for an event that would take place that afternoon, an event so important it would make that day a truly memorable one, a day Chip and Rhonda would remember for years to come. At three thirty that afternoon, Chip was scheduled to sign the final papers to buy the town's only drugstore, a flourishing business for which he'd worked since shortly after he graduated from high school in 1884. And once Chip signed those papers, he and his wife would join the town's elite and enjoy much greater social status and an income over triple their former one.

On a more personal note, shortly after Chip signed all the papers to buy the drugstore, he planned to ride his bicycle from the lawyer's office in the middle of town to the Merritt House, one of the state's largest and most beautiful antebellum mansions at the crest of a small hill a mile to the west. Chip's younger sister, Lucy, of whom he and Rhonda were both extremely fond, had worked in several menial positions at the Merritt House since finishing high school in 1888; and Chip was finally in a position to offer her a much better job as his bookkeeper and sales assistant.

Because Lucy had no idea she'd be offered a much better job shortly after Chip bought the drugstore, she considered the morning of January 17 no different from any other morning. In fact, she had her usual hard time in the mansion's schoolroom during the last two hours before lunch with Becca and Willie, who were nine and ten. Always unruly and hard to control, the Merritts' older children paid no attention to the grammar, history, and arithmetic she tried to teach them that morning. They threw dozens of spitballs at each other and left their desks every four or five minutes to look out the windows into the backyard or race each other down the hall to the bathroom, a great convenience installed only a few years earlier. Each time Becca and Willie returned to the schoolroom after using the toilet, they brought the three little house dogs with them, which forced Lucy to shoo the dogs out of the room as they snapped or barked at her while eluding her clutches for several minutes, causing the children to laugh gleefully at her vigorous but ungainly efforts. By twelve thirty Lucy was almost as depressed as she'd been on the afternoon of her high school sweetheart's funeral thirteen and a half years before.

Shortly after the children rushed down the main staircase to have a fine lunch of country ham, vegetables, and apple tarts with their parents and five-year-old brother Little Robert in the family dining room, Lucy went down the backstairs to the servants' kitchen and had a very different meal. After helping herself to a plate of collards and hominy, neither of which she liked, she sat down at the rickety old table in the middle of that large brick-floored room. The Merritts' housekeeper, Flossie Plowden, was already sitting at the table with her daughter Tulip, who was two years older than Lucy, who would turn thirty in June. Flossie and Tulip welcomed Lucy with big smiles and friendly words; and because of their encouragement and unwavering support over the years, she felt a special bond with them.

Lucy ate several bites of her lunch before Mrs. Merritt entered the room and said in her high-pitched nasal voice, "Don't pick at your food like that, Lucy! It's my hus'bun's birthday and we're havin a dinn'uh party tonight. So I want you to work in the main dinin room all aftuh'noon 'cause the centerpiece and oth'uh arrangements you made a day or two befo Christmas need to be spruced up with some fresh pine and holly branches. But don't spend ov'uh an hour on that 'cause my best soup tureen and sixteen o the julep cups need to be polished, and so do sixteen place settins o my best flat silv'uh, which I expect you to finish by five-thirty. Then you'll help my little angels with their supp'uh befo readin 'em Bible stories until Little Robert's bedtime at eight o'clock." (Little Robert, who'd been named for his paternal grandfather, was so small Lucy's brother-in-law, Dr. Joseph Hanford, the only doctor in town, was afraid he'd be only five feet one or two when fully grown. As for Becca and Willie, who were of normal height, they were allowed to go to bed whenever they liked, which Lucy considered a serious mistake. Whenever they stayed up past ten o'clock, they were rude and irritable when she woke them up in time for breakfast at seven thirty the next morning.)

As Mrs. Merritt left the servants' kitchen, Lucy sighed because she hated polishing silver even more than teaching Becca and Willie, who upset her whenever they became so bored with their games and toys they teased Little Robert until he burst into tears. But she had no choice in the matter, so after eating several more bites of her lunch she pushed her plate aside and finished her glass of water. As Flossie and Tulip tried to bolster her spirits, she stood up and found some clippers in a nearby cupboard and took them and a bucket of water out into the backyard where she cut a dozen pine and holly branches off several bushes and saplings between the barn and chicken coop. After carrying the clippers and bucket of greens inside, she put the clippers away and found an apron in another cupboard. After putting it on over her simple cotton dress, she walked through the main kitchen with her bucket to the butler's pantry where she found several rags and a jar of Hall's Silver Polish, Mrs. Merritt's favorite brand. Although Lucy was convinced several other brands were better and cheaper, an item's price was never a matter of concern for her employers because they never saw any reason to live within their means. They could always sell off another tract of seven or eight acres whenever their creditors became impatient and threatened to cancel their charge privileges unless they handed over at least half of what they owed to their grocer, pharmacist, or the best seamstress in the area, who happened to be Lucy and Chip's mother, Margaret Summerlin. For years Margaret had specialized in making children's clothes for the Merritts and most of the other leading families in the area.

With another sigh Lucy carried her bucket of greens and the rags and silver polish through the family dining room into the main dining room, which was so large the Merritts held their annual Valentine's Day cotillion and several other dances there every year shortly after the servants rolled up the enormous Persian rug and moved it and the banquet table to one side of that truly impressive room. It was admired by all the townspeople lucky enough to have attended a party there for its high ceilings and elaborate crown moldings, its handsome mantels and fireplaces at the room's northern and southern ends, and its nine Chippendale mirrors that reflected the soft candlelight of the magnificent Waterford chandelier with its hundreds of crystal prisms.

After sprucing up the arrangements on the banquet table and massive sideboard on the inside wall, Lucy took a third of the Merritts' best flat silver and julep cups out of the sideboard's smaller drawers and lined them up on one side of the banquet table. With her mind in neutral she worked on those items until four o'clock, when she had them gleaming and returned them to their drawers.

Twenty minutes later, as she was about to finish one side of the Merritts' best soup tureen, Flossie emerged from the butler's pantry and said, "Mist'uh Chip wants to see you on the back porch, Lucy. If yo mama or papa's sick and you need to go home fo an hour or two, don't worry if the old battleaxe comes in and wants to know where you've gone. I'll tell her you had an attack o the trots and are out in one o the privies. That'll stop her in her tracks 'cause she's always complainin about all the smells out there."

Lucy laughed and thanked Flossie as she took off her apron and straightened her hair and dress a bit. She was afraid Chip had come to tell her that their mother's arthritis had flared up again or, even worse, that her father had cut off one of his fingers with his new table saw, which his most capable workman had done ten days before while cutting different lengths of half a dozen maple planks for the sides of a new chifforobe her father, the best furniture maker for miles around, was about to finish. After hurrying through the butler's pantry and both kitchens, Lucy opened the mansion's back door and was relieved to see her tall, handsome brother smiling broadly as he strode around the porch while puffing on a cigarette.

Because they hadn't seen each other in several weeks, Chip tossed his cigarette into a nearby bush and gave Lucy a big hug while saying, "I've just bought Bradley's Drugstore. Isn't that wonderful?"

"Yes, I'm sure it is," Lucy said with an uncomprehending look. "Is Rhonda going to help you run it from now on?"

"No, Lucy, *you're* going to help me run it because this is your ticket to a much better life. Can you believe you're finally in a position to leave this unhappy place?"

"But why isn't Rhonda going to help you run it the same way Mrs. Bradley helped her husband run it for so many years before he died last fall?"

"Rhonda can't do that because Alfred's asthma attacks are still so serious she's afraid to leave him at home with a colored girl who knows nothing about medicine."

"But what would I do at the drugstore? I don't know anything about mixing the liniments and potions you make for the store's hundreds of customers."

"Don't worry about that because mixing those things is my most important duty. You'll be my bookkeeper and sales assistant, and I know you'll do a great job in those roles because you've always been good with arithmetic and you're always so patient with other people."

"I'm sure I could help you wait on customers but I couldn't be your bookkeeper because I know nothing about accounting."

"Don't worry about that either because the store's bookkeeping system is so simple I can teach it to you in five or six minutes."

"I don't see how that's possible and if I worked for you, where would I live? I couldn't live with you and Rhonda because your house is too small, and I'd hate to impose on Joe and Julia because their children are still so young. And I'll never live with Mama and Papa again because despite how wonderful they are in most ways, they'd probably order me around as much as they did while I was in high school."

"Julia and I felt the same way about their bossiness until we got married and moved into places of our own. And because I knew you'd hate to live with them again, I've decided to pay you forty dollars a month, which is an *excellent* salary for this day and age, so you'll be able to rent a cottage of your own. You'd like that, wouldn't you?"

"Yes, I certainly would, but I don't own a stick of furniture or any sheets and blankets or pots and pans. So there's no way I could furnish a cottage of my own."

"Stop being so negative, Lucy! I clearly made a mistake by not preparing you for such a sudden change in your life although Rhonda and Julia and everyone else in the family convinced me to keep you in the dark until I finally bought the drugstore and there was no longer any chance the deal would fall through. After all, if I'd told you last fall what was about to happen and your hopes had risen sky high, you would've been even more depressed if I'd been unable to buy the drugstore and give you a better job. At any rate, I signed all the papers to buy the store less than an hour ago, so you have a chance to leave this terrible place now and get on with your life. And once you do, you'll never have to teach Becca and Willie again and you'll never have to deal with their parents again either."

"That's only partly true because what if Mrs. Merritt comes into the store one day and I have to wait on her? I'd die of embarrassment if that ever happens."

"It'll never happen because she comes to the store only once or twice a year; and whenever she does, she expects me to stop whatever I'm doing and wait on her the same way her husband does. So you'll never have to wait on either one of them, I promise."

"Then I'd love to work for you because I've always hated my life here. The thought of never having to bow and scrape to the Merritts or their awful children again is so wonderful you'll never know how grateful I am for this."

"I have a good idea already but be sure to have all your clothes and other things packed and waiting on the back porch by eight forty-five tomorrow morning. If you'll promise to do that, I'll send Clem Johnson to get you and all your other stuff in the store's delivery wagon shortly after I open the store for business at eight thirty. He'll drive you and all your things to my house, and you can spend the rest of the day getting settled in my study with Rhonda's help. And on Saturday morning we'll leave for the drugstore twenty minutes earlier than I usually do so I can explain the store's bookkeeping system and other duties to you before I open the store for business."

"I can't believe you want me to start working for you this Saturday morning because that's less than a day and a half from now. Wouldn't Monday morning be soon enough?"

"No, because tomorrow's the last day Mrs. Bradley will be able to help me. As I'm sure you know, she's worked for me seven or eight hours a day since shortly after her husband's funeral because she likes to stay busy and felt really grateful to me because of all the things I did to help her run the store during the last months of his life while he was bedridden at home. But she sold her house and most of her furniture two weeks ago to the lawyer who's about to move to town and become George Kahle's partner and—"

"But where will Mrs. Bradley live when she vacates her house and has almost no furniture? She's not going to sleep on a mattress in her backyard, is she?"

"No, of course not," Chip said with a laugh. "She's about to move to Richmond and live with her daughter, Martha Williamson, and her family on Monument Avenue. Martha's due to arrive in town tomorrow afternoon and she plans to spend all day Saturday helping her mother pack her clothes and several small pieces of furniture. I'll take them up to the Hertford station for them on Sunday afternoon in the store's delivery wagon. As for Martha and her mother, Joe's offered to drive them up to the Hertford station at the same time in his and Julia's buggy."

"It sounds like you and Joe are going to be very busy on Sunday."

"That's right because we're both scheduled to be ushers at church that morning, which is another reason why I need your help so much on Saturday. Because Mrs. Bradley won't be able to help me for even an hour that day, I'll be exhausted by the time I close the store at five thirty unless I have your assistance because the only other person who'll be there to help me will be Dillie Hughes, my new soda fountain attendant. Although Dillie's an excellent worker, she has a hard time taking orders because she can barely read and write and most of the store's customers don't like the idea of being waited on by a colored girl. But I'm sure that'll change in several months when they realize how smart and polite Dillie is."

"Hmmmmm, I understand your problem now, and I guess I could start working for you on Saturday morning."

"You'll be a real lifesaver if you do, and I'm sure you'll like Dillie a great deal because she reminds me a lot of Tulip."

"Then I'll probably like her too, and I'll have all my things packed and waiting on the back porch by eight forty-five tomorrow morning."

"Thank you so much because that means a great deal to me, Lucy." After giving his sister an even bigger hug, Chip hurried to his bicycle and rode it out of the Merritts' rear driveway before heading for the drugstore in the middle of town. Since shortly after three fifteen, Mrs. Bradley and Dillie had been helping the store's customers as well as they could.

As for Lucy, she returned to the main dining room and resumed her work. Her spirit soared even more when she realized she'd never have to polish any of the Merritts' silver again or be annoyed and upset by Becca and Willie's behavior for several more years. Although there were bound to be some problems at the drugstore, her work there would probably be much more interesting and satisfying than her work at the Merritt House had ever been.

Half an hour later, after finishing her work on the Merritts' best soup tureen and its platter, Lucy pushed it aside as Flossie appeared again and started setting the table for the Merritts and their fourteen dinner guests. Lucy found several pairs of salt and pepper shakers in the sideboard's smallest drawer and was polishing them when Mrs. Merritt entered the dining room to check on her work. As she was inspecting the tureen and its platter for any remaining specks of tarnish, Lucy screwed up her courage and said, "I hate to bother you, ma'am, but I need to tell you something important."

"Go ahead, but be quick about it!" Mrs. Merritt snapped. "I've got lots of oth'uh things to do befo I go upstairs to bathe and dress for dinn'uh."

Lucy took a deep breath and said, "My brother bought Bradley's Drugstore this afternoon and wants me to work for him from now on. Because he needs my help on Saturday morning, I'll be moving into town shortly after breakfast tomorrow."

"Don't be silly, you foolish girl!" Mrs. Merritt said although she was only four years older than Lucy even if she was seven or eight inches taller. "You can't leave tomorrow mornin 'cause you have teachin duties with my children until the middle o June. Besides, I'm entitled to two weeks' notice in case you've forgotten."

Deeply annoyed by Mrs. Merritt's words, Lucy decided to express her feelings for the first time. "No, I haven't forgotten that or anything else, but I'm leaving tomorrow morning whether you like it or not. I owe my brother much more than I'll ever owe you or your husband, and I'm not going to argue with you about it."

"What's gotten into you, Lucy? You've never been so rude and feisty befo and it's not a bit attractive."

"I don't care how you feel about me anymore because I'm sick and tired of my job here. You've made me work much longer hours than you said you would on the day I applied for the position, and you've never been kind to me. Even worse, you've never supported my efforts to do a good job in the schoolroom, and because of that Becca and Willie have learned a lot less than I hoped they would. And finally, my attic room is even colder in the winter than it's hot in the summer and I can't stand the thought of spending more than one more night there."

"Why didn't you speak to me about your grievances a long time ago?"

"Would it have mattered? Of course not. It would only have gotten me fired."

"Well you're certainly fired now 'cause you're the worst and most disrespec'ful employee I've ev'uh had! I want you and all your things out o my house by the time I come downsta'uhs fo breakfast tomorrow mornin."

"Don't worry because I'll be long gone by then. The less I see of this awful place, the better I'll like it!"

Lucy turned around and rushed through the center hall and breakfast room to the backstairs as Flossie gaped at her in amazement. During her thirty-four years at the Merritt House, Flossie had never known a servant to speak so bluntly to Mrs. Merritt, whose sharp tongue and forbidding appearance intimidated their other servants so much they never uttered a word of complaint. As for Lucy, she was determined to take refuge in her attic room before Mrs. Merritt abused her further.

Shortly after five thirty, Lucy went downstairs to the schoolroom on the second floor and had an equally unpleasant scene with Becca and Willie. They were teasing Little Robert to the point of tears when she appeared, and she was so annoyed by their behavior she decided to let them know exactly how she felt. After slamming the door to get their attention, she said to them, "Stop it right now, you nasty children! It's cruel to tease Little Robert like that, and if you don't stop it right now I'll get really mad at you and you won't like it at all!"

Becca and Willie were amazed because Lucy had never spoken to them so bluntly before. But Lucy suddenly remembered that they were only children although they were several inches taller than her and old enough to be much better behaved. So she did her best to control her temper, convinced it would be wrong to sink to their level. But Willie provoked her again by saying, "Mama will give you a real tongue lashing tomorrow morning when I tell her you blessed us out this afternoon and I can't wait to see her do it."

"Neither can I!" Becca chimed in.

"I'm no longer afraid of what your mother says to me," Lucy said calmly. "Because I'm moving into town tomorrow morning I'm no longer afraid of what your father says to me either."

"But who'll help us with our supper and read Bible stories to us once you leave?" Little Robert wailed.

"I have no idea, Little Robert, and frankly, I don't care. I've tried for years to teach your brother and sister as much as I could. But they've never paid any attention to me, and they've made fun of me dozens of times behind my back by calling me a dwarf because I'm so short. And because of my father's limp, which he got while fighting in the Civil War, I've heard them call him a cripple six or seven times while he and several of his workmen were delivering a new piece of furniture. Becca and Willie should be ashamed of themselves for doing something that rude and arrogant."

"We'll never be ashamed of ourselves for doing a damn thing!" Willie said defiantly. "So you should go back up to your attic room and stay there. We don't need your help getting our supper tonight and we hate the thought of seeing your ugly little face again."

Lucy winced before saying, "That's fine with me, Willie. But I hope Becca or Little Robert tells your mother what you just said to me. She's always wanted you to have good manners and show consideration for the feelings of others. I've tried to teach you those things but you've ignored everything I said, and I'm sure you'll regret it when you're older. People of your station in life are expected to behave like ladies and gentleman, but you and Becca have no idea how to do that and I'm afraid you won't learn much by watching your parents' behavior."

After having her say, Lucy went back up to her attic room and ate an apple and several crackers for supper. It wasn't much of a meal, but she had no intention of going downstairs and seeing one of the Merritts again before she left the mansion for the last time the next morning.

During the next several hours Lucy packed and repacked her meager belongings in a battered old suitcase and several cardboard boxes. When she climbed into bed at eight thirty, she was too excited to fall asleep. So after several minutes she turned on the overhead light again and took out her Bible. After reading several of her favorite passages, she placed it on her bedside table and opened a novel her sister Julia had given her for Christmas and she'd started ten days earlier. She finished that novel, Charles Dickens' *Bleak House*, at ten thirty and placed it on top of her Bible.

Shortly after turning the light off again, she fell into a restless sleep, during which she dreamed that all the Merritts, even Little Robert, were chasing her through the mansion's ground-floor rooms while brandishing butcher knives and heavy clubs embedded with nails and shards of glass. They pursued her through the breakfast room and both kitchens out into the backyard. After cornering her there, they tied her hands together and carried her kicking and screaming for help to the bank of a nearby creek infested with alligators. Flossie and Tulip rushed to her defense and kept the Merritts from throwing her into the creek shortly before Clem Johnson arrived in her brother's delivery wagon. Although Flossie and Tulip knew they'd receive a terrible tongue lashing from the Merritts and might even lose their jobs, they untied Lucy's hands and helped her get into the wagon before Clem drove her to safety at the drugstore.

Chapter 2

Although Lucy woke up at six thirty the next morning, she remained in bed for another hour. After dressing and bushing her teeth in no time, she made several trips from her room to the mansion's ground floor with her boxes and suitcase. During those trips down the backstairs, she was as quiet as a church mouse because she was determined to avoid more insults from the Merritts, which would be impossible if she disturbed their sleep.

By eight fifteen she'd carried all her possessions down both flights of stairs and stacked them on the back porch. After finishing that task, she returned to the servants' kitchen and had some coffee and a piece of toast, her usual breakfast, with Flossie and Tulip.

Tears came to her eyes—and theirs—as Lucy thanked them for all their help and support over the years. "I couldn't have managed without it and several pats on the back from both of you every week. I'll always remember your friendship and I hope we see each other at the post office or Hogan's Grocery Store from time to time."

"We feel the same way about you," Flossie said while patting one of Lucy's hands. "You're such a sweet little thing, and Tulip and I've been so scared yo spirit would be broken by all the crap you've had to put up with in this awful place. I couldn't believe it when you told the old battleaxe off yesta'dy afternoon, and I wish you'd been free to punish her chilluns whenev'uh they misbehaved. I tell you, Lucy, those are the worst chilluns I ev'uh saw, and they need to have the tar beaten out of 'em several times a week for a month o Sundays. If their paw did that, they might be halfway decent by the time they grow up and leave the nest."

"That's right," Tulip said, "although I'm sure Willie will nev'uh do a lick o work in his whole life 'cause he's so lazy and his mama coddles him so much. But, Lucy, I hope Matthew gets back from the barn befo you leaves fo yo broth'uh's house. Matthew told me last night that he'll miss you a heap and hopes to tell you that himself. Serena feels the same way 'bout you."

"Matthew and Serena are such nice people," Lucy said, "and I'm so glad they got married last summer and are so happy together. But what are they doing out in the barn so early today?"

"They're polishin up the Merritts' buggy," Tulip said, "'cause they're goin to a big dinn'uh pah'ty in Edenton t'night. Between you and me, I don't know why anybody but a lunatic would ask them to a pah'ty. I've got several friends in Edenton who've told me Mist'uh Merritt's cheated so many men at po'kuh, a dozen of 'em hate his guts so much they're plannin to kill him one night for cheatin 'em out of hundreds o doll'uhs."

"I've heard that too," Lucy said in a whisper. "But I feel so sorry for Matthew because he tries so hard to get along with Mr. Merritt, but nothing he does ever seems to help for more than a day or two. Mr. Merritt must have a deep grudge against him for some reason I don't understand because he says such cruel things about Matthew whenever he's not around. I've never understood how he keeps his job when Mr. Merritt dislikes him so much."

"Keep this und'uh yo hat, Lucy," Flossie said in such a soft voice Lucy could barely hear her. Flossie knew she'd be fired if one of the Merritts had come downstairs to the main kitchen and heard her gossiping about a family member with someone in the next room. Even so, Flossie continued in a low voice, "Matthew came within an inch o losin his job last week 'cause he knows the old goat's been tryin to trick Serena into goin into the barn with him durin the last couple o weeks. Several days ago Matthew was so worried about what Mist'uh Merritt would do next to trick Serena, he told the jackass that if he values his life he should forget about his wife and find himself anoth'uh colored girl to root around in the barn with. Mis'tuh Merritt got so mad when Matthew told him those things, he told him to pack all his stuff and clear out by noon. But Matthew went straight to Miz Merritt, who values his work so much she ended the problem somehow."

"Yeah, she sho nuff did," Tulip said, "and I heard her doin it. Miz Merritt told her hus'bun in the study that af'tuhnoon that she'd taken a lot o guff off him ov'uh the years, and she wasn't gonna let him fire Matthew 'cause he ain't done nothin wrong and keeps the place runnin like a well-oiled clock. She also told him to behave himself and stop foolin around with pretty colored girls like Serena."

After thinking for a moment, Lucy said, "I've heard rumors for years that Mr. Merritt's taken advantage of dozens of colored girls since he was a teenager. But I've always wondered how much stock I should put on those rumors."

"They ain't rumors, Lucy," Flossie said firmly, "'cause they's absolutely true. And I know that for a fact 'cause he took advantage of Tulip when she was fifteen and my niece, Carlotta Jones, when she was only thirteen. He got both girls pregnant before sayin he'd fire 'em and give 'em bad ref'rences unless they let the colored doc'tuh plum nelly to Hertford get rid o their babies, which he's paid that doct'uh to do dozens o times since I started workin here when I was fo'teen."

"But why has Mr. Merritt paid that doctor to give so many colored girls abortions?" Lucy said to Flossie in wonder. "That makes no sense at all to me."

"He's done it 'cause the old battleaxe made him do it, Lucy. I've heard her tell him dozens o times that she didn't want 'any of his little black bas'tuds runnin 'round the place.' That always made me so mad I could hardly see straight fo the rest o the day."

As Lucy shook her head in even greater wonder, Tulip said, "Mama, tell Lucy what you almost did to Mist'uh Merritt a week o so aft'uh that colored doct'uh ended my baby's life."

"Okay 'cause she'll be leavin soon and I knows she'll be careful 'bout who she tells it to. Lucy, Tulip survived her abo'tion 'cause she was old'uh and a lot strong'uh than her cousin Carlotta, who died from hers. But from the maw'nin Matthew drove Tulip up to that doc'tuh's near Hertford in the Merritts' wagon, she's nev'uh been able to have any chilluns. I was so mad at Mis'tuh Merritt for makin my only child have an abo'tion, which has kept me from ev'uh havin some granchilluns, I decided to kill him aft'uh he fell asleep in his study one night. But Matthew knew what I was 'bout to do when he saw me put a butch'uh knife un'duh my apron. He told me to get ov'uh my ang'uh 'cause if I'ev'uh killed him the law would come down on me like a ton o bricks, and I'm really glad he told me that."

"So am I because Matthew was clearly right," Lucy said to Flossie at once. "But I'll never understand why you and Tulip have stayed here and worked for such a terrible man. Why haven't you left the Merritt House and found jobs somewhere else?"

"But where would we've found oth'uh jobs, Lucy? There just ain't enough work in this neck o the woods for colored folks like us and everybody knows it. Besides, aft'uh Tulip recov'ud from her abo'tion and could work again, Mis'tuh Merritt moved us into the best cabin behind the barn and raised our pay by fifty cents a week. And since then he's nev'uh made anoth'uh move on Tulip 'cause I told him to his face while I was fixin his breakfast one maw'nin that I'd kill him if he ev'uh did. As fo Miz Merritt, she's been much nice'uh to us too since then 'cause she'd hate fo me to tell all the oth'uh maids in town about the way he treated my niece and daugh'tuh. His standin 'round here has always been pretty low, and it would've hit rock bottom if I'd added my two cents' worth to it."

After thinking for a moment, Lucy said "I finally understand why you and Matthew have put up with all the terrible things you've had to endure here. But I just heard a wagon drive up to the back porch, and it's probably Clem Johnson, my brother's delivery man."

Lucy and her friends got up from the table and went out on the back porch. In no time Flossie and Tulip handed Lucy's suitcase and boxes to Clem on the driver's bench so he could put them in the wagon's bed behind his place directly on the bench.

Suddenly Lucy was so overcome with emotion she started to cry. Flossie wrapped her in her massive arms and said, "Don't worry 'bout us 'cause we always finds a way to manage in this misr'ble place. Now go on ov'uh to your broth'uh's house and have yo'self a good life. You deserve a much bett'uh life than the one you've had here for so many yea'uhs."

"But you and Tulip deserve a much better life too, and I wish you could come with me this morning."

"I'm sure the good Lord will help us find bett'uh jobs one day. But you need to get goin 'cause the old battleaxe told me last night to look through all yo stuff befo you leaves the premises. She was sure you'd try to steal some o the flat silv'uh or a couple o her hus'bun's books. If you're already gone when she comes down to the breakfast room, I'll tell her I went through all yo stuff but didn't find nothin that didn't belong to you. Now get up there next to Mis'tuh Clem 'cause it won't be long before the old bag comes down to the breakfast room and starts actin like a jackass's rear end."

"Flossie, you and Tulip have been so good to me I'll never forget either one of you."

"We'll never forget you eith'uh. Tulip, come ov'uh here now and help Lucy get up there next to Mist'uh Clem."

Clem leaned down and offered Lucy a helping hand as Lucy used Tulip's locked fingers as a stepstool. Once she was seated beside Clem, he slid several inches to his right to give Lucy more room. After saying good-bye to her friends again and how often she'd pray for them to find better jobs, she told Clem she was ready to leave for her brother's house. Clem slapped the mule's back with the reins half a dozen times before the stubborn animal moved forward and turned the wagon around in a large circle. In several minutes Clem drove Lucy out of the Merritts' rear driveway and up a hardscrabble street toward her brother and sister-in-law's house a quarter of a mile to the northeast.

Flossie and Tulip braced themselves for another day at the Merritts' beck and call while Clem said to Lucy as the wagon turned a sharp corner onto West Church Street, "You shore was friendly to them nigg'uhs back there. That was really dumb in my opin'yun."

"I didn't ask for your opinion, Clem. And for your information, Flossie and Tulip are two of the finest people I've ever known. They helped me get through some really hard times without expecting anything in return. So I'll be lucky if I make some new friends in town who're as kind and helpful as they were to me during my long years at the Merritt House."

"Nigg'uh lov'uhs ain't much liked in town in case you don't know it."

"Of course I know it but things will change one day. So you'd be smart not to refer to as them as 'niggers.' Let's talk about something else now if you don't mind."

"Why should I mind? I'll call 'em darkies or 'coons if you like that bett'uh but it don't matter what you or anybody else calls 'em 'cause they ain't nothin but trash."

"That's wrong, Clem, and you shouldn't look down on other people just because of their skin color. But I refuse to discuss this with you any longer. If you want to talk about something else, that's fine with me. But if you're unwilling to change the subject, let's be quiet for the rest of the trip."

"That's fine with me too although you're wrong about them darkies. One day you'll realize our guv'ment should've sent 'em back to Africa a long time ago. If it had, we wouldn't have had to fight that awful war against Yankee aggression which left millions o people like us as poor as church mice."

Lucy knew it would be futile to argue with Clem any longer about such a controversial matter and kept her thoughts to herself during the next several minutes.

Rhonda was sitting in a rocking chair on the front porch when Clem stopped the wagon at the end of the Summerlins' front walk. Rhonda left her chair at once and hurried to the street to help Lucy get down from the driver's bench and give her a warm welcome. After hugging her sister-in-law and telling her how glad she was to see her again, Rhonda helped her carry her belongings into Chip's study behind the parlor. But before they could unpack her suitcase or one of her boxes, Lucy's older sister Julia arrived in her husband's horse and buggy, which Joe had taught her how to drive several years earlier so she could run errands and take their children to her parents' cottage a mile from the Hanfords' house with much less trouble.

After coming inside Julia told Lucy not to unpack anything because she would be staying with her family at their house until she moved into a place of her own.

"No, she won't," Rhonda said firmly to Julia. "Lucy's going to live here with Chip and me until she moves into a place of her own and that's final."

"It's very nice of you and Chip to want her to live with you," Julia said just as firmly. "But Alfred's less than a year old and his asthma attacks still cause him to cry for several hours on most nights. Because Lucy will be on her feet seven or eight hours a day at the drugstore, she'll need plenty of sleep every night, which she'll be able to get at our house but not at yours."

"Don't throw your weight around because you're a doctor's wife and the only woman in town who know how to drive a horse and buggy. If you ever showed any interest in Alfred's health, you'd know his asthma attacks have tapered off and become briefer and much less frequent. Besides, his crying won't bother Lucy at all because Chip's study is on the opposite side of our house from my sewing room, where I moved his crib yesterday while Susan played with him on her bedroom floor."

"That's all very well and good, Rhonda, but Joe and I have a *large* guest room where Lucy will be much more comfortable than she'd be in Chip's study. And while I hate to brag, our house has indoor plumbing while yours doesn't."

As Julia and Rhonda continued to bicker about where Lucy would live during the next month or two, she burst into tears because of their obvious concern about her welfare. She'd been all but isolated from her family for almost thirteen years and now she felt loved and wanted again. Such strong feelings of happiness and relief welled up in her breast they overwhelmed her and caused large tears to roll down her cheeks. When Julia and Rhonda noticed her tears, they stopped arguing in order to comfort her.

Once Lucy's mood returned to normal, Julia made it clear she wouldn't take no for an answer. So the three women carried Lucy's belongings outside and put them in the Hanfords' buggy, after which Julia drove her much shorter sister and her meager belongings to the Hanfords' house. Lucy expected to live there for six or seven weeks although she didn't move into a place of her own until the beginning of June.

Olivia and Joey Hanford were delighted by their aunt's presence in their home that spring. Because Lucy loved children and enjoyed their company, she spent long hours with them on Sunday afternoons and on most weeknights until their eight o'clock bedtime. Once or twice a month she made sugar cookies or gingerbread men for them in the kitchen before telling them a story in the study. On other occasions they followed her around the house, Olivia with her favorite doll in her arms and Joey with a stuffed animal of some kind. Because they were unusually verbal for their age (slightly over four and three), they loved their aunt's accounts of the size and splendor of the Merritt House and the Merritt children's nasty behavior, which caused them to giggle or laugh outright. Several times they asked Lucy if the Merritt children were as mean as Cinderella's stepsisters, to which Lucy always said, "Yes, they certainly are! In fact, they're *even meaner* than Cinderella's stepsisters, and I'm sure you wouldn't like them at all because they're so different from wonderful little children like you. And because they're always so nasty and unpleasant, no one but their parents and the servants will have anything to do with them." Those and similar comments about the Merritt children caused Olivia and Joey to laugh even louder and ask more questions about the various ways Becca and Willie teased Little Robert until he burst into tears.

To Lucy's delight, her niece and nephew were as intrigued by the world around them as the Merritt children were bored by it. Olivia was so precocious she already read well while Joey knew all his letters and numbers. But even more than most little boys, Joey had enormous energy and loved to climb trees and play games that involved a physical challenge of some kind. Lucy was extremely pleased to get to know them better because during her long years at the Merritt House, she'd had so little time off she barely knew them at all and was unsure how to treat them at first. That ended after Julia told her six or seven times to act naturally and forget about such a trivial matter.

During her first week at the Hanfords' house, Lucy had very little trouble adjusting to the routine at the drugstore, with its high ceilings and handsome counters and soda fountain, which her father and his workmen had built and installed fifteen years before. The three potbellied stoves, in which Clem Johnson kept fires burning on cold winter days, and the four ceiling fans that whirled softly overhead on hot summer days, kept the large space comfortable during the most unpleasant months of the year. Although Lucy was cautious and a bit unsure of herself at first, she soon enjoyed waiting on customers and ringing up their purchases. To her great relief, she learned the store's bookkeeping system in only five minutes, just as Chip had told her she would. In several days she was posting the previous day's charges as if she'd done that work for years.

Chip was extremely pleased with her job performance and told her so dozens of times to boost her confidence. He was also pleased that Lucy had no trouble getting along with Dillie Hughes, who was surprised and very grateful when Lucy stopped whatever she was doing on slow mornings to help her serve coffee or lemonades to the nineteen or twenty lawyers, bankers, and merchants who came to the drugstore between nine forty-five and ten fifteen to relax and chat with their friends for twenty or thirty minutes.

After her first full week of work, Chip gave Lucy a check for $10.85 because, like Dillie, she preferred to be paid at the end of each week rather than at the end of each month. Chip realized that by paying them a fourth of their monthly salary every Saturday afternoon, he was paying them slightly more a year than he'd promised to pay them. But he was so pleased by how well everything was going he ignored that fact at Rhonda's suggestion. An unusually kind and generous woman, Rhonda had convinced Chip to pay Lucy at least $40 a month so she'd be able to live comfortably in a cottage of her own on the salary she made at the drugstore.

Lucy had never had $10.85 at one time before, not even on the day she graduated from high school and was awarded the five-dollar prizes for outstanding work in Latin and history. So shortly after she retired to the Hanfords' guest room several hours after supper on the afternoon Chip gave her a check for her first seven days of work, she took it out of her pocketbook and gazed at it while wondering what she should do with all that money. Being a person of practical bent, she knew she should save most of it because of the dozens of items she would need to buy once she moved into a place of her own. She was also determined to give the Hanfords a nice present or treat them and their children to a good meal in the dining room at Crumpler's Hotel, the best place in town to eat, for being so kind and hospitable to her.

On the Monday morning after she received her first paycheck, Lucy told Chip she'd like to go to the town's only bank and open a checking account so her money would be in a safe place. Chip considered that a fine idea and offered to accompany her to the bank. She thanked him but said she could handle such a simple matter by herself. Chip smiled knowingly, aware of what she was likely to encounter at the bank. All its officers and other employees were men except for one of the five bookkeepers, a widow and distant cousin of the president, who'd given her a job rather than a room in his home to keep her from living in poverty.

Because it was a blustery day, Lucy put on her coat and bonnet before marching next door to the Bank of Perquimmons City. It had grown steadily since the fall of 1888, when Andrew Ridinger became its second president six years after it opened for business. After entering the bank on that January morning in 1901, Lucy waited in line for several minutes to see one of the four tellers. On moving up to the first vacant window, she handed her check to the slender young man who was waiting to assist her. The sign at his window said he was the head teller and his name was Dennis Payne. As Mr. Payne turned her check over to be sure Lucy had endorsed it properly, she said she'd like to open a checking account and deposit all but fifty cents of her money in it.

"Very good, madam," Payne said with an engaging smile as he handed her an application form to fill out. "I'm sure you won't have any trouble with this, but be sure to include your husband's name and place of work in the blank spaces near the bottom of the first page. They must be included on your application for a checking account."

"I have no husband, Mr. Payne. But I'm a woman of some standing in this town because I was born into a respectable family here. And because I've been responsible for my own finances since I graduated from high school over a dozen years ago, I'm sure my personal information and signature will suffice."

"I understand how you feel, Miss Summerlin, but this bank has rules that must be followed. Do you work in a nearby office or store?"

"Yes, I'm the bookkeeper and sales assistant in a nearby store."

"Very good, but because you're single I need to know your employer's name and address in case you overdraw your account by accident. In that event, we can contact your employer who'll cover any deficiencies you've incurred unwittingly."

"I'm sorry, Mr. Payne, but I can't accept a policy that strongly suggests the bank lacks confidence in female depositors like myself. So if you're unable to open an account in my name only, I'd like to talk to someone who has the authority to do so. By any chance, is the bank's president free at the moment?"

"Yes, ma'am, he's talking to one of our other customers over there by the water fountain now. So I'll go over and ask him to explain the bank's policy in this regard to you more clearly than I've been able to do."

Payne hurried across the lobby and huddled for several moments with Andrew Ridinger. A tall, heavyset man in his early forties, Ridinger had long sideburns and a thick handlebar mustache. Lucy had seen him at church dozens of times; but because he and his wife always sat on one of the rear pews and he always prevailed on his wife not to attend the coffee hour after the main service which he considered a waste of time, Lucy didn't realize how enormous he was until that morning at the bank. Although he was only an inch taller than Chip and Joe, who both stood six feet two, Ridinger weighed almost three hundred pounds, which caused Lucy to consider him a real giant. She hoped his massive size wouldn't cause her courage to falter and submit to a policy she considered unacceptable.

Ridinger was soon at Lucy's side, smiling broadly and extending one of his large, meaty hands in a friendly way. As she placed her much smaller hand in his he said, "It's a pleasure to meet you, Lucy. Chip's told me a great deal about you since he was elected to the bank's executive committee several weeks ago. I've also heard a number of things about you from your brother-in-law, Dr. Hanford, who's also a member of our executive committee. So if you'll give Mr. Payne the name and address of either man, we'll put this matter behind us in no time."

Lucy withdrew her hand from Ridinger's and said firmly, "I can't do that because this is a matter of principle to me, and I refuse to acquiesce in a policy I consider wrong and misguided. Furthermore, this is a business transaction, not a social call, so I'd prefer to be addressed as *Miss Summerlin* by a person I barely know."

"Oh, I see," Ridinger said, amused by such audacity from such a small person, and a female at that.

"Mr. Ridinger," Lucy said loudly enough for everyone else in the lobby to hear, "I've already told Mr. Payne that I'm a person of good standing in this community. I have a full-time job in a local store, and for years I've made a monthly pledge to St. John's Episcopal Church, which I've always paid in a timely way. If you need to verify that, you can always check with the church treasurer, George Kahle, or my brother, who's a member of the vestry and chairman of its Building and Grounds Committee."

"That won't be necessary," Ridinger said at once because his friend Kahle had just entered the bank. Ridinger hated to look foolish in the eyes of the town's most distinguished lawyer, who was always so well dressed and groomed he looked like he might be an important judge or the head of a large business corporation. But Lucy didn't give a fig about Ridinger's dignity. She was determined to achieve her goal, which Kahle's timely arrival made much more likely.

"I have something else to say to you, Mr. Ridinger," Lucy intoned in her best oratorical voice, the one she'd used while delivering her valedictory speech on the night she graduated from high school. "If you refuse to let me open a checking account without having a male guarantor, I'll wait until the Bank of Hertford opens a branch in town this summer. I've heard a rumor that its president and executive committee are planning to open a local branch in July or August, and I'm sure they'll want to attract as many accounts to it as possible. Of course, I'd rather bank here because it's so convenient to my place of work. But I shall do otherwise if you leave me no choice."

Ridinger sighed and said, "Miss Summerlin, you're the most determined adversary I've encountered in many a year, and you shall have your account just as you wish."

Turning to Payne, who'd followed their proceedings with barely concealed amusement, Ridinger said, "Dennis, open a checking account for Miss Summerlin at once because she's probably in a hurry to resume her duties next door." After winking at Dennis, Ridinger whispered to him, "I'll fill out her application form later provided you get her to sign it in the right place."

Lucy realized Ridinger considered her a pest and wanted to get rid of her as soon as possible. But she smiled sweetly and thanked him for his help shortly before he harrumphed his way across the lobby to his office door. As he was about to go inside, Kahle consoled him on his defeat by the smallest adult he'd ever seen in the bank. Ridinger snorted, "George, don't you have something better to do than to annoy me on a morning I have a great deal of work on my desk? Although it's too early to go down to the Combat Café and bicker with Buzz-Saw Beulah, you could always go back to your office and think up some better arguments than the pathetic ones you've used on her during recent weeks. A lawyer like you should be ashamed of the way Beulah argues circles around you every time we have lunch there."

Kahle laughed and said, "You accept defeat so gracefully, Andrew. But I have a question for you now. If you're unable to handle Lucy successfully, when will you get up enough courage to tangle with Buzz-Saw Beulah? She called you a lily-livered coward several times last week; and although Quentin and I did our best to change her mind about you, that turned out to be impossible."

"That's not a bit funny, George, and I can't wait until Beulah has you on the ropes again while I'm having lunch with you and Quentin tomorrow or a day or two after that."

As Ridinger and Kahle continued their discussion in the president's office, Lucy signed the application form for her checking account before accepting two quarters and her deposit slip for $10.35 from Payne. She put them in her purse before thanking him and returning to the drugstore. Chip was waiting for her near the front door with an expectant look on his face when she entered the building and took off her coat and bonnet. With a grin he said, "Well, Lucy, did you have any trouble at the bank?"

Feeling a bit devilish she said, "No, Chip, although the teller who waited on me had to obtain the president's permission to suspend the normal rules of business involving a single woman like myself. But when Mr. Ridinger came over and spoke to me, he was even more pleasant than I thought he'd be. In fact, he said it was high time the bank treated *all* women fairly and hopes my action will prompt other spinsters to come in and follow my example."

Chip's face fell. As he returned to the drug counter, he thought, *That certainly doesn't sound like the Andrew Ridinger I know. I wonder if Lucy's pulling my leg again, the way she did so many times when we were children.*

For the rest of the day Lucy was amazed by her audacity that morning. Of course she'd stood up to Chip and Julia dozens of times while they were children, and she'd even defied her mother in the kitchen occasionally, causing Margaret to rebuke her for being underfoot and hindering her efforts to finish her baking or ironing. But this was the first time Lucy had ever confronted a man as large and imposing as Ridinger. And because she'd stood her ground without wavering, she was very pleased with herself.

Even so, she hated the thought of becoming known as a rude and arrogant person like Mrs. Merritt.

Almost thirteen years before, on the June morning Lucy walked across town for her job interview at the Merritt House, she'd assumed Mrs. Merritt was a true lady with hundreds of friends and admirers in the area. But after several days at the mansion, Lucy's opinion of her employer was completely different because she'd felt the rough side of her tongue several times too often. During later months and years, whenever Lucy joined her family at church on Sunday mornings, she overheard whispered complaints about Mrs. Merritt's rude and condescending behavior. Largely because of that, shortly after she started working at the drugstore in January of 1901, Lucy hoped to forget her unhappy years at the Merritt House but wondered if that was possible because of her bitter memories of her former employer and the other members of her family.

On the first Sunday in March, after having a bowl of soup and a piece of pecan pie with her parents several hours after she walked home from church with them, Lucy mentioned her feelings about the Merritts as they relaxed at the kitchen table together.

"Lucy," her father said after thinking for a moment, "you should forgive the Merritts for the way they treated you while you were on their staff. Your deep dislike of them is hurting you a lot more than it'll ever hurt them. In fact, they probably have no idea you disliked them so much, and I'm sure they'll be surprised if they ever find out."

"No, that's wrong, Papa, because I told Mrs. Merritt exactly how I felt about her on my last afternoon at the mansion. I'd already told her about my decision to quit my job so I could work for Chip, which made her so angry she said some really hurtful things to me. But I know I should forgive her and the rest of her family for my own sake rather than for theirs. But that won't be easy. It'll be almost impossible in fact."

"I understand your problem because it took me twenty years to forgive the Yankee troops whose heavy fire wounded my right leg so much during the siege of Petersburg I've had a bad limp ever since. But all my pent-up bitterness vanished shortly after I forgave them. Besides, if Jesus could forgive His enemies as they nailed Him to the cross, I'm sure you can forgive the Merritts."

"But Jesus was perfect, which no one will ever say about me."

"You're certainly right about that," Charles said with a chuckle. "But you'll be much happier once you forgive them and forget all their nasty insults and criticisms."

"I'll do the best I can but don't expect a miracle, Papa."

Margaret reached across the table and squeezed her daughter's hand while saying, "I'm afraid it'll take you several years to forgive the Merritts for the way they treated you. But who'd like another piece of pie now?"

Charles roared with laughter before saying, "Margaret, you've always thought a piece of your pecan pie would solve all of life's problems, even the worst ones."

"No, that's wrong, Charles. But a piece of my pecan pie will solve a lot more problems than a dose of Lydia Pinkham's Compound ever will. And most of my friends have raved about its healing qualities for years."

"I don't doubt that for a minute although I'm sure your friends have exaggerated the results they've gotten from using Lydia Pinkham's Compound. So cut Lucy and me another piece of your wonderful pie. And make 'em big enough this time they'll solve all our problems until suppertime."

Chapter 3

As Lucy developed a closer relationship with her niece and nephew while living at the Hanfords' house, she also developed a closer relationship with their father. One April evening as Julia was getting Olivia and Joey ready for bed upstairs, Lucy had a long conversation with Joe in the study behind the parlor. He started that conversation by saying how much happier she seemed to be since leaving the Merritt House and getting accustomed to her work at the drugstore. He also said it was a blessing for his children to get to know her better.

She thanked him for those words before asking him why he'd settled in Perquimmons City rather than in Salisbury or another town in the central part of the state where he'd grown up and his parents and most of the other members of his family still lived.

After thinking for a moment he said, "I'm sure you met my mother when she and several other members of my family came to Perquimmons City on the weekend Julia and I were married. So you probably have some idea of why I opened an office here and not in Salisbury or a nearby town like High Point or Thomasville."

"Are you saying you wanted to avoid that area when you moved back to North Carolina from Virginia because of your mother's strong and domineering personality?"

"Yes, although I wish I felt differently about her. She has dozens of fine qualities, and when she's dead and gone I'll probably kick myself for avoiding her during the latter part of her life. But her constant chatter drives me up the wall and so does the way she orders everyone else in the family around, especially my brother and his wife. So during my last few months in Richmond, I decided to establish my practice at least a hundred miles from Salisbury so I wouldn't see her more than once or twice a year, and I've never regretted that decision."

"I'm glad you feel that way, but why did you settle in Perquimmons City and not in a much larger place like Charlotte or Asheville?"

"I've always liked small towns; and during my last three months in Richmond, I visited the placement office at the Medical College of Virginia once or twice a week hoping to see a notice from a fairly small place that wanted to find a resident doctor. On the last Thursday afternoon in April—and I'll remember that day for the rest of my life—I saw a letter in the doctors-wanted file from Dan Wiley, the town clerk here. Dan's letter said the mayor had instructed him to write the placement offices of at least a dozen medical schools in the eastern half of the country about the town's urgent need for a resident doctor. Dan's letter also said how friendly and cooperative most of the townspeople are. But what really caught my eye were his comments about the excellent hunting and fishing in the area. As a boy I loved to hunt and fish on my parents' farm several miles west Salisbury. I'd really missed being able to do that during my seven years in Richmond and figured I'd be able to do them several times a month here. But my patient list increased so fast during my first year in town I've been unable to do as much hunting and fishing as I'd hoped to do. But I'm not complaining because there have been some wonderful compensations."

"You mean Julia and the children, don't you?"

"Yes, although I knew getting married and starting a family would change my life in most ways. But it never occurred to me how much fuller and richer my life would become. Because of Julia and the children, I've gained a new outlook about the things in life that really matter. Besides, I've usually been able to hunt and fish with Chip, Dan, Burt Trumble, and several other friends once or twice a month."

"That's interesting but I have a different question for you now. Several years ago when I had a bad cold I couldn't shake, I came to your office and was amazed to see several colored people sitting on one side of your waiting room while the same number of whites were sitting across the room from them and no one seemed to be annoyed or upset by the situation. I could hardly believe my eyes, and I've often wondered how you brought about a miracle like that."

Joe smiled and said, "It was actually very simple, and I did it mainly because it had been drummed into me by my favorite professor in

Richmond, who'd grown up in Boston, that I should *never* turn my back on someone who needed help, whether that person was black, white, red, yellow, or some other color. And because the only black doctor in the area lived on the outskirts of Hertford when I moved to town and still does, I knew I'd probably have almost as many colored patients as white ones, and I wasn't about to turn my back on a colored person who came to my office for help. Unfortunately, during my first month in town, several dozen whites made it clear to me they had no intention of sitting in my waiting room alongside several blacks who were waiting to see me also."

"I'm surprised you didn't set up two waiting rooms."

"I didn't have enough space to do that, and besides, I saw no reason why blacks and whites couldn't use the same waiting room. After all, people are people, and in my naive way I felt it was high time the area's whites got over their racial hang ups. Even so, I'm convinced we'll all be much better off when we get to that point, which is a lot farther off than I thought it was during my years in Virginia. You're probably unaware of it, but during the 1890s there was a very capable black man named John Mitchell on the Richmond city council. I operated on him one morning for a ruptured appendix and got to know him fairly well while he was recovering from that surgery. In my opinion, he was no different from one of the dozens of white people I operated on for various reasons."

"I'm not surprised to hear you say that because of how kind and considerate you always are to Augusta. But how did you actually solve your waiting-room problem?"

"Well, less than a month after I opened my office here, I realized that dozens of whites who should've come to see me there were arranging for me to visit them in their homes during my office hours. At least three-fourths of the house calls I made during my first month in town were unnecessary and took a great deal of my time, which kept me from seeing dozens of people who needed my help a lot more. So during my fourth week in town, I bought a hundred postcards and had the print shop in Hertford, the one that prints the *Tribune* on Tuesday and Friday mornings, inscribe a brief message on the postcards' blank side. That message explained that from the last Monday in July there would be a two-dollar surcharge for every house call I made and considered unnecessary, and I wouldn't waive that surcharge for anyone, regardless of how rich or prominent that individual was. Shortly after the printer finished that job, I paid Mary Bishop, my nurse-receptionist, five dollars to address a postcard to every adult I'd already visited in his or her home since the week I opened my office. And shortly after Mary completed that job, I took those sixty-three postcards to the post office and paid a clerk three dollars to stamp them during his free time before mailing them at the bulk rate."

"I bet you heard dozens of complaints during the next five or six weeks."

"Did I ever! But I expected to hear them and knew the news would travel fast once those postcards reached the people to whom she'd addressed them. Even so, nine or ten people who hadn't heard about my surcharge arranged for me to come to their homes without much of a reason. And as I was about to leave their homes, I handed them a postcard explaining my policy although I didn't ask them to pay the surcharge for that visit. But by handing them a postcard as I was leaving their homes, I put them on notice about future house calls I considered unnecessary. And in that way I ended them for good by the beginning of September as I knew I would."

"Why were you so sure you'd be successful?"

"Because I'd made a point of meeting the doctors in Hertford and Edenton shortly after I opened my office on East Main Street. They both welcomed me to the area largely because they had so many patients they were no longer willing to spend two afternoons a week here in town as they'd done during earlier years. So when it became clear to the local whites that they could no longer count on Dr. Jacobs or Dr. Wainwright to see them in their homes, they had little choice but to accept my policy unless they were willing to make the trip to Hertford or Edenton or pay my surcharge for unnecessary house calls. The Merritts are the only family on my patient list who still refuse to come to my office although they've complained bitterly about my surcharge since the month I established it. They think I'm unaware of how much they criticize my policy during the social hours at the Presbyterian church on Sunday mornings, but it's hard to keep secrets in small towns like Perquimmons City."

"That's true although I didn't realize the Merritts have been so critical of your policy in regard to colored patients unnecessary house calls. It doesn't surprise me, though, because they consider themselves too good to socialize with most of the people who live here and in Hertford, which explains why most of their friends live in Edenton, which is the oldest and probably the most sophisticated town in the area. But let's not waste any more time on them because I have another question for you now. Do you think your efforts to start a capital funds drive to raise enough money to build a local hospital in five or six more years will succeed?"

"I'm afraid it'll take a lot longer than five or six years, but I suddenly feel very thirsty. So I think I'll go to the kitchen and drink some water. Would you like me to bring you some water when I come back?"

"Thanks but I'm not thirsty now although I'd like to use your powder room for a moment or two. I still consider indoor plumbing a great luxury, don't you?"

"Yes, although I got used to it in Richmond in a week or so and would hate to go back to using privies and chamber pots again. I had to do that during my first six months in town when I lived in the cottage I bought on Second Street . . . You know, Lucy, I've been meaning to talk to you about my cottage because it's probably the right size for you and only a short walk from the drugstore. You're still looking for a place to rent, aren't you?"

"Yes, and I'd love to hear about your cottage when you get back from the kitchen because Julia's told me several times how nice and comfortable it is."

They both stood up and left the study, Joe for the kitchen directly across the back hall while Lucy went to the powder room between the kitchen and Julia's morning room. That large attractive room had been a screened porch until Joe had it enlarged and glassed in for his wife on their first wedding anniversary.

Once they returned to the study and were comfortably seated again Joe said, "Let's see now—I was about to tell you about my cottage on Second Street a couple of minutes ago, wasn't I?"

"Yes, because Julia's told me several times that you took her there fairly often during the last month before your wedding, which explains why Papa got so down on you back then. But Julia liked your cottage so much she would've been very happy to live in it with you."

"I hope you you'll keep this to yourself, but I'm sure your father knew I took Julia to my cottage at least a dozen times during the last month before our wedding and was afraid she'd be pregnant on our wedding day. It took him several years to get over his enormous anger at me for doing that."

"Julia's been aware of that for years because Mama told her she did everything she could to keep Papa from going on the warpath shortly after he made some violent threats against you during the last several weeks before your wedding. On more than one occasion they both heard Papa threaten to set your 'tawdry little love nest' on fire, but his bark's always been a lot worse than his bite."

"I've always assumed that was the case, but how did your parents know what Julia and I were doing at my cottage during the last month before our wedding?"

"They both noticed a large hickey on your neck one night when you brought Julia home at ten thirty and claimed you'd been driving her around town in your buggy since having dinner with them and leaving their cottage with Julia shortly after seven o'clock."

"Gosh, it was really dumb of me not to realize that—almost as dumb as some of the pranks my fraternity brothers and I played on the members of half a dozen other fraternities while we were students in Chapel Hill. We were real hell raisers back then although I'll deny it if you ever tell Julia or your parents I told you that. But let's get back to my cottage now because I'm convinced it's the right size for you. Still, I'd hate for you to feel obligated to rent it just because it belongs to me. I'm sure I won't have any trouble finding someone to replace the current tenant, who plans to move out during the last week of May, if you think it wouldn't be right for you for any reason at all, which you don't need to explain to me."

"It's nice of you to say that, but how many rooms does your cottage have? And is there a good place in the backyard where I could grow flowers and vegetables?"

"It has four rooms and a large backyard where you could grow as many flowers and vegetables as you like. Although the rent might be a bit steep for you—eight dollars a month—I'm willing to adjust it so it'll be in your price range."

"It sounds perfect for me, but what sort of adjustment do you have in mind?"

"I'll reduce the rent to five dollars a month provided you do two things in return. First, although Olivia's only four and a half, she's fascinated by history and wants to learn about the lords and serfs of the middle ages as well as the lives of the ancient Greeks and Romans if you can believe it. Julia's told me several times that you were the best history student the local high school's ever had. So I wonder if you'd give Olivia a brief history lesson on Sunday afternoons until she decides she'd rather do something else, which probably won't take more than a month. And here's the second thing you could do, which would please your sister enormously." Julia, who'd just entered the study and made herself comfortable in her favorite chair, sighed while rolling her eyes at Joe when he said, "My sweetie pie loves to have fresh flowers in the house during the warmer months of the year but she lacks the patience to grow them. After all, aside from the children, her greatest interest is fashion; and whenever she's not making a new outfit for one of them, she's making a new skirt or blouse for herself. I'm convinced I made a big mistake two Christmases ago when I gave her that blasted sewing machine she'd begged me for dozens of times."

Julia stuck out her tongue at Joe, which brought a big smile to Lucy's face. Joe pretended not to notice and continued, "In short, if you'll share some of your flowers with your sister and indulge Olivia's fantasy about learning some basic facts of history, I'll reduce the rent on my cottage by three dollars a month."

Lucy was very touched by the way Joe had presented his offer. He clearly wanted to avoid the impression that he considered her a poor relation who needed financial help. For several moments Lucy was so overcome by his thoughtfulness and the amusing way he'd presented his offer she was unable to respond. Eventually she said, "Of course I'll do those things, Joe, because I'd enjoy doing them and it wouldn't be any trouble at all."

"Good, I hoped you'd feel that way. Now, I'll tell you a bit about my cottage's current occupant, Wilfred Brooks, who's a traveling salesman. He informed me ten days ago that he plans to move out by May twenty-fifth or a day or two before that; and because he's lived there since I vacated it for this house, which I loved the minute I saw it and bought for a wonderful price, I'm planning to have its interior painted before you or another tenant moves in on, let's say, the first day of June, which is a Saturday if I remember correctly. Until then, Julia and I hope you'll continue to live with us because the children have become extremely fond of you, while Augusta says you're always very helpful in the kitchen. Of course, we'll miss you a great deal once you leave us. So we hope you'll come back and have dinner with us on Sundays and several other times a week if you can endure our company that often."

Lucy laughed and said the idea of "enduring" their company was so silly she hardly knew how to respond to it.

Julia laughed at that idea too before saying, "Joe and I truly hope you'll come back several times a week because it's been a real pleasure having you live with us. Our suppers won't be the same without your amusing comments about all the funny things that happen at the drugstore when the town's big shots come in for their morning coffee and go on and on about all the clever things they've done since the last time they saw their friends. Especially Ozzie Crumpler, who's the most amusing man Joe and I've ever met."

"You and Joe give me too much credit, Julia. But I'd love to come back and see you and the children fairly often. But just how often we'll see when the time comes. After all, I'll probably make so many new friends during the summer and have such an active social life by next fall I won't be able to fit you into my busy schedule."

Joe and Julia looked at her in disbelief before laughing outright as Lucy gave them a deadpan look before laughing almost as hard as they were.

A week later, as Lucy walked past Joe's cottage as she was returning to the Hanfords' house after having lunch with her parents after church that day, she knew at once that it would be perfect for her needs. As a result, she could hardly wait for Wilfred Brooks to vacate it during the latter part of May and she could move in and make it her home.

Because Joe had decided to have the whole cottage painted and several other improvements made before she even went inside it, Lucy was unable to see its interior until four weeks later. Julia was with her that afternoon, and from the moment they unlocked the front door and entered the parlor, Lucy was pleased by everything she saw. Its walls sparkled with two coats of fresh paint, and there was a new and more efficient Franklin stove in the fireplace. Joe had also had all the torn window screens replaced and part of the back porch enclosed and fitted up with a toilet, sink, and galvanized tub to Lucy's surprise and enormous gratitude.

While the cottage was being painted and improved in those ways, Lucy had been able to work in the yard and she'd pruned most of the bushes around the cottage because their branches had become too long and leggy. She'd also cleared a large space in the backyard for vegetables and especially flowers, of which she'd become extremely fond as a schoolgirl. She'd worked in her mother's flower and vegetable garden several afternoons a week from the time she was nine, and during her teenage years she'd taught herself how to arrange cut flowers effectively. Because Chip gave her the last week of May off so she could get ready for her coming move, she planted a dozen kinds of flowers in the backyard, including gladiolas, larkspur, dahlias, asters, zinnias, petunias, and dianthus or pinks. She cleared almost as much space for vegetables and planted tomatoes, cucumbers, onions, squash, zucchini, green beans, and several kinds of herbs and lettuce. By the middle of July she was able to give Julia dozens of flowers and vegetables on Sunday afternoons when she walked to the Hanfords' house and gave Olivia a history lesson—actually a short talk about earlier peoples and their most important social and religious customs—before she had dinner with her niece and the rest of her family. Lucy also gave an occasional assortment of flowers and vegetables to her parents, Chip and Rhonda, and even Dillie Hughes whom she already liked a great deal. As for her sister-in-law Rhonda, she was one of Lucy's favorite people as well as an excellent cook who reciprocated by giving Lucy several jars of homemade jams and jellies as well as dozens of tips about simple but inexpensive meals she could fix for herself.

On the morning of June 1, when Lucy finally moved into Joe's cottage with Julia and Rhonda's help, her father arrived in his wagon with a loveseat, two end tables, and a rocking chair he'd made especially for her parlor. He also brought and hung six pairs of curtains Margaret had made from materials she'd found on sale at Miss Edna's Dry Goods Store on West Main Street two blocks from the drugstore. Late that afternoon Chip and Clem Johnson arrived with a chest of drawers, a double bed with new springs and a good firm mattress as well as several hooked rugs for Lucy's bedroom and parlor. They also brought a small drop-leaf table and two ladder-back chairs for her breakfast nook, which Joe and Julia gave her along with Joe's original office desk and file cabinet, which he'd recently upgraded with larger ones. Lucy was especially pleased to get the file cabinet because for almost ten years, she'd collected newspaper clippings, family letters, and other materials for a book about her family and hometown she planned to write one day. She also received from the other members of her family dozens of kitchen items retrieved from attics and basements as well as six lamps, two sets of sheets and pillowcases, two bedspreads, and a heavy comforter for cold weather.

Because of all those gifts Lucy had only a few things to buy, including a desk chair, two blankets, a set of canisters for her kitchen, and half a dozen pictures for her walls. Luckily she already owned a watercolor she'd loved for years, a large watercolor her mother had painted during the Civil War and called "Sunset on the Sound." A gifted amateur painter whose childhood dream had been to be an illustrator one day, Margaret gave Lucy that picture, which her father had framed thirty-four years before, as a special gift on the evening before she moved into her new home.

To show her appreciation to her parents and all the other members of her family for their enormous generosity, Lucy tried repeatedly to take them out to dinner at Crumpler's Hotel where she'd heard the food in the dining room was extremely good. But they refused to let her spend any of her hard-earned money on them. So during June and July, she crocheted three sets of placemats for them, one for her parents and the other two her brother and sister's families, all of whom were deeply impressed by her handiwork and very pleased to receive those placemats.

Shortly after Lucy moved into Joe's cottage, she was welcomed to the neighborhood by Hazel Barlow who lived in a similar cottage a short distance south of hers. A spinster like herself, Hazel was several years older than Lucy; and because she was Estelle Hogan's younger sister, she'd worked for almost twenty years at Hogan's Grocery Store as a bookkeeper and cashier. On the Sunday afternoon Hazel welcomed Lucy to the neighborhood, she invited her to have supper at her cottage that night and gave her half of the pound cake she'd made for their dessert. Lucy knew at once that she and Hazel would be good friends because they had a number of interests in common. They both loved to read and garden; they both enjoyed playing cribbage and double solitaire; and most of all, they loved to spend time with their nieces and nephews. Because Hazel had a number of fine qualities and clearly liked men, Lucy was convinced she was still single because of a large purple birthmark on the left side of her face and neck. She was clearly self-conscious about that blemish, and in several days Lucy realized that Hazel was almost a recluse because of it. Lucy also sensed that Hazel was a needy person who longed to find someone she could spend an hour or two with several times a week. That didn't bother Lucy at all because she enjoyed Hazel's company and considered her a nice and interesting person. *She would've made some man an excellent wife,* Lucy thought one night after Hazel had supper at her cottage and they played several games of double solitaire before Hazel returned to her own cottage. *I guess most men can't overlook a birthmark like Hazel's. That's a real shame because physical beauty isn't everything, which I know from personal experience because I grew up in the shadow of Julia's enormous beauty. Because of that, I've felt like an ugly duckling since I was six or seven, although Jobie always told me I was much better looking than I thought I was. My life would've been very different if he hadn't died during the summer we were sixteen and about to start our senior year in high school. But at least I'm not living and working at the Merritt House anymore, thank God! What a nightmare that was!*

During the next two weeks dozens of other women who lived nearby welcomed Lucy to the neighborhood. They usually called on her in pairs and brought her gifts of kitchen staples like a pound or two of coffee, tea, sugar, or butter while several women gave her kitchen towels or small trivets. A fine little cookbook compiled by the ladies of the Methodist church was an especially welcome gift from Lillian Greenfield, a strikingly attractive redhead with no relatives in eastern North Carolina or southside Virginia.

Lillian worked in the town's office building between Jack's Bicycle Shop and Miss Edna's Dry Goods Store on West Main Street. She was a year or two younger than Joe and Chip, who'd both been born in August 1867. Because she seemed especially nice and admired the work Lucy had done in her yard during May and June, Lucy gave her a tour of her flower and vegetable garden before inviting her to come inside and have a glass of iced tea on the first Sunday afternoon in July.

Although Lucy thought Lillian would stay for only ten or fifteen minutes, she was still chatting away in her parlor almost an hour later. Lillian talked about how friendly and helpful their neighbors were before they discussed their churches for several minutes. But Lillian, whose husband had died of tuberculosis four years before, gradually turned the conversation to Lucy's family. She asked several questions about Joe and Julia before asking almost twice as many about Chip and Rhonda.

"Someone told me that Rhonda grew up in Elizabeth City. Is that right, Lucy?"

"Yes, but she moved to Perquimmons City shortly after she graduated from high school. Her aunt, Edna Wilcox, offered her a job in her store and a bedroom with kitchen privileges in her own home free of charge."

"I've heard Rhonda worked at the dry goods store for several years before she married Chip, and she continued to work there until a month or two before Susan was born."

"That's also right because she and Chip hoped to save enough money to buy a house in several years."

"That was smart of them. But how did Rhonda get along with her aunt? I probably shouldn't say this, but I've always found Miss Edna unpleasant and hard to deal with, especially when several other women are there and no one's buying anything."

"Rhonda complains about her aunt's manner from time to time. But she also says Miss Edna's extremely nice and considerate once you get to know her, provided she's not annoyed by customers who're wasting her time by asking frivolous questions."

"I'm not surprised to hear that because I've always assumed she had a nicer and pleasanter side. If she didn't, her business wouldn't have been as successful as it is."

"It was a successful business when she inherited it from her parents almost twenty-five years ago although she's made it a lot more successful since then."

"I didn't realize her parents started it, but what about Rhonda's weight problem? She hasn't lost much of the weight she gained while she was pregnant with Alfred, and I wonder how Chip feels about that."

"I couldn't say, but most people are unaware that Rhonda's been pregnant *five* times, not just twice. She had two miscarriages before Susan was born, and she delivered a stillborn child during the years between Susan's birth and Alfred's arrival last summer. A year or so ago I read an article in the *Tribune* that said women who've been pregnant several times usually find it much harder to lose all the weight they gained during later pregnancies than they lost after their first two or three."

"That makes sense although I've never heard it before. Still, if Rhonda made a greater effort, she'd probably lose a lot more of the weight she gained during her last two pregnancies, don't you think?"

"Yes, but I don't see why you're so concerned about it."

"I'm not at all concerned about it, Lucy. I said that only because most men get a roving eye when they're in their thirties or early forties and I hope Chip and Rhonda's marriage isn't headed for trouble."

"It's not because they're devoted to each other and their children. I know my brother extremely well, and I'm sure he'd never cheat on Rhonda just because she's twelve or thirteen pounds overweight. But I don't feel comfortable discussing such a personal matter with someone I just met. Besides, I have some important things to do this afternoon if you don't mind."

Lillian stood up at once and apologized for overstaying her welcome. "I'm afraid I lost sight of the time because we were having such an interesting conversation."

Lucy stood up too and opened the screened door for Lillian while saying she'd also lost sight of the time until a minute or so ago. "I really enjoyed your visit and would love to see your garden in several days."

"I don't actually have a garden, certainly not one that's comparable to yours. But I'm so glad you're my neighbor now and hope we'll see a lot of each other in the future."

As Lucy watched Lillian cross the street to her own cottage, she wondered why Lillian was so interested in Chip and Rhonda's relationship. She was bound to have met Chip because he always paid his water bill in person at the town's office building, where Lillian was the head cashier and an assistant bookkeeper. If she was about to make a play for Chip, Lucy was convinced she'd be disappointed because his marriage to Rhonda was a successful one although it was less ardent than her parents' or Joe and

Julia's. Chip loved his wife and children, their small but comfortable house, and his respected place in their church and community. He was too sensible to sacrifice those things for another woman although Lucy realized Lillian was so attractive most men probably found her desirable. She certainly had a better figure than Rhonda's, despite how slender Rhonda had been in June 1891 when Chip married her during a simple ceremony at St. John's Episcopal Church, which they and all the other members of the Summerlin and Hanford families attended. Still, during unguarded moments with old friends at the drugstore, Chip often described his wife as "much too heavy for my taste now." Lucy considered that very unfair because Chip had gained almost thirty pounds during the last ten years and loved the hefty meals Rhonda fixed at his request. Fortunately he stood six-feet-two and had been fairly thin until he married Rhonda. Just as fortunately, he wasn't a lustful man; and aside from his occasional praise of Rhonda's handsome face and figure during their two-year engagement, he seldom commented on a woman's appearance. So Lucy hoped he wouldn't be enticed into a relationship with the widow Greenfield. Lucy was extremely fond of Rhonda and was convinced she'd be devastated if Chip had an affair with her or another woman.

Chapter 4

Several weeks after her awkward conversation with Lillian Greenfield, Lucy gave in to Julia's pleas and accompanied her to the July meeting of the United Daughters of the Confederacy. That organization, the only women's club in town aside from the women's circles of the four white churches, met on the last Friday night of each month except December in the Ladies' Parlor of the Presbyterian church.

Lucy had serious qualms about joining the UDC because she'd loved Harriet Beecher Stowe's famous novel *Uncle Tom's Cabin,* which she'd read twice while she was in her twenties and caused her to feel no nostalgia for slavery or the Confederate cause. Furthermore, her father had told her and his other children dozens of times how bloody most of the battles of the Civil War had been. Finally, as Charles Summerlin grew older, he blamed the South's political and social leaders increasingly for seceding from the Union and causing a conflict that led to 620,000 deaths and condemned the defeated region to decades of grinding poverty. On a more practical level, Lucy hated the prospect of seeing Mrs. Merritt at UDC meetings because several of her forebears in the great Manigault family of Charleston, South Carolina, had been officers in the Confederate army. But Julia assured Lucy that Mrs. Merritt seldom attended UDC meetings. In fact, Julia had seen her at only two meetings since Selma Ridinger convinced her to join the organization in May 1897. On hearing that, Lucy reluctantly agreed to attend its July meeting and was extremely glad she did.

All the members in attendance that night, twenty-three counting Lucy and Julia but not Mrs. Merritt to their great relief, welcomed Lucy as a new member and couldn't have been nicer. In fact, there was immediate talk of Lucy becoming the club's next historian because of her extensive knowledge of local history and genealogy, which the other members admired and praised several times.

During the club's August meeting, Phyllis Kahle nominated Lucy to be the club's next historian because the current holder of that office had submitted her resignation two weeks earlier, her husband having accepted a job in Greensboro two hundred miles to the west. Lucy did her best to decline Mrs. Kahle's nomination on the grounds she was the newest member of the group and knew very little about its policies and procedures. But the other members ignored her objections and elected her its new historian by acclamation, which was very gratifying of course.

For Lucy's formal installation during the September meeting, her mother made her a new dress of white organza with some lovely pink appliqué on the bodice which, with a bit of padding, camouflaged how flat chested she was, at least in comparison to Julia's hourglass figure which was admired for miles around by men, women, and dozens of teenage boys on the cusp of manhood. Margaret also gave Lucy a canister of her favorite face powder and convinced her to wear her hair in a more becoming way. Because Lucy hadn't cut her hair in a dozen years, it hung down her back to her waist unless she wore it in braids on top of her head, which she did whenever she attended church or was working at the drugstore. But several hours before the UDC's September meeting, Margaret insisted on cutting her hair to shoulder length while her curling irons were heating on Lucy's kitchen stove. Lucy shed several tears as her mother cut off three-fourths of her hair with her best pair of scissors. But shortly after Margaret gave her remaining hair a slight wave with the curling irons, Lucy gazed at her reflection in a hand mirror and realized her new hairdo was much more attractive than her previous one had been. In fact, it made her look several years younger although, in her opinion, a bit like the kewpie doll Chip had won at a carnival six or seven years earlier by throwing four out of five tennis balls into a bushel basket.

When Lucy put the mirror down on her breakfast table Margaret said, "Lucy, I want you to wear your hair like this for several years. You've always wanted a family of your own and it's only a question of time before you meet a man you'll like as much as you liked Jobie Caldwell, who would've made you a wonderful husband. But you've grieved for him too long already; and if you continue to grieve for him, you'll never meet another man who'll think you're interested in getting married."

"I'd love to meet another man like Jobie but no one in his right mind would be interested in an old maid like me."

"Hush, Lucy! I hate to hear you run yourself down like that. Besides, you're only thirty and still in the prime of life. You have beautiful cheek bones and a lovely smile that lights up every social gathering you attend. Dozens of men would feel blessed if they had a treasure like you."

After a long sigh Lucy said, "I don't mean any disrespect, Mama, but everyone in town knows I was the runt of the litter and took after your side of the family rather than Papa's the way Chip and Julia did."

"That's a *terrible* thing to say and you should be ashamed of yourself for even thinking it, Lucy."

"I'm just facing facts and it's not my fault I'm so short and flat chested because I'd love to be as tall and pretty as Julia. But as I've heard you say dozens of times, 'If wishes were horses, beggars would ride.' And although I've never told you this before because you and Papa get so many orders from the Merritts and hate to hear Chip or me run them down, they fought like cats and dogs while I worked for them. Largely because of that I'm convinced having a husband is no guarantee of happiness."

"I agree with you about the Merritts," Margaret said while packing her curling irons into a wicker basket. "But most marriages are much happier than theirs. After all, my relationship with your father has always been *wonderful* and so has Joe and Julia's. Unfortunately, Chip and Rhonda's is a lot less successful because Rhonda's gained so much weight since their wedding and disagrees with Chip's ideas far too often in my opinion. I wish she'd stop doing that because it would please Chip a great deal if she did."

"But Rhonda's really smart, Mama, and she has a right to express her views and opinions. Besides, you're bound to realize men as easy to live with as Papa and Joe are extremely rare. But let's change the subject now because I've never liked conversations like this and there's hardly enough time for me to get ready for tonight's meeting and make a centerpiece for the refreshment table, which I promised Joanne Wiley I'd do. She's the club's new social chairman in case you haven't heard."

"I'm sure Joanne will do a fine job in that position, but it's time for me to go home and fix your father's supper. However, I want you to think about everything I've said this afternoon and keep an open mind about it."

"I will, Mama, I promise."

Shortly after Margaret left for home with her curling irons, Lucy ate an apple and a clump of grapes for supper before picking a nice combination of flowers in her backyard. During the next half hour she made a large centerpiece, an unusually nice one in her opinion, which wasn't quite as humble as it had been during earlier years, she feared. After taking a quick bath she put on her new dress and powdered her face a bit before finding a wicker basket for her centerpiece. Shortly after seven o'clock she left her cottage with her centerpiece for the Hanfords' house several blocks away.

Once she rang their doorbell Joe answered it and asked her to come in. As he held the screened door open for her, he gazed at her new dress and hairdo before calling to Julia in the kitchen, "Come quick, sweetie pie. A stranger's here and she's a real knockout. But I have no idea who she is because she won't tell me her name."

Lucy turned crimson and said, "Stop it right now, Joe! There's no reason to say such a silly thing about my appearance." But she made a mental note to wear her new dress fairly often and buy a set of curling irons for herself in a day or two.

"My goodness, Lucy!" Julia said as she entered the front hall from the dining room with a tin of sugar cookies in her hands. "Mama must've made that lovely dress for you and I'm sure she did your hair in such a flattering way. All the other members are going to be *very* impressed by how nice you look tonight."

"Thanks, but let's get going. It's a fairly long walk to the church, you know."

"We won't be walking tonight because Joe went to Sonny's stable a while ago and got Prancer and the buggy so we can use them tonight. Wasn't that nice of him?"

"Yes, but he shouldn't have gone to all that trouble because I like to walk."

"I'm sure you do," Joe said. "But why are you always so uncomfortable when a member of your own family does you a favor?"

"It's not that, Joe. It's just that . . . well, to be honest about it, I'm often confused by the things you say. I'm never sure if you're being serious or just joking around."

"Then you're in good company because Julia says the same thing about me, which makes no sense to me at all."

"Don't pay him any attention, Lucy. He can't stand it when a patient thanks him for doing something really nice for him or someone else in his family."

"Now listen here, sweetie pie, you have no reason to say something like that."

"Good-bye, Joe," Julia said while patting his cheek playfully. "It's time we left for our meeting, and I probably won't get home until ten o'clock because I plan to drive Lucy back to her cottage shortly after the meeting ends."

"You don't need to drive me home tonight," Lucy said firmly. "I'm capable of getting there under my own steam and I'm sure you know it."

Joe laughed and said, "There you go again, Lucy. You hate to feel beholden to someone else and I'm afraid you'll never change. That's so unfair because you do so many good deeds for other people they're disappointed when you refuse to let them do something for you in return."

Julia smiled and said to him, "You've just given us an excellent example of the pot calling the kettle black. But come on, Lucy—we'll be late if we don't leave now. Because Prancer and the buggy are in the backyard, let's leave the house by the kitchen door tonight."

Ten minutes later, when they entered the Ladies' Parlor of the Presbyterian church, there was so much talk about Lucy's appearance she was even more embarrassed than she'd been by Joe's comments in the Hanfords' entrance hall. Rhonda and all the other members paid her lavish compliments while admiring her new hairdo and dress. They also admired the centerpiece she'd made for the refreshment table before agreeing with Mildred Barringer's comment that Lucy had probably been a florist during an earlier life. An unusually nice and capable person who wrote a weekly column for the *Tribune*, Mildred urged Lucy to join the Altar Guild at St. John's Church so she could share her "great talent" with the whole congregation. Lucy loved that suggestion, and in several weeks she not only joined the Altar Guild but became its main flower arranger, a skill she'd honed during her years at the Merritt House. Whenever Lucy heard the Merritts were planning a party of some kind, she offered to make half a dozen arrangements of their garden or greenhouse flowers for their mansion's main rooms as a way of avoiding less interesting work, especially polishing dozens of pieces of their dining room silver.

By taking an active part in the Altar Guild's work and joining the same church circle Julia and Rhonda belonged to, Lucy met or became better acquainted with most of the other women who attended St. John's Church. As they welcomed her into their ranks, she swapped novels with several of them, including Selma Ridinger, Phyllis Kahle, and Josephine Gardiner, a widow for some years who'd played a key role in organizing the local chapter of the UDC in 1888, the same year Lucy graduated from high school. Lucy liked all those women, but she especially liked Phyllis Kahle. An unusually friendly and energetic woman with short curly hair, Phyllis always had a smile on her face; and because she always had several amusing stories to tell, she could pep up any social gathering. As a result, she and her husband were invited to more parties than any other couple in town although the Ridingers and the Hanfords ran them a close second.

By the time Lucy joined the Altar Guild and became its main flower arranger, she was incensed by Clem Johnson's treatment of Dillie Hughes. Shortly after she started working at the drugstore, she realized Clem insulted Dillie several times a week because of her race although never while Chip was in hearing distance because Clem was well aware of his high regard for Dillie's work. Like most blacks of that era, Dillie had something of an inferiority complex because of the way she'd been belittled and insulted by most of the local whites for years. And because she valued her job a great deal, Dillie always turned a deaf ear to Clem's insults although Lucy knew she was hurt and offended by them. As a result, Lucy was so annoyed by Clem's treatment of her she told him whenever she overheard him insulting Dillie to keep his bigotry to himself. She also told him dozens of times that only a few people in town shared his racial views, which he always scoffed at when Chip was busy in the store's office and couldn't hear an argument that was taking place in the store itself.

Because Clem ignored Lucy's complaints about his treatment of Dillie, she decided by the spring of 1902 that she had no option but to urge Chip to fire him, which she did dozens of times during the next six months. Chip finally gave in to her pleas during the third week of September; and in the hope of keeping a similar situation from occurring, Chip hired a black man, Dillie's cousin James Basham, to take Clem's place. Lucy had enjoyed a friendly relationship with Dillie since her first week at the drugstore, but she greatly strengthened it when she convinced Chip to give Clem's job to James. And because Dillie and James told their many friends and acquaintances in town about Lucy's friendship and unwavering support of them, blacks throughout the area began to consider Lucy a true friend and spoke to her politely and usually with great deference whenever they saw her at the bank, the post office, or Hogan's Grocery Store.

Although Lucy failed to realize it for several weeks, Clem felt deep resentment toward James and soon decided to teach him a lesson for accepting "a white man's job." Late one October afternoon, while James was delivering some medicine to the Kahles' house on Magnolia Drive, Clem and two of his friends attacked him as he got down from the driver's bench of the drugstore's wagon. A violent scuffle ensued, and when James yelled for help, two burly black men who'd been splitting firewood in the Kahles' backyard rushed to his assistance. In several moments they knocked Clem and his friends to the ground and freed James before the three of them gave Clem and his friends a real thrashing.

The Kahles witnessed the fight from their parlor windows, and as Clem and his friends were about to slink away, George came out on his front porch with his pistol and fired two shots into the air to get their attention before calling to Clem, "I know who you are because you worked at the drugstore until a month or two ago. You and your friends started that fight and got exactly what you deserved. So don't even think about getting up a lynch party against these three colored men. I saw the whole thing from my parlor windows; and if any harm comes to them, I'll testify in court about what I saw today and how you had a personal grudge against them. Furthermore, because Chief Trumble hates lynching and is doing everything he can to stamp it out, you'll rue the day if you ever go down that road. Because I'm afraid you'll do that anyway, I plan to tell Chief Trumble the next time I see him exactly what I saw this afternoon. So if any harm comes to these three hardworking men during the next five years, Chief Trumble will know exactly where to start his investigation and whom to question first. Now get out of here and don't cause any more trouble you'll regret for the rest of your lives if you do."

Such firm words from one of the town's most important citizens caused Clem to lose face with his friends and allies. A month or two later, he and his wife Mabel and their nine-year-old son Paulie moved away and were never seen in Perquimmons City again. Rumor had it that they moved to Kinston where Clem fomented so many plots against people of color its mayor and town council grew heartily sick of him by the next summer and ran him and his family out of town. As for Clem's wife, rumors eventually spread that Mabel left him for another man shortly after they and their son were driven out of Tarboro and took refuge in Roanoke Rapids a short distance south of the Virginia line.

Shortly after George Kahle's warning forestalled a later attack on James and his friends, Chip bought the house he and Rhonda had rented from her aunt, Edna Wilcox, since their wedding in June 1891. During the years 1903-1904, Chip had their house painted and reroofed before equipping it with electricity and indoor plumbing. He also converted some storage space under the eves into another bedroom for their second son, John, who'd been born in June 1902. From the time John was a week old, the whole family called him Jack and rejoiced that he didn't suffer from asthma the way Alfred still did from time to time. Because of that, Chip and Rhonda felt guilty about making Jack share a bedroom with his older brother when they could afford to build a new room for him. Will Crabtree, the best carpenter in the area, and his sons built that room for Chip and Rhonda in August 1904. A year later Rhonda convinced Chip to pay Will and his sons to build a large rumpus room on the back of their house for their children, who were between two and eight years of age at the time.

While Chip and Rhonda were doing so much work on their house, Joe and Julia were making several improvements to theirs. In November 1904, shortly after Joe paid off his ten-year loan from the Bank of Perquimmons City a year ahead of time, he hired Will Crabtree and his sons to triple the size of the porch behind their kitchen and to screen it in. Because Joe also had it equipped with two ceiling fans, it was a cool place to relax and enjoy informal meals on all but the hottest summer days. At Julia's suggestion, Joe also had their whole house painted, inside and out, and with her help he hung some colorful wallpaper in the upstairs hall, the children's bedrooms, and Julia's morning and sewing rooms. Finally he had their house equipped with central heating and cast-iron radiators. At the same time, he had all the Franklin stoves removed from their home's eight fireplaces, all but two of which Will Crabtree boarded up because the Hanfords no longer used them for heating purposes.

Dozens of other well-to-do families, including the Ridingers, the Barringers, the Kahles, the Richardsons, the Howells, the Hogans, and the Wileys made similar improvements to their homes during those years. So did the older and younger Thomas Stantons, the president and vice president of the local textile mill, which the older Thomas Stanton had established in 1888 with help from his family in New England who owned a string of twenty-two textile mills. Although the local mill, which was known as Stanton's Mill, struggled during its first decade, it entered a boom period that coincided with the outbreak of the Spanish-American War in 1898. Thereafter Stanton's Mill made greater profits every year from its sale of sheets and blankets, bedspreads and quilts, towels, curtains, and table linens, not only in its local outlet store but also in department stores in almost a dozen cities in the upper South, including Raleigh, Charlotte, Richmond, Norfolk, and Baltimore. The profits made by Stanton's Mill, which employed over 330 men and women who worked more regular hours and received higher wages than any other workers in the area, energized the local economy; and because of that, the white elite and mill's fulltime employees lived in greater comfort than ever by the fall of 1906.

On the eastern side of Perquimmons Creek, where most of the town's black population lived—roughly 2,300 of its 5,500 people—half a dozen families made minor improvements to their homes. The families of the black barber, grocer, and undertaker added a screened porch and a third or fourth bedroom to their homes while the pastors of the three black churches did the same. But because most of the black families in the area were still extremely poor and there were no electric lines or water pipes in that part of town, no black families were able to equip their homes with electricity or indoor plumbing.

In September 1906, an explosion of wrath against the Merritts occurred when 192 of their cows escaped from their largest pasture and wandered around the western part of town for a day and a half, doing much more damage to lawns and shrubs than their eighty-four "wandering cows" of 1899 had done. Because of that earlier incident, the town council had passed a measure based on an earlier ordinance enacted by the Raleigh city council which required all cows, horses, mules, and goats to be penned up. Also like the Raleigh ordinance, the local measure of 1899 decreed the payment of heavy fines by the owners of all such wandering animals and the possibility of lawsuits for full or partial restitution for whatever damage those animals did to the property of other families as they wandered up and down the town's streets in search of food and water.

For several years after 1899, William Merritt made a serious effort to keep his pasture fences in a state of good repair. But by the summer of 1903 if not sooner, he lost interest in that effort for two reasons—he was not only a lazy man but he was also convinced that the laws that applied to ordinary mortals didn't apply to full-fledged aristocrats like himself. His great-grandfather, Thomas Merritt, had served in the state legislature for sixteen years before he was elected governor of North Carolina in 1856 although he died only a month after his inauguration from a massive heart attack caused by his obesity. Thomas Merritt's son Jacob was the state's attorney general for seven years before being appointed to a seat on the state's Supreme Court, on which he served for a decade until his death in 1871 without having written a single opinion of any importance. Even so, William Merritt and his wife Marguerite, who'd been born into one of South Carolina's greatest families, were convinced they had a God-given right to dominate political and social life in the extreme northeastern part of North Carolina during the 1890s and first years of the twentieth century.

Largely because of Merrritt's laziness and assumptions about his family's dominant position in local society, he made no effort to keep his pasture fences in a state of good repair after August 1903, which paved the way for the unpleasant events that occurred in September 1906.

During the night of September 4 to 5 of that year, 192 of the Merritts' cows escaped through half a dozen breaks in their fence at the end of Magnolia Drive, Rosemary Lane, Pine Street, and Hertford Avenue, the town's best residential streets. Under the cover of darkness, those cows wandered around the western part of town, doing extensive damage to the lawns and shrubbery of most of the town's most prominent families. The Merritts' cows also ate most of the corn, beans, squash, okra, tomatoes, cucumbers, onions, pumpkins, and other produce in vegetable gardens that, in six or seven cases, covered an acre or more.

The next morning several dozen families could hardly believe their eyes when they gazed through their windows and saw choice shrubs stripped of their foliage and large vegetable and flower gardens all but destroyed. Their disbelief turned to bitter anger when Chief Trumble and the ten special deputies Mayor Ridinger instructed him to swear in by ten o'clock failed to round up all the Merritts' wandering cows by nightfall. Their last two cows were found late the next afternoon chewing contentedly on the remains of a large snowball bush between the Ridingers' chicken coop and smoke house. By then the mayor and his wife were a great deal angrier than they'd been in April 1899, when the Merritts expressed no concern for the damage their wandering cows had done to the Ridingers' lawn and favorite shrubs. In fact, by five o'clock on the afternoon of September 6, 1906, the mayor and his wife were almost apoplectic and were convinced the Merritts owed them at least $300 in restitution, which Andrew explained in a short but very firm letter he mailed to the Merritt House the next morning.

Smaller claims were mailed to the Merritt House by dozens of other property owners, including Joe, Chip, Russell Barringer, Ozzie Crumpler, Walter Kemble, Dan Wiley, Percy Hogan, Floyd Richardson, and Josephine Gardiner, although the Merritts ignored all the complaints they received for several weeks. Their indifference caused forty-five of the town's leading citizens to hire George Kahle, whose lawn and shrubbery had also been damaged by the Merritts' cows, to file a collective lawsuit against them in the local court. Because Kahle added a claim for $320 on behalf of the four white churches in town, whose lawns and shrubs had also been stripped of most of their foliage, the local court soon ruled that the Merritts should pay slightly over $2,300 in restitution to those churches and forty-six property owners in all. In addition, the Merritts were ordered to pay a fine of $975 and almost $230 for all the hay, turnips, apples, carrots, and other fodder the Merritts' impounded cows consumed before they were allowed to recover them.

During the second week of October, Merritt finally took steps to strengthen the fence around his largest pasture to such a degree there was almost no chance it would give way again. But there were smaller breaks in the fences around his other pastures as late as October 29, enabling several dozen other cows to escape from those pastures although several of his farm workers rounded them up a great deal faster. Even so, there was such enormous hostility toward the Merritts by the beginning of November the original fine of $5 for each cow or other large animal that escaped from the Merritts' or another family's pastures and ran loose in town for an hour or longer was increased from $5 to $50 during the town council's November meeting. With much greater fines and claims for restitution staring him in the face, Merritt hired an additional farm worker and ordered him to inspect all his fences at least once a week and keep them in a state of good repair. Although that was widely considered a step in the right direction, bitter conversations about the recent wandering-cow episode and the Merritts' callous behavior continued at the post office, the drugstore, the bank, and Hogan's Grocery Store until the second week of December. Then the approach of the Christmas season with all it festivities caused the townspeople's deep dislike of the Merritts to fade although it never disappeared altogether.

As for the relationship between William Merritt and his wife, which was already strained by his frequent affairs with young colored girls, which Marguerite deeply resented, the wandering-cow episode of 1906 came within an inch of destroying it for good. Although Marguerite supported her husband's actions in public, she criticized them scathingly in the privacy of their home. As she pointed out dozens of times at the Merritt House, her husband's laziness and neglect of their fences forced them to pay almost $3,600 in fines, fodder fees, and restitution to prominent families who'd probably harbor deep resentment against them for years to come. Moreover, to raise that much money, Merritt had to sell all their stock in Procter &

Gamble, which he'd bought in 1894 with a portion of the money his wife had received from her parents' estate and she hated to be lost for such an unnecessary reason.

Merritt bristled whenever his wife reminded him of the unhappy outcome of the wandering cow episode of 1906 before she expressed her deep disappointment with him in regard to two other matters. Although he was the largest stockholder in the Bank of Perquimmons City, he'd never been elected to serve on its board of directors although Dr. Hanford and Chip Summerlin had been elected to serve on it during the last five years. Even more galling to Marguerite, her husband had failed to win a seat on the town council during the elections of 1900 and 1902 when he'd campaigned vigorously for a seat. The first time Marguerite coupled those three issues together, her husband was so furious he refused to speak to her for several days. But the second and third times she coupled them together, he lost all self-control and hit her in the face before knocking her to the floor and forcing himself on her because, he insisted, she'd refused to fulfill her "wifely duties" since the middle of September.

Shortly after his second violent assault, Marguerite wrote her uncle, Benjamin Manigault, in Charleston and begged him to allow her and her children to spend the holiday season with him in the Manigault House, in which she'd spent her teenage years while attending a local finishing school for girls from well-to-do families. Because her uncle's first wife, Dorothy, had died in July and Benjamin Manigault hated the prospect of spending the holidays by himself, he sent a telegram to his niece shortly after he received her letter and told her she and her children were welcome to come and stay in his home as long as they liked.

So on Saturday, November 23, several hours after her husband left town on an overnight hunting trip with two Edenton friends, Marguerite and her children packed their favorite clothes in half a dozen suitcases. Shortly after dinner that night Marguerite wrote her husband a note she left on his desk in the study. That note explained where she and their children would be when he returned to the mansion late the next afternoon, but it said nothing about when they would return to Perquimmons City.

After an early breakfast on Sunday morning, Matthew Harden drove Marguerite, her children, and all their luggage in the family's buggy to the Hertford station, which they reached in time to catch the nine-thirty train to Rocky Mount. There they left the local train and, after a brief wait in the station, boarded an express train that took them to Charleston by four fifteen that afternoon.

Shortly after they reached Charleston, William Merritt returned to the mansion and found it deserted except for Flossie and Tulip. For the first time in his life Merritt was speechless when he read his wife's note. It had never occurred to him that she might take such a bold step, and in several hours he was roaring drunk.

For six weeks Marguerite and their children remained in Charleston with her uncle, the head of the city's oldest and most respected law firm. To her dismay Becca and Willie hated the formality and dozens of rules their great-uncle told them they must abide by while living in his home, one of Charleston's greatest mansions. By the beginning of Christmas week Becca and Willie wanted to return to their own home, and Marguerite eventually allowed Willie to do so, provided he told his father that she and the younger children wouldn't return until William swore he'd never strike her again and allow her to have a bedroom of her own. Willie served as a faithful emissary, and in several days he softened his father's anger at his wife's "treacherous and disloyal conduct," as he'd described her actions in a letter he wrote her during the first week of December. In another letter written nine days after his original diatribe against his wife, although he never mailed it, Merritt had threatened to divorce her on the grounds of desertion and deliberate alienation of his children's affections.

By the end of December Merritt missed Becca and Little Robert a great deal and hoped the family would be reunited by Valentine's Day, when his father had held the first of his twenty-four annual cotillions for the fifty leading couples in the area, almost two-thirds of them from Edenton. Shortly after Robert Merritt's death from pneumonia in December 1882, his son William decided to continue his father's tradition and, in late December of 1906, hated the thought of breaking it. So on New Year's Day Merritt wrote his wife a third letter in which he swore he'd never strike her again and would allow her to have a bedroom of her own if she returned to the Merritt House in time to make all the arrangements for that year's cotillion and plan "a splendid midnight buffet with dozens of rare delicacies our guests will enjoy and remember for years to come. I'm determined that our buffet at this year's cotillion will greatly exceed the refreshments served by puffed-up families like the Ridingers and the Hanfords during their parties, and with your help I'm convinced they will."

By the time Marguerite received her husband's third letter, her uncle was courting a rich and attractive widow from Savannah, Germaine Bergeron, who'd spent the last four months with her sister in Charleston. As a result Benjamin Manigault was eager for his niece and her younger children to return to their own home several hundred miles to the north. So despite Marguerite's skepticism about her husband's oath that he'd never strike her again, she and her two younger children left Charleston for Perquimmons City on January 11; and five weeks later the Merritts' annual Valentine's Day cotillion occurred on schedule and was the grandest one ever held. Even so, the deep fissures in Marguerite's relationship with her husband had only been papered over, not resolved, while their elegant cotillion brought about only a partial restoration of their local prestige. During the months after the wandering cow episode of 1906, their social position had reached its lowest ebb since June 1861, when William Merritt's father, Robert, led a sneak attack on the pacifist, anti-slavery residents of Quakertown, a hamlet several miles east of Perquimmons City. During that brutal attack shortly after dawn, seventeen adults and four children were killed, and those who survived it scattered in all directions before being welcomed a year later by several Quaker communities in Indiana. Although Quakertown disappeared during the summer of 1861, it and Robert Merritt's brutal attack on it were never forgotten. Nor was the wandering-cow episode of 1906 ever forgotten, to the younger man's great misfortune in the fall of 1910.

Chapter 5

Most of the townspeople were unaware of the Merritts' marital problems or ignored them because of greater interest in other matters. In regard to purely local matters, the average family was mainly interested in the weather and its church's religious and social events, while on the national level most people focused on the win-loss record of their favorite baseball team, the Washington Senators, and the dynamic leadership provided by President Roosevelt, especially his decision to build the Panama Canal, a bold project that took almost ten years to complete. But there was an important matter in 1907 that interested almost all the townspeople, black and white alike—the rapid progress of the automobile age and the many different ways cars affected the lives of ordinary people. On the last day of 1906, there were no cars in Perquimmons City, but a year later there were fourteen, and the number grew steadily thereafter until the great New York stock market crash of 1929 and, a year later, the onset of the Great Depression, the worst economic downturn in American hgistory.

The first local man to buy a car was Russell Barringer, the owner of the town's largest and most successful store, a hardware and building-supply company on East Main Street. Barringer's profits soared during the first decade of the twentieth century because new houses, cottages, and bungalows were built in all parts of town while older dwellings were improved and Barringer's store provided most of the materials, including shingles and tarpaper, readymade doors and windows, screws and nails, paints and stains, bricks, gutters and linoleum, as well as a wide range of plumbing and electrical supplies. Barringer's sawmill on Belspring Road, which he owned in partnership with Osgood Crumpler, the manager and co-owner of the local hotel along with his mother Olive, did just as well during that decade. Building contractors for miles around bought almost ninety percent of the flooring and framing they needed from Barringer and Crumpler's sawmill several miles east of town.

During the second week of February 1907, Barringer took the eight forty-seven train from the Hertford station to New Bern, almost a hundred miles to the south, where he bought a Buggymobile made by a local entrepreneur, G. S. Waters. Now in its second year of production, Buggymobiles were small self-propelled vehicles similar in many ways to the Fords, Oldsmobiles, and other cars produced by Detroit companies at the time.

After returning to Perquimmons City in his Buggymobile, Barringer sold it two months later because it was too small to seat more than one passenger in addition to the driver. By the first week of April, he was convinced he should've bought a bigger car, one that could carry his wife and four children as well as himself. So on April 8 he sold his Buggymobile to the Episcopal minister, Robert Thompson, who wanted a small, inexpensive car he could use to visit his parishioners, half of whom lived a mile or so from the church's rectory on a lot adjacent to the grounds of St. John's Episcopal Church at the corner of West Church Street and Magnolia Drive.

Two days after Thompson bought his Buggymobile, Barringer took the first train to Elizabeth City, forty-five miles northeast of Perquimmons City, and bought one of the handsome but much more expensive Maxwells that were extremely popular at the time, partly because of the large brass headlights that protruded from both sides of their hoods. Not only were Maxwells larger and handsomer than Buggymobiles—they could carry five passengers in addition to the driver—they were also much more dependable and less prone to mechanical breakdowns. Owning a Maxwell soon became a status symbol in eastern North Carolina, a clear indication that its owner had arrived in more ways than one.

Impressed and a bit envious of Barringer's second car, Joe and his friends Andrew Ridinger, George Kahle, and Floyd Richardson, the owner of the local funeral home, sent a joint telegram to the president of the Maxwell Automobile Agency in Elizabeth City two weeks later. In their telegram those four men informed the agency's owner, Harold Goodrich, of their decision to buy Maxwells for themselves and their plan to take the first train to Elizabeth City on the second Saturday morning in May, which they did.

Shortly after eleven thirty that morning, Joe and his friends arrived in Elizabeth City and were welcomed to town by Harold Goodrich himself, who drove them in his own Maxwell to his showroom and repair shop a mile away. There the four men from Perquimmons City wrote checks for their cars, after which they received the legal papers for them and a complimentary pair of driving goggles to protect their eyes from gravel and small rocks thrown up by other cars.

For the next two hours, Joe and his friends received driving lessons from the agency's best salesmen and mechanics. Once the four men could use the choke properly and shift gears without much trouble, the agency's head mechanic showed them how to change the engine oil and a flat tire before they started back to Perquimmons City in an impressive procession with Joe leading the way. Luckily, only one car, Andrew Ridinger's, had a blowout on the homeward trip. The other three men stopped at once to help Andrew, the least mechanically-minded member of the group. After Joe and the others jacked up his car, they replaced the flat tire with the spare. As a result, the four men were only five minutes late for supper that night.

A month later Chip Summerlin bought a car for himself and his family, an Oldsmobile that was slightly smaller and cheaper than the five Maxwells that were roaming the town's most important streets now. Shortly after lunch on Thursday, June 13, Chip and his janitor-delivery man, James Basham, set out for Hertford in a buggy Chip rented from Sonny Langhorne's livery stable at the corner of West Church Street and Magnolia Drive. In slightly less than an hour, they arrived at a fairly new automobile agency, the Henry Baker and Robert Osborne Automobile Company, which was already generally known as B & O Motors. Just as Joe and his friends had done, Chip sent a telegram two weeks in advance that said he'd be coming to buy a new car that day. So his Oldsmobile was waiting for him when he arrived, and all the papers were ready for him to sign in Henry Baker's office once he wrote the agency a check for it. On completing that transaction, Chip received a driving lesson from Robert Osborne while James Basham returned to Perquimmons City in the buggy. A fast learner, Chip headed for his hometown an hour later and chugged into Perquimmons City shortly after James did.

That afternoon Chip closed the drugstore an hour early so he and Lucy could take a spin around town before they stopped in front of his and

Rhonda's house. There Rhonda and the children joined Chip and Lucy in the car for a junket through the middle part of town as Jack, the youngest child, sat on his mother's lap. After crossing Hertford Avenue, Chip drove to his parents' cottage on Fourth Street where Lucy and Rhonda got out of the car and sat in rocking chairs on the front porch while Chip drove his parents and children wherever they wanted to go. Susan, Alfred, and Jack waved gaily to everyone they knew during that twenty-minute excursion. They had great fun until they saw the Merritt children's upturned noses in their father's magnificent new Stanley Steamer, which Merritt had bought the previous afternoon in Edenton. The Merritts' vehicle eclipsed in grandeur the town's nine Maxwells, whose owners now included James Howell, Walter Kemble, and Percy Hogan, the owner of the town's largest and best grocery store. They also included both Thomas Stantons, father and son as well as president and vice president of Stanton's Mill. Shortly after the Merritts' Stanley Steamer turned off East Main Street and disappeared up Fourth Street, the youngest Summerlins' good spirits revived in short order.

Less than a week after Chip bought his car, he hired Will Crabtree and his sons to build a *porte cochère* on the eastern side of his and Rhonda's house to shelter it during bad weather. Lucy considered that a much better arrangement than a detached garage, which Joe and most of the other early car owners had built.

In 1907 half a dozen new appliances came on the market, including electric toasters, fans, and waffle irons. Without question, the most popular new appliance was the electric washing machine which Kemble's Furniture & Appliance Store on East Main Street sold in large numbers during the second half of 1907. On July 9, several days after Walter Kemble paid for a full-page ad in the *Tribune* to promote the sale of those machines, Joe and Chip bought one for their wives or maids to use while splitting the cost of a third one for Margaret and Charles. Lucy bought one for herself several weeks later, as did Hazel Barlow, Lillian Greenfield, and Josephine Gardiner. Within two more months, the Ridingers, the Barringers, the Kahles, the Wileys, the Richardsons, and both Thomas Stantons followed suit. By Christmas, almost every family of means had bought a washing machine from the Kembles, whose profits increased so much during the second half of 1907 they built a large rumpus room on the back of their house for their ten-year-old son Tom and his friends to enjoy.

Several weeks after Lucy bought a washing machine, she helped Julia and Rhonda give a party to celebrate Joe and Chip's fortieth birthdays. That party was held at the Hanfords' house on Saturday night, August 24, and almost a hundred people attended it. The only person Lucy was surprised and annoyed to see that evening was Lillian Greenfield whom Julia had invited at Chip's request. Because Lillian flirted with Chip for half an hour in the Hanfords' study, Lucy's fears about them being romantically involved, which had died down during the months after Jack's birth in 1902, sprang back to life. In fact, Lucy took Julia aside forty-five minutes after Lillian arrived and explained her fears to her at great length. Once she finished her spiel, Julia laughed and said she was being silly because Chip would never cheat on Rhonda.

"If that's true, why did he ask you to send Lillian an invitation?"

"How should I know? If you're that concerned about his feelings for her, why don't you ask him about them yourself?"

"That's a good idea and I think I will."

Lucy waited until ten o'clock, by which time most of the guests had left, before telling Chip in the Hanfords' kitchen how surprised she'd been to see Lillian at the party. "She was almost too friendly when I moved into Joe's cottage six years ago, and she asked me dozens of questions about you and Rhonda on the afternoon she welcomed me to the neighborhood. Because I've hardly laid eyes on her since then, I wondered while she was flirting with you tonight how well you know her."

Although Chip's face turned ashen he said smoothly, "I hardly know her at all, Lucy. But whenever I go to the town's office building to pay my water bill, she's always very friendly to me and all the other men who come in to pay their bills in person. I can't remember where I heard it, but I understand she's very lonely because she has no relatives this part of the state and widows are seldom invited to parties. So I asked Julia to send her an invitation, hoping she'd meet some people she'd like and get to know fairly well. I was just trying to be nice but you seem to think I made a mistake."

"No, I'm not saying you made a mistake provided that's all there is to it."

"Goodness, Lucy, you don't think I'm involved with her in some way, do you?"

"I'm afraid that thought occurred to several times tonight."

"But if I was involved with Lillian, how could I have kept it a secret from you? After all, you live directly across the street from her and you've never seen my car or bicycle in front of her house, have you?"

"No, but that doesn't prove anything. There are alleys between all the north-south streets in my part of town, and because of those alleys, it would be easy for you to drive your car or ride your bicycle up to Lillian's back porch and go inside for an hour or two without me being aware of it. Furthermore, you often leave the drugstore for an hour or two on Wednesday afternoons, which is Lillian's day off because she works on Saturday mornings. And you never tell Dillie or me where you've been or what you've been doing when you return to the store on Wednesday afternoons."

Chip blushed again and denied he was involved with Lillian so vehemently, Lucy knew it would be futile to question him further that night. But when she went to bed two hours later, she tossed and turned until she fell asleep. She liked Rhonda so much she'd hate for her to be hurt in any way. Rhonda had always been a loyal and loving wife to Chip and a kind and understanding mother to their children. On the other hand, Chip was Lucy's only brother and she still felt extremely grateful to him for rescuing her from her dismal life at the Merritt House in 1901. So Lucy wondered what she'd tell Rhonda if she ever asked her if she knew anything about Chip's relationship with Lillian. Even worse, how could she be loyal to Chip and Rhonda at the same time if she ever found herself in such a tricky situation? As a result, she hoped and prayed that she'd never be confronted by such a difficult dilemma.

Because the Barringers attended the Hanford-Summerlin party on August 24 and enjoyed it a great deal, Mildred wrote an article about the party that appeared in the *Tribune* six days later. In her article, Mildred discussed how elegant the food and drink had been, how lovely the flower arrangements in the entrance hall, dining room, parlor, and study were that evening and how much everyone had enjoyed the festivities on that occasion. In particular, Mildred's article noted how much everyone enjoyed singing happy birthday to Joe and Chip as they stood side by side in front of the dining room fireplace as Julia directed the singing from a stepstool in the room's bay window "as her own lovely voice soared above those of a hundred other people, all friends and admirers of two of the most popular and capable men in town."

When the Merritts read Mildred's article six days later, they were deeply annoyed because they hadn't received an invitation to it. Of course, they'd never invited the Hanfords or Summerlins to one of their parties or Valentine Day's cotillions, which most of the other leading families in town considered very strange given the fact that Joseph Hanford had been their family doctor since shortly after his arrival in town in 1895. But as the Merritts always were, they were convinced that the laws and customs that applied to ordinary people didn't apply to them. As a result, they were not only deeply annoyed at the Hanfords and Summerlins for what they perceived as a social slight, but they also felt those two families were "upstarts" who should be taught a much-needed lesson about the social hierarchy in town. So shortly after they read Mildred's article in the *Tribune*, they decided to throw a much larger party at their mansion with much more lavish food and drink than the Hanfords and Summerlins had provided their guests.

 The Merritts' party on Saturday night, September 14, was attended by almost two hundred people, but none of the Hanfords and Summerlins of course. Everyone at the Merritts' party was deeply impressed by the extravagance of the food and drink, especially the seemingly endless supply of champagne which caused a dozen women—Marguerite and Isabel Stanton most of all—to become rather tipsy. For that and several other reasons, couples like the Ridingers, the Barringers, the Kahles, the Howells, and the Richardsons, who attended both parties, agreed that the Hanford-Summerlin party had been much more enjoyable. And from that night, those couples and most of the Merritts' other guests were convinced that their leadership of local society was drawing to a close if it hadn't ended already. However, the Merritts were unaware of that growing belief, nor were the Hanfords and Summerlins, who never tried to impress their guests as the Merritts always sought to do. Unfortunately for the Merritts, their efforts to stave off their further social decline by flaunting their wealth and "superior taste and breeding" were doomed to fail because their arrogance and pretentiousness offended most of the people they hoped to impress and, to some degree, cultivate.

 Three weeks after the Merritts' party, Lucy read another interesting article in the *Tribune* by Mildred Barringer. She and her family had just returned from Norfolk, Virginia, where they'd spent three days visiting the hundreds of exhibits and sampling the countless delights of the Jamestown Exposition of that year. That important exposition, which was on the same lavish scale as the Pan-American Exposition of 1901 in Buffalo, New York, commemorated the three hundredth anniversary of the first permanent English colony in the New World. According to Mrs. Barringer's article, she and the rest of her family had had a wonderful time at the Jamestown

Exposition. In fact, they strongly recommended it to everyone who could afford to take the train to Norfolk and spend several nights in a hotel or tourist home near the exposition's 335-acre site.

Lucy yearned to attend that exposition and see with her own eyes the ten exhibits the Barringers and their children had enjoyed most, especially those in the Negro Building, which depicted dozens of aspects of black life in all parts of the country but especially in the states of the former Confederacy. Fortunately for Lucy, her sister and sister-in-law were equally impressed by Mildred's article, and in several days they decided with their husbands' strong support that they and their children would visit the exposition together during the last week of October. The weather would be much cooler then while the heavy rains of the fall equinox would be over.

Five days before they were due to leave for Norfolk, Joe and Chip decided to take Mildred's advice and travel to Norfolk by train rather than by car. Most of the highways of that era were poorly paved, if they were paved at all, while gas stations were few and far between. Even worse, the tires of that period were thin and undependable, causing most families who ventured over a hundred miles from their homes in a car to have at least one blowout. In short, it was safer and faster to travel by train than by car; and if the Hanfords and Summerlins left from the Hertford station by nine o'clock one morning, they would reach Norfolk by noon, whereas an automobile trip would probably take them twice as long.

Not surprisingly, all the other adults in the family agreed with Joe and Chip's decision to take the train to the exposition rather than drive there in the family cars. But on the day before their departure, Charles and Margaret decided not to go on the trip at all. Charles was sixty-seven and none too well, while Margaret was sixty-four and her arthritis almost as painful as it had been during a long cold spell in January 1906, despite the unusually warm weather during recent months. Although Lucy and everyone else in the family was disappointed by the older Summerlins' decision to remain at home, they were relieved when Margaret urged them not to cancel the trip but to attend the exposition and enjoy dozens of fascinating things they could describe to Charles and her shortly after they returned to town.

The next morning Lucy and nine other members of her family took the first train from the Hertford station to Norfolk and checked into a hotel several blocks from the exposition's main gate shortly before noon. Then after a light lunch in the hotel coffee shop, they set out for the main gate and its six ticket booths. In short order Joe and Chip bought three-day passes for their wives and children and split the cost of a third pass for Lucy despite her firm protest that she could afford to pay her own way. After entering the sprawling compound, they realized in several minutes that there was so much to see and do they hardly knew where to start.

The children's favorite exhibit was the Miller Brothers' Ranch whose kitchen, bunkhouse, barn, corral, windmill, blacksmith's shop, and other main features had all been moved to the exposition from the ranch's original site in Oklahoma. The children visited that exhibit several times during their three-day stay and saw cowboys roping calves and steers, gun-toting outlaws trying to stop a speeding stagecoach so they could rob its passengers of their valuables, and a pack of Indians in war paint making a fierce attack on a small but well-defended stockade.

The adults in the family enjoyed that exhibit almost as much as the children although they preferred the larger and much more colorful exhibit known as "Akoun's Beautiful Orient." Visitors to that exhibit received a warm welcome from a Muslim "princess" shortly before they strolled down replicas of Middle Eastern streets lined with small shops and kiosks selling cheap trinkets and other artifacts from Egypt, Lebanon, Syria, Persia, and several other nearby countries. They also saw belly dancers performing brief routines while barkers tried to convince gaping men and teenage boys to buy tickets for risqué shows behind carefully locked doors, during which they would enjoy sensual pleasures they'd never even imagined before. Although Joe and Chip hoped to attend one of those shows, Julia and Rhonda told them repeatedly with great firmness that such shows were off-limits to family men like them.

As for Lucy, she enjoyed every exhibit she saw—almost fifty, by her count. But as all the other adults in her family knew in advance, her favorite exhibits were all located in the Negro Building and depicted hundreds of facets of black life in all parts of the country but especially in the South, where five out of every six American blacks still lived in poverty. Booker T. Washington, the most prominent black leader during the late nineteenth and early twentieth centuries, had visited the Negro Building in July and made a famous speech to an audience of several thousand people. Lucy wished she'd heard that speech and hoped to find a printed copy of it one day so she could read it for herself. But her search was unsuccessful because she never found a copy of it despite how long and hard she looked for one.

When the family returned to Perquimmons City, they found its oldest members in worse health than ever. Margaret's arthritis was bothering her more than it had in a dozen years while Charles had had a stroke a day or two before—at least that was Joe's opinion on the morning he examined him and told him to stay in bed for at least a month. But as most of the other members of the family realized, Charles was temperamentally incapable of remaining in bed for even a week, and five days later he was toiling away in his workshop again.

When Julia informed Joe of that while they were putting Olivia and Joey to bed one evening, he rushed outside to his car and drove at top speed to his father-in-law's workshop. On finding Charles there at eight twenty, he said firmly, "I hate to be so blunt but I told you last week to stay in bed for another month. If you continue to work as hard as you always have, you won't live long enough to ring in the New Year with Margaret and the rest of your family."

"Don't talk to me like that because I'm not a fool, Joe! You're just like all the other doctors I've known during my life. 'Do this but don't do that; avoid fried foods like the plague; take one of these nasty little pink pills with every meal; drink a spoonful of this foul-tasting liquid shortly before breakfast and supper'; and do other worthless things like that. You doctors are such terrible bullies it's a wonder you have any patients at all."

"I'm not being a bully; I'm only telling you the honest-to-God truth! And if you don't believe me, I'll drive you to Edenton tomorrow morning so you can get a second opinion from Dr. Jacobs or his new partner, Dr. Humphries."

"Forget that because I'm not about to stay in bed for another month. I have more than a dozen orders to fill by the middle of December, and if I fail to meet that deadline most of them will be cancelled. I can't let that happen because my workmen have large families to feed and buy presents for. I've always given them a ten-dollar bonus a week or two before Christmas, and I'm not about to end that practice just because you think I'm slightly under the weather."

"You're not 'slightly under the weather,' you jackass! You're in *awful* shape and you should do exactly as I say! I've always admired your generosity to your workmen, but you need to wise up and stop being so pigheaded! If you continue to work as hard as always have, you won't live long enough to give your workmen a Christmas bonus this year, and they'll lose their jobs shortly after you die. So think about their long-term interest and do the right thing now."

"Dammit, Joe, you're the one who's being pigheaded, not me, and I refuse to listen to any more of your bullying! So get the hell out of my workshop and keep your nose out of my business! If you can't do that I don't give a rat's ass if I ever see you again!"

After that fight, their first in ten years, Charles refused to speak to Joe or listen to anything he said before he had a second stroke on December 8. That stroke was much worse than his first one; and his best and most senior workman, Ike Rodman, rode his bicycle to Joe's office at once to tell him about it while Charles's other workmen carried him into his and Margaret's house and placed him on the simple mahogany bed they'd shared for almost forty years.

Joe drove to the Summerlins' cottage at once and did his best to make his father-in-law comfortable. The left side of his body had been paralyzed, and his speech was so slurred no one could understand a word he said except Margaret and she was often unsure about his meaning. She was so worried about him, in fact, she wrung her hands the whole time Joe examined him and took his vital signs that morning. Shortly after Joe told her to keep Charles as still and quiet as possible before he left their home for the drugstore, she read several of her husband's favorite chapters of the Bible to him until he fell into a restless sleep shortly after eleven o'clock.

Meanwhile at the drugstore, Joe explained the situation to Chip and Lucy in several minutes. Once he finished Lucy offered to spend the rest of the day and the coming night at her parents' house in order to give her mother as much help and emotional support as she could. Chip welcomed Lucy's offer before Joe drove her to her own cottage so she could pack a nightgown and some clean clothes for the next day. Then Joe drove her to her parents' cottage, where Margaret was extremely relieved to see her. In several minutes Lucy convinced her mother to lie down and get some rest in the bedroom Chip had used before he married Rhonda and moved into a cottage with her. As for Lucy, she sat in a rocking chair by her father's side as he moaned and gasped for breath until he fell asleep again shortly after three fifteen that afternoon. Then Lucy went into the kitchen and fixed some chicken soup and several peanut butter and jelly sandwiches she and her mother ate in silence at the kitchen table. During the next sixteen hours, they took turns sitting with Charles and getting him a bowl of soup or a glass of water whenever he woke up and asked for something to eat or drink. They also brought him a chamber pot to use whenever he needed to relieve himself. When he woke up at 4:00 AM and was unable to go back to sleep, Margaret read him several more chapters of the Bible until he dozed off again. She and Lucy also said a number of heartfelt prayers for his recovery.

Lucy continued to sleep at her parents' house until her father died shortly after ten thirty on the night of December 19. She and her mother were sitting in rocking chairs on either side of his bed at the time and they both saw him take his final breath. Although his death was extremely sad for both of them, they were relieved that his suffering was finally over. Margaret closed his mouth and pulled the top sheet over his face as tears streamed down her cheeks. She said no finer man had ever lived with the exception of Jesus of course. Lucy agreed and held her weeping mother in her arms for several minutes before telling her to get some sleep in Chip's former bedroom because the daybed in the sewing room suited her fine.

   Mr. Summerlin's funeral took place three days before Christmas. Although it was a cold, dreary morning with a hint of snow in the air, the church was packed. Margaret did fairly well during the first part of the service, but tears streamed down her cheeks during Mr. Thompson's eulogy because she'd loved her husband so much. Shortly after the congregation sang Charles' favorite hymn, "Breathe on Me Breath of God," Chip, Joe, Russell Barringer, Ike Rodman, and the other pallbearers carried his coffin down the center aisle while the choir remained in its stalls and sang "A Mighty Fortress Is Our God." Margaret walked several steps behind the coffin with Lucy and Julia on either side of her to keep her from stumbling and falling. By the time the final hymn ended, the congregation had left the church and reassembled in the cemetery where an open pit was waiting to receive the coffin. Once all the mourners, including Charles' weeping grandchildren, were standing around the pit, Mr. Thompson read several more prayers before signaling the pallbearers to lower the coffin fifteen or sixteen inches into the pit. As they did he sprinkled several handfuls of topsoil on its lid before reading a brief prayer Margaret had adapted from one in the prayer book: "From dust Charles' body came, and to dust it is now returning. Oh Lord, we beseech thee once again to remember the soul of thy dear departed servant, Charles Alfred Summerlin Senior. He always did his best to serve you in humility and deep gratitude for all the blessings You bestowed on him during his life on earth . . . Let us go forth from this place now while rejoicing in the endless love of Almighty God, Father, Son, and Holy Spirit, and in thankfulness for the years we shared with our deeply loved husband, father, father-in-law, grandfather, or friend, Charles. Amen." After those final words, the pallbearers lowered his coffin to the bottom of the pit before covering it with topsoil and, eventually, sod.

   Meanwhile Lucy and Julia guided their mother through the main door of the parish house into the fellowship hall. There a large assortment of sandwiches, cakes, pies, muffins, and cookies prepared by the four women's circles was waiting on several folding tables while coffee, tea, and apple cider were available at the window near the door to the kitchen. More than a hundred people came inside to hug Margaret and tell her how sorry they were Charles's earthly life had ended. Margaret rallied a bit while thanking everyone who spoke to her with great kindness and affection, but she refused to eat or drink anything. When Chip and his family drove her home, she told Rhonda she wanted to be by herself for the next several days although Lucy slept at her cottage on all those nights.

Because of Charles' death and Margaret's deep depression, that Christmas was an unusually sad time for the family. The adults did their best to carry on as usual for the children's sake. But Lucy and Julia were convinced their mother's days were numbered because she never stopped grieving for her husband. She spent all her time in bed unless she wanted to go to the kitchen or the bathroom. Because she refused to do any sewing, Julia finished the clothes she'd started for the Merritt, Barringer, and Wiley children. Worst of all, Margaret ate almost nothing, and by the middle of January she'd lost nine pounds she could ill afford to lose.

By that point Julia was sleeping at her mother's house on weeknights in case she needed help of some kind. On Saturday and Sunday nights Lucy took Julia's place and sat in a rocking chair beside Margaret's bed for hours, holding one of her hands in hers as she lay under the quilt and other covers half asleep. From time to time Lucy read several Psalms or a chapter of the Bible to her, which she clearly liked although she never said so. In her occasional lucid moments Margaret said she was worried about Lucy because she was still single although Margaret was hopeful that the other adults in the family would take care of her during the years ahead. On hearing those words Lucy rolled her eyes in disbelief but kept her thoughts to herself of course.

By the end of January it was clear Margaret had lost her will to live and there was nothing anyone could do about it—not even Mr. Thompson who was usually very persuasive in such situations. Shortly after Julia told the minister how depressed her mother was, he visited her every afternoon to see how she was doing and pray for her recovery as she lay in bed barely conscious of his and Lucy's presence. Several minutes after he administered communion to her on the first Tuesday afternoon in February, Margaret died with an amazingly peaceful look on her face. Lucy was very grateful Mr. Thompson was there at the time because she was convinced she would've gone to pieces had she been there by herself.

When it was clear Margaret was dead, Mr. Thompson pulled a blanket over her face before telling Lucy that she and Julia had done everything they could've done for a dying parent. Then Lucy and Mr. Thompson knelt down together and held hands as they recited the Lord's Prayer before the minister said a long spontaneous prayer for Margaret's soul.

Margaret's funeral two days later was almost identical to her husband's seven weeks earlier. The hymns were the same and the church was packed again, partly because it was a beautiful winter morning, warm and clear. Shortly after the pallbearers carried the coffin outside to the pit beside her husband's grave, Mr. Thompson read the same prayer Margaret had adapted from the prayer book for her husband's funeral with several changes the minister made to it out of necessity.

After that final prayer there was another reception in the parish hall, during which Lucy and several other members of the family broke down and wept openly. In fact, Lucy shed more tears after her mother's funeral than she had after her father's or even Jobie Caldwell's in August 1887 when she'd felt her heart would break because they'd planned to get married in another year or so. Her sadness continued for several months as she helped Chip and Julia get their parents' affairs in order so they could distribute the dozens of items family members wanted as keepsakes. Whatever was left they planned to give to needy families in town.

Lucy took her mother's wedding ring, the pearl necklace her father had given Margaret on their twenty-fifth wedding anniversary, and several of her dresses. They fit her perfectly after Julia let out their waistbands an inch or two. In addition, Lucy took a watercolor her mother had painted as a young woman and called *A Fall Day in Belspring Woods*. Lucy considered it almost as beautiful as *Sunset on the Sound*, which her mother had given her shortly before she moved into Joe's cottage in 1901. As for Julia, she took her mother's silver dressing-table set and two quilts she'd made twenty or thirty years before. Julia also shared with Rhonda her mother's hats, purses, and silver bracelets, which had great sentimental but almost no monetary value.

Chip and Rhonda took one of Margaret's quilts and her only painting of a building that no longer existed in town—the original St. John's Church, a small-frame building that had been struck by lightning and burned to the ground in less than an hour in July 1867. That building was replaced eighteen months later by the existing and slightly larger brick building on the same site. Chip also took the pistol his father had used during the Civil War and one of his hunting rifles while Joe was very pleased to receive the other hunting rifle.

Although the family gave Charles's pocket knife to Joey and his hunting and coonskin caps to Alfred and Jack, no one remembered what Susan and Olivia wanted. They eventually received most of their grandmother's costume jewelry and several shawls they'd admired dozens of times.

That summer as Chip—the court-appointed executor—was taking his first steps to settle his parents' estate, he and his sisters divided most of the furniture in their parents' house and the fourteen finished pieces in Mr. Summerlin's workshop or still on consignment at Kemble's Furniture & Appliance Store. Chip and Rhonda took their parlor and most of their kitchen furniture as well as their double bed and triple chest of drawers. Lucy was glad to obtain their day bed, which she planned to use in her study, and a stunning mahogany highboy, one of the finest pieces her father ever made. As for Joe and Julia, they were very pleased with their share of the furniture, which included a small but extremely fine kneehole desk and ten dining room chairs that were identical to the eight Joe had bought from Charles in the fall of 1895.

Shortly after that distribution of their parents' furniture occurred, Lucy and Julia gave dozens of household items to several black families who lived on the eastern side of Perquimmons Creek. The most important of those black families was the Hanfords' long-time maid, Augusta Walters, and her daughter and son-in-law, Creola and Travis Brewer, and their seven-year-old son Luke. Augusta and her family received sheets, blankets, comforters for two single beds, a set of everyday china, and dozens of clothes in good condition. They included a dozen coats, jackets, and sweaters Joey had outgrown and Luke could probably wear in another year or two.

During the first week of August, Chip sold the workshop with its many tools and raw materials, as well as the small tract on which the building stood to Ike Rodman, his father's best and most dependable employee for thirty-three years, for $1,385. A month later, during an auction of seven different properties in town, the winning bid for the Summerlins' cottage was made by Robert Dawson, the mill's chief purchasing agent. To Lucy and the rest of the family's great surprise, Dawson bid $1,620 for the cottage and several pieces of furniture inside, including a maple chifforobe that was so large it would've been very difficult to move.

Late the next winter, shortly before Chip paid the last of his parents' bills and made the final distribution from their estate, he voluntarily waived his executor's fee. As a result he received the same amount of money Lucy and Julia received: $1,092.85. That much money made Lucy feel like a rich woman although it failed to offset the enormous loss she felt because of her parents' deaths. Chip and Julia felt the same way; and shortly after dinner at the Hanfords' house several nights later, all three agreed that no amount of money could offset the loss of their parents, whom they'd loved so much they knew they'd miss them a great deal for the rest of their lives.

Chapter 6

Long before Chip made the final distribution from his parents' estate, he decided to run for a seat on the town council. Established shortly after Perquimmons City was incorporated in 1852, the town council consisted of nine men who served for staggered six-year terms with three coming up for election or reelection every other year.

Chip announced his candidacy for a council seat in a brief notice in the *Tribune* on the second Tuesday in September 1908; and once he did, all the other adults in the family gave him strong support. But William Merritt had already declared himself a candidate for the third time—the "wandering-cow" episode of 1899 had doomed his efforts in 1900 and 1902 to win a seat. Now, in the fall of 1908, Merritt waged a much more strenuous campaign for two reasons—he was determined to win a seat as a way of silencing his wife about his earlier failures in that regard, and if he won a seat, he might be able to convince four other councilors to support a measure repealing the ten-fold increase in the fine for allowing a cow or another large animal to wander around town for an hour or more. Despite the lingering hostility toward him in 1908, Merritt's great name recognition and financial resources caused Chip and the other members of his family to consider him a dangerous rival. Indeed, by the middle of October Merritt had distributed more campaign buttons and pamphlets stating his position on the most important issues of the day than his four rivals combined.

In Perquimmons City during those years, the voters usually returned two of the three incumbents seeking reelection while admitting only one newcomer to the council each two-year cycle. Because of that custom and the widespread belief that Merritt would be successful this time, Rhonda and the Hanfords wondered if Chip had any chance of success. Lucy was especially worried that her brother's candidacy was doomed to fail because of the rumors in some circles that he'd been involved with Lillian Greenfield for a number of years. But those rumors were either ignored or considered false on Election Day because Chip came in only five votes behind Russell Barringer, the only successful incumbent seeking another term, and thirty-four votes ahead of Merritt, who barely defeated the other two incumbents who hoped to win a second six-year term.

The whole family was elated by Chip's victory, and the Hanfords gave a party in his honor shortly after the results were announced at the town's office building at seven thirty that evening. In a brief speech in the Hanfords' dining room, Joe praised his brother-in-law's "vigorous but clean campaign" while Lucy and Rhonda uncorked a dozen bottles of champagne in the kitchen. Once the family and fifty-two friends and neighbors toasted Chip's victory, Susan and Olivia were allowed to drink a small glass of that bubbly wine for the first time. Joey and the two Summerlin boys drank glasses of white grape juice again although Joey protested so heatedly Julia gave him a sip of her champagne. He wrinkled his nose and told his younger cousins they weren't missing anything before downing his remaining grape juice in a single gulp.

After joyful celebrations on Thanksgiving and Christmas Day, Chip took the oath of office on the second Tuesday night in January when the new council met for the first time and elected Andrew Ridinger to his seventh two-year term as mayor. Because of Merritt's eminence and strong desire for the office of vice mayor, the council elected him to it although he'd received fewer votes in the recent election than Chip or Russell Barringer, whom Chip nominated for the position. Barringer declined the nomination, however, because he was extremely busy with his business ventures and the problems of his younger son, the town's worst juvenile delinquent since Merritt's teenage years. Most of the older townspeople had vivid memories of the many nasty pranks Merritt had played on children younger and smaller than himself and on unsuspecting neighbors. Miss Edna Wilcox, who lived in a rambling bungalow a short distance from the Merritt House, certainly remembered his nasty pranks. Late one October night in 1879, Merritt left the bodies of three rabbits he'd killed with his hunting rifle on the front porch of Miss Edna's bungalow; and when she found them at eight forty-five the next morning as she was about to leave her home for the dry goods store, she was furious and guessed at once who'd left them there.

Merritt's election as the town's vice mayor caused him to overestimate his power and influence. For several days after the council's first six meetings in 1909, Chip complained to Rhonda shortly after he drove home from the town's office building that "King William" had dominated the proceedings and spoken on every issue as if he were wiser than King Solomon, Julius Caesar, Henry VIII of England, or some other great historical figure. Merritt also called so often and loudly for the repeal of the $50 fine for allowing a cow or another large animal to wander around town for an hour or longer, he infuriated his fellow members during the council's first several meetings. Furthermore, whenever proposals were made to increase the property tax to raise more money for the schools or an equally worthy cause, Merritt attacked those proposals with scathing words. Because he was the greatest landowner in the area, his speeches angered most of the townspeople because they knew all but a small portion of his six thousand acres were outside the town limits and not subject to town taxation. So if a tax increase went through, it would have only a minor effect on his bank balance, which he refused to admit. Equally galling to the other townspeople, whenever Merritt felt he'd benefit from a proposal under consideration, he left no stone unturned in his efforts to secure its passage. During most of the council meetings in 1909, there was one issue on which he spoke so long and loudly it made him a laughingstock, which most of the voters welcomed because there was a good chance it would doom his efforts to win another term in 1914, when he was expected to seek reelection and, if successful, campaign vigorously for the office of mayor.

With his wife's inheritance of almost $160,000, which she'd received in 1894, Merritt had equipped his mansion with electricity and indoor plumbing before buying thousands of shares of stock in blue-chip companies like General Electric, Procter & Gamble, Bethlehem Steel, and the Atlantic Coastline Railroad. That railroad took dozens of New Yorkers to Florida every winter for a month or two of fun in the sun. The richest and most forward-looking of those New Yorkers were beginning to buy winter homes in Palm Beach or Miami although Merritt was convinced there was no need for them to travel all the way to Florida. As he pointed out dozens of times, Perquimmons City had mild and extremely pleasant winters with only a brief cold snap or two between November and March during normal years. He also noted that there was excellent boating on the Albemarle and Pamlico Sounds, much safer boating in fact than Florida's coastal waters provided. Last but not least in his opinion, because of the presence of the Outer Banks a short distance off the North Carolina coast, Perquimmons City enjoyed greater protection from the enormous destructive power of summer hurricanes than Palm Beach and Miami did.

In order to attract rich New Yorkers to Perquimmons City, where Merritt hoped to sell them building sites of several acres at greatly inflated prices, he urged the town council to do two things at public expense. First, he called for it to build a large, well-equipped marina half a mile west of his mansion where Merritt's Creek flowed into the Sound because the public dock at the end of Sixth Street was so dilapidated it was unusable. Second, he wanted the town council to build a race track comparable to the ones in Baltimore and Louisville, where the Preakness and the Kentucky Derby took place every spring. Several times he offered to sell large tracts of land to the council for those purposes, always at an exorbitant price of course. But despite his repeated efforts, Mayor Ridinger and seven other councilors turned a deaf ear to his proposals whenever he tried to ram them down their throats.

Although routinely defeated on those matters, Merritt enjoyed eventual success on a third and more important matter. As most of his fellow citizens were aware, his sprawling lands to the north and west of the ten-acre tract on which his mansion and its dependencies stood contained dozens of choice building sites, which rich New Yorkers might buy if those sites were developed and advertised properly. To that end Merritt called for West Main Street to be paved from the middle of town to the bridge across Merritt's Creek. If that was done and several paved streets constructed into his meadows and woodlands, potential buyers would be able to drive into those gently rolling hills and view its hundreds of fine building sites for themselves. In that event Merritt would probably be swamped with demands for lots, causing him to become as rich as his forebears had been before the Civil War, during which their wealth plummeted as a result of President Lincoln's Emancipation Proclamation of 1863, which freed his family's 227 slaves. Almost as harmful to the Merritts' wealth during the "War of Northern Aggression," as the Merritts and most other Southerners called it, the Union navy sank the four commercial ships Merritt's forebears had owned and operated with great success during earlier decades, when New England shipyards bought eastern North Carolina's tar, timber, and turpentine in steadily increasing quantities.

Because Merritt was convinced his fellow councilors would reject a scheme intended to increase his own wealth, he called for all the leading streets in town to be paved at the same time West Main Street was paved. The other streets he included in that group were East Main Street as far as the western end of the bridge across Perquimmons Creek into the black part of town, East and West Church Street, East and West Granby Street, and such important north-south streets as Magnolia Drive, Rosemary Lane, Pine Street, and especially Hertford Avenue, which extended northward from Courthouse Square until it made a long bend and became the Hertford Road. The slightly larger town of Hertford ten miles north of Perquimmons City had the nearest railway station from which wealthy New Yorkers could alight from their Pullman cars and hire a car and driver to take them on to Perquimmons City to view the many building sites Merritt was so eager to sell them.

During the council's April meeting, Merritt introduced his proposal for the paving of almost fifteen miles of hardscrabble streets. To his dismay that proposal seemed almost as visionary to the other councilors as his schemes for the construction of a large marina and race track. Moreover, the other councilors resented Merritt's proposal to use so much public revenue in a way that would greatly increase his own wealth. But on the other side of the coin, the town stood to profit if only one rich Northern family built a winter home in the area, while most of the townspeople would profit if their most important streets were paved. Since 1907 there had been a steady upsurge in traffic as more and more men bought cars for themselves and allowed their wives to use their buggies whenever they liked, usually with the help of a colored driver. However, because Julia Hanford had driven her husband's buggy for almost ten years a dozen other women, including Selma Ridinger, Mildred Barringer, Phyllis Kahle, and Joanne Wiley, had convinced Julia to teach them how to drive their husbands' buggies during her free time, which also contributed to the steady upsurge of traffic on the town's most important streets.

Furthermore, in May 1908, several months before Henry Ford introduced his famous Model T, Osgood Crumpler, the manager and co-owner of the local hotel, had established the Crumpler-Barringer Ford Agency in partnership with his old friend Russell Barringer. Although Crumpler and Barringer had been partners in several earlier ventures, it would be hard to imagine two such different men. Osgood, or "Ozzie" as he was known to his many friends, was short, pudgy, and a bit dainty compared to Russell, a tall, rangy man who reminded his fellow citizens of Abraham Lincoln. Ozzie was excitable and had little conniption fits whenever an important development caught him by surprise whereas

Russell took everything in stride and was unflappable even when his wife Mildred brought several expensive outfits home on approval from Ada Howell's Millenary Shop, where Julia had worked for seven years before Joe moved to town and they fell in love in several weeks. (It wasn't quite love at first sight, although it came very close.) Probably because Ozzie and Russell were so different, they worked extremely well together; and during their agency's second year of existence, it sold fifty-seven Model Ts, a record that stood in eastern North Carolina until the last Model T rolled off a Michigan assembly line in 1928.

Much of the Crumpler-Barringer Agency's success was due to the vigor and enthusiasm of its first sales manager, Grover Beasley, whom Ozzie and Russell lured away from B & O Motors in Edenton. A short but handsome man with curly black hair and a constant smile on his face, Grover had been born in poverty. But he was smart, hardworking, and very ambitious. Because he talked so glibly about the dozens of cars he planned to sell for Ozzie and Russell every year, they often joked that he'd become a millionaire in a year or so if he moved to Alaska and sold bathing suits and other summer apparel to the Eskimos who lived near the Arctic Circle.

Unfortunately for Lucy's peace of mind, Grover was a cousin of Hazel Barlow and rented her smaller bedroom during his first six weeks in town. On the Sunday afternoon he moved into Hazel's cottage, Lucy invited Hazel to dinner that night and told her to bring Grover along if he had nothing better to do. Hazel took her cousin along several hours later because she hoped Grover and Lucy would take a shine to each other and start courting.

Grover took an instant liking to Lucy because he enjoyed her wit and occasional feistiness and considered her height of five feet one a plus because he was only four inches taller. But Lucy never cared for Grover because she considered him somewhat oily because of his glibness and the fact that he had a ready answer and a quick fix for the most complex problems of the period. Furthermore, Grover was different in almost every way from Jobie Caldwell, whose death in 1887 Lucy still mourned from time to time. Worst of all in Lucy's eyes, she was convinced Grover was interested in her, at least in part, for a financial reason.

Grover dreamed of managing an automobile agency of his own in five or six years. But if his dream was ever to be realized, he had to find a financial backer. On his first afternoon in town he was impressed when Hazel told him Lucy's share of her parents' estate had been almost $1,100. He was even more impressed by the fact that her brother and brother-in-law were extremely well-to-do and members of the local bank's executive committee. If Lucy became his wife Chip and Joe would probably give him the financial backing he needed to establish an automobile agency of his own. At the very least they would probably help him obtain a large, low-interest loan from the bank.

Counting on one or both those possibilities Grover made an appointment to see Joe at his office during his first week in town on the grounds that he'd suffered from painful back problems for several years. In fact, he wanted to meet Joe only to impress him with his intelligence and business skills, which Joe grasped halfway through his appointment with him. After getting nowhere with Joe, Grover dropped by the drugstore a number of times to buy several items and chat with Chip about his interest in joining the Elks' Lodge, which Chip had joined in 1892 at Mr. Bradley's urging and was now its president for the second time. Pleased by Grover's desire to become an Elk, Chip offered to serve as his sponsor and speed his admission into the group.

Although Grover had Chip and Hazel's support in his campaign to win Lucy's hand, she never showed any interest in him. Whenever they were alone together for several minutes, the only subjects Grover ever discussed were his two main goals in life—selling dozens of cars a year and dying a rich man—which never impressed Lucy at all. In fact, they caused her to consider him superficial, materialistic, and overly ambitious. Grover also weakened his chances with Lucy by making no effort to cloak his racial views and firm belief that the country should deport its millions of black people to Africa, which annoyed Lucy a great deal. But she never mentioned her annoyance to Hazel because she hated to lose her friendship and was confident Hazel would realize in several weeks that she had no interest in marrying her cousin.

On the August night Grover was inducted into the Elks' Lodge during a dinner meeting at Wilbur's Chicken and Seafood Palace, which most of the women in town avoided like the plague because of its ramshackle appearance from the Elizabeth City Road, Hazel had supper at Lucy's cottage again. As they were enjoying their dessert, Hazel asked Lucy why she seemed so indifferent to Grover when he was clearly smitten by her. Lucy put her fork down on her plate before saying, "For several reasons, Hazel. Our views and interests are completely different, and I'm several years older than him as I'm sure you know. And while I hate to say it, I consider him narrow-minded and even a bit bigoted because his racial views are so crude in my opinion. Finally, I have no desire to join the Baptist church while he's made it very clear he'd never become an Episcopalian just to please me. In view of those differences between us, there's no way we could have a successful marriage."

Hazel thought for several moments before saying, "I understand your concerns about him but I've felt for years that you'd love to have a family of your own, like your brother and sister's. Besides, if two people love each other enough they can make a marriage work despite greater obstacles than the ones you just mentioned."

"That's true, Hazel, and I'd love to have a family of my own one day. But I could never marry Grover because we have nothing in common. And while I hate to use such a crude term, I have no 'sexual feelings' for him at all and know I never will."

"You're sure about that?" Hazel asked Lucy after thinking for another moment. "You have no feelings for him comparable to the ones you had for Jobie Caldwell during the years before he died so suddenly?"

"That's right, Hazel. And I've never been as sure about something in my whole life."

"Well, in that case," Hazel said with a sigh, "I'll explain your feelings to Grover during breakfast tomorrow morning if you'd like me to."

"I'll be extremely grateful if you do that, Hazel. In fact, I'll consider it an enormous favor and feel indebted to you for the rest of my life."

Shortly after Hazel explained the situation to Grover the next morning, he gave up all hope of convincing Lucy to marry him. And several weeks later, shortly after he moved into a cottage of his own on Fifth Street, he transferred his affections to Wilma Puckett, a salesgirl at Miss Edna's Dry Goods Store and the favorite grandchild of a well-to-do banker in Greenville who came to town once or twice a month to take her out to dinner. Although Wilma's uncle considered Grover a fortune hunter and warned Wilma about his motives several times, she was dazzled by his looks, glibness, and lofty ambitions. Shortly before Christmas they were married at the Baptist Church and in quick succession three little Beasleys arrived on the scene one by one. As they did Grover's dream of owning an automobile agency of his own vanished like a puff of chimney smoke on a blustery March day.

Despite the collapse of Grover's dream to die a rich man, he did an excellent job for the Crumpler-Barringer Agency, and its sales remained strong until the New York stock market crash of October 1929 and the great depression that followed it. That the Agency's sales remained strong until the fall of 1929 was due in some measure to Grover's efforts although it was due even more to the "good roads program" the state legislature funded between 1907 and 1913. During those years appropriations for the construction of better roads in all parts of the state tripled, which encouraged more and more men and even four or five widows like Josephine Gardiner and Olive Crumpler, Ozzie's amusing little mother with her enormous gift for gab, which she passed on spades to her only child, to buy cars for themselves.

Because Russell Barringer realized that his and Ozzie's Ford agency would become even more profitable if the town's main streets were paved, he not only gave strong support to Merritt's original paving proposal but he also called for it to be augmented. In fact, Barringer suggested that all seventeen of the town's north-south streets should be paved, not just Hertford Avenue and the other most fashionable residential streets. He also maintained that the sidewalks on both sides of those streets should be paved at the same time. Shortly after Barringer spoke up in favor of Merritt's proposal and called for its expansion during the council's June meeting, it won immediate support and was passed by a solid seven-to-two majority that night. A month later it sailed through the council on its second reading after a brief discussion.

Because the mayor and town clerk had foreseen the proposal's second passage during the council's July meeting, they'd already contacted Harold Dosher, a paving and sidewalk specialist in Elizabeth City, on June 15. Because Dosher was eager to get the job, he submitted a reasonable bid to Dan Wiley two weeks later. So when Ridinger explained that bid to the other members of the council during its July meeting on the night of the thirteenth, all nine members, including Merritt of course, considered it such a good bid it was unanimously adopted after a brief discussion. Although a second *pro forma* vote would have to be taken during the council's August meeting, work on the paving project was already underway by then, to the delight of most of the townspeople who were heartily sick of muddy streets and sidewalks whenever it rained for several days in a row.

Unfortunately for Merritt, Barringer received the lion's share of the credit for the adoption of "the great paving project of 1909," as the measure soon became known. Although Merritt had been the real author of the project, he received no credit for it because his public image was still so tarnished nothing he said during council meetings or on any other public occasion had a positive effect on his image. Although he was deeply annoyed by that, his wife was amused by his frustration, partly because she knew he was having another affair with a young colored girl, one who'd worked at the Merritt House until Marguerite became aware of her husband's liaison with her and fired her without a word of explanation. But because Marguerite was unwilling to risk her husband's anger and the possibility of another beating, she kept her feelings to herself for the first time since their wedding in Charleston, where her husband had been a cadet at The Citadel until he was expelled for low grades and chronic misbehavior, although it almost killed her.

While "the great paving project" of 1909 was making rapid strides, Joe received an unexpected but very cordial letter from his cousin in New York, Frances Hanford Van Landingham, whom he hadn't seen in twenty years. Frances was the oldest daughter of Joe's uncle, Thomas Hanford, who'd left North Carolina for New York in 1869, hoping to land a job on Wall Street and make a fortune in several decades. In less than a month Thomas Hanford obtained an entry-level job with the small brokerage house of Feldman & Baring which specialized in the purchase and sale of stocks, bonds, and government securities which the company managed for its clients, to whom it also gave free advice about investing and estate planning. Through talent, hard work, and sheer good luck, Thomas Hanford rose through the ranks of Feldman & Baring and became one its four vice presidents in 1887. Along the way he married and fathered three daughters, Frances Ann, Doris Mary, and Rebecca Lynn, whom he took every summer between 1880 and 1887 to Salisbury, North Carolina, where they spent six or seven weeks on the large farm owned by Thomas's older brother, Sam, a gentleman farmer and country lawyer, and his wife Lucinda, Joe's parents.

Because Sam and Lucinda had failed to have a daughter as they'd always hoped to have, they doted on their Northern nieces and treated them with great kindness and consideration. Joe and his older brother Sam Jr. were always glad to see their Northern cousins again for two reasons. They not only liked them a great deal despite the difference in their ages; but during the weeks their cousins spent in North Carolina, the boys' mother focused her attention on them and paid no attention to her sons' "grievous shortcomings," which she often discussed with her friends at church or during parties at the Hanfords' large, rambling house a short distance west of Salisbury, to Joe and his brother's great embarrassment.

The three New York girls loved their summers in the South, and Frances developed a huge crush on Joe who was taller and much better looking than his older brother. In fact, Frances followed Joe around the farm like a devoted little puppy. But the loose ties between them ended in the fall of 1887 when Joe was a senior at the state university in Chapel Hill and Frances's father became a vice president of Feldman & Baring. Because Thomas Hanford's wife had died in 1883, his oldest and most socially adept daughter, Frances, remained in New York during the next six summers in order to serve as her father's hostess or "date" at parties and receptions of all kinds because he had no desire to marry again.

By the early 1890s, Frances had become a tall, elegant, and accomplished woman, and in the fall of 1893 she married William James Van Landingham, the president and managing partner of Feldman & Baring, the company's name having recently been changed to Feldman, Baring, & Van Landingham because of Bill's vigorous leadership since April 1886. In only seven years, he transformed the company from a moderately successful brokerage house into the largest and most successful company of its kind in the country between the early 1890s and the mid1920s.

By 1909 Frances and Bill had two children: William Jr., whom they always called Billy, and a daughter, Barbara, whom Billy usually called Babs. Barbara was only ten in 1909 and still lived with her parents in their double brownstone on the southern side of Gramercy Park in lower Manhattan. As for Billy, he turned thirteen that fall and was a second-year student at the Groton School in a small town a short distance northwest of Boston.

Since 1900 Frances's sister, Doris Mary, had been married to a prominent businessman, Gerald Babcock, a native of Winston-Salem, North Carolina, who'd graduated from Princeton before obtaining a law degree from New York University. Doris Mary lived with her husband, now one of the lawyers for the Reynolds Tobacco Company, and their twin daughters in the most fashionable section of Winston-Salem less than fifty miles from Salisbury. Frances's other sister, Rebecca, had married a Connecticut banker in 1903. But he died four years later during a yachting accident on Long Island Sound.

On the second Saturday in October 1909, Joe received a long and unexpected letter from Frances. As Joe was telling Lucy several things about that letter and his Northern cousins the next afternoon, Julia called him from the kitchen. Because Augusta had that Sunday off, Julia needed some help stuffing a capon for dinner. On leaving his desk chair Joe handed Frances's letter to Lucy before saying, "Here, you might as well read this for yourself while I help Julia in the kitchen for several minutes. When I get back I'd like to know what you think of my cousin's letter."

After leaving the study and crossing the back hall to the kitchen, Joe held the capon while Julia stuffed it despite his efforts to distract her by making off-color remarks she did her best to ignore. Although she was successful at first, she eventually giggled and said, "I can't believe you're so horny after all the fun in bed we had last night."

"Don't be silly, you sexy little vixen. It's because of all the fun we had last night that the only thing I can think about is getting into your bloomers again."

"Shhhhhhhh, Joe. I just heard Joey coming down the backstairs, and Olivia's no longer practicing her scales and arpeggios on the parlor upright. What will they think if they hear us talking like that?"

"Who cares what they'd think. I sure don't because if I did, it would keep us from having more fun like this."

"You actually think that's fun?" eleven-year-old Joey asked his father on entering the kitchen. "I don't see how holding a capon while Mom stuffs it could be much fun, and when the heck will supper be ready anyway? I'm starving."

"You're always starving," Joe said to his son. "So go down to the basement and do some sit-ups and chin-ups before using my boxing bags for a while. That'll be good for you and it'll probably cause you to forget about your hunger until supper's ready."

"Sure, that's a good idea," Joey said before opening the basement door as Olivia entered the kitchen and asked if there was anything she could do to help.

"There certainly is," Julia said to her. "Take your father's place and help me stuff this capon. As for you, Joe, I'd like you to go back to the study and stay there with Lucy until supper's ready. That'll take your mind off the things that have been bothering you although they've given me some good ideas for tonight." With a quick little wiggle of her hips and a seductive look she added, "I'm sure you'll like them because they're fairly risqué, if you know what I mean."

"Mom!" Olivia said firmly. "You're too old to act like that; and if you don't stop it at once, I'll get Aunt Rhonda to talk to you and Dad about your behavior tonight. I've never known her act like that or say something so suggestive to Uncle Chip."

Joe burst into laughter and Julia giggled again, causing Olivia to wonder if her parents had gone bonkers.

Meanwhile in the study, Lucy skimmed the first several paragraphs of Frances's letter until she came to its real purpose in the fourth paragraph. That paragraph and the remainder of her letter read:

After a year of mourning for her husband, Rebecca moved back into our father's brownstone on Twenty-second Street and resumed an active social life. She is now engaged to an extremely nice and attractive young man named Martin Feldman, the younger son of another senior partner of my husband's company. As capable as he is devout, Martin is now the Rector of St. Thomas' Episcopal Church on Fifth Avenue, one of the largest and most important Episcopal parishes in the country. He and Rebecca will be married in the ballroom of his parents' house on Fifth Avenue at five thirty on the third Friday afternoon in November, six days before Thanksgiving. Doris Mary and her husband plan to attend the wedding, and so do your parents and your brother, Sam Jr. and his wife Roberta. Rebecca would <u>love</u> for you and Julia to attend the wedding also. And because I knew you much better in Salisbury than Rebecca or Doris Mary did, Rebecca asked me to write this letter on her behalf and extend a cordial invitation to you and Julia to come to New York that week and take part in all the festivities.

Everyone in my family would love to see you again and meet Julia, and it would be an easy train trip from Hertford to New York. My husband and I have a fairly large house, so we could easily accommodate you and Julia while you're in Manhattan. But I must warn you about one thing——because there will be several other people staying with us that week, I'm afraid our home will be fairly crowded. So you might prefer to stay at the Gramercy Park Hotel less than a block away, as your parents and brother and sister-in-law have decided to do. That hotel is extremely nice, and I understand it has large, comfortable rooms that are quite reasonable, certainly less than $12.50 a night. It also has an excellent dining room where my family has dinner on most Sunday evenings because our cook and her helper have most of their Sundays off.

Bill just reminded me from his chair by the fire that his company has a box on the Grand Tier at the Metropolitan Opera House. That box seats eight people very comfortably, and

Bill has arranged for us to have it during the week of Rebecca's wedding. On the Tuesday evening of that week, the great Italian tenor Enrico Caruso will be appearing as the Duke of Mantua in Verdi's famous opera <u>Rigoletto</u>, which I've seen many times because music is one of my main interests. Two nights later, the equally famous French soprano Emma Calvé will be singing the title role in Bizet's <u>Carmen</u>, which she performs so brilliantly she practically owns it in New York. Your parents and brother and sister-in-law have expressed a strong interest in seeing both operas; and if you and Julia are present with them on those nights, I'm sure their pleasure will be even greater.

With great fondness and a deep wish to see you again after so many years and an equally strong wish to meet Julia. Very cordially yours, Frances Hanford Van Landingham.

Shortly after Lucy finished Frances's letter, Joe returned to the study and asked her what she thought of it.

"It's a *wonderful* letter because it's so warm and cordial," Lucy said while smiling up at him. "But I didn't realize how sly you are until I read it."

"What makes you think I'm sly?" Joe said, trying not to smile while making himself comfortable in his desk chair again.

"I'm sure you and Julia would love to go to New York for Rebecca's wedding. But if you make that trip, which you really should, you'll need to find someone to stay with the children while you're away. I wonder if you already have someone in mind for that role."

"Yes, someone who'd be perfect for it. But I'm reluctant to ask her because it would be a great imposition."

"It doesn't sound like an imposition to me, and I'm sure her answer will be yes if you ask her."

"Then you'll do it? You wouldn't mind?"

"Of course I'll do it because it would be enormous fun to stay with Olivia and Joey while you and Julia are kicking up your heels in New York. So while the two of you are having a wonderful time in Manhattan, I'll be having fun with my niece and nephew here in town."

The month before Joe and Julia left for New York was a whirlwind of activity. Joe was determined that he and Julia should have all the proper clothes so they wouldn't be considered poor country cousins. On the last Saturday in October they took the first train to Norfolk where Joe bought his wife a beautiful evening gown with a small purse and a pair of evening shoes in the same color. He also bought her a pair of long kid gloves, a lovely strand of opera-length pearls, and a mink coat with a matching muff and hat for their nights at the opera. For himself he bought a new tuxedo and cummerbund, two new dress shirts, some patent leather dress shoes, a black overcoat and pair of leather gloves, and finally a bowler hat and an ebony walking stick with a crystal knob on top. The next afternoon they modeled their new clothes for Lucy and the children who were very impressed by how elegant they looked.

During a later trip to Elizabeth City, Joe bought a dozen silver goblets at Wentworth & Sloan, one of the best jewelry stores in the area, as a wedding present for Rebecca and Martin. For Julia, who was with him that day, he bought a silk blouse and tweed suit, a fine pair of walking boots, and an English raincoat and matching hat for rainy days. An elegant cocktail dress for late afternoon or evening wear and a velvet dress with a beautiful bodice to wear in the hotel dining room completed his purchases for her. Although he decided to make do with his present raincoat, he bought a new rain hat for himself, a "ditto" or three-piece navy blue suit, and a wine red smoking jacket to wear with his best pair of gray flannel slacks.

During the social hour after church the next morning, Julia told Lucy in a corner of the parish hall that Joe had spent almost fourteen hundred dollars on all those purchases.

"My goodness!" Lucy said at once. "You and Joe will probably be the most elegantly dressed couple in New York that week, and wouldn't the Merritts be green with envy if they knew about your coming trip. Let's see now . . . how could I bring it to their attention?"

"Forget that, Lucy, because I'd hate for you to sink to their level."

"Oh heck, I thought I was about to have some real fun for a change."

The week Joe and Julia spent in New York flew by for Lucy because her niece and nephew behaved beautifully except for a bitter argument on Tuesday night about who should take the first bath, each insisting the other one should go first. Olivia had always won arguments of that kind in the past, but Joey was growing up fast—he'd turned twelve on November 5 and was four inches taller than Olivia and seven inches taller than Lucy. So out of self-interest Olivia had stopped bullying him that summer.

The next night Chip and Rhonda had Lucy and the Hanford children to dinner, and two nights later Lucy, Olivia, and Joey reciprocated by having the five Summerlins over for an equally good meal Augusta fixed for them, after which Olivia played several of her favorite piano pieces for the group on the parlor upright—a Steinway Joe had given Julia on their second wedding anniversary. When Olivia was in the third grade, Julia, who'd taken piano lessons with the best teacher in town for eight years while she was a schoolgirl, taught her daughter how to read music and play several easy pieces. That summer Julia felt Olivia should take lessons from a much better teacher and arranged for her to study with Maxine Brown, the best organist and choir director in the area, with whom she continued to study until she graduated from high school and was about to leave home for college.

By the November evening in 1909 in the Hanfords' parlor, Olivia had studied with Mrs. Brown for slightly more than four years; and because she practiced every day for at least an hour, she played several pieces for her Summerlin relatives with real skill and artistry although Joey insisted he'd heard a dozen wrong notes. Olivia denied his charge vehemently and stuck out her tongue at him shortly before she accompanied Susan as she sang several Stephen Foster songs everyone enjoyed, even Joey. Susan had a beautiful voice similar to Julia's, and Lucy and everyone else in the family loved to hear her sing.

Two days later, when Lucy left the drugstore on Saturday afternoon, Olivia and Joey were waiting for her near the building's side door on Hertford Avenue. Within minutes they crossed the avenue and walked to Hogan's Grocery Store several blocks beyond the hotel on East Main Street. There the children begged Lucy to fix hot dogs and baked beans for supper, which Julia disliked and never allowed Augusta to fix for them. They also chose a number of items for a special meal on Sunday evening to welcome their parents back to town. Lucy bought six pork chops shortly after Joey said they were his father's favorite meat and he always ate two. Olivia suggested they have scalloped potatoes, string beans, and a jello salad with chopped nuts and celery as well as cottage cheese. Joey begged Lucy to make a batch of Parker House rolls, which the whole family loved, and for once he and Olivia agreed they should have apple pie with a slice of cheddar cheese on top for dessert. Lucy paid $2.45 for all those items but that didn't bother her at all because the children were so excited about the meal they'd planned for their parents' homecoming.

After church the next morning and a pick-up lunch in the kitchen, they straightened it and the study up before waiting impatiently in the parlor for Joe and Julia to arrive in Chip's car. The previous Sunday after church, Chip had insisted on driving the Hanfords to the Hertford station and on meeting them there when they returned to eastern North Carolina a week later. As Chip pointed out to Joe, it would be risky for him to leave his Maxwell in an unattended parking lot for slightly more than a week.

On the next Sunday afternoon, four days before Thanksgiving, Lucy and Olivia remained in the parlor, hoping the time would pass faster if Olivia played all the piano pieces she knew, each one several times if necessary. But Joey refused to have any part of that and went down to the basement and did several different exercises before pounding on his father's boxing bags for half an hour. After tiring of that activity, he went outside and jogged around the house and garage several times before doing eight sets of sit-ups and jumping jacks on the front porch. Shortly after finishing his fourth set of jumping jacks, he heard his uncle's car chugging down the avenue. At once he yelled to Lucy and Olivia in the parlor, "They're back, they're back!" before rushing down the front walk as Olivia rushed through the front door and hurried after him. They were both beside themselves with excitement when Chip stopped his car at the curb. After getting out of it, Joe and Julia hugged their children and gave each of them a book and a thousand-piece jigsaw puzzle they'd bought at Macy's, New York's largest department store. Joey loved his beautifully illustrated book about baseball, his favorite sport, while Olivia said she couldn't wait to start her book, Jane Austen's most famous novel, *Pride and Prejudice*, which Julia and Lucy had both loved as teenagers.

After Chip said good-bye and drove off, the children helped their parents carry everything into the front hall. Lucy stacked the suitcases and boxes on the floor in front of the coat rack where Julia said they could stay until Joey took them upstairs shortly before dinner. Then everyone went into the parlor and made themselves comfortable before Joe and Julia gave their children and Lucy an account of their week in New York—how wonderful both operas had been and how beautifully Signor Caruso and Mme. Calvé had sung on those two nights. What a simple but elegant wedding and buffet dinner they'd attended on Friday afternoon at the older Feldmans' mansion on Fifth Avenue. How comfortable the Gramercy Park Hotel had been and how large and attractive the Van Landinghams' house on the southern side of that small park was. Joe and Julia also described the city's amazing new "skyscrapers" which were so tall they seemed to disappear in the clouds. They'd been especially impressed by the Flatiron Building, already one of Manhattan's most famous landmarks although it was less than ten years old, and the Metropolitan Insurance Tower which had been completed only a year before and rose to a staggering height of seven hundred feet.

As Olivia set the dining room table, Lucy helped Julia fix dinner in the kitchen while Joe helped Joey take the suitcases and boxes upstairs. When Joe and the children returned to the parlor and made themselves comfortable again, he told them about the walks he and their mother took on Tuesday morning through Chinatown and Little Italy and their visits two days later to the Metropolitan Museum of Art and the Museum of Natural History, both of which he knew his children would enjoy one day. He also described the rides he and their mother took on New York's famous subway system on the day they spent several hours at both museums. Finally he told his children several things about their second cousins, Billy and Barbara Van Landingham, whom they'd probably meet in several years and Joe was sure they'd like a great deal.

Once the family went into the dining room and sat down around the table, Joe said a short blessing before he and Julia praised the excellent meal their children had planned for their first evening back in town. It was every bit as good, they maintained, as the dozens of fine meals they'd enjoyed in New York. After finishing their dessert and taking all the dishes and silverware into the kitchen, they returned to the parlor where Julia gave Lucy a silk scarf she'd bought for her at Bergdorff Goodman, one of Frances's favorite department stores. As Joe drove Lucy back to her cottage, he thanked her for taking such good care of the children while he and Julia were in New York. He also tried to reimburse her for the groceries she'd bought for that evening's dinner. But she told him to put his money away because she would never accept a penny from him, which he was bound to know by now.

Shortly after all that excitement ended, the family became immersed in the preparations for Thanksgiving and Christmas. They were happy occasions for the family despite the absence of the older Summerlins. Lucy missed them more than anyone else in the family because she lived alone except for the frisky little kitten Hazel Barlow had given her shortly after Thanksgiving. Lucy named her kitten Mr. Jobie in memory of her teenage sweetheart who'd been extremely frisky with her almost a dozen times during the last two months before he died suddenly from yellow fever in August 1887.

During a family party on New Year's Eve at the Summerlins' house, Olivia played several piano pieces before everyone sang popular songs like "Take Me Out to the Ball Game" and "Come Away with Me Lucille, in My Merry Oldsmobile" to their hearts' content. After that party and a relaxing New Year's Day, the family enjoyed several weeks of calm before another period of great excitement began.

On the second Thursday in January, Julia received a letter from Frances Van Landingham with some surprising but very good news. Frances's letter revealed that for almost a year, she and her husband had planned to buy a winter home in Florida; and during the second week of October, they'd scheduled a visit to Palm Beach and Miami during February and March. They still planned to make that trip, without their children of course because they would be in school then. Frances's letter went on to say that she and Bill had enjoyed seeing the Hanfords in New York so much they'd decided to stop by Perquimmons City on their way to Florida. They understood there was a good hotel in the middle of town, and they'd be very grateful if Julia reserved a suite for them on the nights of February 3 and 4. Their train would reach the Hertford station shortly after eleven o'clock on the morning of the third, and Bill would hire a car and driver at the station to bring them on to Perquimmons City. They planned to check into the hotel at once and have lunch in the dining room before resting for several hours. That evening they wanted the Hanfords and their children to be their guests in the hotel dining room. Frances hoped their sudden decision to visit Perquimmons City wouldn't cause Joe and Julia any trouble or require them to change some existing plans. But if it did, Frances was counting on Julia as a new but very good friend to inform her of that fact as soon as possible.

During dinner that evening, Lucy was amazed by Julia's excitement as she told her about Frances's letter. Julia was bubbling with enthusiasm when she said, "I'm sure you'll enjoy Frances's company as much as Joe and I did while we were in New York because she's a delightful person in every way. She's an inch or so taller than me and much more sophisticated although she's not a bit snobbish. She's an excellent pianist, and I can't wait for you to hear her play several of Scott Joplin's rags on my piano. I've never heard anything like it before and Bill begged her to play another rag dozens of times because he really loves the way she plays them."

"She actually plays ragtime music?" Lucy asked in disbelief. "I thought she was a highbrow who loves opera and classical music."

"She does love opera and classical music but she loves popular music almost as much. You'll never meet a nicer person than her because she's so sensitive and considerate of other people's feelings. While we were in New York, she introduced Joe and me to all the other members of her family and did everything she could to make us feel comfortable with them, but especially with her husband who's incredibly important." Turning to Joe Julia said, "Tell Lucy how important Bill is."

"You actually call him by his first name if he's incredibly important?" Lucy asked Joe in disbelief.

"Yes, that's right," Joe said, "because he asked us to call him by his first name shortly after Frances introduced us to him. He also asked us dozens of questions about Olivia and Joey and our lives here in Perquimmons City. But getting back to his great importance, he's one of the true giants of Wall Street, at least according to the article I read about him while we were waiting in the hotel dining room on our first morning in New York for our breakfast to arrive. That article in *The Wall Street Journal* explained how Bill and the great banker J. P. Morgan worked with several other men to keep the dollar from collapsing several years ago and triggering a financial panic that probably would've caused a serious depression in all parts of the country."

"I read the first half of that article too," Julia said, "and Bill's not a bit cold or stuffy, as I was afraid he'd be before we met him. Actually, he's as warm and friendly as Frances is, and they both love their children a great deal. So they're just like us, Lucy, and once you meet them I'm sure you'll find them as pleasant and agreeable as Joe and I did."

The next morning Julia walked down the avenue to the hotel and told the desk clerk she'd like to speak to Mr. Crumpler for several minutes. But the desk clerk said Mr. Crumpler had left the building five minutes earlier for the drugstore where he usually had his morning coffee with several friends. So Julia crossed the avenue and marched into the drugstore with a determined look on her face. She waved to Lucy at the cosmetics counter as she neared the table where Ozzie was sitting with Andrew Ridinger, Russell Barringer, and George Kahle, who were widely known as the town's "four big shots."

As she neared their table Julia said crisply to Ozzie, "Some extremely nice people from New York will be spending two nights in town early next month. They've asked me to reserve a suite at the hotel for them on the nights of February 3 and 4. You do have a suite at the hotel, don't you, Ozzie?"

"Oh, yes, ma'am, Miz Julia," Ozzie said at once. "A lovely suite on the third floor that has two rooms and its own bathroom. I had it repainted last summer and I can let them have it for only nine dollars a night. A suite like that in a good New York hotel would cost at least thirteen or fourteen dollars a night."

"I'll take your word for it, Ozzie, and the Van Landinghams are too nice to quibble about the price anyway. So reserve that suite for them and write it down in your reservation book the minute you return to the hotel. And I'd like a large flower arrangement to be in their sitting room when they arrive and a large box of chocolates as well—you can send the bill for the flowers and candy to Joe. And be sure there are some new towels in the bathroom because these are *extremely* nice people with high standards. I want you to take care of everything yourself so there won't be any slipups."

"Oh, no, Miz Julia, there won't be any slipups because I'll take care of everything myself, I promise."

After thanking Ozzie for his help, Julia left the store as Andrew Ridinger said to his friends, "My word, I never realized it before but Julia's almost bossy as Lucy is! Did I ever tell you about the day Lucy came into the bank and tried to open a checking account without telling Dennis she works right here in her brother's store? Imagine that—a tiny little woman like Lucy insisting on being completely responsible for her own finances and obligations. What will the world come to next?"

"I was in the bank that morning," George Kahle said with a grin, "and it was one of the funniest things I ever saw—big old Andrew kowtowing to tiny little Lucy as if she was the bank's most important customer. It was so funny I wish I had a picture of it."

"It wasn't a bit funny, George!" Andrew said sourly. "One of these days a woman will storm into your office and tell you how to run it. I can't wait to see how funny you think it is when the shoe's on your foot and pinching the hell out of it."

Lucy was helping Jobie Caldwell's mother and grandmother at the stationery counter at the time. The three women overheard the big shots' conversation without making any effort to do so. When the big shots turned to another subject, Lucy and her customers smiled at each other and agreed it was high time for them and all the other men in town to take their ideas seriously. Lucy was especially outspoken about the matter and said there wouldn't be as many problems in the world if women could vote in national elections and help determine who'd hold the country's most important elective offices and make all the crucial decisions.

Charlotte Caldwell and her mother, Evelyn Baskin, nodded their heads in agreement before they urged Lucy to run for the town council at her next opportunity. There was no local ordinance against women holding elective office, Mrs. Caldwell insisted, "because I've looked into it and I'm sure you'd be a successful candidate, Lucy."

Mrs. Baskin agreed and said she was convinced Lucy would shake things up a great deal during her first year on the council. In fact, Mrs. Baskin felt that Lucy, whom she'd taught in the sixth and seventh grades, would be able to convince the male councilors to adopt bolder and more effective policies than they'd ever supported in the past.

"I'd certainly try," Lucy said at once. "But Congress and the President will have to grant us the right to vote in national elections first. And how long do you think it'll take them to do that? A thousand years?"

"Oh no, Lucy, not a thousand years!" Mrs. Baskin said in horror. "I can't believe it'll take them that long to realize it's the right and proper thing for them to do."

"I wouldn't count on it if I were you," Lucy said with a sigh. "Given their age-old practice of considering us the weaker sex, I wonder if they'll ever want our help in cleaning up the terrible mess they've made of things."

"I'm afraid Lucy's right," Charlotte Caldwell said to her mother. "But we need to go to the grocery store now and talk to Estelle. She agreed to meet with us at ten thirty and help us choose the refreshments for our little card party next week."

Lucy rolled her eyes at Evelyn Baskin, hoping she shared the disappointment she felt on hearing Mrs. Caldwell's comment. But because Mrs. Baskin was preoccupied with taking her daughter's arm in hers so she wouldn't stumble or fall, she failed to notice Lucy's disparaging look. Shortly after the two ladies said good-bye to Lucy, they walked slowly to the drugstore's main entrance and left the building as Lucy wondered if anything would change in her lifetime.

Chapter 7

On February 3 the Hanfords left Perquimmons City in time to meet the Van Landinghams' train at the Hertford station. When it came to a stop at the main platform, Bill and Frances got off with their luggage and greeted Joe and Julia warmly. Then as Bill helped Joe carry their suitcases to the luggage rack on the back of his car, Julia and Frances made themselves comfortable on the car's back seat. While Joe was tying the suitcases to the luggage rack, Bill sat down on the passenger side of the front seat. After putting on his driving goggles, Joe cranked the car's engine until it started and climbed into the Maxwell before sitting down behind the steering wheel. After releasing the hand brake he put the car in gear and turned it around before driving it out of the parking lot.

As they headed for Perquimmons City, Bill told the Hanfords they shouldn't have gone to so much trouble because he'd planned to hire a car and driver at the station. Joe said they hadn't gone to any trouble at all, and besides, he and Julia looked forward to showing him and Frances around their town.

The Van Landinghams were an even taller couple than the Hanfords. Frances had dark brown hair similar to Joe's, while Bill had an impressive mane of thick gray hair. Frances was twenty-two years younger than her husband who'd had no children by his first wife, who died in 1877 when they were both twenty-five. Because Bill had been devastated by her death, he devoted the next sixteen years of his life to his business career, and in the fall of 1886 he became the president and managing partner of Feldman & Baring. By 1893 Otto Feldman and Lionel Baring were so impressed by

Bill's leadership, especially his decision to open branch offices in Boston, Philadelphia, Chicago, and several other Northern cities, they changed the company's name to Feldman, Baring, & Van Landingham in February of that year.

A month or so after that, Bill was captivated by Frances, the oldest daughter of Thomas Hanford, one of the company's four vice presidents. Bill admired Frances's beauty and charm, her lovely smile and bright sparkling eyes, as well as her enormous love of music and great skill at the piano. Most of all he admired her poise and gracious manner whenever she served as her father's hostess or accompanied him to a dinner party where she was usually the youngest person at the table. As for Frances, she admired Bill's quiet, confident manner, his polished manners, and his refusal to court her although she assumed from the way she often caught him gazing at her before he blushed and looked away that he found her quite interesting and attractive. That he seemed to be embarrassed because he was old enough to be her father endeared him to her even more. Finally, the fact that he was one of the richest and most respected men in New York and stood six feet four while she was five feet ten made him even more attractive in her eyes.

For several months Frances was frustrated because Bill never made an effort to speak to her except when they were seated near each other during a dinner party at the home of mutual friends. Hoping to break the impasse Frances eventually convinced her father to ask him and Mr. and Mrs. Lionel Baring to a small dinner party at their brownstone on Twenty-second Street. There were eight people at the table that night—Frances, her father and two younger sisters, Bill, and Lionel and Gertrude Baring and their English granddaughter, Edwina Spencer. While they were enjoying their main course, an excellent beef wellington Mr. Hanford's cook had fixed at Frances's request, the subject of her impending social debut in the Grand Ballroom at the Waldorf-Astoria Hotel on the last Saturday night in June came up and was discussed at some length. Eventually Gertrude Baring asked Frances if she'd chosen her principal escort for that important occasion.

Frances sighed and said, "No, I'm afraid I haven't, Mrs. Baring. Men my age or several years older always seem a bit boring to me. They never talk about something of any importance; and while I hate to say it, I find most of them vain and superficial." She gazed at Bill who was sitting directly across the table from her, hoping to see some interest in his eyes. But they remained completely opaque.

"Surely you know a somewhat older gentleman you could ask," Mrs. Baring persisted. "And you mustn't wait much longer, my dear, because the last Saturday in June is only six weeks off."

"Yes, ma'am, I'm aware of that, and there's a very handsome gentleman I'd like to ask. But I'm afraid he'd have no interest in being my principal escort." Bill's eyes suggested a flicker of interest but nothing more.

"That's ridiculous, Frances! Because of your beauty and charm any man would be *delighted* to be your principal escort and there's nothing to be gained by waiting."

"You really think so, Mrs. Baring?"

"I certainly do and I'm sure your father agrees with me."

"Is that true, Papa?" Frances asked her father who was sitting directly across the table from her on Bill's right. "Do you agree with Mrs. Baring?"

"I certainly do, Frances. In fact, I don't understand why you've waited this long."

"Then I'll ask him right now. Mr. Van Landingham, would you be at all interested in serving as my principal escort at this year's ball?" Frances held her breath, knowing she'd taken a big chance and might be embarrassed by his answer. But she considered it a chance worth taking because she was unlikely to have another chance to ask him.

The dining room was totally silent until Bill said, "Frances, I'd consider it a great honor to be your principal escort at this year's ball. I know everyone in the room was amazed—myself most of all—when you asked me to assume that role. But unless your father objects, and I know how to make his life extremely difficult if he does—just a little joke, Tom, so relax—I'll look forward to that night with great anticipation. But I need to warn you about one thing. I haven't been on a dance floor in twenty years. So if you intend to follow through with this, I think we should practice together several times during the next six weeks."

"I do intend to follow through with it, I assure you. So once we have our dessert and adjourn to the parlor, I hope we can put our heads together and find several times when it would be convenient for us to practice together for an hour or two if you can spare that much time from your busy schedule." Turning back to her father Frances said, "That's okay with you, isn't it, Papa?"

"Frances, how can you ask me that with a straight face? Don't you see the Sword of Damocles that's hanging over my head?"

Lionel Baring laughed outright before saying, "Tom, I'll protect you if you have any reservations about Bill and Frances practicing together. But I'm sure that won't be necessary."

Tom laughed too before saying, "I'm also convinced it won't be necessary. I was only trying to make a little joke of my own."

Bill gazed down at him while saying, "A good recovery, Tom, but you shouldn't have rejected Lionel's offer of protection that fast. If you'd like to reconsider, I won't hold it against you for more than several years."

Everyone else at the table laughed except the Barings' granddaughter, Edwina. She saw no reason to laugh because she was only twelve and had no idea what a Sword of Damocles was.

Six weeks after that dinner party Frances and Bill were by universal agreement the handsomest couple at that year's debutante ball. And only four months after that, Thomas Hanford walked his daughter down the center aisle of St. Thomas's Episcopal Church to the strains of "Here Comes the Bride" while a beaming Bill Van Landingham waited for her near the high altar, which was banked with pink and white roses, lilies, orchids, and chrysanthemums. A long article with several pictures of the happy couple in the next morning's *New York Times* described the ceremony as "Manhattan's society wedding of the year."

After driving the Van Landinghams into Perquimmons City on that February morning in 1910, Joe gave them a brief tour of the town before stopping at the hotel's side entrance. As Joe got out of the car and untied their suitcases, a porter emerged from the building and placed their luggage on a trolley he rolled inside to the main desk. As Bill and Frances were about to go inside to register, Joe said he would come for them at six thirty that evening and drive them up the avenue to his and Julia's house for dinner.

Bill smiled and said, "That's very kind of you, Joe. But we hoped you and the rest of your family would have dinner with us in the hotel dining room tonight."

"I know you did, but Julia and I feel very strongly that you and Frances should be *our* guests on your first evening in town. After all, we enjoyed a number of excellent meals in your home last fall and we'd hate for you to consider 'Southern hospitality' just a hollow phrase."

"That's right," Julia said at once, "and I've already given my cook her instructions. Although Augusta's skills can't compare to those of your cook and her helper in New York, I'm sure she'll serve us a good meal this evening."

"I'm sure Bill didn't mean to suggest she wouldn't," Frances said. "I've told him several times about all the outstanding meals my sisters and I enjoyed at Joe's parents' home in Salisbury while we were girls. Because I've loved Southern cooking since those wonderful summers, I'm looking forward to tonight's meal with great anticipation."

"So am I," Bill said, "but there's no need for Joe to pick us up this evening. As we were driving into town he pointed out your house, that handsome Victorian several blocks up the avenue. Frances and I usually take a turn around Gramercy Park in the late afternoon or early evening. So we'll walk up to your house and save Joe the trip."

When Bill rang the Hanfords' doorbell shortly after six thirty that evening, Lucy opened the front door and invited him and Frances to come in. After introducing herself to them, Lucy took their overcoats and hung them on the coat rack in a corner of the entrance hall before leading them into the parlor. A cheerful fire was burning in the fireplace as Julia greeted Bill and Frances warmly again. On turning back to Lucy Frances said, "Julia's told me a great deal about you and how helpful you always are. You sound a lot like my sister, Doris Mary, who lives in Winston-Salem. I wish I could see Doris Mary as often as Julia gets to see you."

"What a lovely compliment," Lucy said. "But Joe and Julia have told me a great deal about you and your husband, all very favorable of course."

Bill smiled down at Lucy—he was fifteen inches taller than her—before asking her to call Frances and himself by their first names because they'd never liked formality.

Lucy gazed up at him and said, "Certainly, Bill, because Julia's told me there's no reason I should be afraid of you even if you are one of the giants of Wall Street."

"My, my," Bill said with a twinkle in his eye, "I'm sorry to hear that. I've clearly lost my ability to inspire fear in other people, which I could do when I was younger by just frowning or snapping my fingers at them. That's one of the hazards of growing old, I'm afraid."

"You're not old," Lucy said at once, "not with a wonderful attitude like that. Old is only a state of mind and you're clearly still very young at heart."

As the Van Landinghams made themselves comfortable in the wing chairs on either side of the fireplace at Julia's suggestion, Joe entered the parlor with a decanter of sherry and five wine glasses on a silver tray, wedding gifts from his brother and sister-in-law in Salisbury. He put the tray down on a side table before handing small glasses of sherry to Bill and Frances before handing another glass to Lucy who'd taken the slipper chair at one end of the sofa. After handing a glass to Julia on the sofa, Joe sat down beside her and took the last glass of sherry for himself before asking Bill and Frances if their suite at the hotel was satisfactory.

The Van Landinghams said it was a very attractive and comfortable suite shortly before Olivia and Joey entered the parlor and introduced themselves. After complimenting their manners Frances asked them about their interests and what they hoped to do when they were grownups.

Joey said at once, "I plan to play professional baseball for nine or ten years before I go to medical school and become a doctor like Dad."

Clearly hoping to top her brother Olivia said, "I plan to be a concert pianist so I can perform with all the leading orchestras in Europe and here in America."

"You must have enormous talent if you're thinking in those terms," Frances said to her. "How long have you taken lessons?"

"Only a little over four years although Mom had already taught me how to read music and play six or seven easy pieces. Luckily for me, I've had an *excellent* teacher since then, and she drills me on my scales and arpeggios during the first several minutes of every lesson so I'll practice them every day and they'll be really clean and fast. During the last ten days I've learned how to play Chopin's *Raindrop Prelude,* and I'll be glad to play it for you now if you'd like to hear it."

Frances said she'd love to hear her play that prelude because she'd learned how to play it when she was about Olivia's age and Chopin had always been one of her favorite composers.

"I like his music a great deal too," Olivia said, "although I like Mendelssohn's almost as much." Once she sat down at the upright and adjusted the stool to her liking, she played the *Raindrop Prelude,* one of Chopin's longest but easiest preludes, with real skill and artistry.

"That was a beautiful performance," Frances said as soon as Olivia finished it. "It was clear and straightforward without any sentimentality. You play like someone a great deal older and more mature than yourself, Olivia."

Bill agreed and so did Lucy and Julia. Joe echoed that opinion before saying to Joey, "What did you think about your sister's performance? We'd like to know how you felt about it too."

Julia held her breath while Joey said, "Well, she played that piece fairly well in my opinion, although its middle section seemed really long and boring to me. If I were Olivia, I'd choose shorter and peppier pieces to play for guests because most people like them much better. Mom's told me several times that Mrs. Van Landingham plays ragtime music extremely well, and I think Olivia should learn how to play several of Scott Joplin's rags because they'd be a much better choice for company pieces."

Joe and Julia were relieved by their son's answer while Lucy was amused by the honesty of Joey's comments about Olivia's choice of what to play that evening. As for Bill, he said, "You're right, Joey—my wife does play ragtime music extremely well, partly because rags are great company pieces just as you pointed out. But I still think Olivia made a fine choice about what to play for us. And she's well on her way to becoming a concert pianist if she's taken lessons for only a little over four years."

Olivia beamed as Joey shrugged his shoulders before asking the Van Landinghams if their son liked baseball and other sports. Bill said his son liked baseball a great deal and always rooted for the New York Yankees. But his favorite sport was football, which he played at his boarding school in Massachusetts.

"I like football too," Joey said, "but not quite as much as baseball. I'm just glad they're played at different times of the year so I can play 'em both."

Several minutes later the Hanfords escorted their guests across the entrance hall to the dining room, where they enjoyed an excellent meal that began with an outstanding oyster stew Augusta had fixed that afternoon. Once they finished it, Augusta cleared the table of the soup bowls before bringing in the main course—a beautifully cooked leg of lamb with mint jelly and large bowls of mashed potatoes, string beans, and two kinds of squash they passed around the table family style. The main course also included a basket of Augusta's wonderful Parker House rolls. For dessert they enjoyed a slice of coconut cake with some vanilla ice cream on the side.

After dinner Olivia followed the three women back to the parlor for some "girl talk" while Joey accompanied Bill and his father to the study where the men had some brandy and a good cigar. Joe had remembered in early January that Bill usually smoked a cigar shortly after dinner in New York. So Joe had ordered a dozen Cuban cigars from a tobacconist's shop in Elizabeth City although he himself seldom smoked a cigar or even a cigarette.

Shortly after the children said good night at nine forty-five and went upstairs to their bedrooms, Bill thanked the Hanfords for an excellent meal and a delightful evening. Because he and Frances were clearly ready to return to the hotel, Lucy said she needed to be on her way too because she was a bit tired from her day at the drugstore. Despite a vigorous protest from her and the Van Landinghams, Joe insisted on driving Bill and Frances down the avenue to the hotel before driving Lucy to her cottage on Second Street.

Frances spent most of the next day with Julia because they enjoyed each other's company a great deal and were never at a loss for something to discuss, whether it was music or the latest fashions, their children's occasional social problems and the grades they made in school, or the magazines they both took and especially liked.

After discussing the latest fashions in Julia's morning room for half an hour, Frances said she'd like to go on a walk and see more of the town. Julia considered that a good idea because it was a beautiful morning, warm and bright. After leaving the Hanfords' house they strolled down the avenue to Church Street, where they turned right and proceeded to the small Episcopal church the Hanfords and all the other members of Julia's family attended. Because the Van Landinghams were Episcopalians too, Frances said she'd like to go inside and look around. So Julia led her through the narthex into the nave and showed her the pews the family occupied on most Sunday mornings. She also pointed out the pulpit and choir stalls before showing her the small pipe organ the church had bought in 1884. It clearly needed an overhaul because it had wheezed and groaned a bit during recent services despite how soft and slowly their organist always played it.

After touring the church Julia and Frances resumed their walk and proceeded farther west on Church Street until they reached Magnolia Drive and turned right. After walking two more blocks they came to the Kahles' residence, a rambling frame house with a large screened porch on the southern side and a sun porch of equal size on the northern side. On the sidewalk Julia introduced Frances to Phyllis, who'd been picking up sticks and pine cones in the front yard. While the three women were chatting about the beautiful weather, Selma Ridinger drove up in her buggy, which Andrew had given her shortly after he bought a car for himself. Julia had taught Selma how to drive her horse and buggy several years before, and during later months and years she'd given driving lessons to Phyllis, Mildred Barringer, Joanne Wiley, and several other local women. Frances was amazed because she'd never seen more than three or four women driving buggies in New York, and only in Central Park or on narrow side streets at times other than rush hours.

After getting out of her buggy Selma tethered her horse to a hitching post and joined the other three women on the sidewalk. Once Julia introduced Frances and Selma to each other, Selma took an active part in the conversation about the Van Landinghams' coming trip to Florida and the kind of winter home they hoped to buy in Palm Beach or Miami. Eventually Phyllis insisted that Julia and Frances come inside and have lunch with Selma and herself, which her cook probably had ready by now. Shortly after they went inside the four women enjoyed a fine meal of chicken salad, several kinds of vegetables, and lemon tarts before they adjourned to the parlor and played bridge until three thirty. After thanking Phyllis for a lovely time, her guests left the house together before Selma drove Julia and Frances back to the Hanfords' house in her buggy. After letting them out at the end of the Hanfords' front walk, Selma drove farther north in the direction of a cousin's house while Julia and Frances went inside and discussed several novels they'd recently read until Olivia and Joey came downstairs from their bedrooms, where they'd just finished their homework. Shortly after they said hello, Joey left the parlor for the home of his best friend, Cordell Richardson, who loved sports as much as he did. On warm winter afternoons, they usually threw a football or baseball around and played horseshoes for half an hour before they had supper with their families.

Shortly after Joey's departure Olivia sat down on the piano stool and played two of Mendelssohn's famous *Songs without Words* at Frances's request. Once she finished the second piece, Frances said she had great talent and should continue her studies until she was a true artist. She should also come to New York that summer and spend some time with her and her daughter Barbara. "She loves music too, and when you come to New York, Bill and I'll take you and Barbara to a concert at Carnegie Hall, which I'm sure you'll enjoy."

Olivia was so excited by the prospect of a trip to New York and attending a concert at Carnegie Hall she wanted to choose a date for that trip at once. But Julia said they should postpone that decision until a later time, to which Olivia reluctantly agreed before telling Mrs. Van Landingham good-bye and returning to her bedroom to finish another Jane Austen novel she'd started several days before.

Shortly after Olivia went upstairs Frances thanked Julia for a delightful day before saying it was time for her to return to the hotel so she could bathe and dress for dinner. "But don't forget, Julia—Bill and I are expecting you and the rest of your family to join us for dinner in the hotel dining room by six thirty. We'll be very disappointed if you send us a message that you're unable to come for some reason."

As Julia escorted Frances to the front door, she assured her that she'd never do something like that. She also said it had been a lovely day for her and urged her and Bill to consider buying some land and building a winter home in or near Perquimmons City. "If you did that we could see each other often and you could also see Doris Mary without any trouble because there's a direct rail connection between Hertford and Winston-Salem by way of Durham and Greensboro."

Frances thanked Julia for pointing that out before saying she would certainly tell Bill that if they failed to find a house in Palm Beach or Miami they liked enough to buy.

Although Frances and Julia enjoyed everything about their day together, Bill's experiences in town were completely different although they started well enough. After having breakfast with Frances in the hotel dining room, they left the building at the same time: Frances for the Hanfords' house a short distance up the avenue and Bill for Ned's barbershop several doors beyond Joe's office on East Main Street. After getting a shave and a haircut from Ned himself, Bill retraced his steps to the hotel before crossing the avenue to the drugstore to buy some toothpaste, a shoehorn, and a copy of the *Tribune* from which he hoped to learn much more about the area, which had impressed him very favorably so far.

When Bill entered the drugstore shortly after nine forty-five, Lucy was busy in the office with some bookkeeping work. But Chip knew at once who Bill was from his great height and handsome frock coat. So he introduced himself and chatted with Bill about the beautiful weather for several minutes before finding the items Bill wanted to buy. After ringing them up on the cash register and accepting a dollar bill from him, he handed Bill his change and purchases in a small shopping bag as Mildred Barringer and her older daughter entered the store. After telling them he'd be with them in a minute or so, Chip asked Bill if he'd like to meet several local leaders who were having their morning coffee together at the time. When Bill said he'd like that, Chip took him back to meet the town's four "big shots" at their usual table near the soda fountain. In short order Chip introduced him to Andrew Ridinger, Russell Barringer, and George Kahle but not to Ozzie Crumpler. Ozzie had probably remained at the hotel that morning to oversee the work of his head cook, who sampled the cooking wine eight or nine times on most days. Ozzie was probably doing his best that day to keep his head cook from getting tipsy because he knew the Van Landinghams planned to have dinner at the hotel with the Hanfords that evening and wanted the food to be as good as possible.

After shaking hands with three of the town's political and business leaders in turn, Bill accepted their invitation to join them at their table before declining Dillie's offer of a cup of coffee because he'd had several cups during breakfast. Then he told the three men that everyone he'd met in Perquimmons City so far had been very friendly and helpful. "But why doesn't your town doesn't have phone service? Most towns as large and progressive as Perquimmons City clearly is have had phone service for ten or eleven years."

Andrew said he and a dozen other men had tried to establish a phone company during the early 1890s. "Our efforts were on the verge of success until the financial panic of 'ninety-three occurred. Unfortunately, several men who'd pledged to support our plan by buying at least a hundred shares of stock in a local phone company lost their shirts and had to cancel their pledges. When that happened the rest of us shelved the plan for five years, which have increased to sixteen unfortunately. I for one feel guilty about letting that happen and think we should rectify the situation as soon as possible."

George Kahle agreed with Andrew before Russell Barringer said he was convinced it was high time for them to take their original plan out of mothballs. "If we did that and found several new investors, we'd probably have phone service in less than a year, which would make life much easier for us and almost everyone else in town."

After thinking for several moments Bill said he might support such a venture by buying several hundred shares of stock in a local phone company. "But I have another question for you now—why doesn't this area have a hospital? I understand the nearest hospital is in Elizabeth City forty-five miles away."

Kahle said that was correct and the area needed a hospital badly, perhaps one located midway between Perquimmons City, Hertford, and Edenton, which formed a large triangle. "If a hospital was built on a site convenient to all three towns, I'm convinced it would be used so heavily it would pay for itself in fifteen or twenty years."

Russell agreed and pointed out that Joe had hoped to see a hospital built since the summer he arrived in town in 1895. "Joe's an excellent doctor with real vision for the future, and he's suggested half a dozen times that a capital funds drive be launched as a way of raising enough money to build a large, up-to-date hospital. But his calls have fallen on deaf ears and we're lucky that his office has become a clinic of sorts. Although it provides excellent care for his patients, Joe has such a long patient list he's unable to add any more names to it at the present time. However, I've heard him say several times recently that he's thinking about taking another doctor into practice with him. And if he does that and finds a larger building to rent, we'll be better served than we are now."

When that group of dignitaries broke up at ten fifteen, Andrew Ridinger invited Bill to accompany him next door to the bank and see its new vault, which was larger and much stronger than its original vault, which had had been installed shortly before the bank opened in 1882. Bill accepted Andrew's invitation at once because he hoped the bank had a ticker-tape machine he could use to check on how well his riskiest stocks were faring on the New York Stock Exchange that morning. Their value had declined by almost five percent during the last two weeks, and if their value continued to decline he planned to sell them at once.

Shortly after they entered the bank Andrew showed Bill the most important features of its new vault before they made themselves comfortable in Andrew's office. They chatted about general matters there for several minutes before Bill asked Andrew if the bank had a ticker tape machine he could use for several minutes before lunch.

Andrew said he'd planned to buy a ticker tape machine for the bank during the last six months because he and a dozen other men, including Joe, Chip, Russell Barringer, George Kahle, Floyd Richardson, and Percy Hogan, had talked about establishing an investment club of sorts. But he'd failed to buy such a machine because the installation of the bank's new vault had required most of his time and attention since the previous fall. Unfortunately, the only man in town who owned a ticker tape machine was William Merritt.

"What's Mr. Merritt like?" Bill asked after several moments. "Is he a friendly and cooperative man who'd allow me to use his machine for several minutes this afternoon? Of course, he's bound to have a large and diverse portfolio if he has a ticker tape machine in his own home."

"I know for a fact that he owns five thousand shares of stock in this bank. I've also heard on good authority that he owns almost as many shares in the Bank of Edenton and thousands of shares in blue-chip companies like Sears and Roebuck, Bethlehem Steel, and the Atlantic Coast Line Railroad."

"He sounds like a savvy investor to me. But is he friendly and approachable?"

"It all depends on the mood he's in and I just heard him talking to one of the tellers in the lobby. So stay here for a minute while I go out and see if he's free this afternoon."

Actually, Andrew had heard Merritt complaining loudly to Dennis Payne about an accounting practice he disliked and felt should be changed at once. Because he was the bank's largest stockholder, Merritt insisted that his suggestion be implemented by its executive committee that very day. Payne considered that impossible but kept his opinion to himself, knowing Merritt would probably vent his anger on him if he expressed an opinion that differed from his own.

As Ridinger left his office to smooth things over in the lobby, he deplored Merritt's arrogant manner and frequent rudeness to the bank's tellers. After speaking cordially to Merritt and calming him down a bit, Andrew invited him to join him in his office and meet an important visitor from New York. Merritt's hopes soared when he considered the possibility of selling a building site to a rich Yankee who was probably unaware that Southern land values were much lower than Northern ones. If that proved to be the case, there was a good chance Merritt could dupe this Yankee into paying several times as much money for several acres of his land than they were actually worth.

Within minutes Merritt was conversing with Bill, an unusually nice gentleman of the old school, as if they'd been friends for years. With no sense of what was right and proper in such circumstances, Merritt said to Bill, "I don't mean to brag, but my wife and I own four thousand shares of stock in the Atlantic Coast Line Railroad, which takes dozens of Yankees like you to Florida every winter. It's foolish of you and your friends to buy winter homes in Palm Beach or Miami when this area has extremely mild and pleasant winters and is much closer to New York than Florida is. You and your friends don't actually enjoy making long train trips between New York and Palm Beach or Miami every winter, do you? I hate them myself and avoid them whenever possible."

Although taken aback by Merritt's brusque questions and undue familiarity, Bill said, "No, I don't enjoy long train trips and neither does my wife or any of our friends. So I'll give some thought to building a winter home in this area. But at the present time I'm concerned about how several of my stocks are faring on the New York Stock Exchange this morning. Because Andrew told me several minutes ago that you have a ticker tape machine in your home, I wonder if I could use it for several minutes this afternoon."

"I'd be *delighted* for you to use it," Merritt said, thinking he could convince Bill to buy one of his building sites for five or six times its real value shortly after he used his ticker tape machine for several minutes. So he said to Bill, "I'm sure my wife would enjoy meeting you and our cook can always rustle up something fairly good when I bring a guest home for lunch. So let's go outside to my car now and drive to my house. And once we have a good lunch with my wife, you can use my ticker tape machine as long as you like."

"That's very kind of you, Mr. Merritt, but I'd hate for your cook to go to any trouble on my account. It might be better if I had lunch at the hotel before walking to your home by two thirty or three o'clock."

"There's no need for you to do that, Bill, and besides, Andrew's probably ready for me to leave. Whenever I drop by the bank for some coffee and conversation, he always says after several minutes that he has some important work to do upstairs in the accounting department, which I'm convinced is only a ruse to get rid of me."

Bill gave Andrew a curious look as if to say, *Should I go home with this man? He seems a bit strange to me.*

Andrew actually had some important work to do that morning and couldn't think of another way to get rid of Merritt in less than half an hour. So he urged Bill to go home with Merritt and have lunch with him and his "charming partner in life, the lovely and delightful Marguerite."

Thereupon Bill left the bank with Merritt, and several minutes later the latter stopped his Stanley Steamer in front of the Merritt House. Shortly after they got out of it and Merritt entrusted his car to his butler-chauffeur, he led Bill up the mansion's broad steps to its large front porch. After crossing the porch and opening the front door, Merritt ushered Bill inside before he saw his wife reading a novel in the west parlor as she squinted at each paragraph through a gold lorgnette. He called to Marguerite, "Come and join me in the entrance hall, my dear, so I can introduce you to a visitor from New York, Bill Van Landingham. Andrew introduced Bill to me at the bank a while ago, and he'd like to use my ticker tape machine for several minutes this afternoon. He's concerned about how several of his 'iffy' stocks are faring on the stock exchange today."

Marguerite emerged from the west parlor and shook hands with Bill before saying, "I'm Marguerite Manigault Merritt from Chal'ston. I'm sure you've heard of my family because they own one of the most beautiful mansions in that cha'min little city, which is famous for its many splendid mansions. What features of the Manigault House did you like best, Bill? Its large windows or high ceilins? Or maybe the exquisite millwork throughout the mansion, or pu'haps the mahv'lous Waterford chandele'uhs in all the most impo'tant ground flo rooms?"

"I'm afraid I've never heard of the Manigault House because I've never been to Charleston and know very little about it."

"I don't mean to interrupt," Merritt said to his wife. "But while you chat with Bill, I'll go back to the kitchen and tell Flossie and Tulip we have a guest for lunch so they'll go to a bit more trouble than usual."

"That's a good idea," Marguerite said to her husband shortly before he left the entrance hall for the main kitchen. On turning back to Bill she said, "Did I hear you correc'ly, Bill? Did you ac'shully say you've nev'uh been to Chal'ston or heard o the Manigault House? It's one o the most chamin cities in the whole country and my family's *magnificent* home has been open to the public two aft'uhnoons a week for some yea'uhs. And durin Gah'den Week, it's open every aft'uhnoon to people who're so eag'uh to see it, the waitin line outside the mansion extends fo aw'most a mile."

"I'm sure the Manigault House is well worth seeing and I'd love to see it one day. But that'll have to wait until I retire because my company has no offices south of the Mason-Dixon Line."

"Oh? Why is that, pray tell?"

"Well, my company specializes in the purchase, management, and sale of stocks, bonds, and government securities. It has branch offices in cities like Boston, Philadelphia, Chicago, Cleveland, and Detroit. But those are all Northern cities, ma'am. We have no offices in the South and have no plans to open one in the near future."

"How strange. I suppose you have a good explanation for that."

"Do you want the truth?"

"Of course I do! Don't shilly-shally with me, sir!"

"I'm afraid my explanation will annoy you."

"Surely you don't expect me to beg you to ans'uh my question."

"No, of course I don't. But as everyone knows, the South has never recovered from the Civil War. It's still a very depressed area and it's likely to remain the poorest part of the country for years to come. The people down here have almost no money to invest, I'm afraid."

"Almost no money to invest you say? And the poorest part of the country fo yea'uhs to come? My word, sir, wherev'uh did you get such wooly-headed ideas? I'll have you know my hus'bun and I own *thousands* o shares o stock in a dozen diff'rent companies."

"I don't doubt that for a minute because of your beautiful home. But you and your husband are only two investors in an extremely large area. So it wouldn't be profitable for my company to open an office in the South at the present time and probably not for thirty or forty years to come."

"But I have *dozens* o relatives in Chal'ston and Savann'uh who have a great deal o money to invest. Is their money not good enough for Yankees like you? And if you think it's not, you should take a long hard look at yo prejudices. I'm amazed by how little you know about one o the most beautiful and cham'in pahts of our country."

"My word, Marguerite!" Mr. Merritt said when he reappeared. "What have you gotten so worked up about? And why are you talking to our guest in such a heated way?"

"Because *yo* guest is one of those misguided Yankees who comes down here and ridicules the South fo no reason at all! He has no idea what the South's *really* like!"

Bill turned to Mr. Merritt and said, "I'm afraid I've offended your wife with my comments about the South's economic problems. So I'll leave and walk back to the hotel now. Because it's less than a mile from here and I'm a good walker, I'll get there in time to have lunch in the dining room. I can always check on the stocks I'm concerned about shortly I arrive in Palm Beach two days from now."

"No, please don't go," Merritt pleaded while thinking about all the money he'd lose if he failed to sell Bill a building site that afternoon. "Our lunch is almost ready and once we enjoy it you can use my ticker tape machine as long as you like. In that way you can find out what you want to know; and once you do, I'll tell you about several of my most beautiful building sites. I'm sure you'll decide to buy at least one of them if only as a good investment."

"You really think I should stay? My comments about the South's economic problems have upset your wife a great deal."

"She'll calm down in just a minute," Merritt said while giving his wife a fierce look. "So let's go to the dining room now and have a pleasant lunch. Marguerite, will you lead the way *please?*"

"Of course I will, William. And, Bill, I'm sorry I disagreed with your views so strongly. Unfortunately, Yankee prejudice toward the South always upsets me a great deal. That prejudice is *completely* unwarranted, I assure you."

From the entrance hall they moved into the east parlor where Bill stopped and said to her, "This is one of the most beautiful rooms I've ever seen." Hoping to mollify her a bit more Bill continued, "Your furnishings seem perfect for such a large, elegant room and that's a *magnificent* secretary over there on the far wall. It looks like an English secretary to me because it's so graceful and beautifully proportioned. In fact, I can say without any reservations on my part that it's the finest secretary I've ever seen."

"Oh, no, no, no, Bill," Marguerite said with a dismissive little wave of her hand. "That's a simple country piece without any venee'uh or delicate inlay, so it's definitely *not* an English secretary. It was made less than twenty years ago by Cha'les Summuh'lin, who was a fine craftsman for this area although he was completely self-taught and had no willin'ness to innovate. For several years I've planned to move it upsta'uhs and replace it with a much fin'uh secretary made in Boston or Philadelph'yuh. Of course, Mis'tuh Summuh'lin's no longer in business. But even if he was, I'd have to wait until I found a much bett'uh secretary in one of the outstandin antique shops in Chal'ston or Savann'uh."

"What happened to Mr. Summerlin?" Bill asked after thinking for a moment. "Did he retire or pass away?"

"He passed away a little ov'uh two years ago and his wife died shortly aft'uh him. They were simple country people but nothin more. Their son owns the only drugstore in town and employs his sist'uh Lucy as his bookkeep'uh and sales assistant. Lucy was without a doubt the *worst* employee I've ev'uh had, and why I kept her on my staff fo almost thirteen years is a mys'try I'll nev'uh und'uhstand. Lucy's sist'uh Jul'yuh is a lovely puh'son to look at, but she's also very connivin. In fact, she's such an awful social clim'uh you'd nev'uh wanna enuh'tain her in yo own home."

"Why do you say that, Mrs. Merritt?" Bill said, convinced the Merritts had no knowledge of his marriage ties with the Hanfords and, through them, the lowly Summerlins.

"Well, shortly after that han'some young doct'uh, Joseph Hanford, moved to town," Marguerite said, thinking she had Bill in the palm of her hand, "Jul'yuh Summuh'lin set her cap for him. And in less than six months she cnvinced him to marry her, which was a *dreadful* mistake on his paht, I assure you. By allyin himself with the Summuh'lins, Dr. Hanford *ruined* himself in the eyes o the world. His daught'uh Olivia has no chance o bein invited to make her debut in Raleigh or Columbia, where I came out some years ago. Our daughter Becca's already scheduled to make her debut in Columbia a little ov'uh a yea'uh from now. But I'm sure Olivia Hanford will be passed ov'uh and wind up marryin a man o no distinc'shun because of how little social cachet her moth'uh's people had. They had no culture or refinement at all, and I've heard on good authority that no one in the family has any interest in music or ah't or poetry, which is really sad, don't you think?"

My God, Bill thought, *how does her husband put up with such mean-spirited claptrap? I wonder if she ridicules other people as much as she ridicules Julia and Lucy, who seem extremely nice and refined to me as does their brother Chip. And Julia's daughter Olivia clearly loves music and has almost as much skill on the piano as Frances although she's a great deal younger than my wife.*

As they moved into the main dining room, Mrs. Merritt said to Bill, "This is the lah'gest and finest room in our home. It's twenty-two feet wide and forty-two and a half feet long, which means we can hold cotil'yons and oth'uh lah'ge pah'ties here whenev'uh we get the servants to roll up the rug and move it and the banquet table to one side o the room. The rug is an outstandin antique Serapi, and have you ev'uh seen a fin'uh rug even in Chal'ston? Oh, I'm *so sorry,* Bill, you've nev'uh been to Chals'ton, have you? Look ov'uh there now, if you will. Do you see the lovely candela'bruhs and silv'uh service on the sideboard? They're all of Spanish origin, and I've always considered Spanish silv'uh even fin'uh than English silv'uh although it's nev'uh been recognized as such except by true conne'suahs like myself. Don't you agree, Bill?"

"*Marguerite!*" her husband almost bellowed, "in case you haven't noticed, Flossie and Tulip have our lunch on the table and I think we should sit down and enjoy it *now!*"

After helping his wife with her chair at one end of the seventeen-foot-long banquet table, Mr. Merritt walked to the table's other end and sat down at his place before Bill sat down at the place that had clearly been set for him halfway between the host and hostess's chairs.

Flossie and Tulip had fixed an excellent lunch—baked ham with wine and raisin sauce, new potatoes with parsley butter, string beans with mushrooms and slivered almonds, tomato aspic, and biscuits followed by a slice of lemon meringue pie for dessert. But to Bill the conversation was as stilted and unpleasant as it had been in the entrance hall and east parlor. After ridiculing several other people in town, including the three big shots Bill had met at the drugstore that morning, the Merritts questioned him about the social clubs and musical societies he and his wife belonged to in New York. Eventually they even asked him about the size and extent of his stock portfolio, which he considered so offensive he changed the subject at once. Finally, as they were finishing their dessert and iced tea, they offered to help him with the plans for his winter home before urging him to make a deposit of at least five hundred dollars on one of their largest and finest building sites without even seeing it. Bill considered that suggestion so outrageous he dismissed it out of hand.

Because he hoped to leave the Merritt House as soon as possible, Bill asked his host the moment he finished his dessert if he could use his ticker tape machine at once. Aware that something was terribly wrong, Merritt agreed and led him across the mansion's center hall to his chestnut-paneled study. On one side of Merritt's enormous desk his ticker tape machine was spewing out yard after yard of stock prices. In only two minutes Bill realized the stocks he was concerned about were faring much better on the stock exchange that day than he'd feared.

At that point Bill followed Merritt through the center hall to the west parlor, where Marguerite was reading her novel again while squinting through her lorgnette even more. Bill thanked her for a wonderful lunch before apologizing for his comments about the South's economic problems in the entrance hall an hour and a half before.

Marguerite twirled her lorgnette around while smiling up at him and saying, "Don't worry about it, Bill, 'cause I'd already forgotten yo comments, which has always been an easy matt'uh for well-born Southen'uhs like myself. I hope you and yo wife have a luv'ly trip to Florida, but don't forget—my husband and I have a *chamin* lot reserved fo you, a lot we know you'll *love* the minute you see it fo yo'self. Good-bye until we see each oth'uh again, and hopefully we'll be neigh'buhs shortly aft'uh that for sev'ral months every win'tuh if not a great deal long'uh than that."

Bill shuddered at the thought of being the Merritts' neighbors for even an hour but merely said, "Good-bye, Mrs. Merritt. It's been a pleasure meeting you and seeing your lovely home today." He hated to tell such egregious lies but felt the situation demanded it. Besides, he was willing to say almost anything to avoid another diatribe or more offensive claptrap from this extremely unpleasant woman.

At the mansion's front door Bill thanked his host for a delightful time and an excellent lunch as well as the privilege of using his ticker tape machine for several minutes. Although Merritt begged him to stay a while longer so he could tell him about one of his best building sites, Bill insisted on leaving the Merritt House at once. He also said he'd rather walk back to the hotel than put Merritt to the trouble of driving him there. To himself Bill thought, *The less I see of this boorish man, the better.*

By the time he entered the hotel Bill had calmed down a bit. But he was still annoyed at six thirty when he and Frances took the elevator down to the dining room on the ground floor to have dinner with the Hanfords and their children. Although Bill did his best to be pleasant during their five-course meal and never mentioned what was bothering him, Joe and Julia sensed that something had upset him a great deal that day. Their curiosity about the matter ended when Frances said to her husband as they were waiting for their coffee and dessert to arrive, "You should forget about all the unpleasantness at the Merritt House this afternoon. It's foolish to let people you've just met annoy you so much. Besides, Mr. Merritt let you use his ticker tape machine after lunch, so you don't need to worry any longer about those 'iffy' stocks you were so concerned about during breakfast. I hope you remember that if you have any more unpleasant memories of the Merritts, who couldn't have been as boorish as you said they were shortly after you got back to the hotel at two thirty."

By the next morning Bill's mood was back to normal. As he and Frances were waiting with the Hanfords on the platform of the Hertford station for a local train to arrive and take them to Rocky Mount where, after a short wait, they would transfer to an express train bound for Florida, Bill apologized repeatedly for his bad mood the previous evening. Once Julia told him not to worry about such a minor matter, Bill and Frances thanked her and Joe repeatedly for a delightful visit to their charming town. But as the Van Landinghams boarded their train, Joe and Julia gazed at each other sadly, convinced they would never see Bill and Frances in Perquimmons City again. And because the Hanfords felt it would be at least five years before they made another trip to New York, what had seemed to be a budding friendship was all but dead on the vine, thanks to those "blasted Merritts," as most of the townspeople had called them longer than Joe and Julia or even Lucy could remember.

Chapter 8

During the next month Joe was so moody and depressed Julia was deeply concerned about him. He blamed himself for the poor outcome of the Van Landinghams' visit and told Julia dozens of times that if he'd only closed his office on their one full day in town, Bill wouldn't have fallen into the hands of "those blasted Merritts," whose boorish behavior had ruined everything. Joe was so upset by what they'd done he was tempted to drive over to the Merritt House after supper one night and give William Merritt a real thrashing or "use his face as a punching bag."

Julia took Joe's threats seriously because he was still a powerful man although he was in his early forties now. During his high school years he'd been an excellent baseball player and one of the leading members of the boxing program at the Salisbury YMCA. Because his height and strength were coupled with hair-trigger reflexes and a fierce desire to win every match he entered, he won his weight class (198-212 pounds) in all fifteen tournaments he entered. Several years later during his senior year at the state university in Chapel Hill, he was the undisputed star of its boxing team and won all but three of his matches by knockouts and the other three by wide point margins.

Several months after marrying Julia in 1895, he rigged up body and punching bags in the basement of their house on Hertford Avenue. But he used them irregularly until the summer of 1907 when Joey and his friend Cordell Richardson, who were almost ten and unusually tall and strong for their age, begged him to teach them how to box. Joe agreed and taught them on weekends and occasional weeknights, causing him to use his boxing bags much more often—several times a week as a rule. That led to a sudden upsurge of his strength and fitness, which approached the level they'd been during his early and mid twenties when he'd belonged to the Richmond YMCA and sparred twice a week with the biggest and best members of its boxing club. So Julia had good reason to worry during the late winter of 1910 that Joe might do serious bodily harm to Merritt if he ever confronted him about his and Marguerite's boorish treatment of Bill Van Landingham during the hour and a half he spent with them in their home.

Julia's fears increased while Lucy was having dinner with the Hanfords and their children on the second Wednesday night in March. During a lull in the conversation Joe mentioned an unpleasant encounter he'd had with Merritt in front his office building that afternoon. "When the jackass made an ugly comment about Bill that was completely false, I came within an inch of slugging him."

"Oh no," Julia said with a pained look. "Tell me exactly what happened."

"Well, as I was returning to my office after making several house calls, I saw Mr. Merritt coming out of the telegraph office. As I parked my car and got out of it, he walked up to me and called Bill 'a pompous old fool masquerading as a gentleman.' That annoyed me so much I told him he'd been rude to a real gentleman whose manners are much better than his had ever been."

"What happened next?" Julia asked with great foreboding as Lucy squeezed her hand and told her to remain calm.

"He called me an SOB and dared me to throw a punch if I had the nerve. I put my medical bag on my car's hood at once so I could teach him a lesson he'd never forget."

"Oh, no," Julia said, drawing back in horror. "I hope you didn't hit him because you're taller and probably much stronger than him. I'm sure you could knock him down with a single punch."

"No, I didn't actually hit him because Burt Trumble rushed over and stopped me in the nick of time. Actually, I'm glad Burt stopped me because I'm convinced I would've broken his jaw or nose if I'd connected with one of them. Bullies like him never know how to defend themselves when they provoke a fight with someone who refuses to be intimidated by their bluster."

"I'm glad Burt was there to restrain you but what happened after he did?"

"Because Burt has even less respect for Merritt than I do, he told the jackass to go on home in his car. And if he didn't, Burt said he would stand aside and let me beat the tar out of him. On hearing that Merritt stomped over to his Steamer and cranked the engine until it started although it took almost twenty seconds for the water to produce enough steam for him to drive off."

"I hope you went into your office while he was sitting in his car."

"No, Burt and I watched him from the sidewalk and joked about his ridiculous behavior. Just before he drove off, he yelled that he would've beaten me black and blue if he hadn't been in a hurry to get home and spend some time with his children before dinner. Burt thought that was the dumbest thing he'd ever heard and wondered how he had the gall to say it."

Like most of the other members of her family, Lucy was amazed by Joe's sudden belligerence because he'd always been easygoing and slow to take offense in the past. On the other hand Lucy agreed completely with all his complaints about Merritt's behavior because she'd disliked him intensely for years. But because she knew Joe's frequent threats against him upset Julia a great deal, Lucy kept her thoughts to herself and said nothing to encourage Joe's complaints about her former employer.

As for Julia, she continued to take Joe's threats seriously whenever he talked about confronting Merritt somewhere in town. On those occasions Julia always told him to calm down because his words were having a harmful effect on Joey's behavior, which became brasher and more belligerent than it had ever been before. Joe's threats against Merritt also had a negative effect on Joey's cousin, Jack Summerlin, who idolized Joey and wanted to be like him in every way.

Julia's fears that her husband might eventually beat Merritt to a pulp peaked one Sunday evening while the whole family was having dinner at Chip and Rhonda's house. As the group enjoyed its main course Chip complained that the Merritts were always several months behind in paying their bills at the drugstore although they complained bitterly whenever he paid the rent on their building a day or two late. On hearing that Joe started another tirade about Merritt's behavior before saying he might drive over to the Merritt House shortly after having his dessert and give the man a thrashing he'd never forget.

Aroused by those words Joey said excitedly to his father, "I'll go with you and take care of Willie and Little Robert while you beat the stuffing out their old man. And I'm sure we can do it because Mr. Merritt and his sons are nothing but cream puffs."

When Jack said he'd go with them and do his part Rhonda said firmly, "Pipe down, you boys! Fighting's the worst possible way for men to settle their differences and I've told you that dozens of times. If I hear any more talk like that tonight you won't get a piece of my Boston cream pie for dessert and that goes for you too, Joe."

When Joe turned crimson and held his tongue, Julia was so pleased she wanted to give Rhonda a big hug, which she did later in the kitchen.

To Julia's relief Joe was so busy at his office during the next several weeks he was too tired to mention his deep dislike of Merritt, which faded as March wore on. As a result, he wasn't surprised—only annoyed—when he saw Merritt waiting for him on the sidewalk in front of his office building on the first Tuesday morning in April.

Merritt had a worried look on his face as Joe drove up in his Maxwell and parked it while hoping to avoid another strained conversation with the man. But Merritt greeted Joe in a friendly way as he got out of his car before telling him that Little Robert had been sick with a high fever for several days. Nothing his wife or servants had done had made the boy feel better. In fact, he seemed even sicker that morning and was clearly in great pain. So Merritt asked Joe to drive to the Merritt House with him at once and examine the boy before telling Marguerite what she and their upstairs maid could do to hasten his recovery. Despite his deep dislike of Merritt, Joe considered his request so reasonable he agreed to it at once.

Joe's assistants, Mary Bishop and Rachel Sutphin, arrived while Merritt was still explaining Little Robert's problem to Joe on the sidewalk. So after unlocking the building's front door, he told Mary and Rachel to keep the office open until he returned from the Merritt House in an hour or so. They could handle minor problems like cuts and bruises but should tell any patients who arrived for appointments made at least twenty-four hours in advance that he hoped to be back by nine forty-five at the latest and would see them then.

After taking his medical bag out of his car, Joe joined Merritt in his Steamer and, in several moments, said a silent prayer as the worried man drove through the middle of town at breakneck speed, scattering bicyclists, pedestrians, and half a dozen dogs as he did. After pulling his car into his mansion's front driveway, Merritt stopped it there before he and Joe got out of the vehicle and hurried up the broad front steps to the porch. After crossing it in several moments, Merritt opened the front door and ushered Joe inside. Marguerite said a curt hello to Joe, whom she now realized was a cousin of Bill Van Landingham's wife, before she led him up the main staircase and down the long center hall to the children's bedrooms in the mansion's rear wing.

Little Robert was lying in his bed while the upstairs maid sponged off his face and chest with a damp washcloth filled with small chunks of ice. His face was deeply flushed and felt like it was on fire when Joe touched his forehead. As Joe felt his right side he knew at once from the boy's shrill cry that he had a ruptured appendix. In fact, Joe was convinced Little Robert would die by mid afternoon unless he removed the diseased organ by noon at the latest.

Because he didn't have any ether or the right surgical instruments in his medical bag, Joe gave the boy several aspirin and some water to ease his pain as much as possible. Then after picking him up as carefully as he could, he carried him downstairs to the entrance hall where he explained the situation to his parents. Marguerite urged her husband to drive Joe and Little Robert to his office, which he naturally agreed to do at once.

On their trip back to the middle of town, Joe held Little Robert on his lap the whole time. When Merritt stopped his car in front of Joe's office building, Joe got out of the Steamer and carried the boy inside. Several people were waiting to see him, but Joe told them he had an emergency operation to perform and would be too busy to see them before eleven forty-five at the earliest. Anyone with a morning appointment should speak to Mary or Rachel, who would reschedule it as soon as possible.

After carrying Little Robert into his operating room, Joe laid him down on the long padded table near the room's double window, through which sunlight was streaming in and he could see extremely well with the help of the overhead light. Once he put on an operating gown and scrubbed up, Joe gave the boy some ether and prepped him for the operation. Shortly after Little Robert lost consciousness, Joe opened his side and almost gagged at what he saw. It was the worst ruptured appendix he'd ever seen, much worse than the sixteen or seventeen he'd removed during his years as a resident in Richmond's best hospital. He went right to work and removed the diseased organ as fast as he safely could. After cleaning out the wound and sterilizing the incision, he sewed it up before setting up a cot for Little Robert at the back of the long narrow room. He stretched the boy out on the cot and closed the curtains across the double window at the room's other end before turning off the overhead light to darken the room as much as he could. In half an hour some color returned to the boy's cheeks and his temperature fell a degree or two, causing him to look slightly better than he had at the Merritt House.

Meanwhile, Merritt had driven home to get his wife, who was beside herself with worry. When Marguerite arrived shortly after eleven o'clock, she made herself comfortable on a chair near Little Robert's cot while Joe went across the hall to his private office and relaxed in his desk chair for several minutes before eating two sandwiches and an apple for lunch. At eleven forty-five he met with the first of several dozen patients he saw before he closed the office at six thirty that evening, an hour later than he usually did, by which time he was almost exhausted. As Marguerite continued to sit with Little Robert, Joe left for home in his car so he could have supper with his family.

The minute Julia heard him enter the house by the front door, she rushed out of the dining room and asked him why he was so late. As he hung his hat and jacket on the coat rack in a corner of the entrance hall, he explained the situation before saying he planned to return to his office by seven thirty because he'd offered to stay with Little Robert that night.

When Julia asked who was staying with him now Joe said, "Marguerite, if you can believe it. She's been sitting in a chair beside cot since shortly after eleven o'clock this morning."

"Of course I can believe it because she's Little Robert's mother. But why can't she or her husband stay with him tonight? You need a good night's sleep because you'll probably have even more patients to see tomorrow than you did today."

"That's true, but the Merritts have gotten almost no sleep for several nights and Little Robert isn't out of the woods yet. If he takes a turn for the worse during the next eight or nine hours, they won't know what to do, so I have no choice but to stay with him tonight. I'll set up another cot in my operating room and I'll probably get six or seven hours of sleep."

Julia gazed at her husband with a mixture of sympathy and admiration while wondering if the Merritts would do half as much for him if their situations were ever reversed for some strange reason. But she kept that thought to herself as she followed him into the dining room where he enjoyed his favorite meal of pork chops and several vegetables while Olivia and Joey had another piece of pound cake. After cutting Joe a piece of cake, Julia told him about the highlight of her day: a meeting of the book club she'd helped Lucy and Hazel Barlow organize for the women in their part of town several weeks earlier.

During the next month Joe made five visits to the Merritt House to check on Little Robert during an unusually long convalescence. The Merritts were so grateful to Joe for saving their son's life they made several overtures to him and Julia to their great surprise. Six days after the boy's operation the Merritts' butler-chauffeur delivered a basket of fresh fruit to Joe's office and a large potted plant to the Hanfords' house. The Merritts also invited them to a dinner party on the last Saturday night in April. Julia had no desire to attend that party because of their harsh treatment of Lucy while she was one of their servants. Julia also pointed out to Joe that the Merritts had never invited them to one of their Valentine's Day cotillions, which most of the Hanfords' friends considered very strange.

After dinner two nights later Julia discussed the pros and cons of attending the Merritts' dinner party with Lucy. Once Lucy thought about the situation for several moments, she told Julia it was time to forget the past and move on. Because Joe agreed with Lucy's comment when he entered the parlor after playing Chinese checkers with Olivia and Joey in the study for almost an hour, the Hanfords went to the Merritts' dinner party and wore the same clothes they'd bought for their trip to New York the previous fall.

During the social hour after church the next morning, Julia told Lucy and Rhonda about the Merritts' dinner party. "The Merritts' other guests looked very stylish and the Merritts were dressed to the nines of course, hoping to impress the rest of us. But Joe and I looked every bit as good as they did—at least that's what Phyllis Kahle and Mildred Barringer told me in the west parlor while Marguerite was checking on several things in the kitchen. Joe looked very handsome in his tuxedo while my pearls and evening gown received compliments from all the other women, even Marguerite if you can believe it. Although I'm sure she didn't realize it at the time, she fingered her much shorter strand of pearls during the starter course as if she was jealous of mine. Isn't that amazing?"

"No, I don't think it's amazing at all," Rhonda said at once. "Your pearls are the most beautiful ones I've ever seen, but what about the meal? Was it especially good?"

"Yes, it was extremely good although it didn't seem any better than the meal Augusta and I fixed for Bill and Frances on their first evening in town back in February."

"That was an outstanding meal," Lucy said, "and frankly I don't see how the Merritts could have served a better one. But what happened after the meal?"

"The men went across the center hall to Mr. Merritt's study to smoke their smelly cigars and drink some brandy while the women played bridge in the west parlor. But the bridge wasn't any fun at all because Marguerite's a terrible player and hates criticism of any kind. When Phyllis pointed out that she would've made a contract had she drawn all the trumps before running a long suit in the dummy, she was so angry she turned blue and yelled at Phyllis that she was wrong about that. If you ever witness one of her fiery displays of temper you'll never forget it."

Lucy laughed and said, "I told you about her terrible temper several times while I worked at the Merritt House but you never believed me. I guess you have to witness one of her blowups for yourself before you realize how dreadful they are."

"That's right, Lucy, because Joe insisted I was exaggerating when I told him about Marguerite's explosion as we were driving home. He refused to believe that she'd been so rude to Phyllis about such a minor matter. In fact, he insisted that real ladies never behave like that, especially to someone as nice and agreeable as Phyllis."

"We could discuss Marguerite's behavior for several hours," Lucy said. "But it's such a depressing subject let's talk about something else now," which they did.

For several weeks after that dinner party, the Hanfords felt they were on the verge of establishing a cordial relationship with the Merritts. But when some serious friction occurred between them and the Merritts in May, the Hanfords realized that was impossible.

Shortly after Joe sent the Merritts a bill for Little Robert's operation and follow-up care, Mr. Merritt mailed Joe a check for $30 rather than for the full amount of $45.00. On the bottom of his check Merritt had written, "Payment in full for Little Robert's operation and Dr. Hanford's later house calls." In a brief accompanying note, Merritt said he considered $30 sufficient for Joe's services in view of the fruit basket and potted plant he'd sent the Hanfords and the recent dinner party they'd attended at the Merritt House.

Joe was almost apoplectic when he read that note. His fee had been no higher than what most of the other doctors in the area would've charged for such an operation and five follow-up visits to the patient's home. Furthermore, Joe had naturally assumed that the fruit basket, potted plant, and the dinner invitation had been tokens of the Merritts' gratitude for saving their son's life rather than partial payment for medical services already rendered. When he came home from his office that Friday afternoon and told Julia in the kitchen what Merritt had done, she was as appalled as he was. She was also afraid he'd drive to the Merritt House after supper that night and confront the man in person. So she urged him to think long and hard about the best way to handle the situation. Luckily she remembered one of her parents' favorite sayings, "Act in haste and repent at leisure," which she told him half a number of times that weekend.

Shortly after supper on Sunday night Joe sat down at his desk in the study and wrote Merritt a polite but very firm letter. Because his first draft was very messy with several marked-out words and phrases, he copied it over on some clean stationery. After signing it with a flourish, he asked Julia to read it and tell him what she thought. She considered it an excellent letter, clear and dignified without being angry or servile in any way. It read:

Dear Mr. Merritt,

I was glad to be of assistance to you and your wife during Little Robert's recent illness. I hope he's doing even better now than he was the last time I saw him at the Merritt House. If the nurse you hired two weeks ago on his behalf would like any help or suggestions from me, please tell her to contact me at my office or home at her first opportunity.

In regard to another matter of great importance to me, I've included with this letter your check for $30, on the bottom of which you wrote that I should consider it payment in full for the operation I performed on Little Robert and the follow-up care I gave him. That care, as I'm sure you remember, included five visits to the Merritt House during the weeks after I removed his appendix.

Although I regret the misunderstanding that has occurred, I feel compelled to charge you the same fees I charge all my other patients. If I don't and accept only partial payment from you and other well-to-do men, the fees I charge my poorer patients will have to increase considerably. I cannot countenance that because it would mean I was placing a heavier burden on families who're less able to afford good medical care than on others with much greater resources.

If you're unwilling to accept my position in this regard, or if you feel the care I gave your son was inadequate in some way, I urge you to keep your check and find another doctor to treat your family's medical problems. But if you wish to remain on my patient list, as I hope you do, I expect you to send me another check for the whole $45.00 within ten days.

I regret having to send you this letter. But like other men in town, I have a family to support and business expenses to pay. Unfortunately, gifts of fruit baskets and potted plants, which are always appreciated, are little help in that regard, as are invitations to elegant dinner parties.

Cordially yours,
Joseph W. Hanford, M.D.

Nine days after mailing that letter, Joe received a check for $45.00 from Merritt without a word of explanation or apology. Joe assumed that he would continue to be the Merritts' doctor although he and Julia would receive no more invitations to social events of any kind at the Merritt House. He and Julia felt no remorse about that development, only deep relief because they had no desire to entertain the Merritts in their home in the future.

Several days after Joe received Merritt's second check, Julia opened a revealing letter from Frances Van Landingham. Frances had written that letter several weeks after she and Bill returned to New York from Palm Beach, where they'd stayed a month longer than they'd planned to. In fact, the best real estate agent in Palm Beach had showed them so many houses they liked they saw no reason to continue on to Miami. Unfortunately, she and Bill had been unable to agree on which house to buy, so they eventually bought a two-acre lot overlooking the ocean, on which they planned to build a six-bedroom house during the coming year. Ten days after returning to New York, they retained a well-known architect and asked him to draw up plans for a Spanish-style house of between seven and eight thousand square feet, for which they hoped to break ground by the end of September. Once it was built and furnished with a decorator's help, she and Bill hoped the Hanfords and their children would join them and their children in Florida for several weeks whenever it was convenient for the two families to get together. Frances's letter continued:

> Although I'm looking forward to having a winter home in Palm Beach, I actually hoped we'd build such a home on the outskirts of Perquimmons City, which I liked a great deal during

our visit in February. Bill and I considered it a real treat to see you and Joe again. We also enjoyed meeting all the other members of your lovely family, whom we liked far more than I could tell you in a fairly brief letter like this. Of course, having a winter home in North Carolina would also make it a great deal easier for me to see my sister and her family in Winston-Salem because of the direct rail connection you pointed out to me on the day I spent with you and enjoyed so much.

After the delightful hours we spent in your home on our first evening in town, Bill gave some thought to my suggestion that we buy some land in or near Perquimmons City because it's much closer to New York than Palm Beach is. Furthermore, boating on the Albemarle and Pamlico Sounds is probably quite safe, which is a matter of great importance to us. Our son Billy loves to sail and has taken lessons for several years from an excellent yachtsman whose home is only a short distance from our summer cottage on Oyster Bay, an arm of Long Island Sound.

Unfortunately, Bill's very favorable first impression of Perquimmons City and its people was dispelled by the Merritts' rude and arrogant behavior which ruined everything, as I'm sure you've guessed by now. Because Bill considers the Merritts the most odious couple he's ever met, he swore the minute he left their home that he would *never* return to a town where 'two such crude and abominable people live,' which he told me that afternoon at the hotel.

I'm still distressed by Bill's decision, but I thought you should know the truth, dear Julia. After all, my husband's determination to avoid Perquimmons City in the future had nothing to do with you or your children, or with your delightful sister Lucy or any of the charming women I met in your company on our one full day in town.

With fondest regards to you and Joe from your devoted and loving friend, Frances Van Landingham.

Julia had tears in her eyes by the time she finished Frances's letter. After supper that night, while Joe was playing Chinese checkers with the children in the study, Julia handed the letter to Lucy in the parlor and asked her to read it. Once Lucy skimmed it Julia asked her how she should handle the situation.

"What situation do you mean?" Lucy asked with a curious look.

"Well, Joe and I've never kept secrets from each other, and he's asked me several times during the last ten days if I'd heard anything from Frances. So what should I tell him if he asks me that again?"

"If you've never kept secrets from him in the past, I see no reason why you should start now."

"But if I tell him about Frances's letter, he'll probably want to read it for himself. And if he does I'm afraid he'll start ranting about Mr. Merritt's behavior again and threaten to beat him to a pulp. Threats like that upset me so much I can't stand to hear another one."

"I know how you feel but you could always tell Joe several things in Frances's letter and hope that's enough to satisfy him. But if he persists you should let him read it for himself. It would be stupid to let the Merritts drive a wedge between you and Joe."

"That's true but what if he goes to the Merritt House one night and beats Mr. Merritt senseless? It would cause a terrible scandal and Joe would probably lose hundreds of his patients. Even worse, I'm convinced it would have a serious effect on the children. Olivia would be so embarrassed she'd probably find reasons to avoid school and all her friends for a month or so, while I'm afraid Joey would decide from his father's actions that it's okay for men to settle their differences by force. I'd hate for Joey to conclude that partly because I'm afraid his decision would cause Jack to conclude the same thing."

"You're making too much of this, Julia. All the people I know would love for Joe to beat the tar out of Mr. Merritt. But don't you remember Rhonda's little speech while we were having dinner at her and Chip's house back in March?"

"Yes, but I'm convinced Joe's forgotten it. So I'm still extremely worried about the situation."

"You shouldn't worry about it so much because Joe's too sensible to do something he'd regret for years."

"I'd like to believe that but my fears about the situation are much greater than yours and there's nothing I can do to change that despite how hard I've tried."

Two nights later, an hour and a half after Olivia and Joey went to bed, Joe and Julia went upstairs to their room. As they were relaxing for several minutes in the overstuffed armchairs that flanked the small round table in the bay window that looked out on their front yard and Hertford Avenue, Joe asked Julia again if she'd heard anything from Frances. Once she said she had and mentioned several things in Frances's most recent letter, Joe said he'd like to read it for himself. With a heavy heart Julia took it out of the drawer of her bedside table before handing it to him.

After unfolding it Joe started to read as Julia said, "Please don't get upset and make any more threats against Mr. Merritt because he's not worth it. No one in town likes him or Marguerite except Isabel Stanton who's almost as snobbish as they are. Besides, we can remain friends with Bill and Frances even if we don't see them as often as we'd like to."

Joe looked up and said, "I haven't even finished the first paragraph yet so please hold your comments until I've read the whole letter. I'm sure it won't upset me as much as you think it will. After all, Frances is so kind and considerate I don't see how one of her letters could upset me."

Julia did as Joe suggested and watched his face anxiously during the next several minutes. Although he frowned several times he said after finishing the letter, "Those blasted Merritts are absolute creeps and I'd be the world's worst fool if I let their actions weaken my relationship with my wonderful wife. Listen, you sexy little vixen, come over here and sit on my lap while we figure out how to forget about them."

Deeply relieved Julia said, "Sure, Mr. Handsome Doctor, once I lock the door. You know how Joey barges in at all hours of the day and night."

"Good thinking but make it snappy, sweetie pie. It's been at least a week since I've had the pleasure of examining your whole body to be sure everything's in good working order. So forget about locking the door and sitting on my lap. Take off all your clothes and get into bed while I lock the door and turn off the lights."

Within minutes their bedside rugs were littered with clothes and underwear, his as well as hers. There were no more sounds in their bedroom for half an hour except for an occasional giggle or moan of pleasure followed by a whispered request for a little more of this or that.

For the next several months life in Perquimmons City was happy and contented as well as calm and uneventful, which suited the Hanfords and most of their friends and relatives just fine. In the opinion of the average citizen the most important social event during those months occurred on June 19. That Sunday evening Lucy, Julia, and Rhonda threw a big party in honor of Maxine Brown, the minister of music at the Methodist church, and Dennis Payne, the head teller at the bank and a leading member of the Episcopal choir, less than six days before their wedding.

Maxine had moved to Perquimmons City in January 1901 with her husband, Quentin Brown, an experienced lawyer who'd recently accepted a partnership with George Kahle. Because of the increasing volume of Kahle's legal work, due mainly to the fact that he'd been the attorney for Stanton's Mill since 1893, he felt he had to take another lawyer into partnership with him; otherwise he would be unable to bicker several times a week with Buzz-Saw Beulah, a busty redhead with green eyes and the unusually argumentative owner of the Dixie Doughnut and Sandwich Shop on West Main Street, which was widely known as the Combat Café. Kahle considered his lunchtime arguments with Buzz-Saw Beulah, especially when Quentin Brown came along and backed him up, the high point of his week—an even greater high point in fact than having his morning coffee at the drugstore with the town's other big shots. Unfortunately, Brown died of pneumonia in February 1902 despite Joe's frantic efforts to save him. Brown's death required Kahle to find another partner, a gifted young lawyer named Earl Yancey, who'd passed the state bar exam while still a second-year law student at the state university in Chapel Hill. But Yancey lacked Brown's debating skills and had little interest in helping Kahle argue circles around Buzz-Saw Beulah, who never took her defeats stoically, to Kahle's enormous pleasure and amusement.

As for Brown's widow Maxine, a lively and attractive woman of twenty-seven in 1902, she decided to remain in Perquimmons City after her husband's death because she loved her house on West Church Street and had made dozens of friends shortly after she became the organist and choir director at the Methodist church in April 1901 and joined the UDC the next fall. Luckily for Maxine, she was the sole beneficiary of a large life insurance policy her husband had bought ten days before their wedding in 1896. In addition, her house on West Church Street was completely paid for. So with the salary she received from the Methodist church and the money she made from the piano and voice lessons she gave Olivia Hanford, Susan Summerlin, and a dozen other local children, she had a good income and lived very comfortably.

Although Dennis and Maxine met each other during the spring of 1902, they didn't become romantically involved until the fall of 1909. On the second Thursday in October the Methodist minister, Henry Philpot, agreed to Maxine's request to increase the size of the Methodist choir with volunteers from the choirs of the three other white churches in town in order to form a choir of at least fifty members. After two months of rehearsals that combined choir would perform *The Messiah*, Handel's most famous oratorio, on the Sunday afternoon before Christmas in the sanctuary of the Methodist church.

Shortly after Maxine sent out appeals to the Baptist, Presbyterian, and Episcopal choirs, twenty-nine volunteers came forward, the first being Dennis Payne. Dennis had an excellent tenor voice and had been a prominent member of the Episcopal choir since the fall of 1900, shortly after he moved to town from Scotland Neck.

By the latter part of October 1909, when weekly rehearsals for *The Messiah* began, Maxine had put together a choir of fifty-four members, who included Dennis and two other soloists. Dennis's enormous enthusiasm for the project was an inspiration to all the other singers. With his vigorous support Maxine held rehearsals twice a week after Thanksgiving despite bitter protests from four members who resigned from the choir during the first week of December. Even so, *The Messiah* received a rousing performance before a standing-room-only crowd at the Methodist church on Sunday afternoon, December 19. Two days later an article in the *Tribune* gave the performance a rave review while a photograph of Dennis and Maxine celebrating together after the performance triggered rumors that they were romantically involved.

During the first week of January, shortly after Dennis and Maxine were conspicuously absent from several New Year's Eve parties they'd both been invited to attend, they became the talk of the town and everyone expected them to announce their engagement at any moment. That announcement didn't occur until the first Wednesday evening in February. When Maxine arrived at the Methodist church at seven thirty that night for choir practice, she had such a beautiful sparkler on her ring finger everyone insisted on knowing when Dennis had proposed to her.

By that weekend Perquimmons City was buzzing with the news, the local grapevine being extremely efficient despite the town's continuing lack of phone service. On the next Sunday morning, shortly after the Episcopal choir vested for the main service in an alcove of the parish hall, Dennis was surrounded by a group of women who included Lucy, Julia, Rhonda, and Muriel Thompson, all of whom were eager to know if Dennis and Maxine had set a date for their wedding.

"Maxine?" Dennis said with a grin. "It seems like I know someone with that name but I can't place her at the moment. Lucy, you or Rhonda should give me a hint."

"Don't be so silly!" Rhonda said while giving his arm a punch. "We've known for weeks that you and Maxine are stuck on each other. So if you don't come clean we'll ignore your wedding and send you and Maxine no presents at all. Is that what you'd like?"

With an even bigger grin Dennis said he'd hate for that to happen before admitting he and Maxine planned to get married on the third Saturday in June. Personally he'd like to get married much sooner than that, but her family couldn't make the long trip to Perquimmons City from their home in Centerville, Tennessee before the middle of June. Although he and Maxine were still trying to decide if their wedding should take place at the Methodist or the Episcopal church, Dennis promised to spread the word shortly after they reached a decision about where and the approximate time the ceremony would occur.

By the middle of March Dennis and Maxine had decided their wedding would take place at the Episcopal church, mainly because Dennis hoped to remain a member of its choir which needed all the help it could get. It had only four members now because the organist and choir director, Grace Akers, was playing the organ slower and more softly than ever and potential members like Joe, Julia, and George Kahle, all of whom had excellent voices, wouldn't even consider joining it despite Mr. Thompson's frantic pleas to them to join it and keep it from collapsing before it was too late.

During April and May there were several showers for Maxine and half a dozen dinner parties in her and Dennis's honor. On the fourth Saturday night in May, his colleagues at the bank honored them with an elaborate buffet dinner at the hotel; and two weeks later the Elks' Lodge, which Dennis had joined in 1903, threw a large, informal party for them at Wilbur's Chicken and Seafood Palace, to which the wives of all the members were invited. Only two attended it, however, despite the restaurant's reputation for serving the best fried chicken and seafood in the area. But the building's ramshackle appearance from the Elizabeth City Road caused most of the women in town to say they'd never go near the place until Marguerite Merritt had dinner there one night. They were convinced she'd never do that because of her widely known and often mimicked insistence on having the best of everything money could buy.

Meanwhile, Lucy and Rhonda helped Julia plan a party at the Hanfords' house in Dennis and Maxine's honor on the last Sunday evening before the wedding. Lucy offered to handle the decorations for the party and, with Joey's help, hung dozens of pink, white, yellow, and pale blue balloons and crepe paper streamers in the Hanfords' entrance hall, parlor, and dining room that afternoon. She also made large flower arrangements for the parlor, dining room, and Julia's morning room as well as slightly smaller ones for the entrance hall, study, and screened porch. As for the refreshments, which were served in the dining room, Julia's morning room, and on several folding tables on the screened porch, Julia and Rhonda took responsibility for them. With help from Augusta and her daughter Creola, who worked for the Ridingers, they fixed two kinds of punch, one of which was extremely popular because it was spiked with rum and apple brandy. They also fixed six chocolate pound cakes, hundreds of brownies and lemon bars, an equal number of crab puffs and fancy little finger sandwiches, six cheese balls and trays of assorted crackers, a variety of pickles, olives, and salted nuts, and scores of celery sticks stuffed with chicken salad or pimento cheese.

Five weeks before the party Julia sent Maxine a copy of the guest list of ninety-four people she'd drawn up with Lucy and Rhonda's help. Julia asked Maxine to review the list and add as many as forty names to it before mailing it back to her as soon as possible. When Lucy glanced at the thirty-seven names Maxine added to the list, she was annoyed to see Lillian Greenfield's name there. While helping Julia and Rhonda address the invitations two nights later, Lucy thought of an easy way to keep Lillian from attending the party, which might revive the rumors that she and Chip were having an affair, if those rumors had actually subsided for several years after Jack Summerlin's birth in 1902.

After helping Julia and Rhonda address the invitations and put stamps on their envelopes, Lucy gathered up all the envelopes and put them in a paper bag before offering to mail them on her way to work the next morning. Julia and Rhonda thanked her for that offer because they seldom went to town before ten thirty and agreed with Lucy that the invitations should be mailed as soon as possible.

The next morning, shortly after Lucy fed Mr. Jobie and fixed herself some cereal and coffee, the envelope addressed to Lillian "accidentally" fell into the garbage pail under her kitchen sink. Lucy hated to waste a two-cent stamp for any reason at all but considered her "clumsiness" necessary to end a serious threat to Chip and Rhonda's marriage. As a result, she never had any qualms about her "unfortunate mistake" that morning.

In any event, the 137 people who attended the party came early and stayed late because they enjoyed it so much. Lucy and Julia loved it when Olivia sat down at the parlor upright before several dozen people gathered round and sang old favorites like "Beautiful Dreamer," "Down by the Old Mill Stream," and "A Bicycle Built for Two." After a great deal of coaxing, Dennis and Maxine agreed to sing a duet of their own choice. While leafing through Olivia's sheet music, they came across Irving Berlin's first big hit, "Marie from Sunny Italy," which they both knew and liked. They performed that song so well to Olivia's skillful accompaniment, loud cheers and applause erupted the moment they finished that extremely popular number.

Half an hour later Olivia performed a loud glissando to get everyone's attention before Julia announced that an important presentation was about to occur in the dining room. In no time that oversized room, the largest one in the Hanfords' house, was packed with dozens of people standing shoulder to shoulder while dozens of others looked on from the entrance hall, the butler's pantry, and even the kitchen by craning their necks as much as they possibly could. As Dennis and Maxine stood side by side near one end of the table, Lucy, Julia, and Rhonda gave them an elaborate present from the three of them—four place settings of their formal china and four place settings of their flat silver, which Julia and Rhonda had bought two weeks earlier at Tolliver's Jewelry Store in Edenton.

A reporter from the *Tribune* was present with his camera that night at Mildred Barringer's suggestion, and in the paper's next issue there was a long article about the party, which Mildred described as "the largest and most successful party in Perquimmons City in many a year." Three photographs accompanied the article. The first showed Dennis and Maxine singing their duet together. The second showed a dozen people clustered around the spiked punch bowl at one end of the dining room table. And the third showed Julia and Rhonda on either side of Lucy as she stood barefooted on a large ottoman in the parlor. All three women were wearing their best party dresses with corsages of pink roses and baby's breath on their left shoulders—corsages slightly smaller than the one Rhonda had pinned on the left shoulder of Maxine's dress shortly after she and Dennis arrived together. The caption under that picture described the three women as "elegant and accomplished hostesses who are fully qualified to assist all the other ladies in the area whenever they're planning large social gatherings."

As Lucy read that caption and gazed at her smiling face, she wondered how the Merritts felt about her now as they, fought, bickered, or avoided each other whenever possible in their stately mansion on West Main Street.

Chapter 9

On the first Tuesday morning in July Robert Thompson, the rector of St. John's Church, opened his office door in the parish house and saw an envelope addressed to him on the floor. The note inside the envelope was from Grace Akers, the church's organist and choir director for thirty-four years. Petulant in tone, Mrs. Akers's note read:

> Although I've given the best years of my life to this church, I've heard nothing but complaints about my playing during the last six months. Those complaints have been very hurtful, and so has the choir's attitude toward me. All four members, but especially Dennis Payne, have questioned my ability, my leadership, and even my musical taste. I therefore submit my resignation as organist and choir director effective at noon on Sunday, July 17. I've enjoyed working with you, Mr. Thompson; and because I'm leaving you in the lurch to some extent, I suggest you contact Maxine Brown, who's recently become Mrs. Dennis Payne unfortunately. Maxine is an <u>excellent</u> musician, and because Dennis is determined to remain a member of our choir regardless of my feelings, there's a good chance she'll resign her position at the Methodist church to become my successor here although that would mean a substantial pay cut for her.

Although Thompson regretted that Mrs. Akers was so unhappy, he was relieved that she'd finally resigned her position because of the dozens of complaints he'd heard about the choir's small size and her unusually soft and slow playing during recent years. After thinking for several minutes about her advice to contact Maxine Payne, he decided to do just that. He and his wife had attended the performance of Handel's *Messiah* the previous fall, which Maxine had directed, and he was convinced his church would profit a great deal if she became its organist and choir director.

Shortly after reading morning prayer with several elderly parishioners in his office, where they planned to discuss that day's epistle and gospel during the next hour, Thompson told them good-bye and left the parish house before walking down the flagstone path to West Church Street. Because it was almost deserted that morning, he crossed it without any trouble and, several minutes later, rang the doorbell of Maxine's house three blocks farther down the street.

Although Maxine was surprised to see him on her front porch, she asked him to come in and have a cup of coffee with her provided he was willing to overlook the chaos inside. She and Dennis, who'd left for the bank at eight thirty, had recently returned from their honeymoon at Blowing Rock and Grandfather Mountain in the northwestern part of the state. As a result they were still in the process of merging their furniture and other possessions, a daunting task.

After telling her not to worry about that, Thompson accepted her invitation to have a cup of coffee and followed her through the maze of furniture and dozens of unopened boxes into her kitchen where, at her suggestion, he took a comfortable chair at one end of the breakfast table. After some chitchat about the weather while she poured him a cup of coffee, to which he added some milk and sugar, he asked her to call him Bob as most of the adults in his congregation did. Once she refilled her cup and joined him at the table, he told her about Grace Akers' resignation and his hope that she'd like to be considered for her position.

"Yes, I would like to be considered for it," Maxine said at once, "although I understand your minister of music makes only fifteen dollars a month."

"I'm afraid that's right but the vestry will be meeting on Thursday night and Chip Summerlin's the Senior Warden now. He and I see eye to eye on most matters, and I'm sure he'll support my efforts to convince the other vestrymen to increase the salary to twenty-five dollars a month plus an extra five dollars during years when Christmas Eve and Christmas Day don't fall on a Sunday."

"If the vestry agrees to increase the salary that much and offers me the position, I'll definitely accept it because Dennis is determined to remain a member of your church and its choir. As for myself, I was very pleased by the way you performed our wedding ceremony. I also love your hymnal with its many fine old hymns."

During the vestry meeting on Thursday night there was some opposition to paying Maxine or anyone else twenty-five dollars a month to be the organist and choir director. But Chip and the rector worked so well together they secured a solid six-to-two vote with one abstention in favor of Maxine's appointment at the higher salary.

On Wednesday night, July 20, Maxine rehearsed with the Episcopal choir for the first time. And shortly before the main service on the next Sunday morning, she played a soft and very slow prelude, a musical meditation of sorts. But once the bell in the church tower tolled half a dozen of times to announce the call to worship, she pulled out all the stops on the little pipe organ, causing it to wheeze and groan so much most of the congregation thought it was about to give up the ghost. When its mechanical noises ended and Maxine knew it was ready, she plunged into a spirited rendition of "I Come with Joy to Meet My Lord," to which the crucifer, Dennis, and the three other choir members almost danced their way down the main aisle to the choir stalls. Mr. Thompson and the acolyte, Cordell Richardson, followed a short distance behind the choir with an equally vigorous spring in their steps.

Lucy was amazed and whispered to Julia, "This is the first time I've ever heard such joyful music in our church and it's wonderful, don't you think?"

Julia whispered back, "I'm not sure because Maxine's tempos are a great deal faster than Grace Akers' ever were. I wonder how the other members of the congregation will react to Maxine's playing."

"So do I," Lucy whispered. "But in my opinion her playing is a big improvement and we've needed to attract twenty or thirty new members for years. My hunch is we'll do that fairly soon now that the music sounds so much better."

"I hope you're right but I'm afraid you're too optimistic, Lucy."

Most of the people in that morning's congregation shared Lucy's optimisim; and during the social hour in the parish hall after the main service, dozens of members gathered around Maxine and gave her a warm welcome. She was very pleased and urged several people, especially Joe and Julia, whose voices stood out whenever the congregation sang a hymn or one of the canticles, to join the choir and attend its next practice on Wednesday night. "We need more singers like you in the choir, and we're gonna have lots of fun from now on with my 'madcap music' or 'hymns with a heart,' as I like to call 'em."

Joe glanced at Julia in disbelief. He was worried about Maxine's approach because it was so different from Grace Akers'. Grace had never deigned to recruit new choir members despite the rector's efforts to convince here to make an effort to do so. When Grace made it clear to the rector that she would "never stoop to something so demeaning," even if he convinced the vestry to give her a raise, Thompson himself did his best to recruit new members for the choir even if their voices weren't especially good. But no one would join it while Mrs. Akers remained the organist and choir because everyone knew the music was unlikely to improve until she was fired or asked to resign.

During dinner at the Summerlins' house that evening, Lucy praised Maxine's playing before Rhonda and Joe disagreed with her opinion. In fact, they were convinced that while Maxine's approach might be appropriate for the other churches in town, it was improper for Episcopalians like themselves because, in Rhonda's words, "We've always prided ourselves on our refined taste and distrust of everything that suggests 'religious enthusiasm' in some way."

Eventually Rhonda's daughter Susan surprised all the adults in the family by saying cautiously, "I don't mean to annoy anyone tonight but I really liked Mrs. Payne's approach this morning. While Mrs. Akers was our organist and choir director, it never occurred to me to join the choir because her tempos were so slow it always seemed like a funeral was going on, which was terrible. But it would probably be fun to be in the choir now and I've decided to attend its next practice on Wednesday night."

Lucy was pleased by Susan's decision because she had an excellent voice. In fact, her solos with the high school chorus always gave Lucy and most of the other members of the audience goose bumps.

Although Olivia didn't sing as well as Susan, she still had a good voice and said she'd also decided to attend the choir's next practice on Wednesday night. Turning to her parents she urged them to attend it with her and Susan because of their strong, clear voices.

Joe dismissed Olivia's suggestion out of hand before Julia spoke up for the first time that evening and said, "The more I think about Maxine's methods, the stranger they seem to me. So I plan to reserve judgment about whether I should consider joining the choir or not." Once she stopped speaking Joe backed her up and said she'd made a wise decision.

"But Dad!" Olivia said firmly, unwilling to give up without a fight. "You've told me several times that you were a member of your high school chorus and sang seven or eight solos during your junior and senior years. Because you have a great baritone voice and the only man in the choir is Mr. Payne, who's a tenor, the choir will need a voice like yours even more when Susan and I join it. So please reconsider and attend its next practice with us. Of course, we'd love for Mom to come too because she has a much better voice than any of the three women in the choir."

"Olivia," Joe said firmly, "I just said your mother made a wise decision to reserve judgment about whether she should consider joining the choir or not. And because I feel the same way, let's change the subject now," which they did to Olivia's great disappointment and Joey's equally great amusement.

However, because of Olivia's constant prodding and occasional taunts, Joe and Julia reconsidered by Wednesday afternoon and decided to attend that evening's choir practice. Still, as Joe and Olivia followed Julia out of the house at seven fifteen, he said to his daughter, "I'm going to tonight's practice only to find out what it would be like to belong to the choir now. So I hope you won't be too hopeful that your mother and I'll join it."

Julia agreed with him at once, causing Olivia to grumble under her breath, "I can't believe how stodgy they are about things like this. They often act like they're twenty or thirty years older than they really are."

"I heard that," Julia said to Olivia as she took her usual place on the right side of the front seat of her husband's car. "And I plan to quote you the next time you complain about your father and me showing too much affection for each other."

Oh brother, Olivia thought as she made herself comfortable on the backseat. *There's no way I can win in this family. Joey's already girl crazy and Mom and Dad act like giddy teenagers who're completely smitten by each other four or five times a week. I'm the only one who has any idea about what's right and proper, and I wonder if I can stand it until I leave home for college. Maybe I'll meet a nice guy during my freshman year who shares my views and doesn't act like a dog in heat all the time.*

Despite their wait-and-see attitude, Joe and Julia were hooked shortly after Maxine welcomed them and Olivia to that night's practice with open arms. In several more minutes she gave an equally warm welcome to Susan Summerlin, whom Chip had driven to the church on his way to a meeting of the Elks Lodge, and to Edna Wilcox, who had an excellent alto voice. Although George Kahle arrived half an hour late, Maxine stopped what she was doing and gave him a gracious welcome. George had a fine bass voice; and until nine fifteen she led him and the choir's other new members along with its four current ones in a spirited rehearsal of the hymns and canticles she and Mr. Thompson had chosen for the main service four days later. So on that Sunday morning, the last day of July, it included ten members instead of the usual four and sounded so much better the whole congregation was amazed and extremely pleased. Especially Chip and Mr. Thompson because they'd lobbied long and hard for Maxine to be named to the position of organist and choir director at a higher salary than one of her five predecessors had ever received.

Several days after the choir sounded so much better, the weather took a sudden turn for the worse. Heavy storm clouds moved in from the southeast on Thursday morning, August 4, and by noon the weather was so bad an old-timer who'd come to the drugstore to buy a dozen candles and several other items predicted that the area was in for a terrible storm, one comparable to the hurricane of 1885.

Chip and Lucy had vivid memories of that hurricane because they'd been teenagers at the time. The lowest part of town, the area between Hertford Avenue on the west and Perquimmons Creek on the east, was only a few feet higher than the level of the Sound; and during the hurricane of 1885, those blocks had been covered with water between five and six feet deep. That flooding had lasted for several days and caused extensive damage to hundreds of stores and homes within a thousand yards of the Sound. Scores of trees were uprooted and the original courthouse and school building were swept away, as were almost fourteen hundred barns, privies, chicken coops, and ice, tool, and smoke houses. Luckily, only three people died during that storm although it took two weeks to clean up all the debris left behind and eighteen months to build a new courthouse and school building. In the meantime, the children attended classes in the social and educational wings of the Methodist and Presbyterian churches while trials and other judicial proceedings were held in the Baptist fellowship hall, the largest and most suitable room in the area.

On the first Thursday afternoon in August 1910, Chip chatted for a while with the old-timer, who lived in a bungalow on East Church Street, before Chip said the area was overdue for another hurricane. It had been twenty-five years since the hurricane of 1885, and on average a storm of that size and strength swept across the area every twenty years. The old-timer agreed and paid for his purchases at once, hoping to return to his home before the wind and rain grew even worse.

Shortly after he left the drugstore by the side door, Julia and Rhonda rushed in through the front door. As they wiped off all the rain on their hands and faces, Chip asked them why they were gallivanting around town in such bad weather.

Julia said she'd driven her buggy from Sonny's livery stable to his and Rhonda's house shortly after nine thirty so she could help Rhonda put in the pleats and buttonholes of a new party dress she was making for Susan. "But as we were about to fix lunch for her and the boys, we realized we were in for a terrible storm that might cause the power lines to break and leave the streets impassable for nine or ten days. So we drove to Hogan's Grocery Store to stock up on milk, bread, cereal, canned goods, and other things like that."

"That's right," Rhonda said at once. "I was still living in Elizabeth City when the hurricane of 'eighty-five swept through the area and most of its streets were impassable for two weeks back then."

"But you should've gone straight home after you bought everything you needed at the grocery store," Lucy told them firmly.

"We would've done that if the grocery store still sold candles," Julia said to Lucy. "I need a dozen of them and six or seven of those cheap little candle holders Chip sells his customers in case the power fails during a storm. And while you're getting those things for me, I'd like several boxes of matches and a bottle of rubbing alcohol as well as two boxes of gauze pads and several rolls of adhesive tape."

As Lucy left the front of the store to find those items for Julia, Rhonda told Chip that she was worried about Alfred and Jack and wondered if he'd seen them during the last twenty or thirty minutes. "As Julia and I were about to leave our house for the grocery store, Alfred said he and Jack planned to go outside and see what a hurricane's really like. Jack also said he planned to walk to town and ride home with you this afternoon. I made them promise to stay inside until Julia and I get back, but you know how headstrong boys their age can be—they never think anything serious will happen to them, only to people who're older or slightly younger than they are. I'm just so worried that they went outside and a tree or a live power line's fallen on them with tragic results."

"Now you've got me really worried about them too," Chip said to Rhonda. "But I haven't seen them since breakfast, and if they broken their promise to stay inside until you get back, they'll get a whipping from me when I get home this afternoon."

"Don't talk like that because they're still so young and you know how much I've always hated corporal punishment."

"I'm aware of your feelings about corporal punishment although I may not respect them this time because going outside during a hurricane is much worse than taking several apples or peaches off one of our neighbor's fruit trees. But here's Lucy with everything Julia wants."

Chip filled out a charge ticket for those items before bagging them and handing them to Julia before saying she and Rhonda should go home at once and stay there even if Alfred and Jack were nowhere to be seen. "If they're wandering around town in a storm like this, it would be impossible to find them. So, all you and Julia can do is pray that they've taken shelter in a culvert or some other place where they'll be safe until the storm's over. And that goes for Olivia and Joey too if they've gone outside to see what a hurricane's really like."

Julia said she hadn't even considered that although she should have because of Joey's fearless nature and great love of excitement. As she and Rhonda were about to leave the store together, Chip heard them agree that they'd be on pins and needles until they were sure their children were safe.

As they disappeared Lucy asked Chip how long he planned to keep the store open that afternoon. "I'm afraid you'll be unable to drive home if you keep the store open after two o'clock because the wind and rain seem to be getting stronger by the minute."

"That's true," Chip said to her, "but I'm convinced I should keep the store open for my regular customers until two-thirty or three o'clock. I'm unaware of any other store in town that sells candles, matches, rubbing alcohol, and other things of that sort. Let's go back to the storage room now and bring dozens of boxes of those items to the front counter so we can help the people who come in to buy them as fast as we can."

When Chip and Lucy were halfway to the storage room, James Basham rushed into the building through the side entrance. He'd been delivering boxes of candles and small candle holders to the hotel and half a dozen stores on East Main Street. As he was about to take off his rain hat and coat, Chip told him to keep them on and leave for his and his wife's cabin on the eastern side of the creek at once because there wouldn't be any more deliveries that day. As James left the building by the front door, Chip told

Dillie behind the soda fountain that she should go home at once too because the wind and rain had tapered off a bit and it would probably be easier for her to get home now than it would be ten or fifteen minutes later.

Shortly after Dillie left the store, Chip and Lucy took several dozen boxes of candles and other items out of the storage room and carried them to the cash register at the front counter. Within half an hour seven regular customers came in and bought all those items, causing Chip to send Lucy back to the storage room for even more boxes of items that were badly needed during a powerful storm like the one raging outside. By two forty-five they'd sold the store's whole supply of candles, candle holders, matches, and bottles of rubbing alcohol, which prompted Lucy to urge Chip to close the store in several more minutes. But half a dozen more customers straggled in until three thirty to buy aspirin, adhesive tape, gauze pads, and similar items. So Chip felt they should "tough it out" a while longer if they could.

By three forty-five the wind and rain had become so great West Main Street and Hertford Avenue were completely deserted. Only one car had driven by since three fifteen and no one was outside on the sidewalks. Diagonally across the street on the courthouse lawn, two towering magnolias had fallen to the ground in an enormous heap. Chip and Lucy were alone in the store when the overhead lights flickered and went off at three forty-nine. Lucy rushed to one of the store's side windows and noticed that the power lines on the eastern side of Hertford Avenue had just been broken by a huge blast of wind while a massive shower of sparks could be seen slightly farther up the avenue. Several minutes later another blast of wind rattled all the windows and shook the whole building, causing Chip to say it was time to close the store and head for home if that was still possible.

Lucy lit a candle to help her find the yellow slicker and matching hat she'd worn to work that morning. As she was about to leave the building by the side door, Chip told her there was no way she could return to her cottage in such bad weather. Besides, her part of town was probably flooded by now. So she should drive home with him and spend the night on the daybed in his study.

Lucy had hoped to hear something like that although she wondered if Mr. Jobie was safe. Luckily she'd left him inside that morning and was convinced he'd survive the storm unless her cottage was totally destroyed.

As Chip hurried to the office to get his jacket and car keys, Lucy watched a maple tree near the hotel's main entrance fall to the ground.

As it did, one of its branches broke the power line that ran along East Main Street, causing an even larger shower of sparks to fill the air. Badly shaken, Lucy joined Chip in the rear hall before they left the building by the back door. Shortly after Chip locked the door behind them, they put their heads down and held hands while hurrying across the parking lot to his Oldsmobile. As they climbed into it the metal awning above the store's back door collapsed and was swept away by a violent gust of wind. Dozens of garbage cans were rolling around in a frenzy of motion, covering the parking lot with mounds of debris. Suddenly a Model T a short distance from Chip's car was destroyed by a towering pine tree that fell across it and broke it in half like a matchbox.

As Chip started his car and drove it out of the parking lot, Lucy wondered if they'd make it to his and Rhonda's house almost a mile away. Fortunately, Chip was an excellent driver and never lost control of the car even when a gigantic blast of wind, the most powerful one they'd felt since the height of the hurricane of 1885, hit the driver's side of his car and came within an inch of turning it over on its passnger side. After that enormous blast the wind tapered off until several seconds before Chip drove the car under the *porte cochère* on the eastern side of his house.

The moment Chip turned the car's engine off, a deafening thunderclap jolted Lucy so much she felt as if death itself was approaching like a horseman at full gallop. After getting out of the car she followed Chip into the house, where they received a warm and very relieved welcome from Rhonda, Susan, and the boys, who'd honored their promise to remain inside despite how much they'd wanted to go outside for several minutes that morning. As Chip and Lucy took off their rain hats and coats, Rhonda peppered them with questions about conditions in the middle of town. Rhonda wondered how much flooding had occurred and hoped the wind and rain wouldn't grow even worse during the next several hours. Chip gave vague answers to her questions, hoping to keep her and the children from becoming even more worried than they already were. But several minutes later Chip asked Rhonda to follow him into the parlor, where he told her there was bound to be widespread flooding in the lowest parts town by now and conditions would probably grow worse before they improved.

After a simple supper of bacon and scrambled eggs, whole wheat toast and fried apples Rhonda fixed on her wood stove, they lit half a dozen more candles and oil lamps they took into the parlor after cleaning up the kitchen. It was only six thirty but it was so dark it seemed like midnight.

For the next two hours they took turns telling stories about their most amusing childhood experiences, hoping to keep their minds off the howling wind and pelting rain outside. That was impossible, especially when two pine trees fell to the ground like pistol shots a short distance from the house.

At nine o'clock Chip said it was time for them to go to bed; and for the first time in years, Susan and the boys agreed without protest. As Chip and the children went upstairs to their rooms, Rhonda helped Lucy make up the daybed in the study. Once Rhonda took a blanket and pair of sheets out of a nearby closet, they put them on the daybed before Rhonda handed her sister-in-law a pillow and pillowcase.

Shortly after Rhonda left the study and joined Chip upstairs, Lucy took off her shoes and dress before curling up under the blanket and top sheet on the daybed in only her cotton underwear. For several hours she listened to the fury outside while praying her cottage would survive the storm. She also said a brief prayer for Mr. Jobie, whom she hoped had taken refuge under her bed, which he usually did during a storm with so much thunder and lightning.

Lucy fell asleep shortly before midnight, and when she woke up at six thirty the next morning, she felt rested and refreshed. She knew at once that the storm was over because several birds were singing in the apple and mimosa trees in the backyard. When she opened the curtains and peeped through the window, she was relieved to see several patches of blue in the still-gray sky. Of course there was debris everywhere, but nothing that couldn't be cleaned up in eight or nine days.

After a hefty breakfast of bacon and blueberry pancakes followed by a prayer of thanks that they'd survived the storm, Chip and Lucy left the house by the side door. Once they climbed into the Oldsmobile, Chip backed it into the street and headed for the center of town while Lucy described the damage she saw along the way. The screened porch on the western side of the Barringers' house had collapsed while most of the shingles on the Paynes' and Kembles' roofs had blown away. But there seemed to be only minimal damage to the Episcopal church and the much larger Presbyterian church a block closer to the center of town. Still, Lucy counted eight cars along the street that had been crushed by uprooted trees before Chip came to the intersection of West Church Street and Hertford Avenue. It was blocked by dozens of tree limbs until Chip stopped his car and got out of it before pulling nine or ten large branches aside. After returning to the car he drove it across the avenue into the eastern part of town as Lucy became increasingly worried about Mr. Jobie. So when Chip stopped in front of her cottage several minutes later, she told him to continue on to the drugstore where she would join him as soon as she could.

Once she got out of the car and Chip drove off, she noticed several dozen branches in her front yard although she realized her cottage had survived the storm with little if any damage. When she unlocked the front door and went inside, Mr. Jobie was so glad to see her he rubbed up against her legs several times before standing almost erect with his front paws on the lower part of her dress. She picked him up and held him close while stroking his head and back for several minutes. After carrying him into the kitchen, she gave him some table scraps from the ice box and a bowl of fresh water he lapped up in several moments.

Dreading what she'd see in the backyard, Lucy opened the kitchen door and went out onto the back porch before gazing at the ugly mess where half a dozen flower pots had been overturned by the heavy wind and their contents scattered on the ground. Several feet from her back fence a small sycamore tree had been crushed by a large branch the wind had torn off a nearby pine tree. As she returned to her back porch, she picked up several shingles that had blown off her roof and placed them on top of the broken flower pots. After scraping off as much of the mud on her shoes as she could, she went inside again and comforted Mr. Jobie for several more minutes before she left her cottage by the front door and hurried to the drugstore.

Because the power was still off when she entered the building by the side door, the large space was lit by half a dozen oil lamps Dillie had found in the storage room and lit before placing them at strategic places in the store. To everyone's relief, the power came on shortly after nine thirty, so Dillie had a pot of coffee ready when the four big shots arrived a short while later.

As Ozzie Crumpler and his friends sat down at their usual table near the soda fountain, they acted as if nothing unusual had happened. When Dillie brought them mugs of steaming coffee, they were discussing the general election that would take place in November and wondered if Charles Hapgood of Windsor, the district's congressman for seven terms, would be victorious again.

Lucy listened to the big shots' discussion in disbelief. When she took another pot of coffee to their table and offered them a free refill, they accepted her offer without comment. As she was filling Ozzie's mug again, she asked him if the storm hadn't caused him some concern.

Ozzie winked at Russell Barringer before drawling, "Oh, come on, Lucy, you weren't worried by that little squall, were you? I've been through storms thirty or forty times worse than yesterday's and I'm sure my friends have too."

When the other big shots nodded their agreement and returned to Mr. Hapgood's chances of winning another victory at the polls, Lucy shook her head in wonder before Dillie muttered, "Ain't them the strangest men you ev'uh saw? You'd think they don't have a care in the world 'cause they're so rich and powuh'ful."

"You're right, Dillie, they're very strange men indeed," Lucy said as she returned the coffee pot to its burner at the soda fountain before leaving for the cosmetics counter. Several teenage girls were discussing how terrible the storm had been while waiting for her to arrive and help them with their purchases.

One of those girls, Lynette Spaulding, whose mother Lucy knew fairly well because she belonged to the book club Lucy and Hazel Barlow had organized several months earlier with Julia's help, told her friends that their home had been destroyed when a massive oak tree fell on it and reduced it to rubble sometime between five thirty and seven thirty. Luckily, Lynette and the rest of her family were having supper at a relative's house at the time because the power had been off for several hours. According to Lynette's father, the whole family would've been killed had they been at home when the tree fell across the middle of their cottage and reduced it to rubble.

I wonder how Ozzie and his friends would react to Lynette's account of what happened to her family's home during yesterday's storm, Lucy thought as she waited until Lynette and her friends decided what cosmetics they wanted to buy. *Would the four big shots dismiss Lynette's account out of hand? Or would they revise their opinion of yesterday's storm as only 'a little squall'? Probably not because most people believe what they want to believe regardless of what they read in a newspaper or what other people tell them on the basis of wild rumors that have no basis in fact. I never really thought about things like that until a minute ago, but the enormous gullibility of most people probably explains why things are so slow to change in small out-of-the-way places like Perquimmons City in all parts of the country.*

Chapter 10

Most of the debris left by the hurricane was carted off in six days, and all but several of the town's streets were clear by the next afternoon and the remaining ones in forty-eight more hours. With only a few exceptions the townspeople pulled together during the storm's aftermath in a friendly and cooperative way. That fact and the news that no one had died during the hurricane caused hundreds of people to consider it as something of a blessing in disguise because it led to greater unity and concord between the often hostile groups that lived on opposite sides of the alley between Hertford Avenue and First Street, a clear social divide. During recent years there had been a growing awareness that the middle part of town was home to most of its poorer families while the town's western part was a citadel of wealth and privilege. The miserably poor black section on the eastern side of the creek seldom entered the white majority's consciousness except during the week or two before Christmas. At that time, most of the families who lived in the blocks west of Hertford Avenue took baskets of food and used clothes and bedding in good condition to their servants' cabins on the eastern side of the creek, a charitable act the black minority welcomed and resented at the same time.

For ten days after the hurricane, men and boys from the western part of town crossed Hertford Avenue dozens of times to help friends, relatives, and even total strangers in the town's middle section. Lucy and Hazel Barlow benefited from that phenomenon. On the Saturday after the storm several men and boys, including Joey and Cordell Richardson, rode up and down Second and Third Streets in a truck Joe and Chip rented from Stanton's Mill while looking for ways to assist people in obvious need of help. After stopping in front of Lucy's cottage one morning, they removed dozens of tree limbs in her yard and carried off the large pine branch that had crushed the small sycamore tree near her back fence. They also cleaned up the mess created where most of her flower pots had been overturned and replaced the shingles that had blown off her roof. As for the damage to Hazel's property, they carted off an uprooted locust tree in her front yard and a towering magnolia that had been toppled in her back yard. They also righted her overturned privy to her enormous relief and gratitude.

On other streets in the middle part of town, hundreds of other acts of good citizenship occurred during the six months after the hurricane. Without question the most important act of that kind was the policy Russell Barringer instituted at his hardware and building-supply store. For two months after the hurricane Russell allowed poor families in that part of town to buy at his wholesale cost whatever materials they needed to repair their homes and outbuildings. Although no black families lived in the blocks between Hertford Avenue and the creek's western bank—most of the town's blacks were clustered together in the area east of the creek—Russell extended that privilege to them as well at his wife's suggestion. For several years Mildred had been moved by Lucy's periodic comments during UDC meetings that its members should be more mindful of the economic plight of the town's black people, who needed a helping hand during all times of the year, not just during the last week or two before Christmas.

Everyone in town, but the blacks most of all, considered Russell's policy a measure of enormous generosity on his part, a clear sign he had no desire to profit from the misfortunes of others. All seven ministers praised his policy in their sermons, and so did a long editorial in the *Tribune*, which urged the town council to pass a resolution recognizing him as the town's Citizen of the Year. Despite his protest the council took that step during its November meeting, the usual time for passing such resolutions.

To no one's surprise William Merritt sought to profit from Russell's generosity in a way that was roundly condemned by everyone but the members of his own family. During the hurricane hundreds of shingles blew off the roof of the Merritt House while their barn, chicken coop, and ice, smoke, and tool houses were badly damaged as were most of the cabins and privies used by the family's black servants. Although Merritt was the richest man in the area, he sought to buy materials from Russell's store at their wholesale cost just as the town's poorest citizens were doing. A week after the storm Merritt confronted Barringer in a fury shortly after his head cashier, James B. Caldwell (Jobie's father), refused to extend that privilege to him. When Barringer defended his cashier's action, Merritt called him and Caldwell "goddamn nigger lovers" before stomping out of the store in a fury. A dozen other customers witnessed that incident with deep contempt if not hatred in their eyes. In several days Merritt's behavior at Barringer's store was condemned everywhere except at the Merritt House. On her part, Marguerite wondered why her husband never kept his feelings to himself and was always surprised when his critics threw his words in his face on occasions.

Merritt brought even greater criticism on himself by sending an unusually bitter letter to the *Tribune,* which printed it a week later. In his letter Merritt condemned the actions of the Albemarle Power & Light Company for restoring power to the other parts of town, even the black section on the eastern side of the creek, before it restored power to his mansion and several nearby houses. In fact, on the day Merritt mailed his letter to the *Tribune,* the power in his neighborhood was still off.

Two weeks later a polite but firm rebuttal to Merritt's letter appeared in the paper. That rebuttal had been written by the president of the Albemarle Power & Light Company, Cyrus Bennett of Edenton, who apologized for the delay in restoring power to the six and seven hundred blocks of West Main Street. But Bennett was convinced that during the aftermath of the recent storm and future ones as well, the interests of the many had to prevail over those of the few. Although Bennett regretted the inconvenience his policy caused the Merritts and their closest neighbors, he considered it unavoidable and expressed no remorse for his belief or actions. If the Merritts and several nearby families disagreed with his policy, they were free to buy generators for their homes or petition another power company to supply their needs whenever they liked.

Lucy was so pleased by Bennett's letter she was tempted to send him a thank-you note for writing it. But she never did because she procrastinated as much as the average person about matters of that kind. However, the Baptist minister, Linwood Price, whose congregation included well over half of the town's poor white families, sent Bennett a letter of sincere appreciation for his policy and a carbon copy to the *Tribune,* which published it several days later. Within a short time Lucy heard so many favorable comments about Price's letter in the drugstore she realized Merritt's influence had been greatly weakened if not completely destroyed, which she saw no reason to lament.

There was another, more fundamental reason why Merritt's influence plummeted during the hurricane's aftermath. The heavy rain had caused extensive flooding in the middle part of town, although on a much lesser scale than the flooding caused by the hurricane of 1885. Luckily for Lucy, the water failed to reach her doorstep although it came within several feet of it and did substantial damage to Hazel Barlow's cottage only twenty feet farther south than hers. All in all, almost a hundred dwellings closer to the Sound than Lucy's were flooded, as were most of the businesses on East Main Street, including Ned's barbershop, Nadine Roberts' beauty parlor, the telegraph office, and Hogan's Grocery Store. The police department and Joe's office were also flooded, while the town's white elementary school and the "English" or raised basement of the courthouse suffered even greater water damage. With only a few exceptions no one in town regarded such widespread flooding as "negligible," as Merritt characterized it to the handful of people who stopped and listened to his harangues at the bank and the post office or during the social hour after the main service at the Presbyterian church on the four Sunday mornings after the storm. Merritt always did his best to minimize the damage caused by the hurricane because of his firm belief that the town council would raise property taxes in order to provide funds for the construction of an embankment to prevent similar or even greater flooding in the future.

Merritt's fear that the council would raise taxes in order to finance an embankment was well founded. Within several days of the storm two identical copies of a petition calling for the council to build an embankment before another hurricane swept across the area began to circulate in the middle and western parts of town. In a few more days both copies of that petition, which had been drafted by Dan Wiley at the mayor's request, had been signed by almost a thousand men and women.

Both copies were delivered to the mayor, who was also the ex-officio chairman of the town council, on the day after the council's regular monthly meeting on the second Tuesday evening in August. But several days before he received those copies, Ridinger conferred with Randall Porter, the town's treasurer for nine years, and George Kahle, a long-time member of the council who handled its legal work for a fraction of his usual fee. During the eleven months since a smaller and much weaker storm caused minor flooding in the same part of town in September 1909, the mayor and his associates had agreed on the urgent need for an embankment to prevent flooding comparable to that of 1885; and by June of 1910, Ridinger, Wiley, and Kahle had devised a plan they were waiting for the right moment to implement. In fact, during the aftermath of the hurricane of 1910 they were determined to strike while memories of the recent flooding were still strong and there was widespread support for their policy.

When questions about an embankment were raised during the council's monthly meeting on August 9, Ridinger explained that the council's charter forbade last-minute changes to the agenda. But because of the urgency of the matter and his understanding that two copies of a petition calling for speedy action would be presented to him in another day or two, he'd already scheduled a special council meeting on Tuesday night August 16. That meeting would take place in the Baptist fellowship hall, which could accommodate a much larger crowd than usually attended the council's monthly meetings in the assembly room at the town's office building on West Main Street. The mayor and most of his fellow councilors hoped at least 250 concerned citizens would attend the meeting on August 16 and support a plan to raise enough money to build an embankment before another hurricane season started on July first of the next year.

Word of the special council meeting on August 16 spread through town like a lightning bolt; and when Ridinger called that meeting to order at seven thirty that evening, almost three hundred people were present. Seated at folding tables at one end of the Baptist fellowship hall on either side of the mayor and treasurer were the eight other councilors, who included Barringer, Kahle, Summerlin, Richardson, Merritt, and James Howell, the town's only real estate and insurance agent. Seated on folding chairs facing those dignitaries were 187 men and women, who included Joe and Julia, Lucy, Rhonda, Rhonda's aunt Edna Wilcox, Percy and Estelle Hogan, Estelle's sister Hazel Barlow, Floyd Richardson's wife Mary Lou and her sister Josephine Gardner, both Thomas Stantons and their wives, and finally the town's four white ministers and their wives. Another hundred men and women were sitting on the floor or lounging against the walls. Most of the men in that group were clad in old T-shirts and faded overalls as they chewed nervously on toothpicks. Lucy and Joe, who were sitting next to each other, were convinced those men were primed for a fight if Merritt and his only ally on the council, Doug Witherspoon, the owner of a nursery and landscaping service on the Hertford Road, found a way to block the construction of an embankment most of the town's poorer people considered essential for their safety during future hurricanes.

Once Mayor Ridinger opened the meeting shortly after seven thirty, Reverend Price delivered a brief invocation before Ridinger thanked everyone for attending the meeting on such short notice. After calling the meeting "a good example of democracy in action," he gave the floor to the treasurer, who delivered a short but very effective speech that began with an assessment of the damage caused by the recent flooding. Porter stressed the damage suffered not only by the courthouse and nearby school but by most of the businesses on East Main Street and dozens of homes in the five blocks directly behind those buildings. After explaining that a majority of the council had long felt an embankment was needed, Porter described how such an embankment would be built, what parts of town it would protect, and how much money it would probably cost. Because he estimated that an embankment would cost slightly over $120,000, a new tax—or more likely a five-year increase in the current real estate tax—would have to be voted before work on the project could begin.

While the treasurer was speaking, an enormous scowl appeared on Merritt's face. As a result only a few people were surprised when he demanded to be heard the moment Porter finished his speech and thanked the crowd for listening so attentively to his words. Hoping to prevent an unseemly squabble, Ridinger gave Merritt the floor for five minutes.

After making several pompous statements about his family's place in local history and society, Merritt insisted there should be no increase in the real estate tax for even a week. After conceding that an embankment was badly needed, he insisted it would be unfair to impose any part of its cost on landowners like himself who owned no property in the low-lying blocks between Hertford Avenue and the creek's western side. He also argued that only a special levy on property in the endangered part of town should be considered that night.

Merritt's statements were interpreted as convincing proof of his total disregard for the losses suffered by the town's poorer residents and, as such, it triggered an outburst of boos and jeers from all sides of the room. To Merritt's even greater displeasure, the next six speakers, who included Joe, Floyd Richardson, Edna Wilcox, and the Baptist and Methodist ministers, criticized Merritt's comments and complete lack of empathy for the misfortunes of others before they expressed their strong support for Porter's proposal for a five-year increase on the current real estate tax.

When the last cheers for those six speakers subsided, Porter noted in a voice dripping with sarcasm that only a fraction of Merritt's property lay within the town limits. So a 30 percent increase of the current real estate tax, which would probably raise enough money to pay for the embankment, would affect Merritt's bank balance much less than he wanted his fellow citizens to believe. In fact, Porter estimated that Merritt's tax bill would increase by only $70 a year, which such a rich man could easily afford.

When Merritt tried to speak again, he was booed so loudly he stomped out of the room in disgust before leaving the building for his car, which was parked a short distance from the Baptist fellowship hall on East Church Street. He sat impatiently in his Steamer until it had a full head of steam and he could drive off. Dozens of people inside, including Lucy, Rhonda, and Edna Wilcox, watched him from the room's large windows with hostile or contemptuous looks.

The meeting continued much more smoothly after Merritt's departure. By the time Ridinger declared it closed at nine fifteen, he and the seven other councilors had voted in favor of a 30 percent increase of the current real estate tax for five years, which Porter estimated would bring in roughly $20,300 a year. So unless the embankment cost a great deal more than his projections indicated, it would be completely paid for in five years. The council's actions that night received a standing ovation from the crowd, which was delighted that an embankment would probably be finished several weeks before another hurricane season started on July 1, 1911.

Because the town charter stipulated that any tax increase voted by the council had to be ratified during another council meeting several weeks later, the second vote was taken during the council's next regular meeting on September 13. The vote that night was eight to one in favor of the same 30 percent increase on the real estate tax that had been voted three weeks earlier. Merritt was the only councilor to cast a negative vote on September 13; and shortly after Ridinger announced the vote's outcome to the 126 people in attendance that night, Merritt accused his fellow councilors of conspiring to ruin him financially. Because he was absolutely sure that was the case, he jumped to his feet and said he felt compelled to resign from the council and his position as vice mayor effective at once. Then as the crowd booed him again, despite the smallering of applause for unusually decision to resign from the council, he left the room before rushing out of the office building to his car again. He stood in front of its hood until he succeeded in cranking its engine before he climbed into the vehicle and drove off as fast as he could.

Because Ridinger had foreseen Merritt's resignation from the council that night, he announced shortly after Merritt left the room that Dennis Payne had agreed to serve in his place until the next general election occurred in November, and Payne might well be a candidate then for the remaining four years of Merritt's term. Ridinger also announced that Chip

Summerlin had agreed to assume Merritt's position as vice mayor until early January, when there was a chance he'd be elected to that office in his own right. Once the mayor explained those changes, George Kahle moved that they be approved by acclamation. Russell Barringer seconded that motion, and in the twinkling of an eye the motion passed without a dissenting vote to more cheers and applause from the crowd.

Several days after Merritt resigned from the council, he sent a second and unusually vitriolic letter to the *Tribune*. When his second letter appeared in the paper a week later, most of the townspeople were amazed by its bitter tone and its assertion that the council was now in the "iron grip of a wicked cabal" led by Ridinger, Summerlin, Porter, and Wiley. After making that vehement accusation, Merritt's letter argued that those four men were "cunning upstarts without any culture or refinement" and, as a result, they felt "deep hostility toward more refined and better-educated landowners like myself." Unless the voters went to the polls in record numbers during the November election, the angry man insisted, the corrupt regime led by that "shameless group of power-hungry crooks" would control the town for years to come. Merritt therefore urged men "with greater honesty and integrity than those who've already declared their candidacy for council seats" to come forward and announce their decision to run while there was still time. Only in that way, his letter insisted, could "that shameless toady and lackey, Dennis Payne," be prevented from serving as his successor on the council for slightly more than years. And only in that way could the "overweening power of a small group of self-serving hypocrites be broken" before it brought about "the total destruction of conscientious men like myself" whose only error had been "to publicize the cabal's wicked designs they refuse to acknowledge in a public forum of any kind."

After reading that amazing letter, Lucy remembered the ancient Greek saying that "those whom the gods would destroy they first drive insane."

Two nights later at the Hanfords' house, Lucy and the other adults in her family discussed Merritt's two letters to the *Tribune* for almost an hour. Joe made a telling point when he said Merritt was under enormous stress at home. "All five times I saw him and his wife at the Merritt House during Little Robert's convalescence last spring, they snapped at each other so angrily it was embarrassing to hear it. Because they seemed so unhappy together, I'm convinced they should separate or get a divorce, which is probably the best explanation for Merritt's irrational behavior since the hurricane."

Chip agreed with Joe's contention that the Merritts were having serious marital problems but insisted there was a great deal more to it than that. Half a dozen times during the last two months, their butler-chauffeur, Matthew Harden, had come to the drugstore to buy small amounts of arsenic and mercury. Each time Matthew came to the store for that purpose, he produced a signed and dated note in Marguerite's distinctive handwriting before Chip added the cost of those drugs to the Merritts' charge account and placed Mrs. Merritt's note in their file at her request. Chip continued, "Arsenic and mercury are the only substances I'm aware of that can be used to treat syphilis. They can't cure it, of course, but they can control its worst symptoms for a year or two in most cases."

Amazed, Joe said it had never occurred to him that Merritt had come down with syphilis because he hadn't seen him as a patient in almost a year. After thinking for a moment he added, "Syphilis attacks the nervous system and causes most of the people who have it to become paranoid and rant and rave about imaginary plots against themselves. And that's exactly what Merritt's been doing since the hurricane. Because syphilis is very infectious during its early stages, I hope Marguerite's found a good way to protect herself from his sexual advances. If I felt more comfortable with her, I'd warn her to be extremely cautious around him at night."

Chip said she was bound to know how dangerous her situation had become during recent weeks. "After all, that's the only explanation I can think of for why she's been using Matthew to buy small amounts of arsenic and mercury every eight or nine days since the beginning of August."

After thinking for a moment, Julia said she felt Marguerite had been buying arsenic and mercury in order to alleviate her husband's pain and suffering.

After considering Julia's opinion for several moments, Lucy argued that Chip and Julia were both right. "Marguerite probably wants to reduce her husband's suffering as much as she can because she's not completely heartless. At the same time she's bound to realize that he's become a serious threat to her own life because of how contagious syphilis is at first. So if I were her, I'd be frantic because I know for a fact that he forced himself on her dozens of times while I worked for them and lived in one of their attic rooms. Of course, there's a possibility that he's lost all interest in having sex with her during recent years although I seriously doubt it. So if I slept in a bedroom directly across the upstairs hall from his, I'd move into another part of the mansion and reduce the danger to my own life as much as I could."

Eight days after that discussion Lucy received a strange communication from Mrs. Merritt. In her brief but unexpected note Marguerite had written:

> Several days ago, while going through some old records I was about to throw away, I discovered that I owed your mother $398.50 for clothes she made for my children during the last several months of her life. Because I misplaced that bill and let it go unpaid for such a long time, I've added $1.50 in interest and hope you'll accept the $400 in cash I've attached to this note with a paper clip as full payment of that debt.
>
> Cordially yours, Marguerite Manigault Merritt.

The next morning at the drugstore, Lucy asked Chip to follow her into the office and close the door behind himself. After he did as she requested, Lucy showed him Marguerite's note and the eight fifty-dollar bills she'd attached to it. "I'm really puzzled by this," Lucy said once her brother read the note and gave it back to her. "What do you think I should do with all this money?" she asked. "Should I keep it and split it with you and Julia? Or should I return it to Mrs. Merritt in several days?"

After thinking for a moment Chip said, "This is really strange because I have no memory of Mama ever mentioning a debt of any size the Merritts owed her and certainly not one as large as this. And there was nothing in Mama or Papa's records when I settled their estate that indicated they still owed Mama almost four hundred dollars. Besides, I wonder why Mrs. Merritt sent you all this money in cash. It seems like she would've sent you a check you'd have to endorse before the bank cashed it and eventually returned it to the Merritts in their next monthly statement for their records. In that way Marguerite would've had clear proof she sent you all this money, which she could've used to insist that you return it to her at once if she ever learned that her husband had paid that bill to Mama without mentioning it to her. But that raises an even bigger question—why didn't she ask her husband point-blank if he'd paid that bill before she sent you all this money?"

"You're right," Lucy said to Chip at once. "Everything about this seems extremely strange. But I still wonder what I should do with all this money. I'd love to have a third of it, wouldn't you?"

"No, because I'd hate to feel beholden to those awful people in any way. So if I were you, I'd endorse her check and put all the money in my bank account before sending her a check for the whole amount in several days. If you do that, you'll have your canceled check as proof that you returned every penny of the Merritts' money to Marguerite in case her husband ever tells her he paid that bill to Mama shortly before she died and asks you to return the whole amount to her at once. Of course, you could always keep the money and split it with Julia on the chance they remain confused about the matter. But in regard to me, count me out because I won't accept any part of it because of how much I dislike them and would hate to feel indebted to them in any way."

Because of Chip's attitude and the fact that Julia shared it once Lucy explained the situation to her shortly after dinner at the Hanfords' house that night, Lucy deposited all of Mrs. Merritt's money in her bank account the next morning. And several days later, when Mrs. Merritt's check had probably cleared, she wrote Marguerite a check for four hundred dollars, which she paid James Basham fifty cents to take to the Merritt House in a sealed envelope when he made a delivery to the mansion two days later. In the envelope with her check, Lucy included a note explaining that she'd discussed the matter with Chip and Julia, and the three of them had no record or memory of the Merritts owing their mother a debt of any size during the last months of her life.

A week later Lucy received a second and even stranger note from Mrs. Merritt. That note began with a statement of appreciation for Lucy's prompt return of all her money, which saved her from a potentially embarrassing situation. Although she had no wish to deceive her husband, Marguerite's second note maintained, she now planned to use that money to assist a worthy colored servant, Matthew Harden, without telling her husband what she'd actually done with that $400. Her husband had never felt any affection for Matthew, whom he'd accused of disrespect and surly behavior on several occasions. But Mrs. Merritt had always considered Matthew respectful and extremely diligent in the performance of his duties. Because of that she'd been hoping to find a way to help him and his second wife, Jamilla, without annoying her husband. Matthew and Jamilla had recently decided to leave the South with all its racial and economic problems in the hope of finding better-paying work in New York, Chicago, or another Northern city. Luckily, Mrs. Merritt had written on the bottom of the $400 check she'd cashed on the Merritts' joint checking account ten days earlier, "Money to pay a longstanding debt to the late Margaret Edwards

Summerlin." And because Lucy had returned all that money to her so promptly, Mrs. Merritt could now use it to help Matthew and Jamilla leave the area without her husband knowing how she'd actually used it. Furthermore, Mrs. Merritt reminded Lucy of her high regard for Matthew and all the other colored servants she'd worked alongside during her long years at the Merritt House. So Marguerite was sure Lucy would approve of the way she'd decided to use the $400 Lucy had just returned to her. Finally, Mrs. Merritt signed her second note to Lucy, "With kindest regards to you and all the other members of your family, Marguerite Manigault Merritt."

Lucy and Chip were even more puzzled by Mrs. Merritt's second note than they'd been by her first one. That a rude and arrogant person like her, one who'd never shown any kindness to her servants, would confide in a former employee seemed incomprehensible to them.

Because Lucy had never understood the reasons for Mrs. Merritt's strange behavior, she forgot about the matter for several weeks. But on October 18, the real purpose behind Mrs. Merritt's notes to Lucy became clear, first to Joe and Burt Trumble, and then the next night to Lucy herself. In fact, Lucy realized, shortly after she had dinner at the Hanfords' house again on October 19, that Mrs. Merritt hadn't confided in her at all. Rather, she'd done her best to deceive her and most of the other members of her family about the real reason she helped Matthew and Jamilla leave the area for a distant but unnamed Northern city. Mrs. Merritt's actual purpose was to ensure that Chief Trumble would be unable to question those two servants about their part and possible accomplices in a crime so heinous it was punishable by death.

Chapter 11

On the third Tuesday morning in October, Willie Merritt got up an hour earlier than usual because he planned to go hunting with his father at eight thirty. So he put on some old clothes and boots before taking his best hunting rifle, which his parents had given him on his nineteenth birthday in May, out of the gun rack in his bedroom. On leaving his room, he walked down the hall to his father's room and knocked on the door several times. When he heard no response, he opened the door and saw no sign of his father, who was probably downstairs eating his usual breakfast of fried eggs and country ham, grits with red-eye gravy, and biscuits with blackberry jam, which Flossie and Tulip had fixed him every morning for years.

After taking the backstairs down to the ground floor, Willie failed to see his father in the breakfast room or the servants' kitchen, where Flossie and Tulip said they hadn't seen him that morning. When Flossie said he might be asleep in the study, Willie hurried through the main kitchen, breakfast room, and center hall to the study's double doors, which were closed for the first time in years. On opening those doors he saw his father lying in a pool of blood on the floor by the sofa. Willie dropped his rifle and rushed to his father's side to see if he was still alive. But he was clearly dead because he wasn't breathing and his throat had been slit from ear to ear. A butcher knife covered with blood was lying near his right shoulder. Because of all the blood on the sofa, Willie assumed that his father had been asleep on it when the killer attacked him and his body rolled off the sofa onto the floor about the time he took his last breath.

Without touching anything Willie rushed upstairs to explain the situation to his mother. He found her coming out of the bathroom in her house coat and slippers. When he told her about his father's death, she fainted and fell to the floor. He rushed into her bedroom and found some smelling salts on her dressing table he used to revive her. After helping her to her feet, he took her by the arm and guided her back to the wing chair near her bedroom fireplace in which the embers from the previous night's fire were still smoking. He urged her to stay in her room while he drove to the police station to report the crime. After agreeing to his suggestion, she asked him to bring her a bottle of brandy and a small glass from the butler's pantry before he left the mansion, which he did.

After rushing down the backstairs again and through both kitchens without mentioning the crime to Flossie and Tulip, Willie left the mansion and cranked the engine of his father's car. After getting into it, he backed it out of the rear driveway, turned it around, and drove at top speed to the police station on East Main Street. Chief Trumble was sitting at his desk with a cup of coffee when Willie burst in and gave him a jumbled account of everything he'd seen and done that morning. Trumble asked him several questions before telling him to return to the mansion and console the rest of his family until he arrived to look for clues about the identity of his father's killer.

Shortly after Willie left the police station and drove off, Trumble finished his coffee before going next door to Joe's office. He and Joe had been good friends and occasional hunting partners since the fall of 1899, when Trumble and his wife Mamie moved to town from Wilmington. A year later, shortly after Trumble succeeded the late Abe Calhoun as the town's police chief, he convinced Joe to become the town's coroner, an unpaid position he held for twenty-seven years. On that October morning in 1910, Trumble asked Joe to go to the Merritt House with him and determine the cause and approximate hour of Merritt's death.

Joe agreed to his friend's request at once; and after telling Mary Bishop to reschedule his morning appointments, he and Trumble left for the Merritt House in the police department's only car: the Buggymobile the town council had bought from the Episcopal minister, Robert Thompson, the previous fall shortly after he bought a larger and more dependable Model T for himself.

On reaching the mansion and getting out of the Buggymobile, Burt and Joe climbed the front steps and crossed the porch before Burt rang the doorbell, which seemed to be out of order, before he pounded on the door a dozen times. Flossie eventually opened it and asked him what he wanted. Once he explained that he and Dr. Hanford had come to investigate her employer's murder the previous night, Flossie told them to come in, which they did and followed her through the entrance hall and down the center hall to the study's double doors, which were still open. A large, busty woman, Flossie made no pretense of sorrow or surprise over Merritt's death as she led them into the room and pointed out her employer's body, which no one had touched. She and Burt stood aside while Joe examined the body for several minutes before informing Burt that the man had probably been dead for eight or nine hours because rigor mortis had already set in although it wasn't well advanced. Joe also estimated that Merritt had taken his last breath around twelve thirty, give or take an hour in either direction.

For several minutes Trumble looked around the room to see if anything of value was missing. When he found no signs that a theft had occurred and Flossie nodded her head in agreement, Trumble asked her if she'd ever seen the butcher knife the killer had clearly used on his victim in the mansion before.

"Naw, suh," Flossie said at once, "I ain't never seen that butch'uh knife befo this maw'nin. It's a lot cheaper than the knives we use in the kitchens here, so the kill'uh probably bought it at the dime sto on West Main Street or from one o the dime stos in Hertford or Edenton."

After jotting those things down on a notepad he took out of his hip pocket, Trumble asked Flossie to go upstairs and tell Mrs. Merritt he needed to speak to her as soon as possible. When Flossie returned in several minutes, she said Mrs. Merritt was still trying to get her nerves under control while comforting the children. So it would probably be fifteen or twenty minutes before she came downstairs.

While waiting for Mrs. Merritt to appear, Burt and Joe examined all the windows and outside doors on the mansion's ground floor and found no evidence of a forced entry. After going down the inside stairs to the basement, they conducted a similar investigation while the family's three little house dogs barked viciously at them from their cages near the door to the root cellar. When they found no evidence of a forced entry through a basement window or one of its three outside doors, they left the basement by the door under the west parlor and looked around the mansion's foundation for footprints in the grass, which was soft and spongy because of the heavy rainfall during the last several days. When they found no footprints, Burt told Joe he was convinced the murder had been an inside job.

Burt became even more convinced of that as he talked to Tulip, an even larger woman than her mother. She stopped sweeping the front porch to talk to him; and when Burt asked her if the house dogs had been penned up the previous night or allowed to move around the mansion at will, she said, "I can't ans'uh that fo sure 'cause me and Mama washed the dinn'uh dishes and all the pots and pans befo we went back to our cabin last night. But it's my understandin that the dogs ain't penned up on most nights as a way o keepin bur'gluhs from breakin in and stealin the dinin room silv'uh or somethin else that's really valu'ble. So I don't ac'shully know if the dogs was penned up last night or not."

"Have you ever known Willie or Mr. Merritt to put the dogs in their cages in the morning shortly after they came downstairs and you and your mother were fixing their breakfast?"

"Yes, suh, I've known them to do that a num'buh of times but nev'uh durin the last couple o months."

"Thanks, Tulip," Burt said. "You've been a big help this morning."

As Tulip resumed her sweeping while humming "Nobody Knows de Trouble I've Seen, Nobody Knows but Jesus," Burt told Joe he was absolutely certain that a man who'd known the dogs would be penned up the previous night had entered the mansion shortly after midnight to commit the crime. He was just as certain that the murder had been planned well in advance and carried out with great skill. When Joe asked him if he already knew the killer's identity, Burt said he had a good idea but was reluctant to mention any names until he questioned Mrs. Merritt and several of her other servants.

As Burt and Joe reentered the mansion, they saw Willie helping his mother down the main staircase with great care. Mrs. Merritt was wearing a long black dress, a veil that covered her whole face, and an enormous, wide-brimmed hat adorned with a large clump of silk flowers on the right side. As Marguerite neared the foot of the staircase, Burt and Joe expressed their sympathy for her enormous loss. She thanked them in a quivering voice before suggesting they follow her back to the breakfast room. They could sit comfortably around the table there and have a cup of coffee and some of Flossie's delicious pecan rolls while discussing the man who'd committed such a wicked crime.

Shortly after they were seated in the breakfast room, Mrs. Merritt took off her hat and veil and placed them on a corner of the Welsh dresser behind her chair so it would be easier for her to hear Chief Trumble's questions. Burt and Joe both noticed that her eyes showed no signs of redness or puffiness, which they probably would've done had she been weeping about her husband's death during the hour or so since Willie told her about it.

As Flossie entered the breakfast room and put a stack of napkins and a platter of pecan rolls in the middle of the table, Tulip brought in four mugs of steaming coffee. Burt and Joe took a napkin and placed a pecan roll on top of it before Willie did the same. After taking a sip of his coffee Burt asked Mrs. Merritt where she and her children had been between eleven o'clock the previous evening and one o'clock that morning. Marguerite said the whole family, including her husband, had gone upstairs to their bedrooms around ten o'clock as they usually did. But she'd heard her husband leave his room and return to his study an hour or so later, which he often did, to read until he fell asleep on the sofa around midnight. He usually woke up around one thirty and returned to his bedroom, where he remained until seven thirty the next morning, when he came downstairs to have breakfast.

After scribbling those things on his notepad, Burt asked Mrs. Merritt if one of the house keys was missing. She turned to Willie and asked him to go to the main kitchen and count the keys they kept in a cupboard near the larger stove. Several moments later Willie returned to the breakfast room and reported that two of the five keys were missing. When Burt asked Mrs. Merritt who had access to them, she said all the house servants did although her husband usually kept one of the keys under the front seat of his car in the event he came home an hour or so after she locked all the outside doors around ten o'clock and followed the children upstairs. Several times a month her husband played poker with his Edenton friends, and their games usually broke up shortly after eleven although they occasionally lasted until midnight or slightly later.

That discussion prompted Willie to go outside and check under the Steamer's front seat. When he returned to the breakfast room once again, he said he'd found no key in his father's car.

"Just as I thought," Marguerite said to Chief Trumble as Willie resumed his place at the breakfast table and helped himself to another pecan roll. "I told my hus'bun dozens o times it was too dang'rous for him to keep a key und'uh his cah's front seat. Most o the darkies who live around here knew he kept a key there, and one of 'em probably stole it several days ago without him realizin it. That explains how the kill'uh entered the house without leavin a speck o evidence that he'd been here."

Burt said that was possible but unlikely before asking Mrs. Merritt where the other house servants were that morning, especially the ones who lived in the attic. Mrs. Merritt said only one servant lived in the attic now; and because that young woman had been on her staff for less than a month, there was almost no chance she'd been involved in the crime.

After saying he might want to question that servant at a later time, Burt asked to see Matthew Harden, the Merritts' butler-chauffeur, and his second wife, Jamilla, a beautiful woman almost twenty years younger than Matthew, who'd married her less than two months before.

As Burt and Joe sipped their coffee and finished their pecan rolls, Mrs. Merritt told them Jamilla had resigned from her staff on September 15, two weeks before Matthew gave her formal notice although he'd continued to perform his duties until four thirty on the afternoon of October 14, when he told her good-bye in the study for the last time. She hadn't talked with Matthew or Jamilla since that afternoon. Nevertheless, when she happened to look out one of the study's windows on the morning of the fifteenth, she saw Matthew moving his clothes and other possessions out of the cabin he and Jamilla had shared since their wedding on the third Saturday afternoon in August. Their jobs and the cabin they'd shared were still vacant because honest, dependable servants were hard to find; and the Merritts had learned from painful experience that it was a mistake to hire applicants who lacked good references.

Burt was especially interested in where Matthew and Jamilla were living now and wondered if they'd moved in with Matthew's parents in the black part of town on the eastern side of the creek. Mrs. Merritt said that was possible although she considered it unlikely because the older Hardens' cabin had only three rooms and she knew Matthew and Jamilla had planned to leave the area for New York, Chicago, or some other Northern city. When Burt asked her to elaborate, she said on the day Matthew gave her formal notice, he told her that he and his wife had decided to try their luck up North where there was less racial prejudice and good jobs were more plentiful than they were in the South. Mrs. Merritt continued, "I hated fo Matthew to leave my staff 'cause he'd been an *excellent* but'luh fo ov'uh twenty yea'uhs. On the aft'uhnoon he told me good-bye, I gave him a lett'uh of unqualified praise fo his work he could show potential employ'uhs up Naw'th. I also gave him fo hundred doll'uhs fo his and Jamilla's trip and first sev'ral months in the Naw'th. Matthew was so grateful fo that lett'uh and all the money, he thanked me profusely fo 'em. I told him he and Jamilla would need that much money if not a great deal mo 'cause good jobs are almost as scarce up there as they are down here."

Clearly skeptical of those comments Burt said, "I find it hard to believe that you gave Matthew four hundred dollars to help him and Jamilla leave the area because that's a great deal of money. In fact, it's more than my wife makes in a whole year as a seamstress at Miss Edna's Dry Goods Store."

"No, it's not *that* much money, Chief Trumble. I usually spend twice as much money as that on my children's win'tuh clothes."

"But you live in a different world from the rest of us as everyone in town knows. Besides, it's hard for me to believe your husband allowed you to give Matthew four hundred dollars because he never liked him and came within an inch of firing him slightly over nine years ago."

Turning to Willie again Marguerite said, "Be a sweet boy and go upsta'uhs to my room. There's a packet o let'tuhs in the middle draw'uh o my dressin table that'll clear up all o Chief Trumble's questions in sev'ral minutes."

As Willie left the breakfast room again Burt said to her, "I'm convinced you gave all that money to your husband's killer."

"No, that can't be true 'cause I'm sure Matthew had nothin to do with my hus'bun's death. They were very fond of each oth'uh even if Mis'tuh Merritt accused Matthew of surliness a couple o times ten or eleven yea'uhs ago."

"Let's not waste any time on games this morning because I know for a fact that your husband had a low opinion of Matthew. Don't you remember their big fight in the summer of 'ought-one? I happened to ride by the mansion on my horse one August morning and saw Flossie and most of the other servants milling around in the backyard because of a bitter fight that was going on in the main kitchen. According to Flossie, that fight broke out when Matthew accused your husband of sleeping with his first wife, Serena. And several days before that fight shortly after Serena told Mr. Merritt she was pregnant by him, he threatened to fire her unless she had an abortion, which the colored doctor in Hertford botched so badly she died several days later. Matthew was so furious about Serena's death he confronted your husband about it in the main kitchen on the August day I neared the mansion on my horse. Furthermore, according to Flossie, Mr. Merritt infuriated Matthew even more by claiming he'd never slept with Serena a single time before telling him he'd clearly confused him with a man in town. At that point Matthew called your husband a liar and threatened to kill him with a meat cleaver he picked up from the chopping block. That caused Mr. Merritt to grab a butcher knife and say, 'Go ahead and try, you dumb nigger! But if you lay a hand on me, I'll kill you with this knife and throw your body to the alligators in the Sound.'"

"Oh no, Chief Trumble, I don't rememb'uh a fight like that at all! You're clearly confusin my hus'bun with someone else in the area. Prob'ly one o the Perdue brothers 'cause they're nothin but po white trash and the whole town knows they've slept with colored girls for years. As for my hus'bun, he slept with sev'ral colored girls until I convinced him he should stop doin it a dozen yea'uhs ago. Besides, he would *nev'uh* have demeaned himself by fightin with a house servant the way you think he did."

"I'm sure you remember your husband's fight with Matthew, Mrs. Merritt. Once I got off my horse that morning and Flossie told me about the fight that was going on in the main kitchen, she begged me to go inside and end it before one of the men killed the other one. When I entered the main kitchen, you were pleading with them to put down their weapons at once. But the minute you saw me, you rushed through the breakfast room and disappeared up the backstairs."

"There's not a bit o truth to that and you know it! My hus'bun was *nev'uh* involved with Serena or any oth'uh colored girls durin the last dozen yea'uhs of his life! After I discussed his behav'yuh with him for a while in the study one night, he admitted his parents would've been deeply ashamed o him had he continued such a cheap and tawdry practice a day long'uh than he already had."

"I'll never believe those things, Mrs. Merritt. Your husband's bound to have gotten Serena pregnant because it's widely known in town that he paid the colored doctor in Hertford to give her the abortion that caused her to bleed to death several days later. Although that doctor's been dead for several years, I'm convinced dozens of colored people in town will swear to the truth of everything I've said when it comes to a trial, which I'm sure it will."

"That threat doesn't scare me a bit, Chief Trumble!" Mrs. Merritt snapped. "No jury will ev'uh trust somethin a darky says in court. And by your own admission, Serena died ov'uh nine years ago. If my hus'bun caused her death either direc'ly or indirec'ly, which I categorically deny, and if Matthew had wanted to avenge her death, which I deny just as categorically, why did Matthew wait so long to kill my hus'bun? Furthermore, there hasn't been a bit o trouble between 'em durin the last dozen yea'uhs. So your charge is *outraj'us* and you know it!"

"That's baloney although I'm convinced the idea of killing Mr. Merritt didn't originate with Matthew. As I see it, someone much closer to him had an even stronger motive for wanting him dead. Furthermore, that person probably paid Matthew several hundred dollars to find another man to cut his throat shortly after Matthew and Jamilla left the area so I wouldn't be able to question them about their part in your husband's death. In my opinion there were at least three people involved in the plot against your husband's life, as you're bound to have known for several days if not much longer."

Although Joe had been following their exchange closely, he was jolted when Marguerite snapped, "I've *nev'uh* been so insulted in my whole life! You have no reason to think I was involved in my hus'bun's death in any way!"

At that point Willie reappeared with the letters his mother had asked him to find in a drawer of her dressing table. In several seconds she flipped through them and found a rough draft of the letter of recommendation she'd written on Matthew's behalf. Shortly after passing that draft to Burt, she passed him the note Lucy had included in the same envelope she'd sent Marguerite a check for the $400 in cash that the latter had sent her several days before. Finally Marguerite passed Burt the rough draft of the note she'd sent Lucy in which she thanked her for returning her $400 so promptly.

As Burt glanced at those rough drafts and Lucy's note to Marguerite, she said with barely concealed anger, "If you'd like to see my actual lett'uhs to Lucy, you can always check with her. I'm sure she's kept 'em because she's a very methodical puh'son and somethin of a pack rat, as I'm sure Doc'tuh Hanford will attest. My correspondence with her proves beyond a shadow of a doubt that I liked Matthew a great deal and helped him and his wife leave the area for a good honest reason and def'nitely *not* because I'd arranged for them to kill my hus'bun fo me. And now, because I'm so upset by his death and your *outra'jus* suggestion that I was involved in his death in some way, I trust you'll be a gen'leman and let me return to my bedroom and lie down. Flossie will show you and Doc'tuh Hanford to the front door if you can't find it by yo'selves. Good day to you both; and until you catch my hus'bun's kill'uh, I see no need fo any fu'thuh contact between us. But to assist you in yo investigation, I plan to off'uh a reward o fifteen hundred doll'uhs for information that leads to the kill'uh's arrest and conviction."

After having her say Marguerite swept out of the breakfast room before disappearing up the backstairs as Willie followed her with her veil and enormous black hat like the dutiful son he'd always been and would remain for the rest of his life.

After leaving the mansion Burt and Joe drove back to the police station on East Main Street, absorbed in their own thoughts and reflections. By the time they entered Burt's office and took comfortable chairs on either side of his desk, they were ready to discuss their thoughts about why the murder had occurred and who'd actually committed it, which took them the greater part of an hour.

Burt started their conversation by saying, "Marguerite gave a great performance this morning. Even a famous actress like Sarah Bernhardt couldn't have played the role any better."

"I'm not sure she was acting," Joe said. "The rough drafts of her notes to Lucy and the draft of her letter of recommendation on Matthew's behalf don't support your view that he killed Mr. Merritt last night or found the man who killed him for her."

"That's true, but those drafts don't support her claim to be completely innocent either. In fact, I'm convinced those drafts are nothing but a smokescreen to mislead me and other investigators about her role in her husband's death. So despite the fact that two of the house keys were missing, I'm convinced she planned the crime and paid Matthew or another man he found for her and ended her husband's life for a third or possibly half of the money she returned to Lucy several weeks ago."

"Even if you're right that Matthew or a man he found for her actually killed Mr. Merritt last night and wound up with a third or half of Marguerite's four hundred dollars, none of the evidence supports that conclusion. Besides, I've heard George Kahle say a number of times—and he has dozens of friends in Edenton—that Mr. Merritt was widely known to cheat at cards and made several bitter enemies as a result. So it seems likely to me that one of those enemies left a poker game fifteen or twenty minutes early one night and took the house key he knew Merritt kept under his car's front seat. And an hour or so after another poker game broke up a week later, that man used the key he'd stolen earlier to let himself into the mansion shortly after midnight and killed Mr. Merritt shortly after he fell asleep on the sofa in the study."

"I'm well aware of the rumors that Merritt cheated at cards, but that theory's too complicated to suit me—correct theories are usually much simpler than that. Besides, if a man Merritt cheated out of some big money during several poker games in Edenton stole the key Merritt kept under his car's front seat and used it after another game a week or two later, how did Merritt get into his house after driving back to it from Edenton on the night his key was stolen, and last night as well?"

"Hmmmmmm, I see your point," Joe said. "But because of my theory's obvious weakness, what are your thoughts about why the murder occurred?"

After thinking for several moments Burt said, "Despite the common view, most murders are committed by a family member, not by a burglar or someone who's bent on revenge because of an earlier insult or injury. Partly because of that, I'm convinced Marguerite was the real instigator of her husband's murder. In my opinion she arranged for Matthew to kill her husband last night and paid Matthew all or most of the money Lucy returned to her several weeks ago. But if Matthew didn't actually commit the crime, which seems plausible, I'm sure he found the man who killed Merritt for at least a third of the money Marguerite gave Matthew several days or a week ago."

"You're probably right about that," Joe said after considering Burt's comments for several moments. "But I'm still troubled by one aspect of your theory. If Mr. Merritt had a bitter fight with Matthew slightly over nine years ago, which Matthew never forgave and played an important part in his decision to kill his employer or find another man to kill him, why didn't Merritt fire him back in August of 'ought-one? Isn't that what most men would've done?"

"Sure, most men would've killed Merritt at the time of their fight over a serious matter like that, and you've and asked me a tough question," Burt conceded. "But I actually heard Merritt fire Matthew shortly after I ended that fight, which had been triggered by Serena's death from her botched abortion several days earlier. But despite how much Matthew hated Mr. Merritt and held him responsible for Serena's death, I'm sure he valued his job and knew it would be almost impossible for him to find another one like it without a good reference from his former employer. So Matthew told Merritt shortly after he fired him that if he was forced to leave the Merritt House and find another job, he'd go straight to the courthouse and ruin his reputation in town."

"I have no doubts Matthew made a threat like that, but how could he have ruined Merritt's reputation in this day and age? Think about it for a minute, Burt—at this point in time how could any colored man have ruined the reputation of a white man as rich and prominent as William Merritt?"

"That would've been impossible for most colored men, but I'm convinced Matthew could've done it because of Merritt's reputation for taking advantage of dozens of colored girls since he was a teenager. Furthermore, several years before he seduced Serena, he slept with another beautiful colored girl named Carlotta Jones, who also died shortly after she had an abortion Merritt forced her to get from the colored doctor in

Hertford. In contrast to Merritt's terrible reputation in town, Matthew was considered an honest and respectable man by all the blacks and most of the whites in the area. So when Merritt fired Matthew in August of 'ought-one and Matthew threatened to go to the courthouse and swear on a Bible that Merritt had been responsible for Serena's death as well as Carlotta Jones' several years before, Merritt backed down and said, 'Oh, you can keep your job, you fuckin nigger. But if you ever threaten me again, I'll kill you with my bare hands, I swear to God I will!'"

"That sounds just like Merritt," Joe said. "He was the worst man I've ever met, and I met some real jerks in Richmond while I was in medical school and doing my residency there. But I'm still having trouble with one part of your theory. If Matthew had a strong motive for killing Merritt from the day Serena died, why did he wait over nine years to cut his throat last night?"

"I can't say for sure although my hunch is this—shortly after Matthew married Jamilla back in August and she joined the Merritts' staff a week later, Merritt made several moves on her. Didn't you ever notice Jamilla in town? She worked for Tom and Louise Stanton for six or seven years before she married Matthew and joined the Merritts' staff at his suggestion. She's even more beautiful than Serena or Carlotta Jones were, and I know for a fact that dozens of men in town lusted after her. At any rate, I'm convinced Matthew was deeply worried that he was about to seduce Jamilla, just as he'd seduced Serena and Carlotta Jones during earlier years. And I'm just as sure Matthew was determined to keep Merritt from having his way with his second wife and getting her pregnant, which might lead to her death shortly after she had a botched abortion at Merritt's insistence. I could be wrong, of course, but I have a hunch Matthew had no plan to kill his employer when he moved Jamilla out of their cabin behind the Merritts' smoke house around the middle of September—at that time he just wanted to protect her from Merritt's advances, which explains why she started living with Matthew's parents or his younger brother and his family. But that turned out to be a stopgap measure because Matthew hated living by himself in the cabin that had been his home for over twenty years. So he and Jamilla decided to leave the area and find better-paying jobs up North where they'd never have to worry about Merritt's lust for Jamilla again. But when Matthew gave Marguerite formal notice in early October and told her about their decision to leave the area, she realized at once that he and Jamilla would need some fairly big money for their trip to New York or Chicago and their first several months in the North because there was almost no chance good jobs would fall into their laps in a week or two. So Marguerite was clearly in a position to use Matthew to kill her husband, who'd abused her for years and embarrassed the hell out of her by sleeping with dozens of colored girls, which he was still doing despite the bald-faced lie Marguerite told us at her breakfast table morning."

"That theory makes perfect sense to me, Burt. But I'm afraid you'll need a lot more than a theory before you arrest Marguerite and charge her with conspiring to have her husband killed by Matthew or another man last night."

"Yeah, you're right about that and my theory about her motive for having her husband killed is much weaker than I'd like it to be. Of course it's common knowledge that her husband's actions upset her for years, but there's bound to be a lot more to it than that. It seems to me she must've been worried by her husband's strange behavior since the hurricane back in August. Joe, you attended the special meeting of the town council on the night of the sixteenth and heard all the ridiculous things he said before he stomped out of the room. In addition, the letters he sent to the *Tribune* during the next several weeks made it seem like he'd lost all his marbles. Because you were his doctor, didn't you ever think he'd gone bonkers during those months of his life?"

"No, although I'm sure he'd come down with syphilis. People who have that disease usually become paranoid and extremely suspicious of other people and their motives. And the wild charges Merritt made against Chip, Andrew Ridinger, Randall Porter, and Dan Wiley in his second letter to the *Tribune* were truly paranoid, don't you think? Besides, Chip told me one night after dinner that Marguerite had been sending Matthew to the drugstore every eight or nine days for small doses of arsenic and mercury, which are the only things I'm aware of that can be used to lessen the pain of people who've come down with syphilis."

"Great balls of fire! Everything falls into place now."

"It does?"

"Sure, because the fact that Merritt had syphilis is the last piece of the puzzle. Marguerite put up with his beatings and affairs with colored girls for years and was probably resigned to endure them for the rest of her life or until he died of natural causes first. But everything changed when she found out he had syphilis. At that point she's bound to have become deeply worried about her own life because of the chance he might force himself on her one night and give her that fatal and extremely painful disease."

"Even if you're right about that, it's still only a theory, isn't it?"

"No, because there's some strong circumstantial evidence to back it up. Several weeks ago I overheard Tulip telling several friends in Hogan's Grocery Store about all the tension at the Merritt House. According to Tulip, Marguerite had been barricading her bedroom door against her husband for six or seven weeks. But when I asked Tulip about it, she clammed up and paid for everything on her list at once. Then she and Flossie left the store and drove off in the Merritts' wagon without saying another word to me or their friends. So Marguerite clearly had a strong motive for ending her husband's life for several weeks before Matthew gave her formal notice. On the day he told her he'd decided to resign from her staff and take Jamilla to a big Northern city, she probably offered to pay him several hundred dollars to kill her husband on the night before they left town so I wouldn't be able to question them the next morning, meaning today of course. But if Matthew had some qualms about committing the murder himself, he agreed to find another man who had no qualms about killing a widely hated white man for, let's say, a hundred and fifty dollars. Furthermore, if it ever came to light that Marguerite had given Matthew several hundred dollars a week or so before her husband was murdered and Matthew and his wife left the area, Marguerite could insist that the money she gave him was only an expression of her deep appreciation for his long and faithful service at the Merritt House."

After agreeing with Burt again, Joe said that theory also explained why Marguerite had sent the $400 she eventually gave Matthew to kill her husband, or find another man to commit the crime for her, to Lucy first on the grounds it was an overdue payment for a debt she owed Lucy's mother when she died in February 1908.

"That's right too, Joe. And because Mrs. Merritt was sure Lucy would return her money to her in several days, it was an easy way to get the money she planned to pay Matthew out of the bank without causing her husband to become suspicious of why she'd withdrawn so much money from their joint checking account. After all, she had to keep him from thinking his life was in danger, which wasn't an easy matter given how paranoid he'd become because of his syphilis."

"Yeah, I agree with all that too," Joe said at once. "But couldn't Matthew have kept all her money for himself if he killed Merritt shortly before he and Jamilla left the area?"

"Yes, but Matthew's a smart guy and I'm sure it occurred to him that if he killed Merritt late night, I'd come looking for him as soon as I heard about the murder the next morning. After all, I'd ended his bitter fight with Mr. Merritt slightly over nine years ago and knew he had a strong motive for wanting the man dead. So I'm convinced he told Marguerite it would be much safer for him and Jamilla if they left the area a day or two before the murder was committed by a man he found to kill her husband and probably gave at least a third of her money to, which would leave him and Jamilla with a fairly large sum they could live on until they found good jobs up North."

Burt was clearly pleased that they'd come up with such a convincing theory of the murder and the motives behind it so fast.

Joe wasn't completely convinced, however, and said to Burt, "I'm afraid I have another question for you now. It seems to me that if our theory's correct, Marguerite took a big chance if she planned the crime the way you think she did. After all, once she gave Matthew four hundred dollars, how could she be sure he'd give a large part of that money to another man who promised to kill her husband shortly after Matthew and Jamilla left the area? In other words, wasn't there a good chance Matthew would cheat her out of all that money and the next morning her husband would still be alive and as much a threat to her life as ever?"

"Yeah, that's true," Burt conceded, somewhat dejected. But after thinking for several moments he said, "I'll admit Marguerite couldn't be absolutely sure Matthew wouldn't cheat her in the way you've suggested. But on the other hand, Marguerite was desperate and probably felt it was a chance worth taking. Besides, four hundred dollars wouldn't seem like that much money to her because, by her own admission this morning, she usually spends twice as much on her children's winter clothes each year. Furthermore she probably felt she could trust Matthew to honor his promise to her because he was still furious about her husband's role in Serena's death nine years earlier. And one last point, Joe——I'll bet you a month's salary that Matthew hoped to find a way to keep Merritt from preying on colored girls in the future as he'd done dozens of times in the past."

"Those are good points but another question just occurred to me. Let's assume that Matthew actually found the man who killed Merritt last night and gave him roughly a third of the money Marguerite had paid him several days earlier. And if we assume those things, how could Matthew and Mrs. Merritt be absolutely certain that man would show up and commit the crime? In other words, couldn't the man who accepted roughly a hundred and fifty dollars from Matthew a day or two before Matthew and Jamilla left the area simply have 'forgotten' about the crime he'd already been paid to commit last night?"

After thinking for a while Burt said to Joe, "You've asked me some tough questions this morning but that's the toughest one yet. In fact, I'm stumped by it."

"No, it wasn't that tough because I've already thought of a possible answer to it."

"You have? Then let's hear it."

"Okay, but I'd like to state several basic points first. Like you, I'm convinced Marguerite paid Matthew to find the man who killed her husband for her last night, and I'm just as convinced they agreed that the murder should be committed last night several hours after Matthew and Jamilla boarded a northbound train at the Hertford station. Finally, I'm convinced that Marguerite realized there was a chance the man Matthew found and gave a fairly large part of her money to in return for killing her husband wouldn't show up and do the deed despite his promise to Matthew. So consider this possible scenario, Burt—Marguerite gave Matthew only two hundred dollars before telling him to inform the man he'd found to kill her husband that he wouldn't receive a penny of his own two hundred dollars until the hour he ended Mr. Merritt's life."

"That makes sense provided they came up with a way to get the killer's money to him shortly after he committed the crime and Matthew and Jamilla were already on a train headed for Richmond and points farther North."

"That would've been easy as long as there was no misunderstanding about the night and approximate time the murder would take place. If I'm right about those things and last night was the agreed-on night, as it clearly was, Marguerite crept down the backstairs shortly after midnight when she was fairly sure her husband had fallen asleep on the study sofa. Once she was on the mansion's ground floor, she checked to be sure that he was before unlocking the back door for the killer and leaving a hundred dollars on the breakfast table, where the killer was bound to see it before she hid in the butler's pantry or possibly the family dining room. A short while later the killer entered the house through the back door and went through both kitchens to the breakfast room where he pocketed the first half of his money, which he saw on the breakfast table. Then he went through the center hall to the study and slit Mr. Merritt's throat at the same time Marguerite put the killer's remaining hundred dollars on the breakfast table before hiding again. Shortly after the killer left the study and picked up the rest of his money, he left the mansion a minute or two before Marguerite locked the back door and returned to her bedroom while the killer vanished into the night. And because she'd never seen killer's face or heard Matthew mention his name a single time, the killer knew there was no chance he'd be linked to the crime in any way."

"I'd agree with all that except for one thing—I told you earlier in our conversation that the simplest theories are usually correct. And it just occurred to me that Marguerite probably killed her husband herself, which would've saved her all that money and kept her from having to depend on Matthew to find another man to commit the murder shortly after Matthew and Jamilla boarded a train headed North."

After thinking about those comments for several moments Joe said to Burt, "Although what you just said is plausible, it has a major weakness in my opinion. After all, it suggests that Marguerite was an even bigger villain than my theory does. Besides, while you were questioning her at the mansion earlier today, she denied any part in her husband's death so vehemently I'm convinced she didn't kill him herself. Besides, her husband was a fairly big man, and what if Marguerite failed to kill him on her first attempt? If she merely wounded him and he woke up and saw her standing over him with a butcher knife in her hand, it's easy to imagine the horror she would've felt. That's why I'm convinced the killer was a man who was big and strong enough to finish him off without any trouble if his first attempt to kill him failed."

"Yeah, those things make good sense and you've tied up all the loose ends of our theory. So in my opinion at least, we've come up with a convincing explanation of why the murder occurred and how it was carried out."

"I agree, but I'm afraid you'll have a hard time finding Matthew and the man who actually commited the crime. After all, you have no real evidence to go on and only a vague idea of where Matthew and Jamilla are headed—it could be New York, Chicago, Detroit, or one of several dozen other Northern cities. Furthermore, if you ask Matthew's brother or parents where they've gone, I'm sure they'll give you a bum steer. Of course Matthew's brother could be the man who actually killed Mr. Merritt last night although I seriously doubt that Matthew involved his only brother in a capital crime. In any event, I'm sure Matthew's brother would swear he knew nothing about the crime in advance while his wife and children would insist he was home with them all last night."

Drumming his fingers on the top of his desk, Burt considered those points for several moments before saying, "I'm sure you're right that Matthew's brother wasn't involved in the crime in any way. But if Matthew actually hired another man to commit the murder, which I'm convinced he did, how the hell could I find him when I have only one full-time cop on my staff and two part-timers? We have only one car, a dumb little Buggymobile whose top speed is thirty miles an hour even in good weather. I can't believe you actually think I could catch Matthew and his wife in a car like that when I have only a vague idea of where they're headed. Besides, I have no money for special investigations; and worst of all, Perquimmons City doesn't have phone service yet. So the only way I can stay in touch with other police departments is through the telegraph system, which is expensive and fairly cumbersome. Given all those facts, what would you do if you were in my shoes?"

"Those are good points, and if I were in your shoes I'd probably punt, which sounds like what you've decided to do. But I hope you'll inform the attorney general's office in Raleigh about the crime. If you don't and the bureaucrats in that office hear about it from another source, you'll be in big trouble, my friend."

"Yeah, that's right, so I'll definitely send them a telegram about the murder in a day or two. My telegram will probably say I have no idea who the killer was and the trail's already fairly cold. Furthermore, it'll say that while I have a hunch it was an inside job, there's only some circumstantial evidence to support that theory because the murder was planned and carried out with great skill."

"Then you're not going to make any effort to bring Marguerite to justice?"

"Jeez, I wish you hadn't put it like that, Joe. If you consider the crime in one light, wouldn't you agree that Marguerite's guilty of nothing more than justifiable homicide, of trying to protect herself from an abusive husband who might give her a fatal and extremely painful disease in another week or two? Besides, I'm convinced the town council won't object if I eventually bury this murder in a drawer of my file cabinet with other unsolved crimes."

"I'm afraid I can't agree with that, Burt. It seems to me that the town council will do everything in its power to help you solve this crime."

"You really believe that, Joe? Most of the council members know how tense the racial situation has been for the last fifteen or twenty years. In places like Wilmington and Danville, Virginia, there have been bloody race riots during recent years—at least those upheavals have been called race riots although the one in Wilmington was actually a brutal attack by a white mob on dozens of poor colored people because of a newspaper article their main spokesman had written a week or two earlier. One of these days, a group of colored people is going to fight back and give white ruffians a taste of their own medicine."

"That's an unusually bleak prediction, don't you think?"

"Yes, but that doesn't mean it's wrong. If I were colored and had seen all my rights taken away by white politicians pandering to the voters' worst instincts—or if I'd seen my son or brother lynched because he whistled or looked at a white woman 'the wrong way'—I'd be willing to stand up and fight back and I bet you would too."

"Yeah, you're right about that, and to be honest I've always considered our town extremely lucky to have political leaders like Andrew Ridinger, Russell Barringer, and George Kahle. They're decent, law-abiding men, and several times I've heard them say how tense the racial situation's been during the last ten years. But that doesn't mean they'll ignore Marguerite's part in her husband's murder even if Matthew and the real killer are never caught. Because Marguerite has only a few friends in town who'll stand by her during a crisis like this, won't public opinion expect her to be punished for her part in the crime?"

"Sure, but she'll be punished for her part in the crime regardless of whether she spends the rest of her life in jail or winds up with a noose around her neck. Of course she might move back to Charleston in a year or two. But if she stays here, as I'm convinced she will, what kind of life will she have from now on? Especially if her children ever suspect she was involved in their father's death in some way. Despite all his other faults, Mr. Merritt loved his children and was a good father. Willie was almost beside himself with grief when he burst into my office this morning and said he'd found his father's body several minutes earlier. So I'm convinced he had nothing to do with the crime. And if he's completely innocent, as I'm absolutely sure he is, the chances are overwhelming that Becca and Little Robert are just as innocent. But there's a good chance they'll eventually have some questions about their mother's role in what happened last night. And what about the dozen or so people the Merritts socialized with from time to time? People like the Ridingers, the Barringers, and the Kahles among others. They're smart people who refuse to accept everything Marguerite says the way Isabel Stanton and her namby-pamby husband always do. Joe, I understand you and Julia have attended several dinner parties at the Merritt House. How do you think Julia will react when you're invited to another one?"

"That'll never happen," Joe said at once. "And for your information, Julia and I have attended only one dinner party at the Merritt House and we've *never* been invited to one of their fancy cotillions. And because we didn't reciprocate after the dinner party we attended last spring, we're convinced Marguerite will never ask us to another social event in her home which is just fine with us."

"Maybe so, but if she invites you to another party at the Merritt House several years from now, do you think you'll agree to spend another evening in the company of an awful woman who reminds me of a female insect that kills and eats its mate?"

"She reminds me of one of those insects too. So even if I continue to be the Merritts' doctor, I'll *never* take Julia to the Merritt House again under any circumstances. And I'm sure I won't hear an objection from her because of how harsh Marguerite was to Lucy during the years she worked at the Merritt House."

"I knew you'd say something like that, and I suspect everyone else I know would answer that question in the same way. So the Merritt House is about to become an even lonelier place than it's been in the past. As a result Marguerite's about to become a prisoner in her own home, don't you think?"

"Yeah, I sure do; and to make matters worse for her, she has to live with her conscience for the rest of her life, which will become even harder as she grows older. Just think how she'll feel when she's facing death and about to kneel before the Lord our Maker. Who the hell would want to be in her shoes then?"

After a busy afternoon at his office, Joe had dinner with Julia and their children. As they were enjoying a simple meal of fried chicken and vegetables Augusta fixed for them, Joe gave his family a vague explanation why the murder had occurred, convinced it would be wrong to explain the details of such a gruesome crime to Julia while Olivia and Joey were at the table.

But the next night it was the Hanfords' turn to have Lucy and Chip's branch of the family to dinner. As a result they had a much more elaborate meal of mashed potatoes, several kinds of green vegetables, a pan of Augusta's wonderful cornbread, and a large shank of venison one of Joe's poorer patients had given him for taking care of his wife during a long illness. After a slice of pumpkin pie for dessert, the five Hanford and Summerlin children gathered around the parlor upright to sing their favorite songs while the adults discussed the shocking events of the last two days in the study. After summarizing everything he'd seen and heard at the

Merritt House, Joe explained his and Chief Trumble's theory about why the murder had occurred and their reasons for believing the culprits would never be brought to justice.

Chip was annoyed and upset when Joe explained why Burt had no plan to arrest Matthew and Marguerite before a grand jury indicted them for the crime and bound them over for trial. But Lucy disagreed and said with more ardor than she actually felt, "Chip, why should Burt make any effort to bring Matthew and Marguerite to justice? Joe's already explained why Burt thinks it would be a waste of time and money to make a serious effort to find Matthew and arrest him. Besides, it was clearly justifiable homicide on Marguerite's part, don't you agree? Although I've never liked her, her life was in serious danger during the last two months and she couldn't allow her husband to live much longer once she learned he'd come down with a fatal disease he'd probably pass on to her at some point."

"No, that's completely wrong, Lucy! All criminal acts should be punished swiftly in direct relation to their severity. Only by doing that and upholding the supremacy of the law can justice prevail."

"I hate to say it but that's just plain stupid, Chip! I can hardly believe you said something so ridiculous in this day and age when the law's completely biased against colored people. If I were colored and Matthew was caught and sentenced to die for his part in Mr. Merritt's murder, I'd be absolutely furious. In fact, I'd be so furious I'd organize a protest of some kind."

Although Lucy wasn't about to tell Chip or another member of her family, she was convinced Matthew hadn't played any part in the crime because she was sure it had been committed by Flossie and Tulip. On the morning she moved out of the Merritt House early in 1901, Flossie had told Lucy in confidence that Mr. Merritt had forced himself on Tulip when she was only fifteen. In fact, Merritt had gotten Tulip pregnant and threatened to fire her unless she had an abortion at Marguerite's urging because she was determined not to have any of her husband's "little black bastards" on the premises. And while Tulip's abortion didn't cause her to bleed to death as the abortions he forced Carlotta Jones and Serena Harden to have several years later led to their deaths. Tulip's abortion made it impossible for her to become pregnant again, which had been an enormous disappointment to Flossie because she'd hoped to have several grandchildren. Furthermore, Carlotta Jones had been Flossie's niece and Tulip's first cousin, and they'd both been extremely upset when Carlotta died from the abortion Mr. Merritt forced her to have in the fall of 1897. Because Lucy never forgot how kind and helpful Flossie and Tulip had been to her during her long years at the Merritt House, she hoped to keep any suspicion from falling on them even if it meant Marguerite would never be punished or even arrested for the way she instigated the crime.

As for Chip, on hearing Lucy's hope that Matthew would never be arrested and brought to trial for his part in the murder, he blurted out, "That's *terrible*, Lucy, and I can't believe you said something so irresponsible! What would Mama and Papa say if they were still alive and heard you make such an inflammatory statement? You sound like a real firebrand to me, one who's almost as bad as that rabble-rouser in New York, Emma Goldman. She incites violence even when she doesn't actually preach it."

"Chip, you can be so pigheaded about things like this! I heard Papa say dozens of times that things have a way of turning out for the best. And Mama said just as often that most people usually get what they deserve in the end. As for myself, I'm convinced Mr. Merritt got exactly what he deserved two nights ago because I'll never forget all the terrible things he said and did during the years I lived at the Merritt House. And while I'll never condone murder, I'm convinced it would serve no purpose to bring Matthew or Mrs. Merritt to trial. Despite how much Marguerite's hated in town, she's almost untouchable because there's no real proof against her because she covered her tracks so well. Besides, I always liked and respected Matthew; and if he took part in the crime, it was only because Marguerite paid him to carry out a plan she'd hatched out of fear and desperation. Although now that I think about it, Matthew was probably motivated just as much by a strong desire to protect dozens of young colored girls from being preyed on by a man with a terrible record in that regard."

"I agree with your last several points, Lucy," Chip admitted after thinking for several moments. "But the other things you said sure make it sound like you're condoning murder in some cases. And because I'll never agree with that, I don't see how Burt can just sit on his hands and make no effort to round up everyone who was involved in the crime and bind them over for trial. After all, murder's murder, as the Ten Commandments made it clear to Moses and his followers several thousand years ago."

At that point Rhonda made several comments that ended the discussion at once. "Chip, before I decide how I feel about whether Burt should make a serious effort to solve Mr. Merritt's murder, I'd like to ask you a few questions. For example, what are *you* going to do to facilitate a long and expensive investigation by the police department? You're the town's vice mayor, and are you willing to urge the council to buy Burt and his staff a much better car than their present Buggymobile? In addition, if Burt's going to make a serious effort to find Matthew and the actual killer, the council will have to grant him and his men special funds so they can do their job. So I wonder if you're going to call for another tax increase so they can conduct a successful investigation. But remember, Chip, 'there's no such thing as a free lunch,' which I've heard you say dozens of times."

"Oh hell, you and Lucy were cut out of the same bolt of cloth. And because neither one of you takes my ideas seriously, let's change the subject now."

Rhonda and Lucy smiled sweetly at each other and accepted Chip's suggestion at once. As for Joe and Julia, who'd been listening closely to the arguments on both sides, they were so amused they came within an inch of laughing outright. But in deference to Chip's feelings, they kept their views to themselves until later in their bedroom when they laughed about Chip's rigid views for several minutes before turning off the lights and enjoying their favorite fun and games together.

Five days later a long article about Merritt's murder appeared on the front page of the *Tribune*. It summarized the facts that were known about the crime shortly before the paper went to press. Rather interestingly, that article implied, doubtless at Chief Trumble's suggestion, that the murder had been committed by an Edenton man the victim had cheated at cards a number of times. That article also announced that the town council of Perquimmons City had decided to double the $1,500 reward Mrs. Merritt had already offered for information leading to the arrest and conviction of her husband's killer and any accomplices that man might have had.

During dinner at the Summerlins' house two nights later, Joe asked Chip if the town council expected to pay the reward it was offering for information that led to the killer's—or killers'—arrest and conviction. Chip's resounding No and suggestion that they change the subject at once caused Lucy and Rhonda to exchange knowing smiles again.

The next afternoon Julia wrote a letter to Frances Van Landingham who'd recently returned to New York from a ten-day trip to Louisville and Indianapolis, where her husband had opened two more offices of his company. In her letter to Frances, Julia summarized Chief Trumble's actual theory about why the murder had occurred but not the theory reported in the *Tribune*, which the Van Landinghams could read for themselves in the newspaper clipping Julia attached to her letter with a paper clip. Julia's letter also explained Chief Trumble's belief that while Mrs. Merritt had been the real instigator of the crime, there was almost no chance she'd ever be brought to trial for instigating the murder and paying her husband's killer shortly before the crime occurred. But even if Marguerite was never punished for what she'd done, she was about to become a prisoner in her own home for the rest of her life.

After writing that letter to Frances, Julia folded it and placed it and the clipping in an envelope she addressed and stamped before leaving it on the credenza in the entrance hall, where Joe would see it the next morning and take it to the post office for her. Julia felt Frances and her husband would find that clipping and the two theories about why the murder had occurred quite interesting.

Chapter 12

Julia was surprised and very pleased when she received a letter from Frances in only nine days because it usually took her several weeks to respond. After a paragraph about the operas and concerts she and Bill had attended during the last month, the rest of Frances's letter read:

> Bill and I were sorry to read about the death of William Merritt. Of course, I never met the man and Bill didn't like him at all. But it's very sad that his wife arranged for him to be killed in his own home. If he was going to die of syphilis in another year or two anyway, it seems to me she should have taken her children to Charleston until someone in town informed her of her husband's death. In my opinion, that would have been a much better way to handle the problem that confronted her.
>
> Now, my dear Julia, I wish to discuss a development that has excited me a great deal. Although I didn't realize it until last night, Bill has had some serious reservations about building a winter home in Florida since that dreadful hurricane in August did so much damage to Palm Beach and dozens of other places in Florida before moving up the coast to the Carolinas and Virginia. A lovely Palm Beach house owned by of one of Bill's clients who had us to dinner several times while we were there last winter was washed away, while the partly finished homes of two other couples we know quite well were flattened like pancakes. Because of the heavy losses our friends suffered,

Bill had decided to buy some land on the eastern shore of Maryland or Virginia when your letter arrived yesterday. After reading it and the newspaper clipping about Mr. Merritt's death, I showed them to Bill shortly after we finished dinner, thinking the time had come to express my views to him with total honesty and candor. I waited until he read your letter and the clipping before telling him that I'd accepted his decision to build a winter home in Florida because that was his strong preference. But now that he's decided to sell our Palm Beach lot even if he takes a loss on it, I see no reason for us to buy any land in Maryland or Virginia. I pointed out that they're only a short distance closer to New York than eastern North Carolina, although probably somewhat colder in winter. Before he could object, I also pointed out that we know no one—not a single person—in either state while we've already met a number of extremely nice people in Perquimmons City, thanks to you and Joe, whose company Bill has thoroughly enjoyed whenever they've been together. In addition, our children are about the same age as yours and your brother Chip's, which would be a great boon to Billy and Barbara. Finally, I told him about the direct rail connection between Hertford and Winston-Salem which you pointed out to me on the lovely day I spent with you and your friends in Perquimmons City. I've missed Doris Mary so much since she and Gerald moved to Winston-Salem five years ago.

After considering my arguments, Bill agreed that we should definitely think about buying some land in or a few miles from Perquimmons City now. He also suggested that we make another visit to the area shortly after Christmas, when our children will be out of school and can come with us. He feels they should see the town and meet Olivia and Joey, whom we're both sure they'll like a great deal, before we buy some land in eastern North Carolina. But Bill made one important stipulation—he's convinced that if we build our winter home in or near Perquimmons City, we should definitely build it on the *eastern* side of town, which he's heard is fairly hilly and so high above the level of the Sound it's never flooded when a hurricane sweeps across the area. Furthermore, a winter home on the eastern side of town would be far enough away from the Merritt House we'll never have to worry about an unexpected visit from Marguerite, whom Bill has no wish to see again.

I hope you're as pleased about our second visit to Perquimmons City as I am, dear Julia.

Julia was so excited by Frances's letter she was eager to tell Joe and Lucy about it at once. So she put on her winter coat and favorite bonnet; and because Prancer and the buggy were at Sonny's livery stable several blocks away, she decided to ride Olivia's bicycle to the drugstore before riding it to Joe's office. In no time she found the bike leaning against one side of the garage and rode out of the driveway on it. As she sailed down the avenue toward the middle of town, she saw Joe chugging in her direction in his Maxwell, probably on his way to see a patient who lived on the Hertford Road. When Julia motioned for him to pull over, he did so with a puzzled look. After coming to a stop he took off his driving goggles as Julia propped the bike against the side of his car and put one foot on the running board. Then she started talking a mile a minute, as she usually did when she was excited about something.

Her summary of Frances's letter caused Joe to smile and say, "That's *wonderful* news, Julia, and let's invite Bill and Frances and their children to our New Year's Eve party so they can meet most of our friends. Tell her about our party when you write her back and how much we're looking forward to seeing them and their children again. But I need to get to the Crumplers' house now and see if Olive's as congested as she was two days ago when I saw her at my office. Ozzie hired a colored girl to stay with her while he's busy at the hotel, but I'm afraid that girl knows very little about medicine."

Julia said she would definitely tell Frances about their New Year's Eve party in her next letter before she resumed her trip down the avenue on Olivia's bike. Meanwhile, Joe put on his goggles again and released the car's hand brake before continuing his trip to the Crumplers' house on a cul-de-sac a short distance beyond the northern town limits.

Shortly after rushing into the drugstore, Julia joined Lucy at the soda fountain where she was helping Dillie at the moment. At a nearby table the four big shots were having their morning coffee. They ended their conversation at once and listened with great interest to Julia's summary of Frances's letter for Lucy and Chip, who'd come over from the drug counter to see what all the commotion was about. When Julia paused to catch her breath, Ozzie asked her from his chair if he should reserve the hotel's only suite for Bill and Frances and the rooms directly across the hall from the suite for their children. He could let them have those accommodations for only $14.50 a night.

A bit annoyed by Ozzie's pushiness, Julia said she couldn't tell him anything definite that morning. But she planned to write Frances that afternoon and would let Ozzie know whatever she could shortly after she received another letter from her.

In less than a week most of the townspeople were buzzing about Bill and Frances's second visit to Perquimmons City and the fact that they were bringing their children with them this time, which suggested that they'd decided to build their winter home in the area. In several more days Julia received invitations from a dozen friends who wanted her to bring Frances to afternoon teas or bridge parties in their homes.

As for the four big shots, they hatched some plans of their own. George Kahle thought of several ways to suggest, very tactfully of course, that he was available for any legal help or advice the Van Landinghams might need during their coming visit. Because Andrew Ridinger felt Bill's financial expertise would be a great boon to the bank, he thought of ways to convince him to buy at least fifty shares of bank stock, which would make him eligible to serve on its executive committee.

Ozzie Crumpler and Russell Barringer cobbled together a plan to sell the Van Landinghams several adjacent tracts of land with excellent frontage on the Sound and the lower part of Hatcher's Creek several miles east of town. During the last decade Ozzie and Russell had stripped their 803 acres of all their mature trees for their saw mill with the exception of fifty or sixty majestic water oaks, which they spared in the event they ever sold those tracts for residential purposes. As it happened, most of the other landowners in the area had followed Ozzie and Russell's lead and stripped their own lands of most of their mature trees, which had led the local lumber market to become so glutted the price per board-foot had fallen by two-thirds since July. As a result Ozzie and Russell's saw mill was unprofitable now and barely made enough money to pay the taxes on the land, causing Ozzie and Russell to decide to sell it as soon as possible. The Van Landinghams' impending return to the area led them to think they might find a buyer for their three tracts much sooner than they'd thought they could.

Luckily for Joe and Julia, they had no inkling about the plans the four big shots hatched so fast. Had the Hanfords been aware of their plans, they would've felt great foreboding rather than the enormous optimism they actually felt.

Julia was normally a calm and patient person. But she was so excited by the Van Landinghams' next visit, she felt the two months before their arrival would never end. In fact, she complained constantly about how long the days and weeks seemed to be. Whenever Lucy suggested they'd pass somewhat faster if she remained busy, Julia complained about that too before saying she didn't want to hear it again.

Despite Julia's peevishness, Lucy enjoyed her company as much as ever. And while Julia complained about Lucy's advice to remain busy, she was soon immersed in projects that took her mind off her impatience to see Bill and Frances again. Because the holiday season was almost at hand, there was lots of cooking and baking to do as well as dozens of Christmas presents to buy or make. During earlier years Julia and Augusta had always made three or four fruitcakes, several pounds of mincemeat, and six or seven gallons of apple cider they kept in large crocks in the coolest part of the basement. That fall Julia decided to make eight fruitcakes and twice as much mincemeat and apple cider as usual because of the dozen people who would arrive in town shortly after Christmas Day. Not only would the four Van Landinghams arrive on the morning of December 28, but that afternoon Frances's sister, Doris Mary Babcock, and her husband Gerald would arrive from Winston-Salem with their three-year-old twins, Jillian and Caitlyn. On the next afternoon Joe's parents and brother and sister-in-law would arrive from Salisbury.

On Monday morning, November 21, when Julia told Ozzie Crumpler at the drugstore about all the people who would arrive on December 28 and 29, he was very pleased and offered to reserve the rear wing of the hotel's third floor for them. Julia considered that a good idea; and shortly after dinner that night, she wrote letters informing Frances, Doris Mary Babcock, and Joe's mother about the rooms that were being held for them.

By Thanksgiving Julia had finished a new party dress for Olivia and a handsome sweater for Joey, who'd turned thirteen on November 5 and was the most popular boy in the sixth grade. Ordinarily Joey would have been in the seventh grade during his thirteenth year. But because his birthday occurred two months after the first day of school during the year he would normally have entered the first grade and his parents felt he wasn't quite ready for school at that time, Joe and Julia held him back a year after a great deal of soul searching. Almost as important as his relative immaturity in 1903, they felt he'd be better off if he was two grades and not just one behind his extremely precocious and competitive sister. Now, at the age of thirteen in the fall of 1910, Joey was extremely tall and strong for his age. He was also an even better athlete than his father had been, partly because Joe encouraged his interest in sports from the summer he was four and played catch with him several times a week. As a result Joey loved football and baseball and excelled at both. He was also well on his way to becoming an excellent boxer because of his father's instruction and his own physical skills, especially his outstanding coordination and hair-trigger responses. Finally, Joey was a gifted student who made all *A*s except for an occasional *B* or *B*+. Olivia ribbed him about his occasional *B*s until he retaliated by making fun of her interest in classical music, which had led his friends to consider her a real "egghead," a term Olivia hated.

On Thanksgiving Day Joey wore a new sport coat and pair of slacks his father had bought him at Shelton & Walters in Edenton, the best men's store in the area. When Lucy saw her oldest nephew in those clothes at church during the Thanksgiving service, she suddenly realized how handsome and grown-up he'd become. During the social hour in the parish house shortly after the service ended, Lucy warned her oldest nephew to be on his guard because one of the prettiest girls in his class would probably set her cap for him by Christmas if she hadn't done so already. Although Joey blushed and seemed embarrassed, he was clearly pleased by the idea that he was old enough to have a girlfriend.

On December 4 the whole family celebrated Susan Summerlin's fourteenth birthday at Chip and Rhonda's house. Susan looked unusually pretty in the new party dress Rhonda had made for her with Julia's help. In fact, Susan looked so radiant that night Chip and Lucy were reminded of Julia's great beauty at the same age.

Ten days later the family celebrated Olivia's fourteenth birthday at the Hanfords' house. Although Olivia wasn't as attractive as Susan, everyone but Joey and Alfred complimented her on how elegant and sophisticated she looked in her new party dress.

As Joe made a toast to both girls' health and happiness that night, Lucy wondered what sort of person Billy Van Landingham was. He was two weeks older than Susan, and his parents were tall and very good-looking. Wasn't Billy likely to be tall and good-looking too? Of course, he might have a girlfriend in New York or the small New England town where his prep school was located. But if Billy didn't have a girlfriend yet, there was a chance he'd develop some feelings for Susan or Olivia. And if he did, would that girl be as interested in him? Probably; but if a serious attraction developed between him and one of Lucy's nieces, how would the excluded girl feel about her more successful cousin? Was the unusually close relationship they'd enjoyed since they were toddlers about to be tested and possibly destroyed? *Interesting and intriguing questions,* Lucy thought before wondering if anyone else in the family was as curious about that matter as she was.

That year's Christmas Eve service went extremely well and every seat in the church was taken, largely because of Mr. Thompson's excellent and fairly short sermons and Maxine Payne's outstanding leadership of the music program. On Christmas Day Lucy had dinner at the Hanfords' house with the rest of her family, and the next morning she puttered around her cottage because the drugstore was closed that day. She read the first six chapters of John Galsworthy's famous novel *The Forsyte Saga*, a Christmas present from Chip and Rhonda, before crocheting the first several inches of a runner for her kitchen table. After a light lunch and a short nap with Mr. Jobie near her pillow, she went next door and spent several hours with Hazel Barlow. On returning to her own cottage, she straightened up her closets and did some ironing before fixing a simple supper of soup and sandwiches for Hazel and herself.

When Lucy returned to work the next morning, she felt rested and refreshed. When the big shots arrived for their morning coffee, she decided to tease Ozzie Crumpler a bit in her devilish way. "Well, Ozzie," she said seriously after handing him a mug of steaming coffee, "is everything ready for all the people who'll be arriving at the hotel during the next couple of days?"

"Yes, ma'am, Miz Lucy, it sure is. I took care of everything myself shortly before Christmas so there won't be any slipups."

"You probably had to scramble when you heard Mr. Van Landingham's cousins and half-sisters decided to come to town at the last minute."

"What cousins and half-sisters?" Ozzie asked with a pained look. "Nobody told me about them and how many are there?"

"Six or seven if I remember correctly," Lucy said while trying not to grin. "Of course, there may be several more than that. But regardless of the number, you'd better do something fast because Julia's told me several times that they're extremely picky and insist on having the best food and accommodations wherever they go."

"Oh, my God!" Ozzie said before jumping up and making a beeline for the side door. The other big shots stifled their laughter until Ozzie was about to leave the building for the hotel. At that point George Kahle called to him, "Come on back and finish your coffee, Ozzie. Lucy was only joking."

Ozzie turned around slowly and unsurely, not knowing what to think. But when he saw Lucy's grin, he ambled back to the table while saying, "That was really mean of you, Lucy. It almost caused me to have a heart attack, and if I'd dropped dead right here in the drugstore it would've been on your conscience for the rest of your life."

"You're right and I apologize, Ozzie. I guess I'm almost as nervous as you are about how everything will go during the coming week."

By four thirty Wednesday afternoon the eight visitors from Winston-Salem and New York had arrived and checked into the hotel. Two hours later they walked up the avenue to the Hanfords' house, where Julia and Augusta, with help from Augusta's daughter Creola and Creola's best friend, Alethea Basham, James's wife, had fixed an excellent dinner for them as well as the ten Hanfords and Summerlins. Because Joe had added all four leaves to the dining room table, it was just long enough to seat eighteen people; and while the room was a bit crowded, no one complained because it was a joyful occasion with a great deal of laughter and merriment. Billy and Susan sat in adjacent chairs on one side the table and were so attracted to each other they played footsie under the table most of the time, to Olivia's dismay and Joey's great amusement. But he was unable to tease Olivia about the situation because his parents were watching him like a hawk and gave him a stern look whenever he was about to make a comment at his sister's expense.

When Lucy finished a sliver of mincemeat pie with a dollop of whipped cream on top, she felt completely full. By that point the Babcock twins were beginning to fret in their highchairs (Olivia and Joey's childhood chairs, which Joey brought down from the attic that morning at his mother's request). As most of the adults at the table waited for Joe to open a bottle of port while Creola and Alethea brought in large bowls of nuts and fresh fruit and a tray of several kinds of cheese and crackers Lucy felt she should avoid because of her growing girth, she offered to take the Babcock twins to the study and read them a story there. Doris Mary thanked her warmly before saying that wasn't necessary.

Lucy persisted, however, and during the next hour she concentrated on entertaining the twins although she felt extremely sorry for Julia at the same time. Julia was slated to give another dinner party the next night for Bill and Frances—their children and the Hanfords' would be having dinner at the Summerlins' house at the time—as well as for the Babcocks and Joe's parents and brother and sister-in-law, who were scheduled to arrive from Salisbury at four fifteen that Thursday afternoon. And two nights after that the Hanfords would give a New Year's Eve party for a hundred people. Fortunately, Joe and Julia loved to entertain and were never upset when several minor mistakes occurred. Only once, when Joey was eleven and dropped a large bowl of eggnog on the kitchen floor, had Lucy ever seen Joe and Julia upset during the course of one of their four or five parties during most years.

On the morning of December 29, almost seven hours before Joe's family was due to arrive at the Hertford station, Bill Van Landingham joined the four big shots at their usual table at the drugstore for a cup of coffee and some conversation. When that group of dignitaries broke up twenty minutes later, Bill told Andrew he'd like to discuss an important matter with him at the bank. Andrew was pleased to hear that, and several minutes later those two titans of the financial world were conversing on a first-name basis in Andrew's office.

After telling Andrew about his decision to build a winter home in the area, Bill asked him about the possibility of a local phone company being established during the coming year because he needed to stay in touch with his New York office whenever he was away from Manhattan for a week or two. To his surprise Andrew said he'd made a dozen inquiries during the last six months and was convinced he could revive the earlier plan to establish a local company, which had been shelved as a result of the financial panic of 1893. When Bill asked how much capital would be required for that plan to be implemented, Andrew said only $35,000 at $10 a share. Pleased to hear that, Bill asked the approximate return the stockholders would receive on the capital they invested in the company. Andrew said between 4 and 5 percent a year, which he considered quite good. Bill agreed with that statement and said he was willing to buy as many as two thousand shares in the company if Andrew felt there was a good chance he could sell the other 1,500 shares to local investors during the next several months. Andrew assured Bill he would have no trouble doing that because he and George Kahle were prepared to buy 150 shares apiece while Joe, Chip, Ozzie Crumpler, Russell Barringer, Percy Hogan, and Floyd Richardson had all agreed to buy a hundred shares apiece. Finally, Charlie Debs of Hertford had promised during a party in Hertford shortly before Christmas to buy at least five hundred shares in the company. Bill was curious about Charlie Debs and why he was willing to buy so much stock in a phone company in Perquimmons City.

"Charlie's a great guy," Andrew said at once. "He's about my age—late forties—and he's probably the best building contractor between Raleigh and Norfolk. Because of the outstanding work his crews do, he makes so much money every year he's always looking for several good places to invest thirty or forty thousand dollars."

"He sounds like a smart man and an excellent contractor, and I should probably get him to build my winter home. Do you know if he's done any work in town I could see without much trouble?"

"Yes, he's done a great deal of work in town, including the embankment several of his crews will probably finish by the end of May because that work's going so well it's almost a month ahead of schedule. Several years ago his men doubled the size of the social and educational wing of the Methodist church and they've also built a dozen houses in town, including my own fourteen years ago. His crews did such a fine job on it, my wife has never complained about anything, which is amazing because she has an eagle eye for faults of all kinds, especially mine."

As Andrew laughed at his own little joke, Bill said he'd like to meet Charlie before he returned to New York on the following Wednesday. "So if I can find the time, I'll arrange a meeting with him on Monday or Tuesday."

For the next several minutes Bill told Andrew half a dozen things about the land he hoped to buy for his winter home, a tract of forty or fifty acres several miles east of town with a good place to build a dock for his son's sailboat. Eventually Bill asked Andrew if he knew of anyone who might sell him that much land for a reasonable price.

After thinking for a moment, Andrew informed him that Ozzie Crumpler and Russell Barringer owned several tracts of adjoining land with excellent frontage on the Sound and the lower part of Hatcher's Creek, where a dock for his son's sailboat could probably be built without any trouble. Although Andrew had no idea what Ozzie and Russell would ask for their land, he was fairly sure they'd sell it for $20 an acre, the going price for undeveloped land in that part of the state.

Bill was amazed because he'd paid $2,995 for a two-acre lot in Palm Beach the previous spring. But he kept that fact to himself and said he'd like to consult his friend Dr. Hanford about the land in question and see it for himself before he made a decision about it. Andrew said he understood and considered that a good idea.

As Bill was about to leave the bank for the hotel, he offered to wire Andrew whatever start-up money he needed for the phone company at a later time. That money would naturally be applied to his purchase of up to two thousand shares of stock in the company shortly after Andrew made all the necessary arrangements for its establishment. Because Bill seemed to be in a bit of a hurry that morning, Andrew decided to wait until a later time to approach him about buying fifty shares of stock in the bank, which Bill would have to do to be eligible to serve on the its executive committee.

During his brief walk back to the hotel Bill thought about the surprisingly low price of undeveloped land in the area and decided to buy a much larger tract of land than he'd originally assumed he would. A tract of a hundred acres or so in a good location would probably be an excellent investment, one his wife would like. He'd heard her say many times how much she and her sisters had enjoyed their visits during the 1880s to Joe's parents' sprawling farm a short distance west of Salisbury.

On entering the hotel lobby, Bill saw Frances chatting with her sister Doris Mary Babcock and Lucinda Hanford (Joe's mother and Frances and Doris Mary's aunt by marriage) in addition to Lucinda's daughter-in-law Roberta. Roberta always agreed at once with whatever her mother-in-law said even when her own views were completely different because of Lucinda's domineering personality. Bill joined them with a cheerful hello and a tip of his hat although he remained silent until the four women left the hotel and started up the avenue to the Hanfords' house, where they'd been invited to have lunch with Julia and Rhonda before spending the rest of the afternoon with them.

Shortly after they left the hotel, Bill entered the dining room and found his children seated at a table between the room's two front windows. He enjoyed a fine meal with them and was pleased when they said they liked the town a great deal and looked forward to spending the afternoon with their cousins and several of their and Susan Summerlin's friends in the Summerlins' recreation room.

Shortly after Billy and Barbara left the hotel an hour later, Bill told the desk clerk he'd like to have a word with Mr. Crumpler if he was free at the moment, which the clerk assured him he was. Once the clerk led Bill down a narrow hall behind the registration desk to Ozzie's office door, he knocked on it several times. When Ozzie opened it and saw Bill standing there, he gave his distinguished guest a worried look, assuming he'd come to voice a complaint of some kind. Because of Ozzie's unease and Bill's desire to dispel it at once, he praised "all the splendid arrangements at your fine establishment," which had impressed everyone in his family circle. Ozzie heaved a sigh of relief and invited Bill to come in and take a chair on the opposite side of his desk which was littered with old magazines and newspapers. As Ozzie straightened them up as fast as he could, Bill sat down in a comfortable chair and said he understood that Ozzie and Russell Barringer owned several tracts of land a short distance east of town. He wondered if any of their land was for sale because he was interested in buying a hundred acres on which to build a winter home for his family and a dock for his son's sailboat.

Ozzie was very pleased to hear that, and as he made himself comfortable in his desk chair visions of doubling an investment of $9.50 an acre in less than a dozen years danced through his head like the ballerinas in *Swan Lake*, which he'd seen in New York several years earlier. Ozzie stroked his chin a bit while saying, "Yes, Mr. Van Landingham, all our land is for sale. I own three hundred and eighty acres along the Sound and the lower part of Hatcher's Creek while Russell owns four hundred and twenty-three acres, most of it on the Sound but a small part of it—only nineteen acres in fact—farther up Hatcher's creek than my land. All that land is connected and we hope to sell it as a unit. If you bought all our land, we could let you have it for twenty-five dollars an acre, which would be an excellent price for land that lies extremely well and has a dozen good building sites and almost as many active springs."

Assuming Ozzie would haggle a bit, Bill said $25 an acre was a much higher price than he'd expected to hear and he had no interest in buying that much land anyway. Perhaps he should speak to Mr. Barringer and see if he'd sell part of his larger tract of 404 acres for $15 an acre, which he considered a more reasonable price.

Ozzie said at once, "It would be a waste of your time to speak to Russell before coming to an agreement with me because there's a serious right-of-way problem. Because of the land's terrain and the way the road into our land curves around and doubles back, it's impossible to get to Russell's larger tract without going through my land first."

"Is that also true of Russell's smaller tract?"

"No, but that tract's located so far up Hatcher's Creek your son could never use his sailboat there because the creek's too shallow. Even worse, that land has none of the best building sites, which are located on my tract and Russell's larger one. In fact, the best building site of all is located on Russell's larger tract while the best place to build a dock for your son's sailboat is on my land."

"Then I should probably buy those two tracts and forget about Russell's smaller one."

"I'd normally agree with you but Russell's told me several times that he has no interest in keeping his smaller tract once he finds a buyer for his larger one. After all, what could he do with nineteen acres that are so steep and rocky only one house could be built there? But that property would provide excellent protection for your winter home."

Bill thought for a moment before saying, "Okay, Mr. Crumpler, you've convinced me to buy all of your and Russell's land if we can reach a mutually acceptable price. So let's get down to brass tacks. What's the rock-bottom price you and Mr. Barringer would accept for all your land?"

"Although I'm not authorized to speak for Russell, I'm fairly sure he'd agree with me that twenty-two dollars an acre is the least we could accept for it."

Bill took a pencil and notepad out of a pocket of his frock coat and did some quick multiplication. On finishing it he said, "I'm unwilling to go that high because if I did, I'd have to pay you and Russell well over seventeen thousand dollars for your land."

"Then how high are you willing to go, Mr. Van Landingham?"

"Frankly, I'd hoped to get out for fifteen dollars an acre."

"Oh no, no, no, Mr. Van Landingham!" Ozzie said with a quick little wave of his beautifully manicured hand. "Russell and I couldn't possibly accept only fifteen dollars an acre for our land. What about twenty-one dollars an acre?"

Bill said that was still a good bit higher than he was willing to go. After several more proposals and counterproposals were made and rejected, they reached a compromise price of $19.75 an acre provided Russell agreed to it and Bill liked the land when he saw it for himself.

When Ozzie agreed to that price and those conditions, he and Bill agreed to meet in the hotel lobby at four o'clock the next afternoon before driving out to see the land together. Because the next day was a Friday and the beginning of the New Year's weekend, there was a good chance Joe and Russell would be able to go with them, which Bill considered extremely important.

Shortly after four o'clock the next afternoon, Ozzie introduced Bill to Russell in the hotel lobby before they went outside and piled into Joe's car, which was parked at the curb on Hertford Avenue near the hotel's side entrance. After releasing the hand brake and adjusting his driving goggles, Joe put the car in gear and drove up the avenue before taking the right fork onto the Elizabeth City Road. After driving two more miles he crossed the railroad spur that led to the loading and unloading docks of Stanton's Mill before he came to an old stone bridge across Perquimmons Creek. After driving across the bridge Joe drove another mile before turning right onto Belspring Road, which marked the northern end of Ozzie's land. After traveling two hundred yards down that narrow dirt road, Joe and his passengers came to what remained of Quakertown, the thriving hamlet that had disappeared shortly after Robert Merritt led a brutal attack on its pacifist, antislavery members in June 1861.

After driving past the stark remains of the Quaker meeting house and the foundations of several dozen stores and houses that had otherwise disappeared by 1875, Joe came to a fork in the road. As he took the right fork Russell said from his place on the back seat beside Ozzie that the left fork led to his tract of nineteen acres. In several more minutes they came to Ozzie and Russell's saw mill, which had been closed since December 3. After passing the saw mill on the right, Joe drove between several large fields in which scores of young maple, pine, locust, dogwood, and wild pear trees were growing as well as several dozen majestic water oaks. Hatcher's Creek gradually came into view on the left as did the dark, still waters of the Sound straight ahead. When Joe's car was within a hundred and twenty yards of the Sound's northern bank, the road made a long bend to the west and continued parallel to the shore until it came to a stone pillar that marked the beginning of Russell's tract of 404 acres. After passing that pillar Joe drove another quarter of a mile before the road ended in a circular turnaround which Joe made with great care, avoiding several deep ruts as he did. Then at Russell's suggestion, he stopped the car so they could get out and walk up the narrow path on their left. As they proceeded up that path single file with Russell leading the way, they startled several kinds of wildlife—fauns, rabbits, raccoons, possums, chipmunks, and even a skunk. Those animals had been drinking from several nearby springs and ran for cover at the sound of the interlopers' approach. Luckily the skunk had been drinking from the most distant spring and didn't spray before it waddled into a nearby thicket and disappeared, which prompted the four men to heave a sigh of relief.

In several more minutes they reached the top of the hill, which was almost sixty feet higher than the level of the Sound. Bill knew at once that it was a wonderful place for a country house, and from his vantage point he could see a dozen fishing boats in the distance on the southern side of the Sound a short distance beyond the broad mouth of the Alligator River. Much closer to the place on which he was standing now, Bill could see the point where Hatcher's Creek suddenly widened before flowing into the Sound several hundred yards farther south. He realized in several moments that would be an excellent place to build a dock for his son's sailboat; and as he gazed toward the northeast he saw ten or eleven excellent building sites on Ozzie's land, all of which overlooked Hatcher's Creek. But as he looked due north he saw the deserted saw mill and the ruins of the Quaker meeting house. Because the saw mill and the meeting house's ruins were only four or five hundred yards from the place on which he and his friends were standing now, he was convinced they should be dismantled to enhance the beauty of the site on which he would doubtless build his winter home. But because dismantling them would cost at least fifteen hundred dollars, he felt Ozzie and Russell should reduce the price of their land by fifty or sixty cents an acre. He realized, however, that there was almost no chance they'd agree to do that without a fight. And because he was convinced he was getting some splendid land for a fraction of its real value, he decided to overlook that matter.

After sealing his purchase of Ozzie and Russell's land by shaking hands with each of them in turn, Bill and the other men returned to Joe's car so they could drive back to town.

After Joe stopped and let Ozzie and Russell out of the car at the hotel's side entrance, he and Bill continued up the avenue to the Hanfords' house. Shortly after they went inside Bill described the land he'd just bought to Frances and the other women who were present at the time. All six were impressed and asked to see the land at once. But it was almost six thirty and too late to drive out and see it that afternoon. Because the next day was New Year's Eve, Joe offered to drive them out to see the land shortly after they enjoyed an elaborate brunch in the hotel dining room as Bill and Frances's guests. Doris Mary Babcock, Lucinda Hanford, and her daughter-in-law Roberta were disappointed because they and their families were scheduled to leave Perquimmons City at eleven thirty that morning for the Hertford station and, ultimately, their homes in Winston-Salem and Salisbury, where they planned to attend several New Year's Eve parties that night. Besides, Gerald Babcock had already arranged for two men to drive them to the Hertford station and felt it would be almost impossible to change those arrangements on Saturday morning. As a result Joe promised to show his mother and the other people who planned to return to their homes the next day the land Bill had bought whenever they visited Perquimmons City again, which he hoped would be in only six or seven weeks if not sooner.

After an excellent brunch in the hotel dining room at ten o'clock the next morning, the fourteen Hanfords, Summerlins, and Van Landinghams said good-bye to the eight people from Winston-Salem and Salisbury before walking up the avenue to the Hanfords' house. There they discussed how to drive out and see the land Bill had bought the previous afternoon. Although Chip was willing to follow Joe's Maxwell in his somewhat smaller Oldsmobile, he pointed out that it would be uncomfortable for fourteen people to ride in only two cars. He therefore suggested that the group make two trips, a suggestion everyone accepted at once.

In several moments Billy Van Landingham said he'd rather go on the second trip provided he could ride in the same car with Susan Summerlin, which caused her to blush with pleasure. Olivia Hanford concealed her disappointment by saying she'd prefer to go on the first trip, just as Joey, Julia, and Frances preferred to do. Once those four people piled into Joe's car, Bill joined Rhonda and the Summerlin boys, Jack and Alfred, in their father's car.

Shortly after those cars drove up the avenue and turned onto the Elizabeth City Road, Lucy realized she was the only adult still at the Hanfords' house with her niece Susan and Billy and Barbara Van Landingham. During the next ten minutes Barbara peppered Lucy with questions about local boys her age or slightly older, especially good-looking boys who were interested in books and music, her most important interests. Lucy was deeply annoyed when she realized that whenever she was preoccupied with Barbara's questions, Billy and Susan left the parlor and went to the study or Julia's morning room, which made it impossible for Lucy to chaperone them properly. So whenever that happened, Lucy and Barbara joined the two wayward teenagers in whatever room they were in at the time, whereupon Barbara asked Lucy six or seven more questions about local boys, causing her to be so distracted again Billy and Susan disappeared once more. When Lucy went in search of them for the third time, she found them kissing in the butler's pantry with their arms around each other, which caused her to scold them before telling them to return to the parlor with Barbara and herself at once. When Billy and Susan disappeared still another time as Barbara's questions were distracting Lucy once again, she realized Barbara was distracting her on purpose and rebuked her for it, fairly gently of course. Barbara giggled and said, "Billy's so stuck on Susan he promised me a quarter if I'd keep you so busy he could be alone with her for several minutes."

More annoyed than ever, Lucy started another search for the wayward teenagers. This time she failed to find them on the ground floor and was relieved when she didn't find them in one of the bedrooms on the second floor, where she'd dreaded to look. Nor were they in the study, the dining room, the kitchen, or even in the most obvious places in the backyard. She eventually found them behind the garage where she hadn't thought to look until she heard Susan say, "Oh, Billy, you're so fresh. But because you're so nice and good-looking, I wouldn't mind if you kissed me like that again. I've never let a boy put his tongue in my mouth before."

Lucy peeped around the corner and was shocked by what she saw. Their bodies were pressed tightly together, and Susan's arms were wrapped around Billy's neck while his arms encircled her waist although his hands were planted slightly lower on her anatomy in a place they shouldn't have been touching at all. His lips were naturally on top of hers and Lucy hated to think where his tongue was. She'd never seen such an ardent embrace and cleared her throat loudly, hoping it would cause them to jump apart at once. But they remained exactly as they were to Lucy's dismay. So she looked away before telling them to come inside in a minute or so and explain their appalling behavior to her in the kitchen.

As she waited for them to appear, Lucy calmed down while remembering a similar incident during her teenage years. On the second Saturday in May during her junior year in high school, her favorite teacher, Mrs. Stover, gave a party at her house on Pine Street for the nine members of the Latin Club, of which Mrs. Stover was the faculty advisor. Lucy attended that party with her boyfriend, Jobie Caldwell, on whom she'd had an enormous crush since they were in the first grade together. At one point during the party Mr. Stover, who owned the town's largest and most successful livery stable, asked Jobie to follow him outside to the icehouse in the backyard and help him cut several chunks of ice for the punchbowl. Lucy followed them into the backyard and watched Jobie from behind a large snowball bush. Once Jobie filled the bucket with ice, Mr. Stover took it inside while Jobie placed a fresh layer of straw on the remaining ice in the zinc-lined chest before latching its lid.

As Jobie was tucking his shirttail into his trousers, Lucy snuck up behind him and said "Boo!" But he'd heard her footsteps and wheeled around before pulling her into the ice house and giving her a kiss in the cool darkness. It was nowhere as passionate as the kiss Lucy had just seen Billy giving Susan, but it was much more ardent than the quick little kisses Lucy and Jobie had exchanged since Valentine's Day and she loved it. In fact, she loved it so much she told Jobie she'd like another kiss like that. He obliged her at once and twice more in the icehouse. Later that afternoon, as he was walking her home from the party, he obliged her whenever they came to a snowball or forsythia bush that was large enough to shield them from prying eyes.

 Because Lucy's memories of that afternoon were still vivid, she decided to go fairly easy on Billy and Susan when they came inside. But they failed to appear until almost ten minutes elapsed; and when they finally entered the kitchen by the back door, they didn't express any remorse or seem a bit sorry for their behavior. In fact, Billy took a coin out of one of his trouser pockets and said to his sister, "Here's your quarter for distracting her and thanks for doing such a good job, Babs. But remember, you're sworn to secrecy."

 Barbara made the situation even worse by saying, "Sure, Billy, I remember my promise and I won't tell anyone else about the way you and Susan made out whenever you could during the last hour. But don't blame me if Lucy rats on you. She's as prudish as my piano teacher and all the other old maids I know in New York. They hate it when kids like us are having fun and they can't keep us from playing spin the bottle and other great games like that."

 Lucy was so upset by Barbara's words she asked Chip to take her home at once shortly after he and Joe pulled their cars into the driveway several minutes later. Everyone was surprised by her decision to go home so soon because they'd thought she'd go on the second trip to see the Van Landinghams' land. But Lucy claimed she had a splitting headache and wanted to return to her cottage and lie down until she returned to the Hanfords' house shortly before seven thirty for their New Year's Eve party. Actually, Lucy was convinced that if she went on the second trip to see the Van Landinghams' land, she would be upset and deeply annoyed whenever Billy and Susan disappeared into the bushes or a thicket of evergreen trees. She considered such behavior completely unacceptable for teenage children but felt it wasn't her place to "rat on them" as Barbara had predicted she'd do.

 Two days later at the drugstore Bill had coffee again with the four big shots, whose company he'd enjoyed during the Hanfords' New Year's

Eve party on Saturday night and, except for Ozzie who was a Methodist, again on Sunday morning during the social hour after the main service at St. John's Church. While having coffee with the big shots at the drugstore on Monday morning, Bill told George Kahle about the land he'd bought from Ozzie and Russell Barringer on Friday afternoon. Kahle already knew about that transaction of course, and when Bill asked him to do all the paperwork for it, Kahle gladly agreed to do so for his usual fee of $5 an hour. Several minutes later, Bill told Kahle he'd like to discuss an important matter with him in his office for several minutes, and the lawyer gladly agreed to that as well.

Shortly after the two men were comfortably seated on opposite sides of Kahle's desk, Bill told the lawyer that he hoped to buy a large tract of land adjacent to the 803 acres he'd bought on Friday afternoon. He hoped Kahle would handle those negotiations for him with great discretion because he had no interest in dealing with the person Joe and Julia had assured him was the sole owner of the land he hoped to buy. If she knew his identity, Bill was convinced she'd increase her asking price by at least $10 an acre.

Kahle guessed at once that Bill was speaking of Marguerite Merritt because her husband's forebears had owned all the land on which Perquimmons City had grown like a weed between 1835 and 1885. During the years since the Civil War the Merritts had sold off large tracts of their land in order to raise money for their current expenses, which they'd never made a sustained effort to reduce despite the emancipation of their 227 slaves in 1863. Despite that, Mrs. Merritt still owned a sprawling tract of roughly forty-five hundred acres near the Merritt House and a smaller tract of almost a thousand acres between the black section of town on the eastern side of the creek and the 803 acres Bill had bought from Ozzie and Russell on Friday afternoon. At least three fourths of the tract Bill was interested in buying from Mrs. Merritt was covered with thick woods. But whether she was interested in selling that land or a large part of it, Kahle couldn't say with any certainty although he was convinced the thought had crossed her mind several times during recent months.

When Bill asked the lawyer why he felt that way, Kahle laughed and said Bill must not have heard about the Merritts' trip to Charleston the previous fall. When Bill admitted he knew nothing about that trip, Kahle started a long account of their comic-opera excursion with a twinkle in his eye.

"Several days after her husband's funeral, which was sparsely attended, Marguerite and her children packed all their their favorite clothes and headed for Charleston in their Stanley Steamer. As they were nearing Wilmington six or seven hours later, they had a blowout; and because Willie was driving too fast on that stretch of the road, he lost control of the car and wound up in a ditch, where the Steamer was hopelessly stuck. Willie and the rest of his family remained in the car until an old truck came along an hour or so later. The driver stopped to see if they needed some help, and Marguerite offered him three dollars if he'd drive them into Wilmington with their smaller suitcases so they could check into a hotel for the night. The man agreed and Marguerite sat in the cab with him while her children sat in the truck's bed with dozens of crates of geese and chickens. That's bound to have been a funny sight because Becca and her brothers were dressed in some of their best clothes I've heard on good authority.

"After breakfast in the hotel coffee shop the next morning, Marguerite had one of the desk clerks call a garage for her. A mechanic arrived in several minutes and drove her and Willie out to the ditch where the Steamer was still stuck. To their dismay its windows had all been broken during the night and the four suitcases they'd left in the car had been stolen. Its four tires were flat, both axles were broken, and the oil pan had been punctured and was bone dry. To make a long story short, the Steamer was in terrible shape and the mechanic said it would take him at least a month to fix it because a new oil pan and all the other parts he'd need to do a good job would have to be ordered from a warehouse in Detroit. So Marguerite abandoned the car and paid the mechanic to drive her and Willie to the Pierce Arrow Agency in Wilmington, where she bought an enormous touring car that set her back almost four thousand dollars. Of course, she had less than a thousand dollars in her purse, and the agency's owner wouldn't accept such a large check from someone he'd never laid eyes on before. So Marguerite sent Andrew Ridinger a telegram asking him to wire her enough money to cover the car's price. Andrew himself told me those things several days after he wired her all the money she needed. Once she paid for the touring car and put its legal title in her purse, Willie drove it to the hotel where she settled their bill for the previous night's lodging and their breakfast that morning. Then she and the children resumed their trip to Charleston with their smaller suitcases, which were nothing more than overnight bags.

"When they finally reached Charleston, they checked into the Francis Marion Hotel, which I've heard is the city's finest and most expensive. They stayed in that hotel's best suite for almost a month although they had dinner on most nights with Marguerite's uncle, Benjamin Manigault, and his second wife, Germaine. Germaine clearly considered the Merritts' appearance on most afternoons shortly after five o'clock a terrible imposition because they never bought a bag groceries or even a bottle of wine with them. Of course during their first week in Charleston, Marguerite had to buy a passel of clothes for her children and herself, and according to Isabel Stanton, Marguerite's only friend in town, she spent almost two thousand dollars on them."

"My word!" Bill said in amazement. "She clearly has no qualms about spending money like water. She's probably unaware of the old saying, 'Waste not, want not,' which my parents drummed into me as a boy and I'll never forget."

"Even if Marguerite's been aware of that old saying for years, I doubt that she's ever tried to live by it for more than several days. In any event, she was determined to make a good impression on Charleston society because the main purpose of the trip was to find a wife for Willie and a husband for Becca. Apparently Willie had no interest in that endeavor because, to be honest, there's something a bit strange about him and his behavior. Furthermore he probably knows that if he ever gets married, he'll have to find a job and stop sponging off his mother. Whether that's true or not, he turned up his nose at all the young ladies he met in Charleston—one was too tall and another too short, one was too thin and another too fat, one had bad breath while another squinted all the time because of poor eyesight: I'm sure you get the picture.

"Although Marguerite was disappointed by Willie's fault-finding behavior, she was delighted by Becca's response to the sixteen or seventeen bachelors who were paraded in front of her like young bulls in a stockyard. According to Isabel Stanton again, Becca was so excited about the prospect of getting married she felt most of the bachelors she met were excellent husband material. So Marguerite left Becca with her great-uncle, who's the managing partner of Charleston's largest and best law firm, and his deeply annoyed wife on the morning Marguerite and her sons started their homeward trip in their enormous car. Apparently Willie had only one accident on that trip because Marguerite ordered him to slow down every couple of minutes after one of her huge, wide-brimmed hats blew off her head and disappeared into the brackish waters of a swamp several miles north of Charleston. Once Willie stopped the car so she could put on another hat that was almost as large and unsuitable for wearing in an open car, she made Willie and Little Robert look for her lost hat for half an hour while she yelled instructions from the car's back seat. But they failed to find her lost hat because they were worried about the swamp's alligators and refused to wade out into deeper and darker waters than the ones they'd already searched. I probably shouldn't say this, but I can just see the deep concern on their faces because of the terrible situation they were in. It seems to me they were bound to wonder which was worse—the alligators' sharp teeth or their mother's equally sharp tongue. If I'd been in their shoes I probably would've considered it a tossup."

"I would definitely have considered it a tossup had I been in their shoes that day," Bill said after thinking about Willie and Little Robert's plight for several moments. "But it sounds like you might have had several run-ins with Marguerite in the past."

"More run-ins than I care to remember," George said at once, "and so has my wife. In fact, it was because of those run-ins that we left the Presbyterian church and became Episcopalians. But to return to the reasons why I'm convinced Marguerite's given some serious thought to selling the land you'd like to buy, several nights ago during a dinner party at the younger Stantons' house, I heard Marguerite telling Isabel and Mildred Barringer that Becca's being courted by a dashing young man named Gaylord Rochambeau, whose family lost most of its money during the war. Apparently Gaylord's extremely ambitious and something of a social climber because he offered to be Becca's principal escort during the Governor's Ball in Columbia on the first Saturday night in May. And when you add all the money Becca's social debut will cost to the enormous sums Marguerite spent on the trip to Charleston and the touring car she bought in Wilmington, I don't see how she can manage without selling a large part of her land. Besides, as I see it, she'd be smart to sell all or most of her land on the eastern side of the creek rather than a sizable portion of her larger and much more valuable tract of land near the Merritt House."

"I'm sure you're right about that, and I can hardly believe how much money she spent on her trip to Charleston," Bill said while shaking his head in wonder at everything he'd just heard about that trip. "But how much do you think she'll ask for the land I'm interested in buying from her?"

"At least thirty dollars an acre because she's as mercenary as they come and can squeeze more blood out of a turnip than anyone I've ever known."

"I'm not surprised to hear that," Bill said after a moment of reflection. "Although I'd hate to pay her a great deal more for her land than I paid Ozzie and Russell for theirs—they impressed me last week as extremely nice and agreeable men—I'm willing to go as high as twenty-eight dollars an acre for her land because it would provide excellent protection for my winter home. Now this is what I propose, Mr. Kahle—I'd like you to handle this transaction for me in such a discreet way Mrs. Merritt won't guess my identity, which would probably cause her to jack up her asking price to forty or fifty dollars an acre. If you can keep that from happening, I'll pay you a five percent broker's fee of whatever the purchase price turns out to be provided it doesn't exceed twenty-eight dollars an acre. And if the deal goes through, I'd like you to do all the legal work at your usual fee of five dollars an hour. I hope my proposal sounds fair to you and you'll agree to handle these negotiations on my behalf."

"Your proposal seems eminently fair, Mr. Van Landingham, and I'll be happy to handle these negotiations for you despite how long and difficult they're likely to be. I'm afraid they'll make my verbal fights with Buzz-Saw Beulah at her eating place, which is widely known as the Combat Café, seem like child's play. But despite that, please call me George, because being on a first-name basis tends to make unpleasant chores seem a bit less distasteful, don't you think?"

"I certainly do, George, so please call me Bill. I have a hunch we'll be doing a great deal of work together during the next several years."

Chapter 13

After leaving George Kahle's office, Bill walked to the telegraph office on East Main Street and sent a message to Charlie Debs in Hertford. Bill's telegram suggested a joint meeting at Debs' office at eleven o'clock the next morning about an important building project. If Debs had a prior appointment at that hour, Bill hoped he would suggest another time in a return telegram to him at Crumpler's Hotel in Perquimmons City, where he and the rest of his family would be staying until Wednesday morning. Bill signed his telegram, "Cordially yours, William J. Van Landingham, president and managing partner of Feldman, Baring, & Van Landingham Brokerage Company of New York City. Branch offices in Boston, Philadelphia, Cleveland, Chicago, Detroit, St. Louis, Cincinnati, Montreal, Toronto, Louisville, and Indianapolis."

From the telegraph office, Bill returned to the hotel and had lunch with Frances and their children. On finishing their meal, they went out into the lobby and were waiting for the elevator that would take them up to the third floor when a delivery boy arrived with a telegram for Bill. In it, Debs said he was free between two thirty and four o'clock the next afternoon and would expect the Van Landinghams then unless they cancelled by one o'clock. Bill handed the telegram to Frances shortly before the elevator door opened. After reading it she said she'd go upstairs to their sitting room with Billy and Barbara and wait for him there until he arranged transportation for them to Hertford the next afternoon.

In several minutes Bill was seated in Ozzie Crumpler's office and telling him about Charlie Debs' telegram. Once Ozzie called Debs the best contractor in the eastern part of the state, he offered to provide a car and driver for the Van Landinghams early the next afternoon at no cost to them because of all the business they'd brought the hotel during the last five days. Bill thanked Ozzie for his generosity before asking him to call him by his first name as most of his friends did. Ozzie smiled and said, "Certainly, Bill, provided you call me by my first name too."

After a slightly later lunch than usual the next day and a leisurely drive to Hertford, the Van Landinghams entered Debs' office building shortly before two thirty. His receptionist welcomed them and led them down a narrow hall to Debs' conference room, which the contractor entered several moments later. After a warm greeting he introduced himself and shook hands with Bill and Frances in turn.

A short but energetic man, Debs had thick gray hair and piercing blue eyes. He was wearing a handsome ditto suit, a pale blue dress shirt, and a navy blue bow tie with polka dots. Extremely friendly and outgoing, Debs was soon on a first-name basis with the Van Landinghams.

After several comments about the weather, Charlie showed them an album that contained dozens of snapshots of houses, churches, stores, and several factories his crews had built since he went into business for himself in 1889. Charlie also explained that as a young man he'd worked for his uncle, Marvin Debs, one of the best contractors in the state during the generation after the Civil War.

Impressed, Bill told Charlie about the land he'd bought four days earlier on the northern side of the Sound and the western side of Hatcher's Creek. Bill also described the hilltop clearing on which he and Frances planned to build their winter home. Charlie said he was familiar with that land because he'd hunted on it with his younger brothers and several of their friends while they were teenagers. If he remembered correctly there was a wonderful view of the Sound from that hilltop.

"Yes, there certainly is," Frances said at once, "and that's why we've decided to call our new home 'Hilltop House.'"

Charlie said that was a fine name before asking her if they'd brought any sketches or rough floor plans of the house they hoped to build.

As he opened a notepad and took a pencil out of one of his pockets, Frances said they hadn't brought any sketches or floor plans with them because they weren't that far along in their planning. "But we'd like our new home to look like a Spanish country house with stucco walls and a red tile roof. It should have a courtyard with a large fountain at or near the center and it should also have a dozen bedrooms and a large terrace overlooking the Sound."

"I hate to disagree with you," Bill said at once to her, "But we won't need a dozen bedrooms because the house we're about to build will be our *winter* home, not a home for year-round use. So I'm sure six or seven bedrooms will be sufficient for our purposes."

Frances disagreed before saying, "I'm convinced we should build a much larger house here in eastern North Carolina than the one we planned to build in Florida. This area's a great deal closer to New York than Florida is, and I'm sure we'll use a winter home here a lot more than we would've used one in Palm Beach or Miami. Besides, I'd love for Doris Mary and the twins to spend six or seven weeks with us every summer. And there's a good chance Martin and Rebecca will come down during July or August when it's frightfully hot in New York, and so will several of Billy and Barbara's friends. So I think we should have at least a dozen bedrooms and a large screened porch as well as a sun porch we can use in chilly weather. And I'd also like the house to have an upstairs sitting room where we can relax whenever the children are having fun with their friends on the main floor or in the basement recreation room."

"But they'll probably hate the thought of spending so much time in the country with us. Because there are so many interesting things for young people to do in New York, they'll get bored after nine or ten days down here with us, don't you think?"

"No, not at all because they'll make dozens of local friends in no time, and I told them several days ago that we're planning to build a tennis court and a swimming pool they can use with their new friends as well as six or seven of their best friends from New York. They loved those ideas just as I knew they would."

Charlie gazed at Bill with a mixture of sympathy and amusement before saying, "You don't actually think you're going to win this battle, do you, Bill? I'm afraid it ended in a serious defeat several days before you found out it was underway."

After a long sigh Bill said, "You're clearly right about that, Charlie. While I was busy buying the land for our new home, Frances launched a massive attack without informing me about it. I hope you're not plagued by a wife who's as smart and clever as mine, Charlie."

Charlie laughed and turned back to Frances. "If you expect to have a dozen bedrooms and a sitting room on the second floor, what about the most important rooms you expect to have on the main floor? I'd like to hear your ideas about them now."

"Well, in addition to a large screened porch and an equally large sun porch, I want a handsome parlor and a cheerful morning room I can use with my local friends. As for Bill, he wants a study where he and his friends can drink some brandy and smoke their smelly cigars after dinner, so that room should have four or five large windows for especially good ventilation. We also want a cheerful breakfast room and an unusually large dining room with a table that can seat twenty people comfortably, and of course we'll need a butler's pantry and several other pantries as well as a kitchen with at least two stoves and several ice boxes. And I especially want dozens of closets and ten or eleven bathrooms and several powder rooms at suitable places throughout the house. And we also want a large recreation room in the basement with easy access to the swimming pool so our children can use it with their friends without any trouble. That room should have six or seven large windows and at least two outside doors. The basement should also have a laundry room and several storage areas for luggage, bedding, and summer as well as winter clothes, which will make our trips between New York and this area much easier than they'd be otherwise."

After scribbling all those things down on his notepad Charlie said, "Frances, you clearly want an extremely large house although you've mentioned only one room for Bill to use with his friends. Because he'll be paying for everything, shouldn't he have a second room—a billiards room perhaps—that he and his friends can use from time to time?"

"He's told me several times that he'd like to have a billiards room. But he hardly ever plays the game anymore, and a billiards table could always be placed in a corner of the recreation room where he could use it with his friends whenever he likes. But I'd like to move on to two more rooms I should mention now. Our children would love to have a ballroom—nothing too large or grand of course—so they can hold dance parties without any trouble. And Billy's eager to have an exercise room with a full set of of Indian clubs and several other kinds of gym equipment. He was a tackle on his prep school's football team last fall and is convinced he could make a college team if he gains twenty or twenty-five pounds during the next eighteen months."

After emitting another long sigh Bill said, "Well, I guess those rooms wouldn't add too much to the cost. But Charlie, how much money is my wife's dream house likely to set me back? I'd hoped to get out for a hundred thousand dollars but that's beginning to sound like a pipedream."

"Yes, I'm afraid it was a pipedream, Bill," Charlie said with a chuckle. "But before I answer your question, what about servants' quarters, Frances?

You'll need six or seven servants to help you run such a large house and where will they sleep? I assume their rooms will be in the attic or in a separate cottage or two."

"I'm glad you brought that up, Charlie," Frances said at once. "Our New York architect hasn't asked us a single question about servants' quarters although we've met with him several times since last spring. But he's always been preoccupied with other matters; and because of that, those meetings with him have been a total waste of time in my opinion."

"But my dear wife, "Bill said firmly, "he told us during our first conference with him that he has half a dozen other projects on his drawing board he has to finish before he can focus on our winter home."

"My point exactly, Bill. I'm afraid if we wait until he finishes his other projects, our new home won't be ready for us to use for several more years."

Before Bill could respond to that comment Charlie said he'd like to ask them several questions about their New York architect. "For example, when did you retain him and has he produced anything at all for you yet?"

Bill thought for a moment before saying, "We retained him on April twenty-second, shortly before we left New York on a cruise to Bermuda, and he hasn't produced a single thing for us yet."

"He's obviously a very busy man," Charlie said. "So I wonder if you and Frances would be willing to go with another architect. One here in eastern North Carolina who does outstanding work and has just finished his fourth project with me."

"That's an interesting thought," Bill said at once. "But what about you, Frances? Would you consider going with a local architect Charlie's worked with a number of times and thinks very highly of? Or would you rather stick with that old slowpoke in New York?"

"It's obvious what your preference is," Frances said to him with a smile. "And because I'd love for us to be able to use our winter home as soon as possible, I'd also rather go with a local architect Charlie's used several times and thinks very highly of. But before we make a decision about that, I'd like to know several things about the architect he has in mind for us."

"Of course, Frances," Charlie said. "The architect I have in mind for you is Alec Kramer who grew up in Elizabeth City and studied architecture at Harvard before he opened an office in his hometown six or seven years ago. Alec has *enormous* talent and a real flair for design; but equally important for your purposes, he works much faster than most architects. I'm sure he'd love to be involved with your project and will take the train down to Hertford on Friday or Saturday so I can explain your ideas to him in much greater detail than I could during a phone call before I drive him to your site so we can walk around it together. I'm sure we could save at least a year if I work with Alec rather than a New York architect who probably won't come down to see your site until next fall at the earliest."

After making those comments, which Bill and Frances clearly liked, Charlie opened his photograph album again and showed them several dozen snapshots of three houses and a church Alec had designed before Charlie built them in Hertford and Edenton during the last several years.

After studying those pictures Bill said to his wife, "In my opinion, Charlie's made an excellent suggestion we should accept."

Frances agreed before saying, "I've hope for months that our new home will be finished by the middle of December so Doris Mary and her family can spend next Christmas with us here and not in Manhattan, which is a hard trip for them with the twins. Charlie, do you think there's any chance of that?"

"Well, let's see now . . . If Alec starts working on the plans in another week or two, I should be able to break ground for Hilltop House during the last ten days of April. And if I assign my six best crews to it, there's a chance I'll have enough of it finished by the middle of December that your two families can use it next Christmas. But I can't make any promises because I haven't seen any sketches or floor plans yet. I'll do my best, though, and I'm sure Alec will do the same."

"Good," Bill said firmly. "That sounds like the best we could hope for under the circumstances."

After glancing at his pocket calendar, Bill told Charlie that he and Frances could come down to eastern North Carolina again in early March to discuss the project with Mr. Kramer in person if there was a chance he could have some sketches and floor plans ready for them to study by then.

"I'm sure he could have some plans and drawings for you to consider by then," Charlie said. After consulting his own pocket calendar Charlie continued, "If it's agreeable with you and Frances, let's plan to get together again on Tuesday afternoon, March seventh, here in my conference room at two o'clock if that's convenient for you."

Bill said that was fine with him and Frances, but he didn't have a checkbook with him that afternoon. "So if it's okay to you, I'll send you a certified check made out to Alec for five thousand dollars on the first day I'm back in New York. That'll be enough of a retainer for him at this stage, don't you think?"

"Yes, more than enough," Charlie said. "And I'll see that Alec gets your check shortly after he accepts your commission, which 'm sure he will."

"Excellent!" Bill said at once. "But, Charlie, I'm convinced I should put a limit on the size of the house Alec designs for us. If I don't, I'm afraid its cost will get completely out of hand."

"There's always a chance of that," Charlie said, "and you were smart to mention that thorny matter today."

"I'm glad you feel that way," Bill said before turning back to Frances. Choosing his words with even greater care than usual he said, "We told our New York architect we were thinking in terms of a house of not more than eight thousand square feet. But now that we've decided to build a much larger house here than the one we planned to build in Florida, I'm willing to increase its size to sixteen thousand square feet, but not a square foot more. Can you live with that, Frances?"

"Probably, although I'd like to know Charlie's opinion of your suggested limit." She and Bill gazed at Charlie while wondering what he'd say.

After thinking for several moments Charlie said to Bill, "I'm afraid your limit of sixteen thousand square feet is a bit low. I'm convinced everything Frances wants Hilltop House to contain won't fit in a house of that size unless most of the bedrooms are fairly small and the house has only half as many closets and bathrooms as she'd like it to have. And because I doubt that you'll ever build another house as large and grand as the one we've been discussing this afternoon, I think you'd be smart to build a larger house and do everything so well you won't regret it later."

After a moment of reflection Bill said, "I agree with that in principle, Charlie. But how large do you think Hilltop House will have to be to guarantee that everything's done to her total satisfaction and I won't hear any later complaints about my tendency to 'scrimp and cut corners?'"

"I think eighteen thousand square feet would be about right," Charlie said after several moments. "However, that figure won't include the servants' quarters in the attic or a couple of separate cottages I'm afraid."

"Well, I guess I can live with that," Bill said after emitting a long groan. "But I hope you'll tell Mr. Kramer that eighteen thousand square feet for Hilltop House itself is my maximum limit *period*. So if he plans an even larger house for us, he'll have to scale back the plans on his own time or I'll have them adjusted by an excellent draftsman in New York my company's used for twenty years. Is that clear, Charlie?"

"Yes, it's perfectly clear. And I see nothing wrong with your approach because Alec, like all the other architects I've used over the years, gets carried away from time to time and plans houses that are much larger and grander than his clients actually wanted. Fortunately you and Frances have given me so much information I won't have any trouble reining him in, and I'll look forward to seeing you again in early March. This is going to be one of the most interesting projects I've ever been involved with and I'm sure Alec will feel the same way."

Although the Van Landinghams and their children left for New York the following day, the next two months in Perquimmons City were an exciting time. In less than a week most of the townspeople believed greatly exaggerated rumors that the Van Landinghams had bought at least two hundred thousand acres between the eastern town limits and the western side of the Currituck Sound. On that enormous tract of land they planned to build a palatial winter home that would cost several million dollars. Those rumors became even more exaggerated during later weeks. By the beginning of March most of the townspeople were convinced that Bill and Frances were about to build a gigantic winter home ten times larger than the Merritt House or even the White House in the country's capital. Isabel Stanton and several other women insisted it would be larger and even more elegant than one of the Vanderbilt mansions in New York or Newport, Rhode Island, including the Marble House and the Breakers. On one occasion Lucy overheard a customer telling several friends in the drugstore that Hilltop House would be almost as large and grand as Buckingham Palace in London and the Czar's Winter Palace in St. Petersburg.

Lucy was amazed when she heard those rumors in the drugstore, which most of the townspeople desperately wanted to believe. After all, the Van Landinghams were so rich there was a widespread belief that the whole area would profit, directly or indirectly, once they were spending several months a year in eastern North Carolina.

That expectation was fed by Bill's other land purchases during those months. On February 21, George Kahle sent a telegram to Bill's office in New York's Flatiron Building, in which the lawyer informed Bill that he'd just completed some long and very difficult negotiations with Marguerite Merritt. Although George had refused to tell Marguerite his client's name, she'd originally demanded $35 an acre for her 987-acre tract on the western side of the land Bill had already bought from Ozzie Crumpler and Russell Barringer. But during his fifth and final meeting with Marguerite, George had convinced her to reduce her asking price to $27 an acre for that land.

Shortly after Bill received George's telegram, he instructed him to accept Mrs. Merritt's price of $27 an acre for that tract. Bill's telegram also directed George to inform her that a cashier's check for $10,000 was on its way as a down payment on her land.

In another telegram four days later, Bill asked George to open negotiations with Russell Barringer who, according to a recent telegram he'd received from Ozzie Crumpler, was interested in selling a forty-acre tract in the middle part of town. That tract would be suitable for a town park and several other purposes Bill had in mind.

On March 6 the Van Landinghams returned to Perquimmons City so they could meet Alec Kramer and see his preliminary floor plans and elevations for Hilltop House the next afternoon. In addition, Bill wanted to discuss an important matter with Andrew Ridinger at the bank before he went to George Kahle's office and completed his purchase of Mrs. Merritt's land.

After checking into Crumpler's Hotel shortly after one o'clock on the afternoon of March 6, Bill and Frances rested in their suite before having dinner at the Hanfords' house again at their insistence. Joe and Julia were delighted to see their friends again and relieved that they seemed to be unaware of the wild rumors circulating in town about the size and splendor of Hilltop House. Because the Hanfords were convinced those rumors would embarrass the Van Landinghams if they ever heard them, they steered the conversation as far away from that subject as they could without being obvious about it.

The next morning, while Frances strolled around town with Julia again, Bill had coffee at the drugstore with the four big shots before accompanying Andrew Ridinger next door to his office at the bank. There he handed Andrew a cashier's check for $20,000, which covered the price of two thousand shares of stock in the recently established phone company. In return, Andrew handed Bill a notarized certificate for those shares in the company.

Several weeks earlier, during an organizational meeting in the bank's conference room, Andrew had been elected president of the new company for a four-year term. Under his skillful leadership the eleven stockholders who attended that meeting decided that the construction of a small brick building on the Elizabeth City Road for the company's switchboard and other electronic equipment would begin in another month. And seven or eight weeks after that, several workmen would begin erecting poles and stringing telephone wires around town. As a result Andrew informed Bill on the morning of March 7 that unless several unexpected problems developed, the company would be up and running by the end of September, which pleased Bill a great deal.

Shortly after Bill returned to the hotel and had lunch with Frances in the dining room, one of Ozzie's porters at the hotel drove the Van Landinghams to Hertford for their second conference with Charlie Debs. During that two-hour conference Charlie introduced them to Alec Kramer, who'd taken the train down from Elizabeth City that morning. A tall, lanky man with a crew cut and ruddy complexion, Alec exuded enormous enthusiasm for the Van Landinghams' project before he showed them the preliminary plans and sketches he'd drawn for their winter home.

Bill and Frances were delighted with the work Alec had done for them and done so fast. Although they suggested several minor changes to the floor plans, they accepted all his basic ideas before they thanked Charlie for expressing their thoughts to Alec so clearly. Finally, Bill suggested another meeting with Alec shortly after he finished his blueprints and elevations for Hilltop House and compiled a list of all the building materials Charlie would need to calculate a firm price for all the construction work six of his crews of a dozen men each would do. When Debs and Kramer finished all that work, hopefully by the latter part of April, Bill and Frances would take the train down from New York again and sign the necessary papers so work on the mansion could begin a week or two later. Once Debs and Kramer agreed to that suggestion, Debs promised to stay in touch with the Van Landinghams in New York and arrange a date for another meeting in his conference room during the latter part of April.

After a stroll around town on the morning of March 8, the Van Landinghams had lunch with Julia and Rhonda at the Hanfords' house. Frances spent most of the afternoon playing bridge with them and Phyllis Kahle while Bill walked to George Kahle's office to sign all the papers and write Mrs. Merritt a check for the remaining money he owed for her 987-acre tract of land. When Marguerite arrived at George's office several minutes later and realized Bill was the man who'd bought her land, she declared angrily that she'd been duped out of thousands of dollars. Indeed, she told George firmly that he should've informed her that Bill Van Landingham was his client because "he has more money than all the Van'duhbilts and Ast'uhs combined." Had George been honest and forthcoming with her, "I nev'uh would've accepted such a *ridiculously* low price fo my land 'cause its timb'uh alone is worth at least ten thous'n doll'uhs! You should be *ashamed* o yo'self fo helpin such a rich Yankee cheat a po widow like me out o so much money, *Mis'tuh Kahle!*"

Despite her bitter anger Mrs. Merritt was in no position to rescind the sale of her land. During a two-week trip to Charleston in February, she'd spent $750 on an evening gown for Becca and all the other expenses attendant on her social debut in May. She'd also bought Becca's wedding dress and trousseau because her engagement to Gaylord Rochambeau had been announced on Valentine's Day. Their wedding was scheduled to take place in one of Charleston's oldest and most beautiful churches on the second Saturday afternoon in December. In addition, Mrs. Merritt had given her uncle $2,500 to pay all the other expenses of Becca's wedding, including a lavish reception with music provided by a small orchestra and several vocalists in the larger ballroom at the Francis Marion Hotel shortly after the ceremony. Finally, Marguerite had deposited $4,500 in a special savings account for the couple's four-month honeymoon trip through Central and Western Europe.

Because Marguerite had already spent three-fourths of Bill's down payment on her land, she had no choice but to sign the papers for its sale. If she refused to sign them, George told her brusquely after she complained about his part in duping her out of a great deal of money, his client would sue her not only for the return of his $10,000 but also for the recovery of all his legal expenses during a judicial proceeding that would probably take several months. On hearing that Marguerite signed all the papers with a heavy heart before snatching Bill's check for the remaining $16,649 out of the lawyer's hand. Then she rushed out of Kahle's office without saying another word to either man.

After her abrupt departure Bill thanked George for his fine work and paid him for handling that transaction before asking him how his negotiations with Russell Barringer were going. According to the lawyer, Russell had had some second thoughts about selling his forty-acre tract in the middle part of town, a tract that extended from Perquimmons Creek on the east to Fourth Street on the west and from the Elizabeth City Road on the north to East Granby Street on the south. But Kahle was willing to continue those negotiations if Bill was still interested in buying that land. Bill assured him he still wanted to buy it because it would be a good site not only for a town park and recreation center but also for a volunteer fire department, which Bill was convinced the area needed, partly to provide assistance in case there was a fire at Hilltop House of course.

After discussing that matter for several minutes, Bill told George that he was also interested in buying a narrow strip of land on which to build a new highway that would link the Hertford Road with the Edenton Road. After acquiring the land needed for that purpose, Bill planned to buy a fourteen- or fifteen-acre tract near the new highway's midpoint, on which a large up-to-date hospital would be built in another year or two at his expense. That hospital would serve the people of Perquimmons City, Hertford, Edenton, and several other towns within a thirty- or forty-mile radius. Bill felt the area needed a hospital just as much as it needed a fire department and a local phone company like the ones established by small groups of Hertford and Edenton businessmen during the mid 1890s.

Because Bill knew Frances would wonder why he wanted to acquire so much land in or near Perquimmons City, he discussed his ideas with her for almost an hour while they were returning to New York on March 9.

Shortly after their train pulled out of the Hertford station and picked up speed, Bill reminded her that he would turn sixty in November; and because of a bad cold he'd caught in January and had been unable to shake for six weeks, he'd recently become very conscious of his age. He went on to say that he'd made a great deal of money during his career before pointing out that the current value of all his stocks, bonds, and other assets was roughly $72,000,000. Although he'd supported dozens of charitable organizations during the last thirty years, he'd always wondered if his gifts to them had helped ordinary people, which had always been his main goal. In most cases the organizations he'd supported had bought or leased larger and much more elegant headquarters for themselves or given overly large raises or bonuses to their officers and the dozens of men who sat on their executive boards. That had been a great disappointment to him; and because he probably had only four or five years left at most, he'd decided to make some important changes in his philanthropic work.

Before he could continue Frances insisted he shouldn't feel so gloomy about the future. He was in excellent health, largely because he had a strong constitution and had gained less than five pounds since their wedding more than sixteen years before. In addition he had two smart and attractive children who were as devoted to him as she was. Finally, he'd made dozens of new friends in Perquimmons City, men and women he truly liked and whose company he thoroughly enjoyed whenever they were together. So once their new home several miles east of town was finished, their lives would become even more enjoyable than they'd been in the past.

Although Bill agreed with her comments, he said she failed to understand where his comments were headed, which prompted her to give his hand a squeeze before asking him to continue.

"Although I've never told you this, Frances, I've heard my old friend Andrew Carnegie say dozens of times that a man should spend the first half of his life making his fortune and the second half of his life giving it away. Of course, my life is far more than half over and I've made only a fraction of the money Andrew made during the course of his career. But I'm still in a position to give away two or three million dollars a year for the rest of my life without endangering your and the children's security when I'm gone. In any event, I plan to get started right away, because I don't have a crystal ball and can't predict with any assurance when my life will end. I hate to say it but I could fall in front of a car or truck on Broadway or Fifth Avenue several days from now."

"Hush, Bill, I hate to hear you talk like that. You'll probably be around for twenty or thirty more years, which I hope and pray you will. Furthermore, if you can afford to give away several million dollars a year, I hope you will if it makes you truly happy."

"No, Frances, I'll never give away that much money because I have you and the children to think about. But I'd like to ask you a question now, a question I've been mulling over for several weeks. As I'm sure you know, I've always admired your judgment and common sense; and because the children are capable of handling most of their own needs now, you have a lot more free time on your hands. So I'm convinced you're the right person to help me evaluate the dozens of proposals I'm likely to receive when it's widely known that I plan to give away fourteen or fifteen million dollars. I'm assuming of course that you're willing to help me evaluate those proposals."

"I'd love to help you evaluate them because I've always thought people with great wealth have a moral obligation to assist the poor and less fortunate of the world. But I've never been so naïve that I've thought poverty will ever be completely eradicated despite the efforts of people like us."

"Because I've heard you make comments like that dozens of times, I was sure I could count on you. And because I plan to use roughly half the money I give away to help the people of eastern North Carolina, which is a very poor area, I'm grateful that I've made some good friends in Perquimmons City—men like Joe, Chip, Andrew Ridinger, George Kahle, Russell Barringer, and even Ozzie Crumpler. Although Ozzie's a bit of a lightweight compared to the others, I'm sure he means well. Anyway, I consider the others to be men of real ability and great integrity while Ozzie knows the area like the back of his hand because he's lived there all his life. So I'm thinking about asking them to work together as an advisory committee that will evaluate the dozens of proposals we'll probably receive during the next several years. I'll also ask them to pass the most promising proposals on to us for our acceptance or rejection. What do you think of that idea, my dear?"

"I think it's an excellent idea but what about adding Charlie Debs to that committee? When you make it clear we're interested in receiving proposals of all kinds, I'm sure Joe will push for the construction of a large, up-to-date hospital, which the area needs as much as anything else in my opinion. And when the time comes to build a hospital, Charlie Debs will be the right man to build it to plans Alec Kramer draws with Joe's help and advice. So if Charlie belongs to our committee from the start, it'll probably save us a great deal of time."

Bill said she'd made an excellent suggestion before asking her if she had any more suggestions to make.

"Yes, I do have another suggestion I'd like to make. So far we've agreed on seven men we'd like to serve on our advisory committee, but I think we should enlarge it with at least two women. I can think of two who'd be valuable members of it."

"You're thinking of Lucy and Julia aren't you?"

"Yes, because they've spent their whole lives in Perquimmons City just as Ozzie has, but also because their judgment and common sense are every bit as good as mine if not even better. Don't you think it would be smart to add them to our committee?"

"Yes, although if we have a committee of nine members and four of them are Hanfords and Summerlins, most of the townspeople will probably think we're hitching our wagon too closely to theirs—that we're in their hip pocket, so to speak."

"That's possible although I think it's a minor danger at most. But if that perception develops, we could always enlarge the committee with several people who have no ties with the Hanfords and Summerlins. But I'd like to point out something else to you now. For your plan to be truly effective, we should probably spend six or seven months a year in eastern North Carolina in the future. And for us to be able to do that, you'll have to reduce your duties in New York a great deal. Have you thought about stepping down as the president and managing partner of your company?"

Bill said he'd not only thought about resigning as the president and managing partner of his company but he'd already made up his mind to do it in a year or two. Frances was pleased to hear that but wondered if he'd made that decision for a specific reason of some kind.

Bill said he no longer enjoyed his work as much as he had during earlier years. His original partners, Otto Feldman and Lionel Baring, had been dead for almost a dozen years, and their sons and successors were less ethical men in his opinion. They were too aggressive and took much greater risks than their fathers had. They also spent very little time with clients who weren't millionaires already, and they tended to dismiss his ideas and opinions out of hand. As a result he'd slowed down a great deal during the last several years and had accepted less than a dozen new clients since 1907, when he helped J. P. Morgan and several other bankers find ways to avoid a financial crisis that would probably have triggered a serious depression throughout the country. Furthermore he'd already sold almost a third of his stock in his own company and invested it in safer places in the event Feldman, Baring, & Van Landingham failed six or seven years after he died. Although he took no comfort in predicting the eventual demise of his own company, he was convinced it might happen if the "young Turks" continued on their present courses, especially their unspoken goal of making large commissions for themselves at the expense of steady gains for their clients, which they did in various ways that were legal but unethical in his opinion.

Frances was stunned by his worries and asked him why he hadn't discussed them with the other members of his company's executive committee.

"But I have, Frances, dozens of times in fact. Unfortunately, most of my colleagues are convinced I'm too conservative, a relic from the last century, as it were. Because of that I plan to sell all my remaining stock in the company in another year or two."

"Where do you plan to put all the money you realize when you sell your remaining stock in the company?"

"I'll put a large part of it in six or seven insurance companies in New York and Hartford, Connecticut—they're all doing extremely well and I'm sure I won't go wrong by investing heavily in them. I also plan to buy more stock in blue-chip companies like General Electric, Sears and Roebuck, and the Ford and Chrysler automobile companies. And finally, I intend to buy much more stock than I already own in half a dozen North Carolina companies, especially Cannon Mills, the Wachovia Bank, and the Reynolds and American Tobacco Companies."

"That sounds like a sound strategy to me, but I'd rather talk about something more interesting now, especially your plan to help the people of eastern North Carolina. That's something I'm extremely interested in and it's a place where I might be able to make an important contribution as your assistant."

"You'll be much more than my assistant, my dear. I consider us equal partners in the work we're about to begin together."

Ten days after Bill and Frances returned to New York, the nine individuals they'd agreed to name to their advisory committee received personal letters from them. Those letters explained the committee's purpose and the Van Landinghams' hope that all nine recipients of their letters would agree to serve on their committee. Those letters went on to say that Bill and Frances would be returning to Perquimmons City on April 24 to approve the final plans and elevations for Hilltop House, and they hoped everyone on the committee would meet with them in the hotel's conference room on their second night back in town. At that time they would discuss the first important project they planned to fund—the construction of a large, up-to-date hospital that would serve the people of Perquimmons City, Hertford, Edenton and several other towns within a thirty- or forty-mile radius of the hospital.

Bill and Frances's letter to Joe asked him to spend as much time as possible during the coming month thinking about the size and general layout of the hospital and all the technical equipment it would need. In their letter to Andrew Ridinger, Bill and Frances asked him to start the planning process for a new highway that would link the Hertford Road with the Edenton Road. Somewhere along that highway, at a point easily accessible from all three towns, there should be a good site for the hospital and a large parking lot; and they hoped Andrew would locate that site and find out how it could be acquired and at what cost. Finally, in their letter to George Kahle, Bill and Frances asked him to think about the charter, or legal instrument, that would be needed if they established the hospital as a nonprofit corporation, which they considered the most logical course.

Although the Van Landinghams' letters to Lucy, Julia, and the other men on the committee assigned them no special task, they were as elated as Joe, Andrew, and George were because the letters they received were clear and convincing evidence that the Van Landinghams had decided to establish permanent ties with the area. As a result the people of Perquimmons City, Hertford, Edenton, and several smaller towns stood to profit from their leadership and generosity for years and maybe even decades to come.

Chapter 14

When the Van Landinghams arrived in Perquimmons City for the fourth time on April 24, Ozzie Crumpler welcomed them back to the hotel like royalty. After a leisurely meal in the dining room while Ozzie hovered over them trying to anticipate their every wish, they rested in their suite for most of the afternoon. Then after strolling around town for half an hour, they walked up the avenue to the Hanfords' house for dinner.

As they were enjoying their main course, Bill asked Joe about the size and layout of the hospital he envisaged for the area. Joe made several comments before Frances said they should postpone a detailed discussion of that matter until the next night, when she and Bill would meet with their advisory committee for the first time. Frances said she'd hate for most of the members to think everything had been decided in advance. Bill agreed before saying Joey and Olivia probably weren't interested in the hospital anyway.

"No, I'm really interested in it," Joey said at once. "After all, I plan to go to medical school after I play professional baseball for nine or ten years."

"You'll never play on a major-league team because you're not good enough," Olivia scoffed. "And you won't get into a good medical school unless you spend a lot more time on your homework."

"But I get all *As* and *Bs* without keeping my nose in a book the way you do, Miz Smarty Pants. I couldn't stand to study all the time and become an egghead like you."

"That's enough!" Julia said firmly to them. "What will our guests think if you keep that up?"

Frances smiled and told Julia not to worry about it because their children bickered a great deal too. "But I hope Olivia will play something on the piano for us after dinner. I'd love to hear her play a piece she's learned since our last visit."

When Olivia said she'd be glad to play the first movement of a Beethoven sonata she'd been working on for several weeks, Joey muttered, "Oh brother, what a bore."

"Cut it out, Joey!" Joe said at once while giving him a stern look.

Olivia smiled archly as Joey dug into his dessert, one of Augusta's outstanding fruit cobblers with some vanilla ice cream on top.

Although Lucy tried to hide her partiality for Joey in fairness to her other nieces and nephews, he was her clear favorite. Blunt and straightforward, there was nothing sneaky or tricky about him as there was about his cousin Alfred, who was a whiner and complainer as well. Joey was very tall for his age and extremely good-looking. Masculine in every way, he resembled his father so much it was uncanny. Lucy was convinced Joey would be an excellent doctor one day. She also felt there was a good chance he'd play professional baseball for nine or ten years before going to medical school. If her hunch proved correct, she was sure everyone in her family, herself included, would attend one of his double-headers each summer, especially if he played for the Washington Senators or the Philadelphia Phillies because train trips to those cities would be fairly easy and inexpensive.

Late the next morning one of the bellhops at the hotel drove Bill and Frances to Hertford in Ozzie's new car, a luxurious twelve-cylinder Packard, for another meeting with Charlie Debs and Alec Kramer. After a fine catered lunch in Charlie's conference room, Alec produced his final floor plans, elevations, and materials list for Hilltop House, which would consist of 17,987 square feet on three floors. The mansion would be the central element of a complex that included two servants' cottages (1,344 square feet each); a four-car garage with a storage loft above; a fenced tennis court; a swimming pool and adjacent cabana with changing rooms, showers, and toilets for men and women alike; and finally a dock and boathouse for their son's sailboat on Hatcher's Creek. After Bill and Frances studied the plans for all those structures for an hour and approved them, Alec unrolled a topographical map of the site and pointed out where an impressive entrance avenue from the Elizabeth City Road to the mansion's garage and a parking lot for Bill and Frances's guests could be built with a minimal amount of grading and paving. Alex had also marked on the map where dozens of magnolias, crepe myrtles, and clusters of boxwoods, azaleas, camellias, and forsythias could be planted to excellent effect on both sides of the entrance avenue and around the mansion's walls and those of its dependencies. The Van Landinghams studied that map for twenty minutes before commending Alex for his outstanding work before accepting his plans and proposals for the whole complex.

When Bill asked the total price of the project with baited breath, Charlie said it would be $267,585, which included the remainder of Alec's fee and the landscaping as well as the paving of the entrance avenue and a parking lot that would contain forty-one spaces for cars. As a result, whenever Bill and Frances gave a big party or reception, their guests would have ample places to park. Bill heaved a sigh of relief because he'd assumed the total cost would be at least $350,000, which it probably would've been in Florida or New York.

As Charlie was about to explain the construction schedule he planned to follow and the monthly payments Bill would need to make for the work to continue without interruption, Frances said she had no interest in technical matters like that. So she excused herself and left the building because she wanted to see more of Hertford, which seemed like an attractive little town.

When Ozzie's driver returned Frances to Charlie's office building an hour later, the three men were about to sign three identical copies of the complex's legal contract: one for Charlie's files, one for Alec's records, and the third one for the Van Landinghams to keep wherever they liked. After the men signed all three copies, Charlie congratulated everyone on a job well done before saying it was time for a small celebration. He sent his secretary to the building's kitchenette to get five wine glasses and a bottle of champagne from the icebox. When the secretary returned with them, Charlie uncorked the bottle and poured a glass for everyone. Then the five people clinked their glasses together before Charlie made a toast to the work already completed and the construction that would begin in another week and hopefully be far enough along by December 15 that the garage, one of the servants' cottages, and most of the mansion would be usable. However, the rest of the complex, especially the tennis court, the swimming pool and cabana, and the dock and boathouse for Billy's sailboat, wouldn't be finished until the end of March at the earliest.

That night the Van Landinghams met with Charlie and the other members of their advisory committee in the conference room of Crumpler's Hotel. Because the Van Landinghams had already explained the purpose of that meeting in their letters to the committee's nine members a month earlier, they saw no need for a rehash of that subject. So after several words of welcome, Bill asked Joe to come forward and explain his concept of a large, well-equipped hospital for the area, which was the only topic that would be considered that night.

After leaving his chair for the lectern, Joe opened a folder and took out a list of the most important points he planned to make. After clearing his throat a bit nervously several times, he said the hospital he envisaged for the area would have at least seventy-five beds, two operating rooms, two delivery rooms, and an emergency-room suite where as many as three sick or badly injured patients could be examined and given whatever treatment they needed at the time. Such a hospital would need a staff of several doctors and seven or eight nurses, while the doctors in Hertford, Edenton, and other nearby towns would be granted operating privileges for a nominal fee. The hospital would have its own laundry, laboratory, cafeteria, and commercial-grade kitchen for the preparation of meals for patients and their families as well as the hospital's administrative and custodial staff. Finally, although Joe was afraid his next point would be controversial, he felt the hospital should accept black as well as white patients because the medical problems of the black people in the area shouldn't be ignored.

Clearly skeptical of such an arrangement, Ozzie asked Joe if he thought most of the local whites would patronize an integrated hospital. Because Joe had thought that question would be asked, he was prepared for it and said at once, "I see no reason why blacks and whites can't be treated in the same building. During the years I was a resident in Richmond's largest hospital, I never heard a white patient complain because a black person was being treated in a different wing or on a different floor of the same building."

"But this area's probably much more conservative than a city like Richmond," Ozzie said.

"I agree with Ozzie about that," Julia said at once. "And while I'm only playing the devil's advocate here, what if a large part of the local population boycotts our hospital out of racial prejudice? If that happens, won't it fail in less than a year?"

"That's possible but highly unlikely," Joe said with obvious conviction. "With the exception of several local families who don't need to be named,

I doubt that many people will boycott a hospital in our area and travel forty-five miles to the smaller and more poorly-equipped hospital in Elizabeth City. If you think more than several families will boycott our hospital out of racial prejudice, I urge you to visit my office on any weekday morning. I have only one waiting room and I've always treated blacks and whites on a first-come, first-served basis unless there's an emergency of some kind or someone on my patient list arrives for an appointment made at least twenty-four hours in advance. If that's not good enough for my white patients, they're free to find another doctor with my blessing."

"Well said, Joe!" Lucy blurted out.

"Yes, it was well said," Julia said to him. "Although I knew what you'd say and I agree with all of it, I thought it was important for the whole committee to know how strongly you feel about our hospital being open to black as well as white people."

After expressing his full agreement too, Chip pointed out that if the hospital was built on a site roughly midway between all three towns, it would be almost four and a half miles from the black section of Perquimmons City on the eastern side of the creek. "And because only a few blacks own cars and buggy rides are fairly expensive, it'll be hard for them to get sick or badly injured people to the hospital. So in my opinion a special provision of some kind should be made for them."

"That's an important point," Joe said at once to Chip, "and I hoped someone on the committee would make it. Just as you do, I feel a special provision should be made for the blacks who live on the eastern side of the creek although that would increase the hospital's cost a great deal."

Joe and all the other members of the committee gazed at Bill and Frances while wondering what they'd say.

After thinking for a moment Bill asked Frances to explain to the committee their thoughts about an important matter like that. "I'll be glad to," Frances said to her husband before addressing the committee's members from her chair. "What Bill and I hope to learn from tonight's meeting is what the committee would like to see done without any regard to cost. Our actual goal is to see that the people of this area get medical care comparable to what the people of Boston, New York, and other large cities have gotten for years."

After saying how glad he was to hear that, Joe added that if money wasn't a consideration, which was hardly ever the case, he'd like to see a clinic opened on upper Sixth Street a block or so beyond the point where there was no record of any flooding since the town's incorporation in 1852.

He was convinced a clinic in that part of town would be heavily used by blacks and whites alike who lived within a mile or so of the building, especially if its fees were no higher than the ones the hospital charged. Such a clinic would need a fulltime doctor and two nurses to handle routine problems although the most serious problems would be referred to the hospital's medical staff roughly four miles away. Richardson's Funeral Home had recently bought a Cunningham hearse, the best vehicle of its kind on the market, and Floyd Richardson had assured him that it could double as an ambulance for thirty-five cents a ride. Moreover, by the time the hospital opened its doors, the town would have phone service. So the clinic's secretary-receptionist could call the funeral home and arrange for its special vehicle to transport patients in serious condition from the clinic to the hospital in less than ten minutes.

After thinking for several moments Bill said those ideas seemed very sound to him; and if they were implemented properly, the town and surrounding area would have first-rate medical facilities, which was the goal he and Frances had in mind, as she'd already explained.

Once Joe returned to his chair, Bill asked George Kahle if it would be possible to establish the hospital and associated clinic as a single, nonprofit institution.

George said that would be no problem provided the hospital and clinic had a single director and executive board.

Clearly pleased by George's answer, Bill suggested that someone make a motion that the new hospital and clinic should be established as a single nonprofit entity with a single director and executive board. Russell Barringer made that motion at once and Lucy seconded it. When Bill opened the floor to a discussion of the motion, no one made an objection or even suggested a friendly amendment. So Bill called for a vote by a show of hands. The motion passed unanimously, triggering a smattering of cheers and applause.

Bill smiled and poured himself a glass of water from the pitcher Ozzie had placed on a card table beside the lectern. After drinking several sips of water Bill asked Joe to confer as often as he could during the coming summer with Alec Kramer as he drew up the plans and cost estimates for the hospital and clinic buildings. Once Joe said he'd gladly do that, Bill said he hoped those plans and cost estimates could be considered during the committee's next meeting in September, when he and Frances would be in town again to check on the progress of Hilltop House. They planned to spend most of the summer at their cottage on Oyster Bay, which they'd recently agreed to sell to Martin Feldman's older brother shortly after Labor Day.

Eventually George Khale asked Bill if he and Frances planned to finance only the construction of the hospital and clinic buildings or if they also planned to establish an endowment for the hospital and clinic so they would function without any financial constraints and their employees would receive their salaries on the first or second day of every month without fail. In response to that question, Bill said he and Frances had decided to endow the hospital and clinic with stock worth at least a million dollars, the dividends from which would be reserved for their employees' salaries, periodic repairs to the buildings, and the purchase of new and improved equipment whenever it became available. A murmur of approval spread through the conference room before loud cheers and applause broke out. No one on the committee, not even Joe and Julia, had thought Bill and Frances would be that generous.

As Bill was about to adjourn the meeting, Frances reminded him to call on Andrew Ridinger, who'd been asked to locate a good site for the hospital. While standing in front of his chair Andrew explained that he was currently involved in some negotiations with William Pollard of Edenton, a banker like himself for almost thirty years. Mr. Pollard owned a sprawling tract of slightly over six thousand acres that stretched from the outskirts of Edenton on the west to the Hertford Road on the east. The southern boundary of that tract was half a mile north of the Perquimmons City town limit; and Pollard was extremely interested in the hospital because it was intended to serve the people of his town as well as those of Perquimmons City, Hertford, and several smaller towns in the area. So he'd offered to donate fifteen acres for the hospital's site as soon as the highway linking the Edenton and Hertford Roads was built on a narrow strip of land Bill had recently bought with George Kahle's help for that purpose.

After thanking Andrew for his report, Bill adjourned the meeting shortly after nine o'clock.

As most of the other committee members left the conference room, Bill conferred for several minutes with Joe and Charlie Debs about a tentative budget for the hospital and clinic buildings as well as all the technical equipment and furniture Joe felt those buildings would need. Bill asked Joe and Charlie to hold everything to $1,250,000 if they could. But if that proved impossible, they could go as high as $1,500,000 without obtaining his and Frances's approval.

Several minutes later, as Joe and Julia were driving Lucy home, they praised Bill's conduct of the meeting because everything had proceeded smoothly even when Ozzie asked Joe if the hospital would accept black as well as white patients. The Hanfords were even more impressed by the fact that Bill and Frances were willing to donate as much as $2,500,000 for the buildings, their furniture and technical equipment as well as a permanent endowment to ensure that the hospital and associated clinic always operated smoothly.

From her place on the backseat Lucy said, "Who would've thought Bill and Frances were prepared to be that generous? In my opinion Perquimmons City has just acquired a pair of guardian angels, which is wonderful for everyone in the area."

"It certainly is," Julia said from her place on the front seat beside Joe. "Other places should be so lucky."

Joe suggested that the Bill and Frances's generosity might inspire other wealthy Americans to follow their lead and be more civic-minded. "Because there are thousands of millionaires around the country now, just think how much could be accomplished if fifteen or twenty percent of them were as generous as Bill and Frances."

"That's a wonderful thought," Lucy said, "but it'll never happen. The more money most people have, the more they feel they need, which is ridiculous when you think about it."

"You're such a pessimist," Julia said over her shoulder to Lucy. "If I'd told you before tonight's meeting that Bill and Frances were willing to be that generous, you wouldn't have believed it for a minute."

"You're right, I wouldn't have believed it," Lucy said. "And I bet Joe wouldn't have believed it either."

Joe laughed and said, "She's got you there, sweetie pie, because no one else on the committee would've believed it either."

The next morning Lucy was helping Jobie Caldwell's mother and grandmother at the cosmetics counter when Frances entered the drugstore. She waited near the stationery counter while Mrs. Caldwell paid for her and her mother's purchases and Lucy bagged them and handed them across the counter to her before telling the two women good-bye and they walked slowly toward the store's main entrance. Only then did Frances move to the cosmetics counter and tell Lucy hello before they chatted for several minutes about how well the previous night's meeting had gone. Eventually Frances said she'd just invited Julia and the rest of her family to come to

New York for several weeks in July. Julia loved that idea, partly because Olivia had begged for months to go to New York and attend a concert at Carnegie Hall with the Van Landinghams and their daughter. But Joe was too busy to leave town for more than a few days. So shortly after he declined to go the trip, Frances decided to ask Lucy to take his place and she truly hoped Lucy would.

Although flattered and pleased by Frances's invitation, Lucy thanked her for it before saying she couldn't leave town for more than a few days either.

"Oh that's *exactly* what Julia told me you'd say!" Frances complained. "But she's convinced you'd enjoy a trip to New York because you had so much fun when you went to the Jamestown Exposition with the other members of your family almost four years ago. So I hope you'll reconsider and come to New York with Julia and her children in July, when Bill has to be in the city for several meetings before we return to Oyster Bay for the rest of the summer."

Lucy promised to think about Frances's invitation before wishing the Van Landinghams a safe and comfortable trip back to New York.

Once Frances told Lucy goodbye and went to the drug counter to get some toothpaste and cough syrup for Bill, Lucy helped Dillie wait on the big shots at their usual table. They'd overheard Lucy's conversation with Frances at the cosmetics counter; and when she took a pot of coffee to their table and offered to refill their mugs, George Kahle winked at Russell Barringer before saying to Lucy, "I'm glad you decided not to go to New York with Julia and her children in July because Dillie couldn't fix our coffee and serve it to us by herself. In fact, she wouldn't even know where to start unless Chip stopped what he was doing at the drug counter and showed her exactly what to do."

From the soda fountain Dillie said, "I heard that, Mist'uh Kahle, and I've fixed yo coffee and served it to you and yo friends every maw'nin fo ov'uh ten yea'uhs although Miz Lucy helps me whenev'uh she ain't busy with a custo'muh. But I've been waitin for the right time to tell you and the oth'uh big shots somethin really important—it wouldn't hurt you a bit if you brought yo mugs ov'uh here to the soda fountain as soon as you're ready fo a refill."

"You stand corrected," Russell Barringer said to Kahle with a grin. "Dillie has a good point there."

"I sure do, Mist'uh Barring'uh. But my point applies to you and Mist'uh Riding'uh too, and even to Mist'uh Ozzie although he's a spring chicken compared to the rest o you guys. I don't know why you're so sure women like Miz Lucy and me was put on earth just to serve coffee to big shots like you. Well, I got some big news fo you now—it ain't true, and I think Miz Lucy should go to New Yawk this summ'uh and have herself a great time regardless o what you big shots thinks about it."

"You don't mean that, Dillie," Barringer said in his deep voice. "I can't believe you think Lucy should go on a trip and leave her brother and his thousands of customers in a terrible bind. That would be very inconsiderate of her, don't you think?"

When Chip arrived from the drug counter to find out what all the arguing was about, Dillie explained the situation to him in several seconds. With feigned seriousness Chip said at once, "The big shots are right, Dillie, because I can't let Lucy take a full week off in July although it's our slowest time of the year. Whenever she's a bit under the weather and stays home for several days, we make dozens of mistakes and the whole store falls into chaos. We need her here every day to keep us on our toes."

"Oh 'shaw, Mist'uh Chip, I knows you's just joshin me. I don't need Miz Lucy or nobody else to keep me on *my* toes and neither do you. So I say she should go to New Yawk and have herself a great time, which is 'zac'ly what she'll do aft'uh she thinks about it fo a while. Servin coffee every day to a bunch o silly old men ain't much of a job, and neither is sendin out all the bills on the same day of each month. If the bills are a week or two late, who the heck's gonna complain about that?"

Turning to Lucy Chip said firmly, "I forbid you to pay any attention to Dillie's views. She's just trying to stir up trouble and you know it."

With a frown Lucy said just as firmly to Chip, "You have no right to order me around like that! If I decide to go to New York, you'll just have to accept it. End of argument, you hear?"

As Lucy stomped back to the store's office to post the rest of the previous day's charges, she heard more guffaws from the big shots' table. Those guffaws continued until Dillie said, "You big shots think you're *so gol-darn smart*, don't you? Well, Miz Lucy's gonna show you a thing or two this summ'uh, I'm sure as shootin she is!"

During the next several hours Lucy considered Frances's invitation and the pros and cons of a trip to New York with her sister and her niece and nephew. Such a trip would probably be great fun although much more expensive than her trip to the Jamestown Exposition had been. Still, she hadn't been out of town a single time since 1907 and she wasn't getting any younger. In fact, she would be forty on June 16 and she hadn't spent a penny of the money she'd received from her parents' estate in 1909. For several hours after eating her bag lunch in the store's office, she asked herself repeatedly what her parents would expect her to do if they were still alive. She knew they'd be pleased that she'd put all the money she'd inherited from them in her savings account at the bank and had added two dollars a week to it since Chip gave her another nice raise in the fall of 1910. With all the accrued interest, her nest egg came to $1,387.63 now; and she was convinced if her parents were still alive, they'd ask her what she was saving all that money for. Luckily, she'd always paid her monthly pledge to St. John's Church in a timely manner and gave ten or eleven dollars to her favorite charities nine or ten times a year. But did she ever spend any money on herself? Did she ever spend a dollar on just having a good time? Not unless she counted all the fun she had while having dinner with the Hanfords and Summerlins, for which she thanked them with gifts of flowers and vegetables from her garden during the warmer months of the year and boxes of candy or large bags of citrus fruit from Florida she bought at Hogan's Grocery Store during the year's colder months.

In view of those things couldn't she afford to spend ninety or a hundred dollars on a trip to New York? The main expense would be the cost of the train ticket, which would be slightly over $24 including tax. But because she and Julia and her children would be staying with the Van Landinghams, she wouldn't have to pay her share of the cost of a hotel room she'd normally share with her sister and niece or for over six or seven meals in the train's dining car and several New York restaurants. But on the other hand, she would definitely buy a nice present of some kind for Bill and Frances on her last day in Manhattan. She would also insist on buying her own ticket to a concert at Carnegie Hall and several taxi and subway rides. But this was a golden opportunity that might not come again, and Lucy couldn't think of a convincing reason why she shouldn't go on the trip. In fact, she decided by three thirty that it would be foolish not to go on it.

Once she got off work two hours later, she walked up the avenue to the Hanfords' house, where she was having dinner that night. To her surprise Julia met her on the front porch and led her into the parlor at once. There Julia told her make herself comfortable on the sofa and listen to her reasons why she should go on the trip. Lucy was deeply amused as Julia paced around the floor while lecturing her as if she was a schoolgirl again. Julia was about to explain her fifth and last reason why she should go on the trip when Lucy said firmly, "Stop all this fuss and bother, Julia! You've been wasting your time because I decided to go on the trip over two hours ago."

"You did? You actually decided to go on it while you were still working at the drugstore?" Julia asked with an amazed look. "I can hardly believe it!"

While suppressing a grin Lucy said, "I don't see why you feel that way because I can afford to go on such a trip and I haven't been out of town a single time since I went to the Jamestown Exposition with you and the rest of our family. Didn't it ever occur to you that I enjoy going on trips and seeing other places as much as other people do? I'd hate for you to think I'm so peculiar I never want to leave town."

After a moment of speechlessness Julia burst into peals of laughter as Joe opened the front door and came inside. As he entered the parlor he said, "What's so amusing, sweetie pie?"

"It's so funny I can hardly believe it, Joe! I've spent the last ten minutes trying to convince Lucy to go to New York with the children and me in July. But she just told me I've been wasting my time because she decided to go on the trip more than two hours ago while she was still at the drugstore."

"That's good to hear," Joe said with a smile. "And because her fortieth birthday's coming up fairly soon, I'll buy her a new dress for the trip. I want her to look like a real fashion plate while she's hobnobbing in New York with the Van Landinghams and their social set."

Although touched by Joe's offer, Lucy said she couldn't accept such an expensive present from him.

"I don't see why not," Joe said at once. "But if you refuse to change your mind, I'll give you a new mixing spoon or can opener for your birthday. You'd like that a lot better, wouldn't you?"

"Don't be so sarcastic!" Julia said to him. "You know how much Lucy values her independence."

"I value my independence too," Joe said with a grin. "But I also like nice presents and it'll be a cold day in hell when you and the children don't."

On the evening of June 16, shortly after the family enjoyed an excellent dinner at the Summerlins' house and sang "Happy Birthday" to Lucy, she blew out the ten candles on the birthday cake Rhonda had made for her, one candle for every four years of her life. As Rhonda cut the first piece of cake for "the birthday girl," Joe handed Lucy a beautifully wrapped box from Ada Howell's dress shop. It contained one of the prettiest dresses Lucy had ever seen, one Julia had probably chosen because she knew Lucy's size and the styles she liked best. Lucy couldn't believe how generous Joe and Julia had been; but to her amazement, Julia handed her another box that contained a silk blouse she'd also found at Ada's shop and a skirt she'd made out of some beautiful material she'd found at Miss Edna's Dry Goods Store. Lucy's favorite pin, the garnet brooch Jobie Caldwell's grandmother had earmarked for his wife and given Lucy a day after Jobie's funeral, would go perfectly with her new blouse and skirt. So many other presents followed—a new bathrobe and pair of bedroom slippers from Olivia and Joey, a hat and matching purse from Chip and Rhonda, several lace handkerchiefs from Susan, and some new gloves and silk stockings from Alfred and Jack—Lucy burst into tears because she was so overcome by her family's enormous generosity to her. Although she couldn't think of what to say at the time, there was no mistaking how deeply she felt about the rest of her family and how grateful she was for their many thoughtful gifts that evening.

Three days later, shortly after Lucy fed Mr. Jobie and fixed a fried egg and piece of toast for her own breakfast, Lucy cleaned up the kitchen and left her cottage for the drugstore. After walking several blocks she saw Sadie Jones, the best midwife in the area, the one Joe urged all his pregnant patients to use except those he suspected would have long, difficult deliveries and would probably need his greater skills and expertise. Sadie was standing at the corner of Hertford Avenue and East Church Street, waiting for several cars and half a dozen men on bicycles to ride by before she crossed the widest street in town and continued on to her cabin in a small colored enclave on the Edenton Road. Most of the blacks in the county called that enclave "Plumnelly" because it was several miles beyond the western town limits and, in their opinion, "plum nelly" (or almost) to Edenton although it was actually less than halfway to that town.

"Hello, Sadie," Lucy said with a smile, "it's nice to see you again. You look really good today because you've probably lost twelve or thirteen pounds since the last time you came to the drugstore to stock up on the supplies you need for your work."

"Thank you, Miz Lucy, although I ain't lost that much weight. I still weighs almost two hundred pounds I'm afraid."

"Even if you still weigh that much, you look like you feel much better than you did back in March because you had a bad cold that morning and sneezed the whole time I waited on you. But why are you up and about so early today?"

"It ain't early for me 'cause I been up all night deliverin a baby fo a lady who lives across the street from where yo mama lived until the day she died. She was such a kind and carin person I knows you miss her an awful lot."

"Yes, I do miss her a lot and my papa too. But do you still see Flossie and Tulip fairly often?"

"Yes'm, I sees 'em on most Sun'dy maw'nins 'cause we still goes to the same church."

"Good, because I hope you'll give them a message for me the next time you see them if it's not too much trouble."

"No'm, it won't be any trouble at all. What would like me to tell 'em?"

"Tell them I'm really worried about them and hope they haven't told anybody else about their part in Mr. Merritt's murder last fall. I'm convinced they were deeply involved in that crime because Flossie told me on the day I moved out of the Merritt House that she almost killed him a week after he threatened to fire Tulip if she refused to have the abortion that kept her from becoming pregnant again. I haven't mentioned that to another soul and never will because Flossie and Tulip were so good to me during the years I worked at the Merritt House. I wouldn't have been able to make it without their support and encouragement several times a week."

"Flossie didn't have nothin to do with that awful man's death 'cause the spirit o the Lord really came ov'uh her a year or so aft'uh you left the Merritt House and started workin fo yo broth'uh."

"That's news to me because I was sure Flossie and Tulip killed Mr. Merritt in his study last fall."

"Even if Flossie had nothin to do with Mist'uh Merritt's death, Tulip was up to her ears in it just as you thought she was. But she didn't ac'shully kill him."

"She didn't? Then who did?"

"I did 'cause I've always believed in the Old Testament verse 'an eye fo an eye an a tooth fo a tooth.' After all, that man ruined my whole fam'ly and caused me to lose all the folks I loved more'n any others in the whole world."

"I don't see how he could've ruined your whole family, Sadie."

"Well, as I'm sure you know, he got my sweet little Carlotta pregnant when she was only thirteen and forced her to have the abo'tion that caused her to bleed to death a couple o days lat'uh. A month or so aft'uh that, when my hus'bun Sam came home from pickin cotton and t'bacca on some farms near Dunn, I told him what had happened to Carlotta an he almost lost his mind he was so upset. He rushed ov'uh to the Merritt House aft'uh supp'uh that night with our sons Sam Jun'yuh and Marcus to have it out with that evil man. They got into a big fight behind the barn, and when Sam called Mis'tuh Merritt a kill'uh, he took out his gun and shot Sam in the heart. He also shot my boys in both arms and threatened to kill 'em if they ev'uh spread any stories 'bout him in town. Then he had Matthew Harden drive my boys back to Plumnelly in his wagon; and as they got out of it, Matthew gave 'em ten doll'uhs apiece from Mist'uh Merritt and told 'em they'd be smart to use that money to leave this neck o the woods as soon as they was well enough to travel. And that's 'zac'ly what they did, Miz Lucy. They left Plumnelly several weeks lat'uh after tellin me everything Mist'uh Merritt did to them and my wonduh'ful Sam that awful night. And 'cause I ain't heard nothin from my boys since the maw'nin they left my cabin, I has no idea if they're dead or alive."

"Oh, Sadie, I'm so sorry to hear all that. Matthew told me and the other house servants on the morning after Sam died that Mr. Merritt had caught him inside the barn shortly after nightfall as he was about to steal two of his best saddles. Mr. Merritt took out his gun and tried to stop him, and when Sam charged him with a butcher knife, he had no choice but to shoot him in self-defense. The police never questioned that because Matthew Harden swore that was exactly what happened and he'd been there at the time. But I've always wondered if that was true because Flossie and Tulip always said Sam was the most honest man they'd ever known."

"They was tellin the truth 'cause my Sam was so honest he nev'uh stole nothin in his whole life, I swear to God he didn't."

"Sadie, that's the saddest story I ever heard and it's easy to see why you were determined to get even with Mr. Merritt one day. But you should've let God do that, and I'm sure He would've done it on Judgment Day if not a lot sooner."

"Yes'm, I knows I should've done that now. But when Tulip told me one maw'nin aft'uh church last fall that Miz Merritt wanted Flossie and her mama to kill her hus'bun but Flossie wouldn't have nothin to do with her plan, I said I'd take her mama's place without even thinkin 'bout how I'd feel lat'uh."

"That's a shame, Sadie, but I won't mention a word of this to another soul, I swear I won't."

"I knows you won't 'cause Dillie Hughes and Agus'tuh Wal'tuhs has told me what a fine person you are, and so has Creola Brew'uh and her hus'bun Travis. They all say you don't look down on colored folks like us the way most o the white folks in town do."

"That's right, Sadie, because the color of a person's skin has never mattered to me and never will. I just hope a lot more people realize in a year or two that God and Jesus have always hoped we'd feel that way about each other. But tell me this, Sadie—it sounds like you've had some second thoughts about the way you helped Tulip kill Mr. Merritt last fall. Is that right?"

"Yes'm, 'cause I've had some terrible nightmares 'bout what we did to him that night. Tulip stuffed a dishrag in his mouth and held his shoulders down on the study sofa while I sat on his chest and cut his throat from ear to ear. I'll nev'uh fo'get the look in his eyes when he woke up and saw the knife in my hand and knew what I was 'bout to do to him. I just hope God has mercy on my soul when I kneels befo His throne on Judgment Day."

"I can't speak for God of course—no one but Jesus and the Holy Ghost can do that. But what you and Flossie did to Mr. Merritt that night reminds me of the old saying that 'God works in strange and mysterious ways.' Maybe God chose you and Flossie to be his agents on earth to end the life of that terrible man before he hurt dozens of other nice girls like Carlotta and Tulip and also Serena Harden if he'd lived much longer than he did."

"I never thought about it like that 'cause my mama taught me to believe in the old sayin that 'two wrongs don't make a right.'"

"I was taught to believe that saying too although I've never seen it anywhere in the Bible. Besides, you'll feel much better if you think of yourself as an agent of God's judgment on a truly evil man on the night you and Tulip killed him."

"Hmmmmmmm, you're right about that, Miz Lucy, 'cause I feels bett'uh already."

"Good. But from the things you just told me, it sounds like Matthew and Jamilla didn't have anything to do with Mr. Merritt's death."

"That's right although Miz Merritt wanted you and everybody else in town to think they planned the crime and carried it out by 'emselves. That's why Miz Merritt helped 'em leave town fo New Yawk on the same night Tulip and me killed him as a way o keepin Chief Trumble from lookin into the crime the next maw'nin the way he should've done."

"Are you saying that Mrs. Merritt used Matthew and Jamilla only as decoys?"

"That's right, Miz Lucy, and she gave 'em only thirty doll'uhs apiece fo their trip to New Yawk, not a couple o hundred doll'uhs the way most people thinks she did. From the beginnin Miz Merritt planned to have Flossie and Tulip kill her hus'bun and offered 'em fifty doll'uhs apiece if they'd do it fo her. But when Flossie refused to have nothin to do with his death, Tulip convinced Miz Merritt to let her ask me to take Flossie's place aft'uh Tulip told her I'm her aunt and I'd nev'uh gotten ov'uh my poor little Carlotta's death and the death o my wonduh'ful Sam. So I agreed to help Tulip sev'ral hours aft'uh Matthew and Jamilla took the last train from the Hertford station to Rich'mun one af'tuhnoon last fall. After waitin at the Rich'mun station till the next maw'nin, they took anoth'uh train to New Yawk, where I've heard they found good jobs in a shoe fac'try in Brooklyn."

"Did Tulip give you half of the money Mrs. Merritt promised her if she and Flossie killed her husband?"

"That's right, she sho nuff did. Miz Merritt put fifty doll'uhs on the breakfast table sho'tly befo we entered the mansion by the back do 'bout twelve thirty that night. We took that money befo we went to the study and did our work. And once we finished what we'd promised to do to Mist'uh Merritt in his study, we found anoth'uh fifty doll'uhs waitin fo us on the breakfast table. I tell you, Miz Lucy, that was the easiest fifty doll'uhs I've ev'uh made. I usually has to deliv'uh a dozen babies to make that much money."

"You make less than five dollars for delivering a baby?"

"That's right, and a real skinflint like Mist'uh Merritt paid me only two-fifty fo deliverin Becca and his sons. Aft'uh he got Carlotta pregnant and she died from the abo'tion she had aft'uh he threatened to fire her if she unless she had it, I was sho glad he didn't ask me to deliv'uh his wife's next baby although Flossie told me sev'ral yea'uhs lat'uh that little girl had been born dead and Miz Merritt never got pregnant again aft'uh that. I hate to think what I would've done to that sweet little baby if she'd been born alive and I'd been Miz Merritt's midwife that day."

"You would've done the right thing, Sadie, I'm sure you would. You're too good a person to have taken the life of an innocent child because of her father's evil ways. But you look really tired, and you'd probably like to go back to your cabin and sleep for the rest of the day. But the next time you see Flossie and Tulip, I hope you'll tell them how grateful I still am for all their help and support during the years I worked and lived at the Merritt House."

"I'll tell 'em that the next time I sees 'em, Miz Lucy, I promise I will. You have yo'self a nice day now."

"You have a nice day too, Sadie. I've really enjoyed talking to you this morning and I hope you find a way to forget what you and Tulip did to Mr. Merritt last fall. What's done is done and besides, I'm sure God used you and Tulip to get rid of that awful man before he destroyed several more families the same way he destroyed yours."

"That's how I'm gonna look at it from now on, Miz Lucy, 'cause I'm hopin it'll end my nightmares 'bout the awful thing I did to him that night."

"I hope so too, Sadie, and I wish you all the best in the future."

"Thank you, ma'am. I wish you all the best too 'cause you're just as kind and carin as your mama was."

Poor Sadie, Lucy thought as she watched her cross Hertford Avenue and a vacant lot to the sidewalk on the southern side of West Granby Street. *Because she's such a nice person, it's a real shame Mr. Merritt's impact on her life and happiness is as strong as ever although he's been dead for eight months. I sure hope she remembers the things I told her this morning so they'll help her forget all the sad events of her last fourteen years and she can start a new and happier chapter of her life in a day or so.*

Chapter 15

On the morning of July 6, slightly over two weeks after her conversation with Sadie Jones, Lucy left the Hertford station for New York with Julia, Olivia, and Joey. All four of them waved to Joe on the station's platform as long as they could see him. As the train rounded a long bend and picked up speed, they made themselves comfortable and discussed all the things they hoped to see and do in Manhattan. Lucy couldn't tell who was more excited, her niece and nephew or herself. Despite Julia's insistence that she wasn't a bit excited because she'd been to New York less than two years before, she was soon talking a mile a minute like the others.

An hour or so after they finished an early supper in the dining car, their train came to a stop at one of the many platforms in New York's vast new Penn Station which had opened the previous year. They marveled at the size and height of the building's main concourse as they walked through it with their suitcases. In several minutes Joey saw the exit to West Thirty-fourth Street, which they took just as Frances had instructed Julia to do in a recent letter. As they emerged from the building and were about to join the taxi queue, they saw Mr. Van Landingham waving to them from the front of a long black car. After welcoming them to the city, he told them that the city's taxis were too small to carry four passengers and their luggage at the same time. So he'd come to the station to welcome them to New York and take them to his home in Gramercy Park in his company's limousine. One of his personal aides was driving it for him because he'd never even tried to learn that skill, convinced he was too old. Once Joey helped that aide tie the luggage on the back of the car, he sat in the front with him while Bill sat on the back seat with Julia while Lucy and Olivia sat on the fold-down seats attached to the back of the car's front seat.

When the limousine arrived at the Van Landinghams' brownstone on the southern side of Grammercy Park twenty minutes later, Frances was waiting on the front steps with Billy and Barbara to welcome the four visitors to their home. In no time the North Carolinians felt they were with old friends again. Billy was eager to talk to Lucy in private and ask her several questions about Susan and if she ever thought about him and the things he was doing in Manhattan and Oyster Bay that summer.

"I couldn't say," Lucy said while suppressing a grin, "because she doesn't confide in me about such personal matters. But she asked me to deliver a letter she wrote you a day or two ago." Billy grinned as Lucy opened her purse and took out a thick envelope addressed to him. When she handed it to him with a smile, he thanked her for bringing it to New York and said he'd read it later in his bedroom.

After Billy and Joey carried the four suitcases into the house, Bill and Frances ushered the others inside and chatted with them and Barbara in the front hall for several minutes while two of their servants took the suitcases up to the guest rooms on the third floor. Eventually Barbara led the visitors up to their rooms where she told them to freshen up and rest as long as they liked. Whenever they were ready her parents would like them to come down to the parlor on the main floor for some coffee and desert before they planned their activities during their time in New York.

Shortly after eight o'clock Lucy, Julia, and Julia's children came down to the parlor, where Bill and Frances welcomed them to the city again before one of their maids wheeled in a mahogany tea cart that held a silver service and several kinds of desserts as well as small stacks of china, silverware, and small linen napkins. Everyone had a cup of coffee and several delicious little cookies or a slice of coconut cake or Boston cream pie. Billy and Joey sampled all three desserts and eventually had a second piece of Boston cream pie shortly before they finished the remaining cookies.

For almost an hour the Van Landinghams made suggestions for the coming week once Julia explained that was as long as they could stay. Olivia and Joey loved the idea of spending several hours at the Metropolitan Museum of Art and the Museum of Natural History on opposite sides of Central Park, both of which Julia had enjoyed a great deal in November 1909, when she and Joe were in New York for Rebecca's wedding. The collections in both museums were so large and impressive Julia was pleased by the chance to visit them again and see dozens of things she'd missed during her first trip to Manhattan. Frances also suggested tours of the city's largest and most beautiful churches, St. Patrick's Cathedral and St. Thomas' Episcopal Church, which were located a short distance from each other on Fifth Avenue. Billy offered to lead them on a walk across the Brooklyn Bridge, which was always an interesting experience, while Barbara said a boat ride around Manhattan was an excellent way to spend several hours. Bill suggested walks through Chinatown and the financial district as well as a stroll to Union Square on a day the fiery socialist leader Emma Goldman was urging large crowds from her soapbox to adopt her radical ideas. All those suggestions appealed to Lucy, Julia and her children so much they did everything the Van Landinghams suggested.

On their second night in the city the four visitors and all the Van Landinghams except Billy, who'd been invited to a good friend's birthday party, attended a concert at Carnegie Hall by Josef Hoffman, whom Frances and most of New York's music critics considered the world's greatest living pianist. Everyone enjoyed that concert a great deal, especially Olivia, who was awed by Hoffman's brilliant playing. Three nights later, after spending several hours at the Museum of Natural History and having lunch at Tavern on the Green, which Julia and Lucy insisted on paying for, the four Southerners and all four Van Landinghams attended another concert at Carnegie Hall by the great Austrian violinist Fritz Kreisler, which Lucy enjoyed even more than Hoffman's concert. In fact, she enjoyed Kreisler's playing so much she vowed to buy herself a gramophone and several of his recordings shortly after she returned to Perquimmons City, which she did.

The visitors' week in New York came to an end on July 14. They were amazed by how much they'd seen and done, and Lucy was especially glad she'd made the trip because it exceeded her expectations in every way. Her parting gift to the Van Landinghams was an orchid plant in full bloom in a beautiful jardinière, both of which she bought at Frances's favorite florist shop on Third Avenue. Although Lucy spent $23.50 on that gift, she was convinced it was an inadequate expression of her gratitude for the Van Landinghams' hospitality and many kindnesses.

Despite how much she enjoyed the trip, Lucy was glad to see her cottage and Mr. Jobie again. Hazel Barlow had taken care of her cat while she was away, and he'd been very annoyed by Lucy's absence. In fact, he was quite standoffish until Lucy fixed him a special supper of canned tuna with a scrambled egg on top. He wolfed down that meal, accepting Lucy's apology in the process, and slept beside her pillow that night.

The next morning at the drugstore, Chip and Dillie welcomed Lucy back with open arms. But when the big shots arrived for their coffee shortly after nine forty-five, they said nothing about her absence and ordered her around more than ever. After several minutes Ozzie started laughing and asked Lucy for a hug because he'd missed her so much. Once she gave him the requested hug, he asked her if she'd brought him a present of some kind. The other big shots burst into laughter before asking Lucy if she'd brought them presents too. George Kahle said he'd expected a necktie or some socks while Russell Barringer said he'd been hoping for a new pair of shoes.

From her place behind the soda fountain Dillie said, "Lawsy me, I ain't never heard such silly talk from grown men. Of course Miz Lucy didn't bring you big shots any presents. And from the way you've been actin, I'm sure the old lady who's waitin at the drug count'uh fo Mist'uh Chip to fix her some cough syrup thinks you've lost all yo marbles."

Although it had never occurred to Lucy to bring Ozzie and the other big shots a present, she'd brought Dillie something she hoped she'd like—a straw purse she'd found on sale at Gimbel's, one of New York's leading department stores, while shopping for some cologne or special bath soap for Hazel Barlow. She gave Dillie that purse shortly after the big shots finished their coffee and returned to their places of work. Dillie was very touched that Lucy had thought about her while she was in New York and carried that purse every summer until it fell apart fifteen years later.

Shortly after her trip to New York, Lucy's life became more complicated than it had been since the summer Grover Beasley had tried to court her for monetary as well as personal reasons. Now, two years later, another man was deeply attracted to her for personal reasons only, just as her high school sweetheart, Jobie Caldwell, had been for a number of years before he died very suddenly in August 1887.

Edward Stanton, a New England widower of thirty-four, moved to Perquimmons City several months before Lucy left for New York on July 6. Edward was a nephew of Thomas Stanton Sr., the founder and president of Stanton's Mill, to whom he became a special assistant on the second Monday in April. Edward rented one of the few furnished apartments in town and joined the choir of St. John's Church shortly after enrolling his children, Kevin and Dodie, in the Sunday school program.

Lucy met Edward and his children during the social hour after the main service on the last Sunday morning in April. She liked them at once, especially Edward, who was only five feet five, the same height Jobie Caldwell had been. Also like Jobie, Edward was quiet, sensitive, and very intelligent. He had a dry sense of humor and loved books and flowers almost as much as Lucy did. He was also an excellent father to his children who missed their mother a great deal. She'd died the previous fall, two years after being diagnosed with tuberculosis.

Because of the great sadness of his wife's last years, Edward decided to leave his hometown of Lowell, Massachusetts for a year or so, hoping it would help him and his children develop a new perspective on life. When he learned his uncle in Perquimmons City was looking for a special assistant, he applied for the position and won it easily because his qualifications were superior to those of the other twenty-two applicants. He knew the textile business inside and out because he'd worked alongside his father and other uncle in the family's first and most important mill since shortly after he graduated from Yale in 1898. He'd attended Yale rather than Harvard, as most of his male forebears had done, because he truly believed the New England maxim that by the time they were forty, almost twice as many Harvard men worked for Yale men as vice versa. Even more important, Edward had no desire to be a freshman at the same university where his older brother, Gordon, was a junior and what was generally known at the time as a big man on campus just as he'd been known at Groton, the boarding school they both attended during their high school years. Much more serious and reserved than his older brother, Edward distinguished himself at Yale; and during the spring of his junior year, he was inducted into Phi Beta Kappa and was one of a dozen men elected to membership in Scroll and Key, one of the three senior societies that played an active role in dozens of aspects of student life. Since the late seventeenth century, almost all the members of the Stanton family had been Presbyterians or Congregationalists, but Edward preferred the Episcopal Church, which his wife had convinced him to join shortly after their wedding on the Saturday after Thanksgiving in 1899.

During his first six weeks in Perquimmons City, Edward made such a strong impression on the rector of St. John's Church, he appointed Edward to the church's finance and building and grounds committees. As a member of the latter committee Edward worked in the church garden for an hour or two on most Sunday afternoons just as Lucy did. She admired his skill with plants and flowers and his willingness to do whatever the chairman of that committee, Mildred Barringer, asked him to do. Lucy also admired his generosity and frequent provision of cookies and apple juice for the children in the Sunday school program to enjoy during the fifteen-minute interval between the end of the main service and the beginning of their Sunday school classes, which Lucy taught from time to time.

On the third Sunday in May the younger children celebrated Dodie's fifth birthday with a small party. Lucy brought a tin of homemade cookies and a small gift for Dodie that morning. Dodie loved her gift, *The Wizard of Oz*, and climbed into Lucy's lap so she could show her the book's beautiful illustrations. Then as a dozen other children gathered around Lucy's chair or sat on the floor near her feet, they listened while she told Dodie how a powerful storm known as a tornado blew Dorothy and her little dog Toto in her aunt and uncle's small frame house on the drab plains of Kansas to the beautiful land of Oz thousands of miles away. There Dorothy and Toto had several exciting adventures with flying monkeys and tiny little people known as Munchkins. When Dodie asked Lucy if Munchkins were as small as her Lucy said, "Oh yes, Dodie, they're much smaller than me, almost as small as you in fact. But when you grow up you'll be a good bit taller than them."

From that morning Dodie considered Lucy a special friend and always looked for her after the main service so she could hold her hand during the fifteen minutes before her Sunday school class started. Lucy realized Dodie considered her something of a replacement for her mother and was very touched by that. In several weeks she became extremely fond of Dodie and almost as fond of Kevin, who was more independent than his younger sister and a bit standoffish at first. But in several more weeks Kevin decided Lucy was okay and wanted to hold one of her hands too during the fifteen minutes before his class started. That was fine with Lucy although Edward was embarrassed by the way his children were imposing on her. During the social hour on July 2, he took them aside and scolded them for taking so much of Lucy's time.

Lucy overheard him scolding them and told him they hadn't been taking too much of her time. "They're such sweet little children I'm flattered that they enjoy spending some time with me. I've always loved children; and because my nieces and nephews are older than your children and would rather be with their friends, which is normal and natural, I hope you'll let me enjoy Kevin and Dodie while I can."

He smiled and asked her if she truly felt that way. "I'm afraid you're just being nice about my children's attention because we're still new in town they've made only a few friends this soon."

"No, that's wrong, Edward, and I'm sorry you feel that way."

"Then you don't resent the way they've been imposing on you?"

"That thought's never even occurred to me and I hope you'll bring them to Joe and Julia's picnic on Tuesday afternoon. For years they've held a picnic for all the members of our family and at least a dozen friends in their backyard on July fourth. Because that picnic's always a relaxed and informal occasion, I'm sure you and your children would enjoy it."

Edward smiled again and said, "I think we'd enjoy it too and Joe and Julia both invited me to attend it and bring my children along while we were taking off our choir robes shortly after the service ended. But I wondered if we should intrude on a family occasion like that. Now that you've asked us to come too I think we will."

"Good, and I'll look forward to seeing you and your children there."

Two days later Edward pulled his Model T into the Hanfords' driveway shortly after five o'clock. After helping Kevin and Dodie out of the car, he took several watermelons out of the backseat and, with Jack and Joey's help, carried them to the tub of ice Joe had waiting for them on the back porch. Within minutes Susan and Olivia took charge of Dodie while Jack and Joey taught Kevin how to play mumblety peg while Alfred watched them from a folding chair with a bored look on his face. Meanwhile Lucy fixed Edward a cup of lemonade with several pieces of ice, and from that moment they felt so comfortable with each other they were inseparable until the picnic ended at nine thirty. Because Kevin and Dodie had fallen asleep on the study sofa by then, Edward carried Kevin outside to his Model T while Lucy carried Dodie. After making the children comfortable on the back seat, Edward insisted on driving Lucy home because he wanted to spend some more time with her while saving Joe or Chip the trouble.

Kevin and Dodie were asleep when Edward stopped his car in front of Lucy's cottage, and to her great surprise he leaned over and gave her a quick little kiss on the cheek. She was even more surprised when he told her he'd enjoyed her company so much during the picnic he'd like to see her again in a day or two if that was okay with her.

Before getting out of the car Lucy said, "I enjoyed your company during the picnic too, but I'm leaving for New York on Thursday morning. I'm really looking forward to the trip because I've never been there and I've heard a great deal about the sights of Manhattan."

"Are you going to New York with another member of your family?"

"Yes, I'm going with Julia and her children, and we'll be staying with one of Joe's cousins at her home on one side of Gramercy Park. She and her husband are the people who're building a winter home several miles east of town."

"You're talking about the Van Landinghams, aren't you?"

"Yes, that's right. Have you ever met them?"

"No, but my aunt and uncle met them during the Hanfords' last New Year's Eve party and liked them a great deal. My uncle says they've agreed to build a large hospital Joe and dozens of other people are convinced the area's needed for years."

"Yes, that's right too, and Joe's as pleased as punch that we're about to get a wonderful new hospital, thanks to Bill and Frances's great generosity."

"My uncle told me something else that surprised me a great deal—the new hospital will accept black as well as white patients."

"Joe pushed really hard for that but why were you so surprised when you heard it?"

"Because I assumed . . . well, to put it bluntly, almost everyone I've met here since April seems to be extremely prejudiced against blacks."

"I'm afraid you're right about that because most of the whites around here are extremely prejudiced against black people. But no one in my family is, and neither are dozens of other people I know including the Ridingers, the Barringers, the Kahles, the Howells, and the Wileys. And the Thompsons and the Richardsons don't feel any prejudice against blacks either."

"It's clear from Mr. Thompson's sermons that he and his wife aren't prejudiced, and I'll take your word about the other people you mentioned. But getting back to your trip to New York, how long will you be away from town?"

"Only slightly over a week. The Van Landinghams hoped we'd spend two weeks with them, but Julia feels we shouldn't impose on them that long and I feel the same way. Besides, my brother's told me several times that he hopes I won't be away from the drugstore for more than eight or nine days because I'm 'indispensable' there. Although that's not true at all, I'm glad he thinks it is."

"I'm sure it's truer than you think it is. Even if it's not, I'm sorry you're leaving for New York on Thursday morning although I still hope you have a wonderful trip. If it's okay, I'll get in touch with you shortly after you get back to town."

"I'd like that, Edward, I'd like it a great deal in fact. Good night."

As Lucy got out of Edward's car and walked up the flagstone path to her front porch, he waited in his Model T until she went inside and closed the door before he drove off.

Until Lucy fell asleep two hours later she thought only of Edward and his children. They were so nice and agreeable and they certainly seemed to like her a great deal. Was it too farfetched to think Edward might have a romantic interest in her? Was there a chance he was thinking of proposing partly because his children needed another mother? But after several moments Lucy realized she was putting the cart before the horse because she and Edward barely knew each other, and it was much too soon to have thoughts like that. Besides, she was six years older than him, which didn't bode well for a successful relationship.

During her week in New York Lucy was so busy she thought about Edward and his children much less than she thought she would. Even so, she sent them a postcard of the Statue of Liberty on her second day in Manhattan; and the next afternoon, while shopping at Gimbel's for presents for Hazel Barlow and Dillie Hughes, she bought Edward and each of his children a book and a tooled-leather bookmark.

On the trip back to Perquimmons City, she wondered if she'd been right to buy them those presents. What if Edward didn't get in touch with her shortly after she returned to town as he'd said he would? In that event it would be a mistake to give him and his children those presents. Of course she could always put them away until shortly before Christmas and give them to his children then. Or she could give them to two other children she knew fairly well from their visits to the drugstore with their mothers.

Lucy's worries proved groundless. Shortly after ten thirty on her first day back at work, Edward came to the drugstore and told her how much he and his children had missed her. They'd enjoyed the postcard she sent them and wanted her to have dinner with them that night. Pleased and very relieved, Lucy accepted his invitation at once.

But shortly after he left the drugstore, she realized she needed to tell Julia that she'd be unable to have dinner with her and her family that evening. So shortly after she ate her bag lunch in the store's office, she walked up the avenue to the Hanfords' house and explained the situation to Julia, who was so surprised she asked Lucy several questions about her feelings for Edward. Those questions caused Lucy to blush and say she wasn't sure how serious her feelings for him were at that moment, which piqued Julia's curiosity even more.

Shortly after Lucy arrived at Edward's apartment at five forty-five, she gave him and his children the books and bookmarks she'd bought for them in New York. They were very pleased; and when Edward went into the kitchen to check on their meal, Lucy remained in the parlor and opened Kevin's book, a romanticized account of medieval life with an emphasis on the daily routines of the lords and serfs during that period of a thousand years. Once Kevin and Dodie admired the book's illustrations, Lucy asked them to join her on the sofa so she could read them the first chapter. They were intrigued by it and asked Lucy several questions about medieval farming and the three-field system of crop rotation shortly after she read that part of the chapter to them.

As she was about to read another part of that chapter to them, Edward stuck his head through the parlor door and said dinner was ready. So Lucy and the children joined him at the kitchen table where they enjoyed an excellent meal of baked chicken and fresh vegetables he'd cooked. Once they finished their dessert, a lemon meringue pie he'd bought at Hogan's Grocery Store on his way home from work that day, Edward sent Kevin and Dodie outside to play with several children who lived nearby.

Once they left the apartment, Lucy helped Edward clean up the kitchen and wash all the dishes and pots and pans. On finishing that work, he took her in his arms and kissed her on both cheeks before kissing her squarely on the mouth. Because she clearly enjoyed it and made no effort to turn her head away, he kissed her again and asked her to spend the night with him. She was jolted by his request and said she was amazed he'd made it.

"Why? I've heard several people say you were deeply in love with your high school sweetheart and were probably intimate with him during the summer before he died after a short illness."

"Those things are true but Jobie died a long time ago and I've never kissed another man since then. So I'm not about to sleep with you tonight or any other night because as the old saying goes, 'I'm older and wiser now.'"

"But you'd sleep with me if we were married, wouldn't you?"

"Of course I would because I know marriage is partly about sex."

"Then marry me in a week or two," Edward said at once. "I thought about you the whole time you were in New York and I'm sure we'd have a wonderful life together. We like all the same things and my children adore you as much as I do. In fact, they said dozens of times while you were away how much they'd love for us to get married so you'll live with us."

"That's very flattering, Edward. But I'm sure you don't adore me because I'm an old maid and a fairly homely one at that."

"That's a figment of your imagination, probably because you've spent your whole life in the shadow of Julia's enormous beauty. But even if it was true, I've always considered physical beauty overrated."

"You have? Why?"

"Because my older brother was unusually good-looking and six inches taller than me. By the time we were teenagers, I was sick and tired of hearing everyone say how handsome he was compared to an average-looking guy like me. For years he heard hundreds of flattering comments about his looks and great athletic ability—he was a baseball and rowing star at Harvard, which was one of the main reasons I went to Yale. By the time he graduated from college, he felt the world owed him a living; and largely because of that, he never held a job for even a year and was a great disappointment to our parents. They considered him an immature playboy, which he could afford to be because the uncle for whom he'd been named left him a large trust fund when he was thirteen and could use however he liked from the time he was twenty-one."

"I understand why you were annoyed by all the flattery he received for years. But because you spoke of him in the past tense, I wonder if he's still alive."

"He died two and a half years ago while he was skiing with several of his college friends at a resort in Idaho and was killed by an avalanche late one morning. But getting back to you, you're much more attractive than you think you are and you have a wonderful inner beauty that makes you a real pleasure to be with."

"No one's ever told me I have an 'inner beauty', and I've always wondered what that term means. I wish you'd explain it to me."

"Okay, because everyone's entitled to fish for compliments every now and then. But before I explain it to you, let's go into the parlor and sit on the sofa."

Lucy agreed; and once they were sitting on the sofa together he said, "To me, your inner beauty consists of several different things, but especially your enormous kindness and great sensitivity to the feelings of others although you can be a bit feisty whenever someone else does or says something that annoys you. Even so, I'm convinced you don't have an ounce of cruelty in your body and you'd never hurt another person on purpose the way Gordon did hundreds of times without giving it a second thought."

"Those comments are so flattering I wonder if I should take them seriously."

"I knew you'd say something like that because you're so modest and reluctant to hurt other people's feelings. And you're doing your best not to hurt my feelings now, aren't you?"

"What do you mean by that?"

"Unless I'm mistaken you're trying to let me down as gently as possible because you don't have any romantic feelings for me. I hope I'm wrong about that because my feelings for you are so strong I'd love for us to get married in a week or two."

"Edward, I do have some romantic feelings for you, much stronger ones than I realized until several minutes ago. But this is happening so fast there's no way I could agree to marry you in a week or two. We barely know each other and besides, I'm six years older than you."

"I don't see why that matters. It certainly doesn't matter to me because Sylvia was four years my senior and it never mattered to us or anyone in our families. So I hope you'll consider my proposal while we're getting to know each other much better during the next several months."

"I'll definitely consider your proposal provided you don't push me too hard. I'd hate to be maneuvered into a hasty marriage I regretted later."

"That's understandable but have you always been so cautious?"

"Yes, and I'm too old to change now."

"No, that's wrong; and while I'll do my best not to push you too hard, I hope you'll agree to marry me during Thanksgiving week because that's a wonderful time for a wedding. I know that from personal experience because that's when Sylvia and I got married in her hometown."

"I might be able to give you a definite answer by the beginning of November. I'll certainly keep an open mind about it while we see how our relationship develops."

As he put her arms around her and kissed her again, she made a mental comparison between him and Grover Beasley, whom she considered inferior to him in every way. She also compared him to Jobie Caldwell and rated them roughly equal in most ways.

During the next two months things went so smoothly for them Edward sensed that Lucy was on the verge of accepting his proposal by the second week of September. So on the second Saturday of that month, he drove to Edenton and bought her a beautiful engagement ring from Tolliver's Jewelry Store, one of the best stores of its kind in the area. After arranging for a babysitter to take care of Kevin and Dodie several nights later, he told Lucy he'd like to take her to dinner on Wednesday night at a popular restaurant in Edenton. He planned to propose to her again while they were at the restaurant; and if she accepted his new proposal, he would give her the ring then.

But shortly after nine thirty on Tuesday morning, he received a telegram from his mother in New England with some terrible news. His father, a diabetic for fourteen years, had gone blind ten days earlier, and on the previous afternoon he suffered a massive stroke and was now in the intensive care unit in a Boston hospital. Because his life was hanging by a thread, Edward should return to Massachusetts at once if he hoped to see his father alive again.

Several minutes after Edward received that telegram in his office in the mill's administrative suite, he drove to the drugstore and showed Lucy his mother's telegram. Once she expressed her sympathy and deep concern for his father's health, Edward told her he felt compelled to leave for Boston that afternoon with his children. His cousin in town, Thomas Stanton Jr., would drive them to the Hertford station in two more hours so Edward wouldn't have to leave his car in an unattended parking lot for several weeks or a month.

"I understand," Lucy said at once. "Is there anything I can do for you and your children while you're away?"

"Thanks, but I can't think of anything at the moment."

"I'll say a prayer for your father every night at bedtime until I see you again. Is there a chance you'll be back in a month or six weeks?"

"It all depends on my father's health. As my mother's telegram suggested, he could die at any moment, which I hope and pray he doesn't. Unless of course he's in great pain."

"I feel the same way because my father suffered so much during the last six weeks of his life it really tore me up."

"I certainly understand that," Edward said before telling Lucy goodbye and leaving the drugstore.

As he disappeared Lucy had a premonition that she'd never see Edward and his children again. Lucy's premonition proved correct because, despite Edward's plan to return to Perquimmons City by the end of October if possible, he never returned to North Carolina. A week after he arrived in Boston, his father died, and his funeral took place four days later in Lowell.

To Edward's great surprise his father's only surviving brother, William Stanton III, the president of the family's chain of two dozen textile mills in Massachusetts, Rhode Island, and New Hampshire, offered him his father's former position—vice president for advertising and marketing—at five times the salary he'd been making in Perquimmons City. Although Edward knew he might lose Lucy if he accepted that offer and remained in New England, his mother urged him to accept his father's position, which he'd held for thirty-four years. She pointed out dozens of times that Edward hadn't planned to settle in Perquimmons City when he and his children moved to North Carolina the previous spring. She also insisted that this was probably the best offer he would ever receive. Edward's sister Lois and her husband, Daniel Cosgriff, the mills' executive vice president, made the same argument and also insisted that his children would be much better off in Massachusetts than in Perquimmons City, where the schools were poor and Kevin and Dodie would be so far from their cousins they'd be lucky to see them and their other relatives for a week or two once or twice a year.

After agonizing about the matter for a week, Edward accepted his father's position and called Lucy at her cottage that night with great foreboding. After describing the duties of the position he'd been offered, he explained why he'd accepted it that afternoon. He hoped she understood and would take the train to Lowell as soon as possible so she could meet his family and see how comfortable and enjoyable his life in New England actually was because he still hoped she'd marry him by Thanksgiving week if not shortly before weeks before. He also told her that because of his much higher salary, they would be able to travel fairly often and could visit her family in Perquimmons City several times a year in the future. They could even continue to rent her cottage on Second Street if she'd like to do that.

Although Lucy was noncommittal over the phone, she promised to think about everything he told her during that phone call for the next several days. She also promised to send him a clear answer in a letter in a week or less.

During the next several hours Lucy fretted about the matter and what her decision should be before she fell into a restless asleep. The next morning at the drugstore, she continued to think about the situation whenever she wasn't waiting on customers or helping Dillie serve coffee to the big shots and a dozen other customers. Whenever she tried to post the previous day's charges in the office, her mind wandered back to Edward and whether she should join him in New England or not.

By four thirty she'd made up her mind and told Chip she needed to write an important letter. Because she'd been so distracted all day, Chip knew something serious was afoot and was tempted to ask her about it. But he held his tongue and told her to feel free to use the office as long as she liked. After entering the office and finding a box of the store's stationery, she wrote Edward a letter she'd already worked out in her mind. Its most important paragraphs made the following points:

During the last month, I truly hoped to become your wife by the end of November. But during yesterday's phone call, I was amazed when you made it clear you expected me to move to Lowell as soon as possible and marry you there. That caused me to reconsider our relationship because if I did as you suggested, I would be turning my back on the only place I've ever lived and my whole family. Especially my nieces and nephews, whom I've always expected to see grow up, marry, and have children of their own one day. Because I've never met anyone in your family, not even your mother or your sister Lois, and I've never set foot in New England, I would feel marooned and completely isolated there if things didn't work out well for us. And I'm convinced they wouldn't because I'm six years older than you although you've told me several times that the difference in our ages doesn't matter to you at all. But it does matter to me—it matters to me a great deal and always will because I've always been very conventional about things like that. And while I'm sure you'll disagree with my next point even more, I'm convinced you deserve a younger and more attractive wife than me, a wife who'd be a much better hostess for you than I could ever be as well as a more capable and energetic mother for Kevin and Dodie. Furthermore, despite how unlikely it probably seems to you now, I'm convinced you'll meet such a woman in another month or two, a woman who'll keep you from feeling as lonely and depressed as you've been since your Sylvia died almost a year ago.

So you see, Edward, my answer has to be no, and I'm sure you'll understand my decision and accept it in several weeks. By Thanksgiving if not sooner, you'll probably be glad my answer was no because I'll always be a Southerner at heart while you're a New Englander with very different ideas and traditions than mine, which might cause serious problems for us if we ever got married. There are several other reasons why I've decided to end our relationship, but those should be sufficient for now.

Please tell Kevin and Dodie how much I enjoyed getting to know them; and I also hope you'll give them several kisses for me and tell them how fondly I'll always remember them and wish them enormous happiness and great success in all their worldly endeavors.

With deep affection always, Lucy.

After folding her letter and placing it in a stamped envelope, Lucy sealed and addressed it before putting it in a pocket of her skirt.

On leaving the drugstore at five thirty, she walked to the post office and mailed the letter before heading for her cottage several blocks away. During the first part of that walk, Lucy felt enormous sadness and shed several tears, knowing there was little if any chance she'd ever see Edward and his children again. In addition, she was convinced she would just rejected the last marriage proposal she'd ever receive and her only chance to have a family of her own.

But as she neared her cottage, she took stock of her life and realized how much she enjoyed it. She also realized how far she'd come during the last dozen years. In the fall of 1899, she'd been the Merritt children's teacher with several other duties she disliked even more. Furthermore, in 1899 she felt no affection or respect for her employers, who were deeply disliked by most of the people she knew and had no concern for her emotional or intellectual needs. But now, in the fall of 1911, she was an important member of her community and an integral part of a large, extended family that was highly respected for miles around. That family enjoyed her company and included her in its activities several times a week. It also took her ideas and opinions seriously, whereas the Merritts had ignored or ridiculed her ideas the whole time she worked for them. Almost as important, Lucy was a personal friend of the Van Landinghams in 1911 and a member of their advisory committee, which included eight other highly respected people in the area. She was also a prominent member of her church and its altar guild, partly because she was its leading flower arranger. She was known for miles around because of her work at the drugstore where she had a secure job she loved. She was in good health and had a devoted neighbor in Hazel Barlow and a loving pet in Mr. Jobie. Blacks and whites alike greeted her affectionately wherever she went, and during the previous July she'd spent a week in New York, which only a handful of her friends and relatives had ever visited.

After entering her cottage and feeding Mr. Jobie, Lucy combined in a mixing bowl all the ingredients for a meatloaf she planned to cook for her and Hazel's supper that night while thinking, *That's pretty good for a former house servant with average looks and abilities. So there's no reason I should have any second thoughts about my decision to remain in Perquimmons City rather than move to a place in New England I've never seen or heard much about. With a wonderful family like mine and great friends like Hazel and the Van Landinghams, I don't see how my future could be any brighter than it is, especially if I can find a way to get Chip to end his affair with Lillian Greenfield. If I fail in that regard and news of their affair leaks out, not only will Rhonda be deeply hurt but most Chip's customers will turn against him, causing the drugstore to lose so much business a rival drugstore, maybe a Walgreens like the one in Edenton, will probably open on Main Street. In that event I might lose my job or have to take a large pay cut, causing my comfortable standard of living to decline. So I've just got to find a way to convince Chip to end his ties with Lillian, who's so selfish and self-centered she never thinks about anyone but herself. But I can think about that problem tomorrow because it would be unfair to Hazel if I fretted about it so much during the next several hours we didn't enjoy our evening together.*